REMNANTS OF THE LOST

THE ELDER STONES SAGA BOOK 3

D.K. HOLMBERG

Cover by Damonza.com

If you want to be notified when D.K. Holmberg's next novel is released and get a few free books and occasional other promotions, please sign up for his mailing list by going here. Your email address will never be shared and you can unsubscribe at any time.

www.dkholmberg.com

PROLOGUE

THE WIND HOWLED OUTSIDE, OCCASIONALLY GUSTING INTO the cell, and Rsiran sat with his legs crossed in the center of the small space, trying to ignore it. Pain throbbed throughout his body, everything within him hurting, the kind of pain he had come to know far too well over the last few months of his captivity. In all that time, he had struggled to maintain his calm, to ignore the constant torment, but it had grown increasingly difficult.

It should not be so easy for him to be confined in a cell like this. He was Rsiran Lareth, master of Sliding, a man who had held each of the great crystals of Elaeavn. Despite that, he had been unable to prevent his captivity.

And he had been unable to find any way to escape. So much for the plan he and Carth had discussed. This was to have been a brief stay, an opportunity for him to finally find Olandar Fahr. Now he was captured.

Footsteps thudded nearby, and he did nothing. He no longer even looked up as he once had, knowing that it didn't matter. How could it, when torment would come regardless of what he might do?

A shadow moved in front of him, something he noticed through his closed lids, and still he refused to look. Opening his eyes took far more effort than he was willing to give, and with all the pain he felt, everything he had experienced, he knew there was no point.

"Do you think that you can ignore my presence?"

Rsiran had come to hate that voice, much the way he had once come to hate the voice of his own grandfather when he had chased him. That had been years ago, long enough that he had begun to feel a semblance of peace, but then it had been a false peace, something he had convinced himself was real, all while hunting down the Ai'thol.

Why had he ever believed that he was untouchable? He had known they would come after him, and they had held him captive him once before, though never so securely, and never in such a way that left him believing he would not be able to escape. In this case, his captivity left him feeling helpless.

"I have nothing to say to you," Rsiran said without opening his eyes.

Olandar Fahr laughed darkly. "You have managed to withstand my questioning so far, and I must admit that I did not think I would have to push you quite so hard."

"Did you think that I was soft?"

"Yes."

With that, Rsiran opened his eyes and looked over to Olandar Fahr. He was a muscular man, quite a bit older than Rsiran, though he carried the weight of confidence. Power seemed to swirl around him, and Rsiran understood all too well how—and why—he was able to possess such power. This was a man who had held many of the Elder Stones, and because of that, his power had grown.

He still hadn't managed to acquire the sacred crystals in Elaeavn. If nothing else, Rsiran intended to prevent him from doing so, though he had attacked the Elder Trees, and in a way that even Rsiran hadn't managed to overcome.

"Good," he said, barely looking up at Olandar Fahr.

"Good?"

Rsiran smiled. "If it caused you to underestimate me, then it was good. What else did you want me to say?"

"All you need to do is answer the questions and you will be granted peace."

"By peace, you mean death."

"Yes."

Rsiran stared at him for a moment, not sure what he could say. The cold way that Olandar Fahr had confirmed what he suspected left him not only uncomfortable, but still troubled. He had been around hard men before, but this man might be one of the hardest.

"I don't intend to die."

"All men must die."

"Do you intend to philosophize with me?"

"I have no interest in debating with someone like you."

"And what do you mean by that?"

"Only that your capacity to challenge me in any such debate is limited."

Rsiran grunted, closing his eyes once again. There was comfort in keeping them closed, the same sort of comfort he felt when ignoring Olandar Fahr. Eventually the torment would begin, and when it did, he would struggle to ignore anything, so these moments, however brief they might be, were all about him taking what control he could of the situation—even if it was limited.

"If you don't want to debate me, then continue with your torment."

Olandar Fahr stepped through the bars. Rsiran noticed it as a stirring of power, though little more than that. He didn't have the same ability to pass through the bars. If he had, he would have Slid free of here long ago, but there was something unique about the cell that held him. It wasn't heartstone, though he would never have expected the Ai'thol to make that mistake. They knew his ability over that metal far too well. In all the time he had been captive, he had continued to search for answers, trying to understand what they were using to confine him, but those answers had not come.

"It's almost as if you look forward to this torment," Olandar Fahr said.

"The only thing I look forward to is your defeat."

"And yet, were you able to see the game board, you would know that my victory is nearly at hand."

Rsiran blinked open his eyes, looking over at the other man. He grunted, shaking his head. "Game board? If this is a game to you, it's one that you will lose."

"And who will stop me?"

"You fear her."

Olandar Fahr tipped his head to the side, regarding

Rsiran for a moment. Shadows swirled around him, reminding Rsiran so much of the way they swirled around Carth when she was using her connection to the shadows. It was one sort of magic that he didn't fully understand, though it wasn't the type of magic he needed to comprehend. It was tied to the Elder Stones, much the way all magic was tied to Elder Stones, and unfortunately, that sort of power could be acquired by those who were never meant to harness it.

"And why should I fear her?"

"Because you know that she can defeat you."

"She has tried and she has failed. I don't fear Carthenne Rel, no more than I feared you."

"You feared me enough to send your men after me."

"That is less about fear and more about a desire to remove any sort of obstruction that might prevent my victory."

"What is the need for that other than fear for how I might prevent your victory?"

"What makes you think that I fear anything? I have complete control of the situation. And you can go nowhere."

"For now," Rsiran said.

"You will not manage to escape. You are my captive, from now until the day you leave this world."

"That may be, but you are still mistaken if you think that means I fear what you will do to me."

"Why fight it? If you know it is inevitable, why resist?"

"Because I know what you would do with that sort of power."

"I would rule. Is that so different than what you did with the same power?"

"I never intended to rule."

"And yet you did. Perhaps you didn't mean to do it, but your people looked to you, wanting to be tied to the power you possessed, and with it, they expected you to take on a role where you would lead."

"If you knew anything, you would recognize that leadership and ruling are quite different."

"Oh, I am well aware that they are different. Only, there comes a time when a man must step forward, no longer fearing his place in the world, and accept the power that has been thrust upon him."

Rsiran said nothing. He looked at the backs of his eyelids, steadying his breathing, preparing himself for the pain that would soon come. It was the only way he knew to get ready for it, even if he couldn't fully prepare. How could he ever adequately prepare for the torment? When it came, everything hurt, and he could focus on nothing else. There were times when he contemplated telling Olandar Fahr what he wanted to know, but he never did. While it might end his torment, it would cause people he cared about to suffer far more than Rsiran was willing to allow. He cared too much about them to do that to them.

"You will fall," Olandar Fahr said.

"I have already fallen," Rsiran whispered.

"You believe that you can't fall any further?"

"You can torture me, but there is nothing more you can do that you have not already done to me."

Olandar Fahr laughed, the sound grating and painful. Rsiran had heard it often enough over the months of his infrequent visits to hate that sound. Olandar Fahr didn't come every day, but he came often enough that Rsiran had grown to despise it, and each time he came, he had a new torment for him, something Rsiran had not been able to prepare for.

"If you believe that, then you are quite mistaken."

Rsiran opened his eyes, glancing over at the other man. He crouched in front of him, now close enough that Rsiran could almost grab him, but he knew that if he were to try, he wouldn't be fast enough. His speed was tied to the other man's magic. Not only was he incredibly intelligent, but he was powerful in a way that Rsiran—even with his connection to all of the great crystals within Elaeavn—was not.

He reached into his pocket, pulling out a strange dark bar of metal. It wasn't the first time that Olandar Fahr had brought metal into the room with him during the torment. He seemed to enjoy that almost as much as he enjoyed anything, and he relished testing Rsiran, seeing how much pain he could withstand from the various alloys that the Ai'thol had control over. For the most part, Rsiran had found that he could tolerate much of what they did to him. It wasn't the first time he had been tortured, and his experience had granted him a certain fortitude when it came to such things, though he wished it weren't necessary.

Something about this bar looked a little different. It was a deep black, almost inky, and as he stared at it, he noticed shadows swirling around the bar.

Rsiran glanced up at Olandar Fahr, and the other man grinned.

"You recognize what this is. Good. Then you will understand just what it might be able to do. It has taken me considerable time to create this, and while I had another purpose in mind, the fact that you continue to fight has proven to me that I must use this with you."

Rsiran said nothing. He had no idea what the metal bar was, but he wasn't about to let Olandar Fahr know that. Let him believe Rsiran was more knowledgeable than he actually was. He already underestimated him; admitting inexperience with this would only convince Fahr that Rsiran was every bit as ignorant as he believed.

"What do you want to know?" Rsiran asked, eyeing the bar. There was something unsettling about it, and if he was right and they had somehow infused it with the shadow magic that both Olandar Fahr and Carth had access to, then it was the kind of thing he wanted nowhere near him.

"I have told you what I want to know. The question is whether you will be willing to share with me just what it is that you do know."

"If you promise not to harm my people."

"The way you promised not to harm mine?"

Rsiran said nothing. What was there for him to say? He had attacked the Ai'thol, killing many of them, blaming them for what had happened to his people over the years. And they deserved the blame. They were responsible for what had taken place, led by Olandar Fahr, killing countless people. All because Fahr wanted power.

And he was close to obtaining everything he wanted. He already had demonstrated considerable strength, and while Rsiran didn't know how many of the Elder Stones he had not yet claimed, he doubted it was very many.

"What is the secret to holding the crystals?"

"There is no secret."

"There is a secret. You are the only one who has held each of the crystals. No others have managed to successfully hold more than one."

"The crystals decide, not me."

"The crystals decide." Olandar Fahr laughed bitterly. "Even if I believed that, there is much more to it." He paused, studying Rsiran for another moment. "Perhaps you don't know. I should not be too surprised by that, considering how little you have proven to know so far."

Rsiran just stared at him. There wasn't anything for him to say. He didn't know, and it made no sense for him to tell Olandar Fahr just how little knowledge he possessed. The crystals did choose, and because of that, he had been chosen to handle not just one of the great crystals, but all of them. It wasn't anything he really understood. Then again, it wasn't his place to understand such things. The crystals were powerful, ancient, and all he needed to know was that he had been granted power by them, and through that power, he had been given aspects of the Great Watcher, a chance to see the world from the vantage the Great Watcher had. It was a perspective that very few ever were granted, and he was thankful that he had been so blessed.

"You don't understand the Elder Stones as well as you believe if you think there is a way to force them to behave as you want."

Olandar Fahr regarded Rsiran for a moment. He said

nothing, merely watching him. After a while, he stood, holding on to the bar, and started to turn. "Perhaps I gave you far more credit than you deserved."

"Perhaps you did."

"And perhaps your ignorance is greater than I had ever believed."

Rsiran looked over at him, and all he could do was shrug. "Perhaps that is true as well."

"Or perhaps you merely want me to believe you don't know these things." He held out the black bar, shadows swirling around him, stretching toward the bar before spinning away. "You would have me believe you know nothing about this power, and yet, you have much experience with it. I doubt that you would have been so successful over the years without knowing more than what you have shared. You might not have enough understanding of the Elder Stones to be able to claim each of them, but you do know something about them, more than most. And you have successfully avoided my ability to find you, which tells me that you do know more than you let on."

The shadows began to push away from Olandar Fahr, stretching not only from him, but away from the long bar, reaching toward Rsiran. They streamed toward him, pushing outward, almost something palpable.

Rsiran recoiled, the first time he had moved since Olandar Fahr had come into the room. Everything in his being told him that he wanted nothing to do with that power, that he wanted to run away away from it, but where was he to go? What was he to do?

When the shadows reached him, they were warm.

That warmth increased, becoming hot.

Suddenly, Rsiran thought he understood.

He sucked in a sharp breath, and Olandar Fahr laughed darkly once again.

"Did you think that we failed?"

Rsiran looked to the bar, much more afraid than he had been before. He thought they had prevented Olandar Fahr from reaching the Elder Stone in Nyaesh, but could they have failed?

With his captivity, Rsiran wouldn't have known.

The heat flowing from the bar suggested that Rsiran was right, that Olandar Fahr had managed to acquire the power of another stone. With that, not only did he gain increased power, but he now had the key to countering the abilities Carth possessed. How many more Elder Stones would he be able to acquire? Was there anyone who would be able to withstand him and his people?

All Rsiran had ever wanted to do was protect those he cared about. It was the reason he had avoided training his son—a mistake, but one he had begun to rectify. Even that might not have been soon enough. If Olandar Fahr had managed to connect to this much power, there might not be anyone—or anything—that could stop him and his steady march toward acquiring the power of each of the Elder Stones.

The shadows continued to swirl around him, moving with increasing speed. The heat pressed painfully down upon him, and he tried not to cry out, but his ability to withstand the torment was battered down quickly. He screamed, some distant part of him aware that Olandar

Fahr laughed as he did, but there was nothing Rsiran could do to stop himself.

The pain continued, burning through him, tearing a part of him away, and he began to wonder if he truly would be able to withstand this torture. How much longer could he hold out? And would he be willing to sacrifice himself to avoid telling Olandar Fahr and the Ai'thol what they wanted to know, information that could destroy their chances of keeping themselves safe?

1

HAERN

Shadows flickered along the street, and Haern crouched on the rooftop, looking down. A series of lorcith coins, each barely large enough for him to See in the darkness, drew his attention. He had placed them carefully, *pushing* them along the street, positioning them in such a way that he would be able to detect them, but even now, he wondered if perhaps they weren't too small for him to fully discern.

He searched for movement. Rumors had led him here, to the small city of Baland far to the south of Elaeavn, and he had convinced one of his friends from Elaeavn to bring him here. If he had the ability to Slide, he wouldn't have needed anyone else's assistance, but unfortunately, that wasn't one of his gifts.

As he sat, focusing on the sense of lorcith all around him, he tried to detect any other outlying senses but couldn't come up with anything.

That fact bothered him.

There should be something here, though the longer he

remained crouched on the rooftop, watching out into the night, the less he was able to come up with. Sitting here as he did, he felt like his father, if only a little. He knew he could never have his father's ability, nor did he have his skill, but training over the last few months with Galen had taught him to use his knives in a way that at least resembled what his father was able to do. Prior to his father's abduction, he had helped Haern learn how to better control his connection to lorcith, granting him an opportunity to understand just what was needed to use it to navigate above the city streets. It was that ability he needed now, if only a little.

The sense of lorcith moving caught his attention.

He *pushed* off the rooftop, *pushing* from one small piece of lorcith to another. He didn't move them. They were small enough they would go generally unnoticed by anyone other than himself—or Forgers. And by the time the Forgers noticed the lorcith, he would have already completed what he wanted to accomplish.

The city was smaller than Elaeavn, smaller than most cities he'd been in, but still larger than many of the villages he had traveled through over the last few months, hunting the Forgers, searching for any information he could find about his father. He was determined to uncover where they had kept him. Once he found that, Haern was going to go and rescue his father, whatever it took. He owed the man that much.

He paused on one of the thatched roofs, resting his hand cautiously. These weren't nearly as secure as the rooftops within Elaeavn where he'd practiced this, nor were they as stable as the roofs within Asador, where he had first learned how to do it. He had to be more cautious on the thatch. Any misstep could lead to him tumbling through, landing in someone's hearth. But he was careful, placing lorcith down so that he could *push* off it as he went.

The movement didn't come again.

Had he made a mistake?

No. Haern was certain he had detected the movement of lorcith. It wasn't such a common metal that anyone would carry it. The only people who carried it were Forgers or those from Elaeavn. It was why he used lorcith to hunt them. And if he could figure out where they were, and if he could take out one more Forger, interrogate him, he could find his father again.

It was what he had told himself over and over again the last few months as he had searched for Forgers. He had only found a handful, and had only ever engaged one of them, forced to kill him before he had a chance to question him.

The sense of movement came again, this time from the north of the city.

Haern *pushed* off, flying above the city. When he had discovered how to do this, he had marveled at the possibilities, learning that his connection to lorcith granted him far more capabilities than he had ever believed. While he didn't have his father's ability to Slide, having this connection was *nearly* as good.

He paused again, this time near a two-story building, clutching the brick of a chimney as he remained precariously above the street, looking down. Several people walked along the streets, most of them dressed like locals in flowing brightly colored silks. None of the Forgers he had ever seen wore silks like that, so they weren't the ones he was looking for.

As he paused, he felt lorcith moving again.

This time it was different. This time it was *his* lorcith.

Had someone uncovered what he was doing?

It wouldn't be all that difficult to discover. Placing the small coins around the streets was really only a matter of convenience for him. He could *push* and *pull* them out of the satchel he carried, though the ones he had placed around the city allowed him to navigate far more rapidly.

Several of his small coins had been moved.

That couldn't be coincidence.

The coins were smooth, flat, and unremarkable, so no one would have any way of tracing them back to him. The only unique thing about them was that they had been forged out of lorcith.

He needed to find whoever had moved his coins.

He pushed off, traveling east now, pausing every so often to search for the connection to lorcith. As he neared the most recent coin to have been moved, he felt a sudden surge of lorcith.

Great Watcher!

The sense of it bloomed nearby, powerful enough he practically fell from his perch along the roof. He was careful not to take a step and *pushed* off to keep himself arranged carefully—yet precariously—before looking down.

A Forger moved along the street.

There was a distinctiveness about Forgers. It came not only from their dress—jacket and pants made from charcoal-colored wool—but also from the sense of lorcith that moved with them. It was an implant, though Haern didn't fully understand how they managed to create them. He'd seen what had happened with Lucy when lorcith had been implanted into her, but most of the Forgers he had encountered didn't have implants like Lucy's. Then again, Lucy's had been placed by someone other than Forgers.

The lorcith exploding from this Forger was powerful. Why hadn't he detected it before?

The man flickered along the street, and Haern thought he understood. He was Sliding.

Haern continued to watch, preparing for his attack. He needed to incapacitate the Forger as quickly as possible, but doing so involved using lorcith, so he had to do it in a way that would surprise the Forger. He had plenty of experience in fighting with them over the last few months. His personal assault upon them had granted him that experience. And there was something unusual about this Forger.

He was alone.

Usually the Forgers traveled in pairs, sometimes in threes. Being able to Slide meant they could travel wherever they wanted, and the fact they did so together made them more formidable. It made it far more difficult for him to continue his campaign against them. Haern suspected the key was to attack simultaneously, surprise them, and once he did, incapacitate them.

He waited, focusing on a sense of lorcith that never came. Coins continued to move throughout the city, and he realized they were being swept up by this Forger.

Could he be the only one here?

He didn't want to wait any longer.

Unsheathing a pair of his lorcith knives as slowly as possible, he *pushed*.

The Forger spun toward him, looking directly up at him.

Great Watcher!

The Forger knew he was there.

Of course he did. He had an ability with lorcith, so he would have been able to control it the same way Haern could. As the knives streaked toward him, the Forger stopped them in midair, spinning them back.

Haern *pushed* off, soaring above the street, and *pulled* on the knives, shifting their direction, arcing them toward the Forger.

The Forger flickered, disappearing in a Slide.

Haern landed on the roof, waiting for the man to reappear, but he didn't.

A mistake. He had revealed himself too soon. He could have chosen a different approach, using the coins to attack.

Lorcith suddenly exploded near him, and he barely reacted in time.

The Forger appeared on the rooftop next to him, and Haern *pushed* off, dropping to the street, using a knife to catch himself and *push* off again, switching the direction, swinging the other knife toward him. At the same time, he focused on the coins in his satchel, streaking all of them at the Forger.

The man managed to catch them all, sweeping them back at Haern. Haern *pushed* off, shooting higher into the air, using that to *push* even higher, forcing the coins—and his knives—toward the ground.

As he hovered for a moment, he realized his mistake. He was outmatched.

He tried to *pull* on the coins, sending them toward the Forger, but the other man was able to *push* against them, resisting every attempt Haern made to direct the coins at him.

Haern's strength began to wane. He lowered to the ground, prepared to fight, grabbing for the poison-tipped steel knives he had brought to use against the Forgers in a situation like this.

The Forger appeared in front of him, just out of reach. He eyed Haern, a long scar splitting the center of his face. Deep brown eyes looked back at him. "Someone from Elaeavn. Have you taken an implant?"

"Some of us don't need an implant," Haern spat. He readied the steel knives, preparing to throw one, though he needed to time it just right. With his enhanced eyesight, he could See when the Forger prepared a Slide, but if he went too early, the knife would miss. If he went too late, the Forger would Slide. If he could catch him in mid Slide, he could stop the Forger.

"You have some talent."

"I'll take that as a compliment."

"And with an implant, you could have *incredible* talent. All you need to do is serve."

"Serve the Forgers?"

"You have it mistaken. The Ai'thol. That is who you would serve."

"I have no interest in serving the Ai'thol."

"No? You are outside of Elaeavn, which means that you have been exiled. Forgotten, as I believe your people like to call it. If they would banish you, why would you claim them? I can offer you something more."

"What makes you think I was banished?"

The Forger cocked his head to the side, regarding Haern for a long moment. "Ah. Then you have come of your own volition. A mistake."

"You made the mistake."

"Did I? Am I the one who came pursuing power I don't understand?"

"I understand your power."

"You understand nothing, child of the Elvraeth. All you understand is what you have been told rather than what you have experienced. You don't grasp the nature of the power that exists in the world, thinking your meager talents matter in the grand scheme of things."

Haern frowned to himself. Why was this man saying anything?

Almost too late, he realized there was another sense of lorcith.

It approached slowly, almost imperceptibly, but he became aware of it.

Great Watcher!

Haern *pushed*, trying to launch himself into the air, but found himself held in place.

He glanced down, realizing the lorcith on him, his buckle, the knives he had hidden in his pockets, even the few remaining coins he had, were all holding him in place.

"I think you will stay here," the man said.

Haern flicked his wrist, sending the knife streaking, but the Forger Slid.

As he did, Haern pushed again, timing it so that as the Forger Slid, he could get airborne. He barely managed to do so in time, and as the Forger reemerged, Haern flicked his wrist, sending another knife streaking. This one grazed the Forger.

It wasn't much. A small bead of blood appeared on the man's hand, but with the terad poison he'd used on the blade, he hoped it was enough to bring him down. From what he'd been taught, there were some who had developed an immunity to this poison; he hoped the Forger wasn't one of them.

The man staggered before finally falling to his knees and then collapsing.

Haern dropped, looking around, then pulled his knives and the coins toward him as he searched the streets for signs of the other Forger he suspected was out there.

There had to be something. He *had* detected movement.

It was time for him to go. He had removed one Forger, but even that had been difficult.

Lorcith suddenly exploded near him.

Two Forgers appeared.

He tried to *push* off, but he was held no differently than he had been before.

These men had no scars, and both had deep green eyes that stared at him. Their heads were shaved, and they wore the clothing of the Forgers. One of the men glanced down at the fallen Forger before turning his attention back to Haern.

"You would hunt the Ai'thol?" he asked in a strange accent. It wasn't the accent of Elaeavn, despite his green eyes.

"I hunt you the way you hunt us."

"We hunt nothing. But if you would chase death, you will have it."

Haern tried to *push* off again, but again he failed.

If he didn't manage to get out of here soon, Thoren would arrive looking for him. He had significant ability with Sliding, and a hint of connection to lorcith, but he wasn't a fighter. If he chased the sense of lorcith, he would be in danger. If nothing else, Haern needed to escape to keep Thoren out of harm's way.

He tried to *push* again and reached into his pocket, searching for the coins, wanting to drop them on the ground, but he couldn't even move them. They were holding him in place.

The Forgers started toward him.

One of the men smiled grimly as he approached, the darkness on his face nearly enough to make Haern shiver.

Haern tried to run, tried to move, and couldn't.

This had been a mistake.

If he didn't manage to get away, it might be the *last* mistake he made.

For his father, he wasn't about to allow that to happen.

Haern tried to run, and though his legs moved, nothing else about him did.

As the nearest Forger approached, he went completely still. Haern waited for him to grab for him, for him to do anything, but he remained frozen… almost as if he had been held.

Could there be someone else in the city who had the ability to hold one of the Forgers?

The pressure on him lessened, and he *pushed*, overpowering the Forgers holding him in place. He hovered slightly in the air, at least out of reach of the other Forger. He looked around, searching for whoever might be intervening, but Saw nothing.

The other Forger stiffened.

Haern shot into the sky.

Everything that had been holding him back was suddenly lifted, and he tried to get control of himself before shooting too quickly, and as he did, he came crashing back down.

He scanned the street, looking for whoever had helped, but couldn't See who it was.

As he backed away, glancing at the Forgers, he saw a dart jutting out of the neck of each one.

Galen.

And if Galen was here, it meant Thoren had brought him.

Haern pushed off, searching the streets until he Saw Galen. He was farther than he would've expected the other man to be, and Haern landed on the roof next to him. Thoren stood a pace behind, barely grasping the chimney.

"What do you think you're doing?" Galen snapped.

"I thought I was trying to find my father."

"By convincing this one to escort you out of the city?

Is that where you've been going in your time away from the city?"

A warm flush washed over Haern's neck, but he held Galen's gaze. "I don't have to answer that."

"If you want me to continue to work with you, you do." Galen glanced down at the street. "We should get back to the forest before others come for those two… three."

"Why would they come for those three?"

"Do you even know where you are?"

"Balend."

"Do you know anything about this city?"

Haern glanced over to Thoren, but the other man looked down. "Only that Forgers were here."

"You know they're here, but you don't understand *why*. They control the city. Of course you're going to find Forgers here, and in far more quantities than you can withstand."

"I've been here for several hours and I haven't seen any Forgers before these three."

"Perhaps they didn't want you to see them."

Haern frowned, staring at the two still standing—and completely stiff—Forgers, along with the one he had attacked. Had that one moved?

"What poison did you use?"

"Now isn't the time for those sort of questions."

"I've never seen anything quite like that. What is it?"

"It's called stoneleaf. It's particularly nasty, and… it doesn't matter. What matters is that we need to get out of this city before more come our way." He motioned to Thoren. "Are you ready?"

Thoren nodded quickly. "I'm sorry, Galen Elvraeth."

"I'm no Elvraeth. Are you ready?"

Thoren nodded and grabbed Haern and Galen, Sliding them.

It happened with a flicker of colors and a sense of jarring movement. When they emerged, they were within a darkened forest. The Aisl forest was home to a great number of people from Elaeavn, though fewer now than even a year ago. The attack on the Elder Trees had changed things, making it so that fewer and fewer people felt safe.

Once they were back, the pull of lorcith came everywhere around him. Haern said nothing as Galen strode toward the darkened shape of the Elder Trees in the distance, and he dreaded where Galen was leading him.

"I'm sorry, Haern," Thoren whispered.

Haern shook his head. "It's not your fault. It's mine. Why don't you head back to the city?"

"Are you sure?"

"You don't need to deal with this."

"What's going to happen?"

"Who knows? Maybe nothing."

Thoren glanced up to Galen for a moment before disappearing with a flicker of colors, indicating his Slide. When he was gone, Galen slowed a step, waiting for Haern to catch up.

"How long?"

"How long what?"

"How long have you been up to this? Has it been since your father disappeared?"

"You say that like he had a choice in the matter."

"Has it been?"

"Not right away, but shortly after."

"All while you've been telling me you were off on your own."

"I *was* off on my own."

"You understand how dangerous all this is? If something had happened to you, no one would have known."

"My father went off like that."

"Your father was better prepared to go off like that. And even he should not have."

Galen locked eyes with him for a moment before spinning and continuing through the Elder Trees. As Haern followed, a strange tingling washed over his skin. It hadn't always been that way, but ever since the attack on the trees, there was that sensation, a strangeness that he hadn't been fully aware of before. Perhaps it was nothing, but it didn't feel like nothing when he detected it. There had to be some meaning behind it, some purpose.

The trees were fading, changing the longer they had the strange implants, and no one knew what exactly it meant for those to be present. It was possible that it signified nothing, that the Forgers had not truly changed anything, but he couldn't help but feel as if there was something to it, and it was something that he failed to grasp.

"Where are you bringing me?"

"Back to your home."

"Are you going to tell my mother?"

Galen stopped, turning to look at him. "You're old enough that you shouldn't be worried about such things. The fact that you are tells me you aren't ready for the challenges you're throwing yourself into, even if I hadn't Seen what happened to you tonight."

"You Saw it?"

Galen nodded. "They held you. You depend so much on lorcith, thinking it will be the key to defeating the Forgers, despite knowing they have the same ability over the metal. You need something more, something they aren't able to do."

Haern swallowed. He didn't know whether or not he should thank Galen for not reporting him to his mother. It was foolish for him to fear her still at his age, but after losing his father, he doubted his mother could stand losing someone else to the Forgers. It was part of the reason he had kept this to himself, but Galen was right. He couldn't keep doing that.

"Will you keep working with me?"

"Will you keep running off on your own?"

"Not without telling you first."

Galen fixed him with his hard stare. His eyes were not a deep green like most of the Elvraeth, but there was something in the way he looked at him that intimidated Haern much more than any of the other Elvraeth he'd been around. "I think it's time for me to be harder with you."

"Harder?"

"If you think you can run off like this, perhaps it's time for me to take a different approach. We need to change your dependence upon lorcith."

"Lorcith is what sets me apart."

"No. It's a crutch for you. Had you another way of

fighting, you wouldn't have been overwhelmed by the Forgers tonight."

"I tried using the steel knives."

"After they were already aware of you. You can't simply act. You need to think, to plan, to strategize. And I'm going to break you until you do."

Haern met Galen's gaze, suppressing a shiver. Galen had already been hard on him, and if he intended to be even harder, Haern wasn't sure what that meant for him.

"Do you still want to work with me?"

"My father is still missing."

"That's not an answer."

"I do."

"Then be ready for a challenge. I will no longer take it easy on you."

2

DANIEL

DANIEL CROUCHED NEAR THE SHORE, THE CAMP IN VIEW, and stayed as low as he could, trying not to draw any notice. He'd been here for the better part of an hour, and all that time, he'd remained nearly motionless. His body ached, but he was determined to uncover anything he could.

Wind gusted out of the north, carrying cold and a few flakes of snow. He still hadn't managed to get over the fact that there was so much snow in the north, though he'd Slid far enough through these lands to have seen quite a bit of it. Each time he Slid, he attempted to move farther and farther from familiar lands, wanting to explore, but there was something else he was after. He wanted to find evidence of the Ai'thol, needed to know where they were moving.

He'd found nothing usable so far, though that wasn't for lack of trying. He continued to Slide, traveling from place to place, discovering the entirety of the continent in a way he never would have considered before. As he went, he found cities that were different than any he had been to, villages that had welcomed him, and he'd found remnants of a time long ago, buildings that were no more. Those interested him the most. Partly it was because he didn't know if any of these represented places that Carth had come from. He knew she had come from a land in the north but not exactly where. She considered Nyaesh part of her home, though even that wasn't completely accurate.

One of the men down on the shore moved. Daniel watched for evidence of Sliding, anticipating anyone who might be flickering in and out of existence, a telltale sign that the Ai'thol might have traveled here. There was nothing. He maintained his mental barrier, prepared for the possibility that if he did encounter the Ai'thol, they would be able to Read him somehow, though so far, he hadn't come across anyone like that.

As the day stretched on, the overcast sky darkening, it was time for him to go. He took a step, preparing to Slide, and found that he couldn't.

Settling himself, Daniel grabbed the hilt of his sword. He had Slid here to begin with, so he knew that he had been able to reach this place once. Whatever had changed had happened over the last hour or so that he'd been here observing.

It was possible they didn't know he was here, but it was equally possible they did and had placed some sort of barricade around him to hold him.

There was a time when he would have been more concerned. In the past, Daniel would have been worried about coming here in this way, but he had been training, developing his ability to fight with the sword if necessary, to overpower various strategies designed to suppress his Great Watcher–given abilities. And Carth had been teaching him how to strategize. More than anything, that had value, especially as it allowed him to think through alternatives in a way he never would have before.

If he couldn't Slide, there wasn't anything holding him from walking.

More than that, the fact that he couldn't Slide suggested that whoever was here had knowledge of that ability, and possibly knew how to suppress it—unless this was an accident. Daniel doubted it was accidental. When it came to suppression of his Great Watcher–given abilities, there weren't many accidents.

He backed away from the small ridge he'd been looking down. As he did, he unsheathed his sword. It was a well-made blade, forged entirely out of lorcith by Lareth, one of the finest sword makers in Elaeavn.

Perhaps he shouldn't have been bringing lorcith blades with him. Knowing what he did about the Ai'thol, it was likely that they had some way of detecting it, and possibly using it.

Maybe they didn't know he was here at all. Maybe what they knew was that someone carried lorcith.

He crept toward a tree, jamming the blade into the trunk before grabbing a pair of knives in his pocket. These were simple steel blades, nothing more than that, and he held them ready. It wouldn't be nearly as easy to fight with knives as it would be with the sword, but he also wouldn't have to fear someone uncovering his connection to lorcith this way.

With every step, he attempted to Slide, trying to move small distances. There was no restriction on him Sliding within this island, so whatever it was somehow contained him to the island in general.

He Slid toward a cluster of trees. Within them, shadows stretched, and he hesitated, looking around and searching for anyone within who might have the ability to control shadows. It was a rare enough ability, but now that Nyaesh had fallen—at least, the Ai'thol had managed to acquire stone infused with Nyaesh's Elder Stone—he worried they might have gained the ability over shadows. He needn't have feared that, though. The A'ras within Nyaesh had a connection to fire and not the shadows. He still didn't know what had happened to the Elder Stone that represented the shadows and whether the Ai'thol had somehow acquired that ability, but seeing as Carth was still able to use it against them, he doubted they had.

Sliding into the trees, he looked around. There was no one here.

How were they able to prevent him from Sliding?

There were a few metals that stopped it. In Elaeavn, heartstone limited his ability to Slide, and while he had never managed to overpower it, there were others who could. It was unlikely the Ai'thol would use a metal like heartstone to defend themselves against the Slider, especially knowing it was ineffective against Rsiran Lareth—a man they feared as much as they feared Carth. That meant there was likely something else.

It would be useful for him to learn what that was.

He scanned the area outside the edge of the trees, finding no movement. Sliding back to the ridge where he'd been watching the men, he looked around. The movement down on the shore was less than it had been before. Small dinghies made their way toward ships anchored in the deep water, and he stayed where he was, observing. The other men on the shore did nothing but wait. Some had a fire burning, as if they were readying to camp for the night, but others were sitting along the shoreline, watching the water as it splashed and caressed the rocky shore.

It was odd.

Then again, tracking the Ai'thol was often odd. He hadn't managed to uncover evidence of them in the months he had tracked them. That troubled him as much as anything else. Carth seemed reassured by the fact that he hadn't come across any Ai'thol, but he was less comforted. They were out there—he knew they were—and if they weren't in the north, he suspected the only reason was because they already had everything they needed from these lands. Any Elder Stones that might be here would already be captured.

These men didn't look like they were with the Ai'thol. None of them did, though he hadn't been able to determine exactly what—or who—they were. The Ai'thol would come to places like this—at least, he suspected they would—but they wouldn't need the ships these men had.

It was time for him to question.

He found a man making his way along the shore. He was heading toward a distant cluster of rocks, and during his time watching, Daniel had seen others doing the same thing, each time returning to the rest. They had used it as their latrine.

It was unlikely they would notice one man missing very quickly.

When the man reached the rocks, Daniel Slid, grabbing him, and then Slid him to the trees. He pushed him away before the man had a chance to react, pointing his knives in the direction of the man.

"What? Who are you?" the man asked. He was thin and of average height, and he wore tattered clothes. His face was deeply tanned, and the tattoos on his exposed skin reminded Daniel of so many of the smugglers he'd encountered. There was something about those tattoos, as if they branded their wearers in a way, tying them to a certain group of men, though that was something Carth had not yet taught him.

"I'll do the questioning."

"What is this?" the man asked again.

Daniel took a step toward him, flickering in a Slide, wanting to be as intimidating as possible when he did. He jabbed one of the knives at the man, drawing just a small droplet of blood. He Slid back, getting away from the man and making sure that no one else neared. As far as this man knew, they were someplace far from the island.

"What are you doing here?"

"Nothing. We're sailors."

"Smugglers."

The man frowned. "We aren't smugglers. We're—"

Daniel shook his head. "Smugglers. I recognize the style of ship." If nothing else, the time spent with Carth over the last few months had taught him about sailing and about ships, things he never would have learned had he remained in Elaeavn. While there were plenty of people in

Elaeavn who sailed, it wasn't something any of the Elvraeth did. "And what are you smuggling?"

"Like I said—"

"Are you going to keep going through this? I've already told you that I know what you are." And he knew they weren't with the Ai'thol. At least, he didn't think they were. The fact that he wasn't able to Slide off the island was troubling, but this man had none of the scars of one of the Ai'thol and didn't seem to possess any connection to magic the way the Ai'thol did.

"This was a job. Nothing else," the man said.

"What kind of job?"

"The kind that paid."

Daniel Slid toward him, jabbing the knife again. He poked the man in the shoulder, drawing another droplet of blood before Sliding back again. "You'll find that I don't have time or patience for such glib responses."

"We were hired to drop some stones in the water around the island. That's it."

"Stones?"

The man nodded. "It was a strange job, but the pay was good. Who were we to argue?"

As he tried to think through what purpose there would be in the stones, the fact that he wasn't able to Slide left him wondering if perhaps these stones were the reason.

"How many did you drop?"

"You'll have to ask the captain."

Daniel glanced beyond the man, toward the edge of the forest and even beyond there. More likely than not, the captain had already returned to the ship, and since he was unable to Slide offshore, Daniel wouldn't be able to easily travel to the captain and question him. "Seeing as how he's not here, I'm asking you. What can you tell me?"

The man shook his head. "I can't tell you anything more than what I have. We brought rocks, dropped them in the water, and we were getting ready to leave."

"Where was the last one dropped?"

"From where you grabbed me."

That would explain why he had been suddenly unable to Slide. It had to. And if they were placing something that prevented the ability to Slide, it had to be on behalf of the Ai'thol. Why protect this island, make it so that those with the ability to Slide couldn't reach it?

Unless that wasn't the purpose of the protection. Maybe it was less about preventing someone from reaching it and more about containing them once they were here.

He shook away the thought. "I need you to show me one of the stones."

"Like I said, the last one we dropped was—"

"I don't want to see the last one dropped. I want to see one where you don't have quite so many men."

The man licked his lips and swallowed. "I'll show you, but can I do something first?"

"It depends. What is it?"

The man looked around, shaking his head. "Well, seeing as how you snatched me as I was heading to take a piss, I..."

Daniel stared at him for a moment. "Are you kidding?"

"I wouldn't kid about something like that. I really have to go, and you kept me from it."

"Go near the tree."

The man sauntered over, heading toward the nearest tree. He started relieving himself, humming under his breath, and Daniel averted his gaze. There was no point in watching the man do his business, and seeing as how he couldn't go very far, he—

The man suddenly appeared in front of him, a sword in hand.

Not just any sword, but the sword Daniel had left.

He brought his knives together, blocking the thrust, twisting off to the side. The man flickered, Sliding as he twisted, and Daniel cursed himself as he Slid as well, emerging near the edge of the forest.

Had he made a mistake?

Somehow he'd underestimated the man and had failed to realize that he was one of the Ai'thol. Daniel had seen no evidence of scars like most of the Ai'thol had, their way of marking themselves, giving themselves increased abilities.

Daniel Slid, watching the other man emerge from his Slide, and he jammed a knife into the man's shoulder. He dropped the lorcith sword, and Daniel kicked it, but the sword came streaking back, forcing him to duck and roll to avoid being impaled.

Not only could he Slide, but he could control lorcith.

Daniel Slid, emerging only a step away, jabbing his other knife into the man's other shoulder. He pinned him down, holding him to the ground. Sitting on the man's chest with his knives in his shoulders, he glared down at him.

"What are you doing here?"

"Seeing as how you felt the need to grab me, I'm guessing you already know."

"What are these stones?"

"Ah, well, that's really the beauty of it. You won't be able to find out."

"Why?"

The man met his gaze, looking up at him, and he started to laugh. "Why? You've already seen why. You won't be able to reach any of the stones, and now that you're here, you won't be going anywhere."

"A trap? That's all this is?"

"That's not all it is, but it's effective for those like yourself. You would have done well to remain in Elaeavn."

"You would have done well not to reveal yourself. I would have brought you back."

"And now I will be the one bringing you back."

The man started to shimmer.

Daniel threw himself back, grabbing his knives, and the man Slid. Somehow he'd managed to do it without taking a step, a technique Daniel still didn't know how to manage. Rsiran could do it, but Daniel's ability to Slide wasn't anywhere near as strong as Rsiran's. There weren't many who had reached that level when it came to Sliding.

With the man having disappeared, Daniel Slid back to the ridgeline, looking down. The other man had reappeared on the shore, and he waved his hands, getting everybody moving rapidly.

Daniel couldn't stay here. They'd soon come after him, and the longer he waited, the more likely it was that they would be able to reach him, and if they did…

How was he going to escape? He couldn't Slide off the

island, but now that he knew these stones ringed it, somehow preventing him from Sliding, he wondered if perhaps there was another way.

He Slid to the far side of the island. In the time he'd been here, he had explored a little bit and found this area to be empty. He emerged on a rocky cliff. White stones stretched down toward the waves crashing along the shore. It was at least a hundred feet, possibly more, down to the water. There were other places on the island from which he could more easily reach the water, but as far as he knew, each of them would be guarded. This was his best bet.

It still wasn't a great idea.

He took a deep breath and jumped.

As he fell, he tried to Slide, but he was still restricted, as he'd expected. If these stones were in the water as the Ai'thol had claimed, then he would still be within the borders. What he needed to do was swim beyond the edge of the stones, reach a place where he could get past it, and then perhaps he could Slide away.

Then find one of the stones. Figure out what it was the Ai'thol were doing and how they were able to use them in a way to restrict Sliding.

Yet even if he found one, he wouldn't be able to travel with it.

When he hit the water, it was like slamming into rock. His breath squeezed out of him, and he plunged beneath the surface. Waves crashed on him, threatening to throw him back into the rock, and Daniel kicked away.

As he did, he traveled further and further from shore.

With each stroke, he made an attempt to Slide. None of them worked.

At one point, he paused and floated, looking up at the rock. The sheer white edge taunted him, and he wondered if he could Slide back up if he needed to, but the sudden appearance of three men looking over the rock forced him to turn and plunge beneath the surface of the water. He stayed there, kicking, still trying to swim away. With each stroke, he was getting further from the island. Hopefully he was getting closer to a way that he could escape.

He had to come up for air. When he did, he floated on his back, looking up at the rock. The three men were still there, and they were watching him.

They knew he was there.

Daniel turned his attention back to swimming, taking stroke after stroke as he pulled himself through the water. Waves continued to crash on him, and he fought through them, battling for each stroke. Each time he did, he focused on trying to Slide, thinking that maybe he could pull himself through a Slide, swim through it in a way he hadn't before.

It didn't work.

How far out were these stones?

If he could find that border, he would have a better sense of what to look for when he returned. And he knew he would need to return, especially if the Ai'thol had discovered a way of preventing Sliding.

A massive swell struck, sending him plunging beneath the water.

Daniel kicked. He wasn't a particularly strong swimmer as it was, and being forced to swim away from the island was difficult. He stayed underwater, looking around, but saw nothing but murkiness. What they needed was Rsiran and his ability with metals to see if he could uncover anything here that restricted Sliding. But then, Rsiran likely wouldn't be trapped here, either.

Another kick, and another attempt at Sliding.

He felt a trembling sense of movement.

Pain built in his chest. He was running out of air and knew he needed to come to the surface, but he didn't dare if this were going to work. He continued to swim, pulling himself forward, and attempted to Slide once more.

This time, he was drawn forward.

He focused on where he wanted to emerge, keeping it at the forefront of his mind, and pulled himself forward.

With a painful, almost excruciating, sensation, Daniel plunged forward, drawn through the water, and he emerged on dry land. He coughed, taking a ragged breath, looking up at the gray sky. A gull soared overhead. He watched its path as it flew, and breathed out heavily.

After a while, he sat up, looking out over the river. This wasn't where he necessarily wanted to be, but it was close to Nyaesh, and close to others he knew would help. And they needed to know about what had happened, though Daniel wasn't certain he wanted to go back there if he couldn't Slide away. He might need to if they were going to get answers, but it left him scared.

The gull circled around him again, cawing, and Daniel got to his feet, making it toward the edge of the water, where he could look out. Ships moving through here drew his attention, and he decided to stand and watch just a little while longer.

3

LUCY

THE MAN WALKING ALONG THE ROCKY SEASHORE IN FRONT of her had a stooped back, and he paused every so often, looking back at the tower. Lucy found herself following the direction of his gaze, curious whether there was anything he might be able to detect from the tower itself, but in all the time she watched, she found nothing. Perhaps there was something there, but she wasn't aware of it.

More than that, he exuded a certain warmth. He practically glowed, and the more she watched him, the more certain she was that the glowing she observed was real. She knew very little about Ras, other than that he had trained Carth, and now he was training her, though Lucy didn't know what she was expected to learn from him.

When she looked back at the tower, following the direction of his gaze, there were shadows circling around it. There was power to those shadows, and it was a power she couldn't help but marvel at.

Somehow, the C'than had managed to capture the essence of the Elder Stone within the tower itself. Though she didn't understand how, she could feel that power and was fully aware of what it did.

"How long have the C'than been here?" she asked, still keeping her gaze on the tower. There was something incredible about it, and the longer she stared, the more certain she was that she was supposed to know something, as if there was some answer to what she observed, and yet she could figure out nothing about it.

"For a long time," Ras said.

"Why here?"

"Why this place, or why here in general?"

Lucy tore her gaze off the tower and looked over to Ras. "I suppose both?"

"The answer to the first is perhaps easiest. This is isolated, and it gives us an opportunity to observe it from a distance. For years, the C'than have moved in the shadows, watching, ensuring there was safety."

"And yet, even though you move in the shadows, you aren't all powerful the same way as Carth."

"No. There are some who are, and we did pursue Carth because of her connection to the shadows, but also because of her natural abilities."

"And what about me?"

"I think I would say that you pursued us."

Lucy watched him. That was as accurate as anything, and she wasn't entirely sure what she should have done otherwise. She had needed to go after the C'than, but partly that was because of the way Carth had encouraged her. She had wanted Lucy to understand the C'than, to see if there was anything she might be able to uncover, and in doing so, Lucy had gained a certain understanding.

Not only that, but because of Lucy, she had helped free women from C'than capture.

"How long have the C'than been here in general?"

"We have an extensive library that might offer you some answers," he said.

Lucy offered a half smile. "I've seen the library."

"You aren't interested?"

She thought of the massive rows of shelves, the towers of books, and knew that whatever else the library might hold, the secrets of this place would be difficult to find. How could she uncover them if she was struggling to decide where to start? She knew there had to be some organizational structure to the library itself, but she had never found it.

"I'm interested. As you recall, I did train as a caretaker in Elaeavn."

"Yes. I am aware. I would argue that perhaps your talents were wasted."

"You don't think I would've made a good caretaker?"

"I wonder if perhaps you were always meant to be more than just a caretaker."

Lucy shook her head. She wasn't sure if that was the case or not, but she did know that in trying to work as a caretaker, she had felt a mixture of emotions. Partly it was a sense of comfort. The library was one place that had always been home to her, a place where she had been welcomed. Until she'd met Haern and begun to spend time in the forest. The other side of it was that in the library she was all too aware of what existed outside of the city. There was so much beyond the borders of Elaeavn, and yet her people remained isolated, as if they feared what they might encounter outside of the city itself.

Lucy sighed, turning to stare at the water. Most of the time she found the waves comforting, reminding her of her home, and yet there was something about this place that was not nearly as soothing as she thought it could and should be. Perhaps it was the violence with which the waves crashed along the rocks, the loud explosion of power as they slammed into the shore over and again. Perhaps it was something about her, her own fear, some aspect of the isolation that existed on the island.

Whatever it was, even though she had been here for the last few weeks, she continued to feel uneasy.

Ras had been welcoming. Carth had seen to that, though when she was gone, there was no reason for Ras to remain accommodating to her. It wasn't as if Lucy was trapped, either. She wouldn't have agreed to stay if she were, mostly because there were others who now depended upon her. She wasn't sure what to do with them quite yet, though she thought she'd found a place for them. Hopefully, she could keep them safe now.

"I always wanted to see the world," she said.

"Many people want to see the world until they do, and then they often change their mind."

"I don't know that I'm going to change my mind."

"That's good. Now that you're here, there is much you can learn."

"I don't know how long I can stay here, either," she said.

"In order to truly be a part of the C'than, you need to embrace what we represent."

"I'm trying, but I feel as if there's more I need to be doing."

"There's always more that we can be doing, but sometimes what we need to be doing is nothing."

She met his eyes. Ras had a flat-eyed stare, and he looked at her, watching her with an expression she found difficult to interpret. It always seemed as if he had something burning behind his eyes, but then, perhaps it was only the fact that he glowed that gave him the appearance of knowing more.

"Come with me," he said.

He continued to walk along the island, winding around the rock, and as he did, he stared out at the water. "You have asked about the C'than, and I've told you. And yet, there is something more you need to know about the C'than."

"What?"

"We have tried to remain neutral, but there is one who has been working against us for years."

"I know about Olandar Fahr."

"Perhaps it's him," he said.

"You don't think it is?"

"I don't know. That is more important. Thinking and knowing are different things, and when it comes to what we must do, we need to *know*."

Lucy stared, not certain what to make of what he was saying. She had believed Olandar Fahr responsible for everything that happened, and yet, every harm she had experienced had come from the C'than—at least, a branch of the C'than. Perhaps rather than Olandar Fahr, the problem was with the C'than itself.

"I imagine you worry the C'than are to blame."

She looked over, wondering if he could Read her. She didn't think Ras had that ability.

"I do wonder if that's possible," she said.

"I admit the C'than must be considered complicit, especially as so much has happened on our watch, and yet, we have done everything in our power to try to ensure we remain neutral. Unfortunately, there have been some who have been influenced otherwise."

"Influenced?"

"The idea came from somewhere. I have yet to learn where that was."

Lucy smiled to herself. Ras didn't believe the C'than could fall victim to a desire for power? From what she'd seen, anyone was capable of that.

"Where did the C'than learn how to place augmentations?"

Carth hadn't even known that answer, and though Lucy had questioned several of the C'than, there had been no real answer from them. She tried to Read Ras, but as usual, she could uncover nothing. It was part of the reason that being around him, being here of all places, was peaceful. It was relaxing not having so many different thoughts intruding upon her.

In other locations, a deluge of thoughts was nearly overwhelming, and the more she experienced, the more she wondered if perhaps there was another way, a way that didn't require her to suffer through all those thoughts trying to crush her.

"It's not something of the C'than," Ras said.

"It must be of the C'than. The technique is different than what the Ai'thol use."

"Are you sure?"

"Very." She touched the back of her head. "I've seen the way the Ai'thol have placed augmentations." Then again, she hadn't seen it firsthand, but she had observed the effects. "And I have seen what the C'than have been able to do. There is a distinct difference between the types of augmentations. The C'than augmentation is far more refined."

"Unfortunately, I must agree with you."

"So the question remains where they learned to place such augmentations."

"If only I was able to answer that, but unfortunately, I am not. I have spent some time searching for those answers, but they remain difficult for me to determine."

"You have no idea?" Lucy found that hard to believe. Given everything she had experienced with the C'than, she had expected some answers here. But if Ras didn't know, then who would?

Perhaps the only way for her to know would be to go looking for those answers.

How, though?

It would involve finding more of the C'than who had betrayed their vows, such as they were, and she had spent considerable time searching for them already. But if there were others who had been experimented upon, Lucy thought she needed to go and search for those for information.

"Unfortunately, we have yet to uncover the key to it." He turned away from the water, meeting her gaze. "As much as we've looked, we have not discovered how they learned that technique."

That was troubling, and not only because they weren't aware how the C'than learned how to place augmentations like that, but because the one person who should know remained in the dark about it.

"What's being done about it?"

Ras regarded her, seeming to glow a little brighter. Was he attempting to Read her? Or did he have some other way of understanding her? Perhaps he was analyzing her, the same way Carth analyzed people she encountered, preparing for how she would have to confront them in a game.

"Are you questioning whether we are pursuing others?"

"I think it's a fair question. When Carth and I went looking, it didn't seem as if the C'than were invested in finding out those answers."

"Perhaps not, and that was a mistake."

"Mistake or not, it's what happened. I think it's reasonable for me to question."

"It is. We have been looking for answers, and yet, we haven't come across anything that would explain things. If the answers are out there, they aren't any place that the C'than can easily reach."

"What about places they can't easily reach?"

"Such as?"

"Seeing as how I don't know how extensive the C'than reach is, I'm not sure."

"The C'than exist all throughout the known lands."

"Are there unknown lands where they haven't extended?"

Ras clasped his hands together, watching her for a moment. "We are not in all places, Lucy Elvraeth. As much as we might try to be, we still have not visited every land in the world. Perhaps you can change that."

"Is that why you wanted me to be here?"

"I believe we have established that you sought us out."

"I did, but I have a feeling you would have sought me out otherwise."

"Perhaps," he said.

Ras turned away from her and continued along the shoreline. Lucy followed Ras, not sure where he was going. There wasn't much on the island other than the tower, and in the time she'd been here, she hadn't really explored much else. The tower was impressive, with multiple levels, and though she had spent considerable time here, she still hadn't uncovered everything about it. The library itself was the most impressive aspect of the entire tower, something she suspected Ras knew would appeal to her.

"If you would begin to understand your studies, you must have a better grasp of what it means to be one of the C'than," Ras said.

"I have been working on my studies," she said.

"You have, but you have also limited yourself," Ras said. "You keep yourself reserved, and you disappear, traveling back to the mainland. If you keep doing that, you will never learn what you need to learn here."

Lucy offered a wry smile. "I think I can manage."

"I understand that your powers are considerable. Carth speaks quite highly of you, and she speaks of your connection to them, along with the control you have over your abilities. There aren't many who have your capacity to Travel, and some would say that only Lareth rivals you."

Rivaled. At least she understood she still wasn't Rsiran's equal. Not that she would have thought she was. She acknowledged Rsiran was something beyond what she could be. Regardless of how much she had learned and how far along she had come, she still had quite a ways before she reached his level. And he had no augmentation. What he did was all his own power.

It was possible she would never reach Rsiran's level. Though she had discovered how to anchor her Slides, the same sort of thing Rsiran had done, she still didn't think she was as powerful as him. With his control over the metal, his way of Sliding was far different than hers, and yet, perhaps that didn't matter. Having a different technique only allowed her to understand there were many ways in which to Slide.

"I will stay as much as I can," she said. "There are others who depend upon me."

"What about the C'than?"

"Would you have welcomed me to the C'than if I weren't helping the other women?"

Ras studied her, and a hint of a smile crossed his face. "Do you want the answer?"

"I think it's fair."

"It is fair, and yet, I'm not sure you want the answer."

Lucy shrugged. "It doesn't matter. You have me as part of the C'than now, and because of that, you have to deal with me."

"Deal with you? You make it sound as if this is some sort of torment for us."

"Isn't it?"

"Lucy Elvraeth, we are pleased to have you with us. You have abilities we can benefit from, much like we have abilities you can benefit from."

"You have knowledge I can benefit from. That's what I'm hoping to gather."

"Perhaps," Ras said.

She smiled. She found him interesting, partly because of his way of addressing her, and partly because she never quite knew where she stood when it came to Ras.

Some of that had to do with the fact that he was powerful in his own way, and perhaps it was in a way similar to what Carth possessed, and part of it was because she knew Carth respected him, almost as much as she respected anyone.

In Lucy's mind, that mattered. Carth was particular about whom she spent her time with, and having Carth decide to respect someone meant something to Lucy, enough that she thought she should trust Ras.

"You haven't begun to teach me," she said.

"Haven't I?"

He continued along the shoreline, picking his way among the rocks. Ras moved easily, and yet, with his back stooped as it was, with his silver hair, she couldn't help but wonder how old he was. He had an air of incredible age about him, and Lucy had been around people like that before who left her uncertain. Carth had an agelessness about her, and though she knew the other woman was probably at least twenty years her senior, possibly more than that, she didn't look it.

"Is this part of your teaching?"

"We can take lessons from everything, Lucy Elvraeth."

When she had first come to the island, arriving at the tower with the opportunity to learn, Lucy wasn't sure what she had expected, but it certainly wasn't this. She had known that Ras had taught Carth, and in doing so had used the game of Tsatsun as a way to hone Carth's mind. Lucy had never played much, but she didn't feel as if she had much of a mind for the game, and for the most part, it didn't matter. She didn't really want to play. It was a game of strategy, a game where she would develop skills, a way she might be able to overpower Olandar Fahr, but the longer she spent trying to learn it, the less she felt compelled.

Whatever else she did, Tsatsun wasn't going to be in her future, and it wasn't something she thought was critical for her understanding of how to conquer Olandar Fahr. There were others who were far more skilled with Tsatsun, not just Carth. Even Daniel had proven to have a certain competence, and she thought he could become more skilled than Lucy ever would be. Daniel had trained his entire life, working with his father, learning about strategy and various things like that. Because of it, she had to believe that Daniel would be a better fit for learning those lessons.

"I guess I expected you to try to teach me games."

"Games?"

"Tsatsun. The way you taught Carth."

"Carth is a unique case, as I imagine you know. And though she is now a master of Tsatsun, that wasn't always the case, and she has benefited from time."

"I think she said she benefited from working with you."

"Perhaps," he said again, smiling and turning toward the water. "How will you benefit, Lucy Elvraeth?"

"Like I said, I'm not much of one for games."

"Do you believe Tsatsun is only a game?"

"Isn't it?"

"Some would say that it is, but others would say it's a way of seeing the world."

"Which others would say that?"

"Those who truly understand it."

"I see."

"But, I won't force you to try to grasp the intricacies of Tsatsun, not if you have no interest in it. Perhaps there's another way we can work together, and in doing so, I might be able to help you find your way of learning, your way of serving the C'than."

"Is it only about serving the C'than?"

"We all must find our way to serve," he said.

Lucy watched him disappear, moving easily along the shoreline. Something occurred to her. It didn't seem as if he climbed over the rocks so much as glided above them.

How powerful was Ras?

Not knowing much about the man, she couldn't help but wonder if he was far more powerful than she had believed. She had known he was skilled, but this was something more—something that suggested a certain type of power.

How did she want to serve?

That was a question she didn't have the answer to. She wasn't sure whether she even wanted to serve. She wanted to learn, and she wanted to be a part of something greater, but what if it wasn't the C'than?

Carth seemed to think it was, and that was part of the reason Carth had brought her here, setting her up with Ras, allowing her the opportunity to learn from him, thinking the two of them would be able to work together in the same way that Carth had once worked with Ras. Lucy wasn't sure if that was a good fit for her. She didn't know if Ras was going to help her the way she needed to be helped.

And perhaps service wasn't what she wanted. At least, not this kind of service. What she wanted was to better understand what happened to the women who had been abducted and tormented, to see if there was any way to help them understand their abilities.

At the same time, she also wanted to better understand the C'than, to see if there was anything she might do to ensure they didn't continue to harm others.

Without the opportunity to spend time with the C'than, to know their intricacies, it was possible she wouldn't be able to learn those things.

And it was her way of serving.

More than anything, she thought Ras knew that.

As she hurried to catch up to him, he glanced over, a knowing look in his eyes. She smiled, ignoring it. She would continue to work with him, and she would learn what she could from him, but she wouldn't be beholden to the C'than as she served.

Ras smiled at her, and once again, she couldn't help but feel as if he were somehow Reading her.

4

RYN

Ryn Valeron twisted the figurine in her fingers. She had spent the last few weeks looking at these figurines, trying to understand if there was something she might be able to learn from them, and in all that time, she hadn't come up with anything. Olandar Fahr viewed these as something important, but she didn't know why or what they were. For whatever reason, he used these figurines, playing a game with them, searching for this mysterious opponent.

She slid one of the pieces along the surface of the game board, looking up at Olandar Fahr. They sat in a small windowless room, the stone walls pressing in around them. The hearth was unlit, a fire unnecessary in the warm room. The wooden chairs were far more decorative than she would've expected for a place like this.

"Is that what you want me to do?"

He offered a hint of a smile. Ever since she had agreed to come with him, leaving the safety and solitude of the temple, some part of him had changed. He treated her differently, and though she was no longer certain why, she doubted it mattered. All that mattered was that she worked as he asked, doing what he wanted of her, and eventually, he promised to show her power.

In order to do the things she wanted, to gain the vengeance she sought, she needed power. Having spent as much time with Olandar Fahr as she had, she believed he could do what he promised, and that there was some way to reach for far more strength than she had managed on her own.

"I have been trying to instruct you on the nature of this game, but…" He moved another piece, and Ryn had a sinking suspicion that her position in the game was far more tenuous than she had believed. She'd thought she had been playing well, but it seemed she had not.

"Why this game?" There were plenty of other games she could work on with him. Growing up in Vuahlu, she had known several different games. Many of the old fishermen liked to play a game they called sticks, dropping small rods of varying lengths onto a game board. It was one she had understood, even if she had never played it well. Even in these lands, Ryn had seen dice thrown at taverns they had visited and knew that though the rules might be a little different in various parts of the world, it was a game played all over. "It seems as if this one takes so long to learn."

"Which is why it is more exciting."

Ryn stared at the pieces. Exciting didn't necessarily describe her experience with it. Exciting would make more sense if there was anything she could fully grasp about this game. The longer she played, the less certain she was that she knew the rules, let alone the overall goal. Somehow, he wanted her to learn how to play so that she would be prepared for another threat, some mysterious opponent he claimed he was playing against.

"I still don't understand why you think I need to know how to play this."

He cocked his head, glancing at her before making another move. "Perhaps you don't need to know how to play, but you can continue to observe."

"How does that help?"

"Do you see how I'm moving this piece?" He took one of the strange animal-like figurines and slid along the side of the board. It wasn't his turn, but Ryn knew better than to argue with him and to challenge him on fairness. "Do you see how it's moving out here?"

She nodded, uncertain what else to say.

"And this one?" This time, he moved a piece along the other side of the board, and once again did so out of turn.

"What's the point?"

"You don't need to know the rules to recognize the move."

"Why would I care?"

He fixed her with a hard-eyed stare. There was always something about the way he looked at her, some expression in his dark eyes that made it difficult to know how to read him. Some of the time, she believed it was anger that caused him to look at her in such a way, and other times, she saw compassion in his eyes.

"Because I care."

She really needed to be more careful with him. It didn't make any sense for her to challenge him on something as silly as a game like this. She knew how important this game was to him and how much he believed it determined everything, even if she didn't necessarily agree.

"And so you want me to notice whether there are other moves made?"

"I think that you can."

"Why me?" She turned her attention back to the board, thinking through how she would move now that he had taken three turns in a row. It disrupted the flow of the game, though she wasn't certain that she cared or that it mattered. If she moved one of the central pieces, she would get closer to what he had told her was the goal, yet she had never been very good at playing. In all the time he had been working with her, she hadn't managed to get to the point where she could even disrupt any of his moves.

"I believe in you, Ryn Valeron."

"Why me?" She forced herself to look up and meet his gaze as she repeated the question. She needed to hear the answer, even though it would be difficult for her to understand. She thought she needed him to admit to her why he had chosen her, and why he continued to work with her.

She had been offered the opportunity for a different sort of safety, but she had chosen otherwise. By agreeing to come with him, by agreeing to serve, she had allowed herself to be a part of this—whatever this was.

Ryn hadn't thought he would continue to work with her, trying to demonstrate how to play a game, but when it came to Olandar Fahr, he often did strange things she didn't fully understand.

"There is much you can see that I cannot."

"I'm not so sure about that."

He smiled at her, sliding another piece along the board. She still hadn't taken another turn. "In time, I believe you will be able to do far more than you know."

Ryn looked back down to the game board. As far as she could tell, there was no other move she could make that would be effective. It was probably what he had wanted anyway, and yet why had he given her a turn? It was unlikely she would have been able to challenge him in the time it had taken him to take those three turns, but it would have been fair, at least.

"Come," he said as he stood from the board. "It's time for us to go."

Ryn looked around the inside of the room. It was a strange place, once again within one of the temples that Olandar Fahr liked to visit, and this one he had simply traveled to, not bothering to visit with the priests like he normally did.

"Where are we going?"

"It's time for you to observe," he said.

One of the things he had asked of her was to observe. As she did, she wasn't sure she had managed to see anything that would be of any use to him. The longer she looked, the more she tried to find answers on his behalf, the less certain she was that she could do so.

"What if I don't find anything?"

"All I ask is that you tell me what you do see." He took her arm, and they traveled.

It was a strange sensation each time they did. There was a sense of movement, but as it passed, she felt a hint of nausea deep in the pit of her stomach. They stepped free under a bright sun. It was warm, but not quite hot. The wind gusted out of the south, carrying with it a strange odor that forced her to wrinkle her nose.

"What is that?"

Olandar Fahr hurried forward, unmindful of the question, and stomped over the hard-packed earth. There were dried grasses all around, and something that made her believe this place had been destroyed by fire. Maybe that was what she smelled.

The landscape was flat, and in the distance it ended abruptly, a large swath of blue stretching beyond.

The ocean.

Why would he have brought her here?

She followed him, trailing after as he picked his way across the ground. His hands were balled into fists, and his back completely stiff. Something unsettled him.

It put her on edge. In the time that she had traveled with Olandar Fahr, she had seen quite a bit, and yet she had been kept from any dangers. That wasn't to say that she hadn't been in danger. There were times when he had traveled to various places and she had risked herself in order to follow him. It was part of whatever test he had for her, his way of trying to ensure she would understand what he wanted, and yet they had never encountered any real, active threat.

This time seemed different somehow.

With just the two of them here, if they came across the real threat, was there anything they might be able to do to get themselves to safety?

She'd never seen Olandar Fahr fight, though from the way men within the temples they had visited regarded him, it seemed he was viewed as some sort of skilled fighter.

Maybe it would be better for her just to stay close to him, prepared for the possibility they might need to escape at a moment's notice.

Other than the strange odor in the air, Ryn didn't see anything. There was no movement, nothing that suggested they were in any danger.

"What is it that—"

Olandar Fahr spun toward her, raising a finger to his lips. Intensity burned in his dark eyes, and he scanned the land around them. With a flicker of movement, he appeared next to her and leaned close, whispering in her ear. "Say nothing."

She nodded.

Her heart hammered wildly, though it felt as if she were reacting to him rather than to any real threat.

If there was a threat, why would he have brought her here?

Ryn remained silent as instructed, searching for anything that might explain what they were going to encounter. The longer she looked, the less certain she was that she would find anything to explain what had unsettled him.

It was possible he had only brought her here to scare her. But that didn't fit with what she knew of the man. When he took her places, there was always a purpose behind it.

What had he wanted from her?

Observe.

Ryn turned slowly and looked everywhere around her.

What if he wanted her to look in a different direction? To see beyond the obvious?

She felt as if something were changed, as if something about this place was wrong, and the more she focused on it, the more certain she was. The damage seemed to be caused by fire, as if the entire land had been burned, almost as if to…

"What are they hiding?" She whispered it, before remembering he had warned her to silence.

Olandar Fahr turned back to her, his brow furrowed. "Hiding?"

Heat worked up her cheeks as she flushed. "I'm sorry. You told me to be quiet."

He took her arm and they traveled. They stepped free near the water, waves lapping at the shore with a soft murmur. Sand pressed beneath her boots.

"What did you observe?"

She turned back toward where she thought they had been, though she wasn't certain whether she was even looking in the right direction. When they traveled like that, it was difficult for her to know where they appeared and what direction they went. She thought they had been directly to the east, but it was possible he'd brought them north or south along the shoreline.

"I'm not exactly sure. All I know is the fire seems to be significant."

"Fire?"

"Wasn't there a fire?"

He pressed his fingers together. "It's possible that there was. What did you detect?"

Ryn thought about the strangeness, the odor in the air,

and the overall feeling she'd had. Maybe it wasn't a fire at all. It was possible it was something else entirely, and it was possible that she was completely wrong about what she had sensed.

"I just thought there might have been a fire," she said, looking down at the ground. Here he had wanted her to try to observe in a different way, to see if she might be able to uncover anything, and all she had done was make a fool of herself. "I'm sorry I let you down."

Olandar Fahr started to chuckle, and she looked up at him. "You didn't let me down. As I told you, you might be able to observe things I cannot."

"What happened there?"

"The better question would be where we were."

"Why?"

"It is nowhere near any land you would easily have visited." He stared over the water. "Until I developed my ability to travel, such places were isolated for me. I had to travel by ship, and going that way is almost painfully slow."

He stepped toward the edge of the water, and an occasional wave sent it rolling over his boots, but Olandar Fahr seemed not to mind.

"When we first encountered some of these isolated places, we thought they were devoid of any life, but the longer we spent here, the more we realized there was something else taking place."

"What?"

Olandar Fahr took a deep breath. "Unfortunately, I don't have those answers. I've been talking to you about understanding the game, and knowing various moves, and you wondered why I have been spending my time like this. Well, this is the reason. I have been trying to understand what exactly is taking place. There are things I don't see, and I need someone like yourself to help." He turned toward her, watching Ryn for a long moment. "Are you willing to help?"

It seemed as if this were some sort of test, and that answering incorrectly would lead to her not only disappointing Olandar Fahr but also finding herself perhaps exiled from him. She still wasn't sure exactly how she wanted to serve, but she did know that she didn't want to be sent away.

"I am."

Olandar Fahr watched her for a moment and then smiled. "Good. There are a few other things I need to show you first, and then we will see about your blessing."

He took her arm, but as he did, she trembled.

5

HAERN

Darkness surrounded Haern, and he looked around, feeling as Sightless as if he were without any abilities at all. Normally his ability to See kept him from having this sense of helplessness, but within the mines of the Ilphaesn Mountain, darkness so complete that all he managed to see were small gradations of shadow overcame him.

The sense of lorcith pressed all around him. The metal was dear to his people, causing great heartache over the years, and for a while had been believed to be incredibly rare. It surrounded him, nearly overpowering him, which was exactly the reason he was here.

"Can you use it?" Galen asked.

His voice came from behind Haern, but near enough it almost felt as if he should be able to reach out and touch the man, though he doubted he would have that opportunity. Galen was Sighted, much like Haern, though his Sight was much more powerful, tied to the time when he had carried one of the great crystals.

"I don't feel anything different."

"You need to focus. You need to—"

Haern grunted, cutting off the other man. "I know what I need to do."

Irritation surged within him, mixed with a sense of helplessness. He hated that it seemed as if there were nothing for him to do. His father was missing, taken by the Forgers, injured—possibly dying and perhaps even dead already—while he did nothing other than continue to train. While his abilities had improved, nearing the point where he thought he would be able to withstand another Forger attack, he still felt impotent when it came to figuring out how to reach—and help—his father.

In the time since Galen had rescued him, he'd pushed Haern but had done so by returning to basics. It was incredibly irritating.

"There's no point in taking out your anger on me," Galen said.

"I know you're only trying to help. It's just I can't pick out the sense of lorcith from within here."

"Your father could."

Haern squeezed his eyes shut. It did little but make it that much darker. He clenched his jaw, forcing down the frustration. "I know what my father would have been able to do. He had more talent with lorcith than I do."

"Only because he worked with it. You can do the same. That's all I'm demanding that you do."

Demanding. That was the difference now. Before, he'd asked. Now Galen didn't take it as easy on him.

Worse, Haern knew he shouldn't get frustrated with Galen. The other man was only trying to help him use his abilities in a way that would allow Haern to find his father

—and have a chance at rescuing him when he did. The people he was going against had far more experience using lorcith, in ways that were beyond what he was capable of doing. And that meant he needed to continue to practice.

He'd seen it himself. He'd failed to understand it, but Galen was determined to help Haern realize just how much he needed to learn.

"My father could use metals other than lorcith."

"You don't think you can?"

"I've had no ability with any other metal."

"Because you haven't tried to foster it."

"I've tried."

"No. You pay lip service to your attempt, but you haven't really tried. If you had, then you would have discovered some way."

"How do you know?"

A soft shuffling told him that Galen came closer. "Has your father ever told you much about his time within these mines?"

"He told me that he was sentenced to serve here." It was something Haern still struggled to understand. The mines had once been a punishment to the Elvraeth, something he couldn't fathom. Why would men be sentenced to come in here blindly? Now the mining guild, along with those of the smith guild who had a connection to lorcith, pulled the metal from the walls of these mines. They worked together, the way the Great Watcher would have wanted.

"It was here that he discovered his full ability with lorcith," Galen said.

"He had an ability with lorcith before then. That was why he was sentenced here," Haern said.

"But it was here that he began to fully understand the depth of that connection and what that meant for him. Surrounded by lorcith like this, how could he do anything else? It's why I have brought you here. I want you to explore it in the same way he did."

"My father had no choice but to explore his connection. If he didn't, he would've been trapped here."

"With his ability to Slide, your father was never trapped."

"My father was not all-powerful."

"Not at first. It took him time to reach the point where he would become nearly impossible to stop. All of that stemmed from his experience and his training."

"I'm not my father."

"Which is what you keep telling yourself." Galen was nothing more than a shadow in front of Haern, close enough now that he could feel the other man breathing on him. There was a faint awareness of lorcith coming off him, but it was difficult for Haern to ascertain whether that came from something Galen carried or the lorcith within the walls of the mine shafts. "You compare yourself to him, regardless of whatever else you tell yourself. You like to think you aren't his equal."

Haern coughed. "I'm *not* his equal."

"You are something different. You are both your father and your mother, and both are strong."

Haern bit back the first response that came to mind. His mother was strong, but in a different way than his father. His father's abilities were what mattered now.

They needed Rsiran and the powers he possessed, not the Sight Jessa had.

"Galen, this is pointless. Let's get back to the forest, where we can continue our training. I made a mistake. You've proven that."

"You did make a mistake. And until you begin to hone your abilities, I think you need to experience something similar to what your father once suffered."

"You intend to sentence me to the mines?" he asked, laughing nervously.

"Yes."

"There's no way. The guilds spend too much time here, and even if they didn't, we would have to..." Haern frowned. It seemed almost as if the wind whispered a different way through the mines than it had before. "Galen?"

No answer came.

"Galen?"

His voice echoed off the walls, a muted sound that carried, reverberating throughout the mine shaft, disappearing.

Could Galen actually have abandoned him here? Haern wouldn't have believed that before, but the old assassin *was* angry with Haern over leaving the city, so maybe it was possible.

He had to be here somewhere. Galen could move more quietly than Haern could manage, but he thought he would have noticed. Then again, maybe not. Anytime Galen made a noise, he did so intentionally. Much like when he had stepped toward Haern within the mines.

Great Watcher.

Was he truly trapped?

Without any way to Slide himself to freedom, he would be stuck here, which was exactly Galen's point.

Presumably, the reason they had come down into the lorcith mines was so Haern could get some experience using his connection to the metal, trying to pick out something as small as one of his knives while surrounded by all this lorcith. But while he did have an awareness here, it wasn't one he felt he could do anything with. The lorcith overwhelmed him. It filled the walls and the floor and the ceiling of the mine, coming from everywhere. His father once had told him that the metal could guide him, that he could use it to navigate, but Haern didn't have that same ability. As he had told Galen, he wasn't his father.

Now that Galen had disappeared, he had to wonder if the other man had planned this all along. What would he ask of Haern?

To escape. *That* was what he asked of him.

Haern tried to focus on the knife he knew was on the ground. Maybe Galen was waiting nearby, counting on Haern discovering his connection to lorcith in a way he approved of, and once he did, Galen would come to him, allowing him to leave. Even if he didn't, Haern thought he could navigate out of the mine, though it would take time. They had Slid in, and supposedly they were going to be Slid out, though if Galen had intended to leave him here, Haern wondered if perhaps that wasn't going to happen as promised.

Focusing on the knife brought him no closer to being able to grab it with his ability.

He crouched down, swiping it off the mine floor in frustration, and pain shot through his hand.

Great Watcher. Now he'd cut himself on his own lorcith-forged blade.

He clenched his hand tightly, squeezing it into a fist, trying to ignore the way it throbbed, but it continued to pulsate. At least it took his mind off the fact that he was here.

He could wander out of here, but how long would it take? When Galen had guided them here, he had instructed Erric to Slide them deep within the mines. Haern doubted he would easily find his way free. Worse, he had no idea which way he needed to go.

He was tempted to wander off, head out into the rest of the mine, but if he took a wrong turn, then Galen wouldn't be able to find him when this test was over. And it *had* to be a test.

Haern took a seat. What else could he do? He was trapped, and without any way of getting free, he might as well focus on lorcith, searching for some way of connecting to the metal. Whatever way that was would have to be greater than his typical connection. That connection had been honed by his father, a way of reaching for the metal that Haern had never managed before. But then, Rsiran had taught him to do so in a way that allowed him to fight, *pushing* and *pulling* with lorcith so he could practically fly. That wouldn't be helpful here.

He swore to himself.

It was a helpless feeling, one he had known far too much these days. Ever since his father's capture, Haern had felt completely helpless. The only way to escape the feeling would be by coming up with some way of saving his father.

He focused on what he knew of the metal, the tricks his father had suggested he would be able to perform when he began to master that connection. According to his father, lorcith would practically glow, though he had no sense of that now. It was dark, pitch black in here, and he wished it would glow if only to light his way.

His stomach rumbled. He'd already been training with Galen for several hours before the other man had decided to pull this trick on him.

"You can come back at any time," he called out. His voice echoed off the rock. "I'm just going to sit here and wait until you come back."

A soft breeze billowed through, whispering across his face. The air smelled of the strange metallic scent of lorcith. It was a distinctive odor, and down here in the mine, a steady and consistent breeze gusted through, and the smell of the metal was nearly overpowering.

He lost track of how long he sat. Moments stretched into minutes, which stretched into hours. In all of that time, he came no closer to understanding lorcith. Somehow, when his father had been trapped within the mines, he had come away with a greater understanding of the metal. That didn't seem to be Haern's fate.

After a while, he got to his feet. The breeze had to be coming from somewhere. What if he followed the tunnel's breath? If he did, he could track it out and chase down Galen, and demand he not pull anything like that again.

Only, if he didn't get challenged in such a way, he

would never fully explore his abilities and would never rescue his father.

As he wandered, he tried to think of the lessons his father had taught him about his connection to lorcith. There weren't many. One of the issues he had with his father was that he hadn't worked with him. His father had always been so busy chasing after the Forgers that he was never at home. If he had been, maybe Haern would be better prepared for this.

At one point, he found a branching off of this mine shaft and turned, heading in a different direction. He continued to follow the steady sense of wind coming through the mines, and he thought the light began to change. At one point, he paused, staring and trying to determine if that was real or not. He thought it was, though with his connection to Sight, he might only be Seeing more. Then again, he hadn't been able to See all that much before.

At another branch point, he turned, once again following the steady breath of wind coming through the caverns. His mind continued to wander. It was possible he could roam these caverns for days before coming across anything. The Ilphaesn mines were extensive. Maybe he should have stayed where he was, but stubbornness had won out, and now he had no idea whether he could even turn back. There had been enough turns along the way that he could be lost here.

After taking a few more turns, Haern stopped, looking around him. This was a mistake. He should have known better. Where was he now? As far as he knew, he was getting no closer to any way out.

He tried not to let the rising panic within him overpower him, but it was difficult.

Was this what it had been like for his father when he had been sentenced? If so, it would have been an awful feeling. He felt helpless and that was even knowing he wasn't meant to be here indefinitely. Galen didn't want to trap him, but he also intended to force Haern to find some way out, to connect to his Great Watcher–given abilities in a way that he had not yet managed. When his father had been sentenced here, it would have been for much longer than this. His father wouldn't have had the same hope of escape, the same belief that someone would come for him, rescue him.

That would have been worse.

Then again, when his father had been here, there had been others with him. Granted, they were prisoners much like his father, essentially slaves, banished by the Elvraeth as a penance that preceded their exile, but it was quite a bit different to be trapped in here alone.

As he continued to wander, he felt increasingly certain the path was lightening up. That had to mean that he was getting closer to the exit. And when he reached it, he decided that he would have to say something to Galen. This wasn't the kind of training he wanted.

Another few turns, each time following the sense of the breeze, and he couldn't help but feel as if he were even more turned around than when he had first come in here. While it did seem to be getting lighter, he still couldn't see anything. The sense of lorcith continued to press all around him.

And maybe that was a problem. It shouldn't be

pressing all around him. There should be a void within it he could pick up on. That void would indicate the opening to the tunnel, and it should be both in front of and behind him.

Was there any way for him to pick up on that sense?

There had to be, didn't there?

Maybe not here. Maybe if he reached a branch point, he could use that to help him find where those voids might be.

Haern continued, taking step after step, now hurrying as he wanted to find one of those branches within the tunnels. When he came across one, he paused.

He stood in the middle of the intersection of the mine shafts, focusing on lorcith. It was all around him, pressing upon him. Some of it had a particular quality to it, and as he listened, he thought he could hear it the way his father had wanted him to, a song that called out to him. It was as if the lorcith demanded his attention.

What he wanted was to find an emptiness within it. Once he located that, he could see if there was anything else he could do. As he focused, he thought he picked up on emptiness.

It was there; it had to be.

And yet, concentrating as he did, he realized it wasn't emptiness that he felt so much as emptiness that he *saw*. The shifting shadows revealed something else, something different, and it seemed as if more than just the darkness swirled around him.

Strangely, the walls seemed to glow.

Haern took a step toward them, focusing on those walls, reaching out, and when he touched it, he knew he wasn't imagining it. The mines here weren't getting lighter at all.

It was him. He was detecting lorcith differently.

He focused on it, searching for anything different within it, taking a moment to unsheathe his knife and set it on the ground. When he did, he stared, looking to see if he could See the difference, and it was there.

Haern *pulled* on the knife. It returned to him as it should, and he *pushed* on it again, sending it streaking down the tunnel before calling it back.

"Galen! I did it. I figured it out."

He waited for an answer.

None came.

"Galen?"

Once again, there was no answer.

Could Galen have truly left him here?

He wouldn't have expected the other man to do that, but then he had wandered off, so any abandonment would be his own fault.

"Galen!"

Even though he might have succeeded at reaching for the lorcith in a different way, he was still trapped within the mine. Somehow, he would need to find his way out. Without any way to Slide, it would have to fall upon him.

At least he was no longer trapped here in the dark. And at least he could use his connection to lorcith. Maybe he could use it another way, but that would involve him finding some great connection he didn't yet possess.

Now that he'd had some success, at least he believed he could have more.

6

HAERN

Night had fallen by the time Haern finally managed to reach the entrance to Ilphaesn Mountain. He stood above the water crashing on the rocks far below, an opening that he would have no way of navigating down from. His heart sank.

After all that time wandering through the mines, now he wouldn't even be able to get out of them?

He stared out at the water. It was almost peaceful from up here, with nothing other than the waves crashing around him, the sense of lorcith all around behind him, and silver strands of moonlight reflecting off the water. From here, staring down as he did, he could almost imagine the Great Watcher looking down over them, protecting his people.

And yet, if the Great Watcher were observing from on high, why wouldn't he be willing to protect them from the Forgers? Why leave them abandoned, feeling as if there was nothing he was willing to do for his people?

As he stared out over the water, Haern experienced that mixture of emotions, a combination of peace and tension he didn't know how to deal with. Worse, he had no idea how he was going to get out.

Something had changed for him, and he should be thankful for that. Now that he was able to detect lorcith in a greater way than he had before, he should appreciate what Galen had done to him, but all he felt was irritation at the fact that Galen had left him stranded. What would've happened had he not managed to find his way out?

Even now, there might not be any way for him to completely get out of here. There was one thing he could try. He *pushed* on his lorcith knife, sending it out from him, holding on to his connection so that it hovered in front of him. It took a combination of *pushing* and *pulling* in order to maintain that hovering before him, a measure of control he had only begun to obtain.

From here, he wondered if he could *push* off, send the knife out, and use that to prevent him from crashing onto the rocks far below. But doing so would involve exquisite control over the lorcith.

Could he lower himself slowly?

He let the knife down, dropping it toward the rocks, and once it was down, he focused on his connection to lorcith. As he did, he took a deep breath and then jumped.

The jump carried him out. He hovered for a moment, suspended over the knife, but then he started to fall.

Haern *pulled* on the knife and sent it streaking along the shore, *pushing* off again as he soared farther away. He *pushed* and *pulled*, using the movements of the knife to draw him along the shoreline, and gradually descended from the point up on the mountain itself.

When he landed, finally coming down to rest along the rocks of the shoreline, he plucked the knife off the ground and stood panting, struggling to catch his breath as he stared outward.

He had done it.

Haern had used his knives in a way that would carry him before, but never from such a height, and never with so much control. What he'd just done showed that he was capable of something he hadn't known before.

"You look pleased with yourself."

Haern spun to see Galen standing behind him. Erric was with him, though he remained a few steps back.

"How did you find me?"

"I never left. Not really."

"You left me in the mines."

"I let you believe that I left you. I wasn't going to let you wander through there aimlessly."

"How long was I in there?" It seemed like hours. Why hadn't Galen come to him sooner? Why leave him wandering?

"The better part of the night."

Haern turned his attention back out toward the moon. It had descended far enough that he realized Galen was telling him the truth. It had to have been hours.

"All of that to prove that I could find lorcith?"

"I didn't care that you reached lorcith," Galen said. He rolled a pair of darts between his fingers. Ever since he started working with Haern, training him, Galen had begun to reassert his own abilities, and there was a nervous energy to the man, a twitchiness Haern didn't remember seeing when he had first ventured out with him.

"Then why?"

"You needed to know that you could."

"All of that to prove I was capable?"

"There's value in confidence."

Haern glanced back to Erric, but the other man stood partially turned away. He had some ability of his own beyond Sliding, though Haern wasn't entirely sure what it was. It might only be something as simple as Sight. He didn't think the other man was a Listener. That ability was fairly rare, and he didn't have the tilt to his head Haern associated with Listeners. Most of them twisted so they could keep both ears focused on the conversation, though perhaps that was only Haern's perception.

"I found a way to detect lorcith more strongly."

"I expected you would."

"What if I hadn't? How long would you have given me?"

"I was prepared to wait days. Longer if it were necessary."

"You would have tormented me like that?"

"I would have encouraged you. I've told you what I went through during my training."

"You nearly died. You've tried to teach me a different way."

Galen grunted. "I haven't done anything with you near what I experienced. I wasn't sure that method of teaching was appropriate, but then you went off to face Forgers on your own."

Haern glared at him but softened when Galen didn't look away. "I could handle it."

"Maybe, but *I* didn't handle it all that well." He sighed. "I'd prefer not to have to teach that way. While there are lessons you can learn through experience, not everything needs to be experienced to be fully understood."

"Such as dying?"

"That would be one thing. Besides, you have an ability I did not, and with your connection to lorcith, you can fight in a way I could not. But you have to find a way to use it without being solely dependent upon it. I think there is value in you continuing to learn and master the various healing arts—"

"Healing?"

Galen shrugged. "They are healing arts, regardless of what you might believe. Just because we don't use them to heal others doesn't mean they don't have that purpose. It's why you need to continue to work at them."

"I have been."

Galen watched him for a moment, continuing to roll the darts. Haern worried he'd use them against him, but then he stuffed them back into his pouch. "Are you ready to return to the city?"

Haern glanced back at Erric before shaking his head. "Not yet. I think… I think I might stay here a little while."

"It's a long way back."

Haern pulled on one of the knives. "I don't have to walk."

"No. I suppose you don't." He turned his attention

back to Erric and grabbed the other man's arm, waiting a moment before they disappeared in a rapid Slide.

Haern stood for a while, staring out at the water. There really was something peaceful about it, and the longer he was there, looking outward, the more relaxed he felt. It was strange that water crashing along the shore could relax him, yet it did. It put him at ease, calming him in a way that very few things ever did.

He stood motionless while watching the water before eventually deciding it was time to turn back. Grabbing two of his lorcith-forged knives, he *pushed* off on them, sending himself soaring into the air, and *pushed* and *pulled*, making his way along the shore. He preferred traveling that way, though it might be a more roundabout path. The sound of the waves crashing around him was soothing, with a steady rhythmic quality that seemed to guide him, washing him toward the city. On foot, it could take days to reach Ilphaesn, while Sliding could take them there in the blink of an eye. This way was slower than Sliding, but quite a bit quicker than walking. Besides, traveling in this way gave him an opportunity to continue to practice using his knives.

It also helped him think through what he would have to do. Eventually, he would have to find a way to use lorcith in smaller quantities. His father had made that clear, especially with the way the Forgers were able to use lorcith themselves. If he could master it, if he could find a way to do so with smaller and smaller quantities, fully grasping the intricacies of the alloy, he wouldn't be in such danger if things didn't go right. And, unfortunately, too often things didn't go right, such as when Galen had had to save him.

How would he ever get to the point where he could travel without fearing the Forgers overwhelming him? Most of the Forgers he had come across had enough potential with lorcith that he worried he wouldn't be able to overpower them using lorcith alone. If they controlled it while he was fighting them, he ran the risk of losing a fight before it even began.

He dropped to the ground, pulling another knife from his pocket. This one was an alloy, an even mixture of lorcith and iron, and he used that, *pushing* off so he would be forced to hover above the ground. As he did, he stayed there long enough that he felt confident he could do it.

Making his way further along the shore, he headed back toward Elaeavn. As the city came into focus, he slowed his progress. It wasn't that he regretted approaching the city, but there was something quiet and peaceful about traveling out by himself. He had never loved being alone the way his father seemed to, but he didn't necessarily fear it, either. He had spent most of his time surrounded by other people, so to be here alone like this was calming in a way.

When he reached the edge of the city, he dropped back to the ground, collecting his knives and stuffing them into his pocket. It wouldn't do for him to travel through the city this way, though it did seem a shame to have to walk now that he had begun to master traveling like this.

From here, the city spread up from the shore. Along the shore itself, rows of massive warehouses lined the road. The occasional guard patrolled, and Haern watched.

Most of the soldiers who patrolled the warehouses were sellswords, hired by the Elvraeth to guard items that had long belonged to their family. Haern had often wondered what the Elvraeth kept in these warehouses, though he had never taken the time to attempt to force his way in. There was no point in doing so, as it would only serve to raise the wrong sort of questions. He wasn't Elvraeth, anyway, so even if he were curious, going into the warehouse would be a violation.

There were other places along the road. Noise from a few different taverns drifted out into the night. There was a certain merriment to the taverns, the sounds joyous and happy, and on a whim, he realized where he needed to go.

When he reached the Wretched Barth, he paused. It was his uncle's tavern, and the place where his parents had first come together, meeting with his uncle and planning their eventual overthrow of the Elaeavn. Every time he was here, he was reminded of his namesake, a man he'd never met but whom his mother had clearly cared deeply for.

He paused with his hand on the door, hesitating as he listened to the sounds inside. There was singing and rhythmic stomping from dancing, and over it all came the steady sounds of a lute playing.

"Are you going to go in or are you just going to stand there?"

"Uncle Brusus," he said, looking over at him. His uncle had deep green eyes and a quick smile. He'd gone gray, but he kept his hair cut short, giving him a more youthful appearance than he would otherwise have had. The cut of his jacket and pants demonstrated a certain flair and signified the wealth he knew his uncle to have. Not all of it was honestly obtained, though that was part of Brusus's charm.

"You look as if you've been tormented," Brusus said.

"Galen has been working with me."

Brusus's face clouded briefly, the same reaction his father had when dealing with Galen. There was much about what had happened between them that Haern still didn't know, though it was so far in the past that it shouldn't matter any longer.

"I suppose he would be the best one to prepare you with your father missing."

"He's not missing. We know the Forgers have him."

"That's not what I was getting at, Haern."

"I know, it's just that I—"

"I know. You want to do anything in your power to get your father back. I understand that. If I were younger, I would go with you."

"You keep saying that you're too old to help, but you're not. Not really."

Brusus smiled, though it was a sad smile. "Perhaps I'm not. It might be that I'm afraid, Haern. It was one thing when we were battling the Hjan. At least I knew what they were. This, the Forgers, these Ai'thol, they're something else."

"They're all the same, Uncle Brusus."

"They are the same, but different. The Ai'thol have gained power beyond what I can counter. Even though I've held one of the crystals, and it changed me"—he grinned widely, and this time it spread to his eyes—"I still don't feel I'm the best person to combat them. Your father, on the other hand, really is, but he's not enough."

"I'm not sure that I'm enough, either."

"You have youth, and you have something I never did."

"What's that?"

"It's what made your father so effective."

"His ability to Slide? I don't think that I'm going to develop that ability. Even if I were able to hold all of the crystals, that's not something they've been known to grant." Holding the crystals typically augmented other abilities of the Great Watcher. Those who managed to hold them, people like his parents and Brusus and countless others within the city, all found aspects of their Great Watcher–given abilities augmented, sometimes in obvious ways such as with Brusus and his ability to Push, something related to Reading, but different at the same time. Others were granted unique abilities, such as Della and Darren. Unfortunately for Haern, he had not been granted any increased abilities by the sacred crystals. If only he had been, perhaps he would be more formidable.

"Your father was powerful for another reason. His ability to Slide was useful, I'll give you that, but that isn't what made him what he was."

Haern ignored the comment about what his father *was* rather than what he *is*. It suggested to him that Brusus had already begun to believe his father was truly gone. It was possible that was true, but it was equally possible he could be rescued and returned. That was what Haern counted on.

"What reason was that?"

Brusus studied him for a moment, cocking his head to

the side and making Haern wonder if he weren't Listening. "Why don't we take a seat? Your aunt has been cooking all evening, and I'm sure she can provide you with something even your mother can't argue with."

"I..." His stomach started to rumble, and he changed his mind about protesting. Besides, where was he going to go tonight anyway? "That sounds great."

Brusus smiled and waved at the door as if Haern was going to choose nothing else. Once inside, Haern's gaze swept around the tavern. Circular tables surrounded by chairs took up much of the floor space, though a section near the back of the room was kept free for dancing, giving the musicians space. There was a raucous sort of activity within the tavern, an energy that had a buoyancy and vibrancy to it, along with a certain joyousness Haern didn't necessarily feel.

Brusus nodded to a few people closest to the door, clapping one man on the shoulder and leaning in to whisper something, shaking another man's hand, weaving from table to table as he greeted people. Within the tavern, his uncle was truly in his element. Regardless of what Brusus might say about his age preventing him from taking on the Forgers, Haern suspected there was a much more practical reason. The tavern suited him. In reality, Haern had a hard time seeing his uncle as anything other than a tavern owner. In all the years he had known his uncle, he'd been like this, always working a room, clearly at ease with the crowd, and always smiling as he visited with his patrons.

Haern wasn't nearly as comfortable within this environment. It wasn't that he minded crowds, but they didn't suit him the same way they suited Brusus. Even his parents seemed to be a better fit for places like this. And as his aunt Alyse emerged from the kitchen, carrying a plate heaped with steaming food, he was reminded why.

Brusus patted him on the arm. "I'll be right back, boy."

He swept away, heading over to his aunt Alyse and kissing her quickly on the cheek. She shot him an admonishing look before dropping the tray onto a nearby table and heading over to Haern.

"Has your uncle been corrupting you again?"

Haern smiled and gave his aunt a quick hug. "Not yet."

"Only because he's already been corrupted. With that father of his—"

Alyse arched a brow. "You blame his father and not the uncle who corrupted his father?"

"I did nothing to corrupt Rsiran."

"You would blame his mother, then? I'll make sure to let Jessa know the next time I see her."

"You would do no such thing."

"You don't think so?"

Haern laughed softly. There was a playfulness between them and an obvious affection despite the age difference. His aunt had to be ten years Brusus's junior, but that clearly didn't matter. There was a happiness to them even his parents didn't have, though Haern blamed his father for that, along with his frequent and extended absences. Had Rsiran been around more, perhaps his parents would have the same good-humored banter, though he had a hard time envisioning that from either of them. His father, for one, was far too serious to have Brusus's playfulness. And his mother spent most of her time worrying about his father.

"I think the boy is hungry."

"And you intended me to whip something up for him?"

"You *are* his aunt."

"And you're his uncle. You can scurry back to the kitchen and see what you can prepare for him."

Brusus gave her a wide grin, leaning in to peck her on the cheek before sauntering off toward the kitchen, though not before weaving through the crowd a few more times, pausing every so often as he visited with various people at different tables. Alyse watched him go, a smile quirking her lips.

"How are you?" she asked as she turned back to Haern.

Something within her medium-green eyes softened as she looked at him, and Haern shook his head, lowering his gaze. It was easy to lie to his uncle, to try and keep strong for him, and even to try to convince him he was okay with all the training. It was the same thing he did with his parents.

With his aunt, it was something else. It wasn't so much that she was able to Read him, though he suspected she could. Alyse was known to be a potent Reader, augmented by her time with the sacred crystal. Yet, it was more than that. It was the way she looked at him, the compassion that shone in her eyes, and the fact he had always felt welcome with her. As much as his father had been absent over the years, his aunt had always been there for him. Sometimes she was simply someone for him to confide in, and other times she advised caution.

"I'm going to be fine," he said.

She touched his arm, and Haern looked up, meeting her eyes. "Fine. All of us are fine, Haern."

"For now."

"You worry about the Forgers returning?"

"They've already attacked."

"And none since Rsiran disappeared."

"He didn't disappear, he was—"

"Abducted. I am quite aware. And he is my brother. I care quite deeply about him, but I wonder why the attacks ceased once they abducted him."

"They were after him all along," Haern said.

"They must have been, but what is it that your father had access to that made them want him?"

Haern shook his head. He wasn't entirely sure. The protections placed around the city had been designed and built by his father, but despite the absence of the one person who was most capable of ensuring the lorcith and heartstone barriers around the city were secured, there hadn't been any further attacks.

"I fear for him."

"As do I. Yet your father is strong. Stronger than me. Stronger than most."

"I know he is. He's been through this before, but…"

"You feel this is different."

"This *is* different. I was there when he was taken, Alyse. They stabbed him with a lorcith rod, and he was dying."

Alyse took his hands, guiding him to an empty table and helping him to sit. She sat across from him, still holding on to his hands and keeping his gaze locked on hers. "I know you don't want to hear this, but it's possible that your father is already gone."

"I... I know. It's why I've been preparing."

"From what I understand, you haven't been preparing. You've been *training*. That's not the mark of someone who's accepted the fact that his father might be gone. It's the mark of someone who intends to risk himself to go after him."

"I've already done it once and succeeded."

"That was different."

"I know," Haern said, looking back down. He couldn't meet his aunt's gaze.

A tray was set on the table, and Haern glanced up to see Brusus standing next to Alyse, worry etched on his face that matched his wife's. "What is this?"

"It's nothing but an aunt and her nephew having a conversation. Did you need to intervene?"

"I brought him food like you told me to."

"And now I need you to go and check on the rest of our patrons."

Brusus locked eyes with Alyse for a moment before smiling and turning away. He began to work through the crowd, stopping at table after table, whispering a few words or clapping a patron's shoulder before moving on.

"What happens if he's really gone?" Haern asked.

"We must be prepared."

"Which is what I've been doing."

"You've been training yourself. We need to train others. It's what your father once had done."

"He hasn't tried to train others in a long time," he said.

"No, since he began to wander out of the city on his

own, he abandoned his commitment to training others. Most who have been here believe that was a mistake."

"He kept the Forgers away from the city for years."

Alyse patted his hands, and he looked up, meeting her eyes. "It's okay for you to admit your frustration with what he did. He felt he needed to go it alone, that his ability was enough to overcome the Forgers."

Haern took a deep breath before nodding. She was right, and he knew it. He had felt the same frustration over the years as well, hating the fact that his father had gone off frequently, feeling as if he were solely responsible for countering the Forgers. Instead, all he had managed to do was anger them, draw more attention to himself, and prevent others within the city from having the necessary experience to counter the Forgers. Perhaps his father had weakened the city by trying to go it alone.

"You've made your point, Aunt Alyse."

She squeezed his hand and stood. "I hope so. Now eat. There are others within the city you can continue to work with. I know Galen has been training you, and from what I understand of his history, he might be the best to help you become as capable as you can be. But there are others who will want to fight. There are others who will *need* to fight."

She left him, and Haern began to pick at his food, enjoying the savory meats. Brusus might have brought the tray to him, but the quality of the cooking told him that his aunt had been responsible for it. His stomach calmed as he ate, and his mind began to clear. Perhaps he had been too consumed with trying to get to his father.

Brusus took a seat across from him, sliding into the

chair as he looked down at Haern for a moment. "How is it?"

"It's wonderful. Thank you."

"Thank your aunt. She's the one who made it."

"I know," he said in between bites. "You never told me what made my father as effective as he was."

"Ah. Well. The key to what made him so successful was something that I didn't have until later." Haern looked across the tavern, locking eyes once more with Alyse.

"Aunt Alyse?"

Haern looked back at him, meeting his eyes. "No, they weren't close until much later. I'm talking about your mother."

"My mother?"

"She was always his anchor. She kept him grounded when others could not. Far too many overlook the fact that it was Jessa who kept him from losing himself when he could have done so easily."

"You're saying I need to find someone like my mother?"

"If there's a special someone?" Haern shook his head, turning his attention back to his food, and Brusus laughed. "I'm saying you need to realize that you can't go it alone. No one can. We all need someone to keep us anchored. For as powerful as he was—"

"*Is.*"

"Is," Brusus said, nodding. "He still needed something to anchor him. As do you. As do we all. It doesn't have to be a love interest. But you need to find your anchor or you'll go floating off and perhaps lose yourself in the process." Brusus stood, glancing around the tavern once more before turning his gaze back upon Haern. "Enjoy your meal, boy. I'll stop back after you're finished."

Haern watched his uncle disappear back into the kitchen, chewing slowly. How was he going to find his anchor? What would keep him from losing himself?

If he couldn't find that, did it even matter?

7

DANIEL

The ship bobbed in the water, and Daniel glanced over to Rayen. Her dark hair caught the breeze, fluttering, and she pulled it behind her head, gripping it with one hand, the other resting on the wheel as she navigated the ship.

Daniel approached, glancing at her for another moment before looking over to the water again. "We're getting close."

Rayen nodded, not taking her gaze off the bow. Every so often, she glanced from side to side, and she tipped her head, as if listening.

"We haven't seen any ships come through here. I think they're gone."

"There haven't been any ships, but there is something odd about this water," she said.

"Odd?"

A particularly large swell caught the ship, sending Daniel staggering. He braced himself, trying to roll with the waves as Carth had taught him before righting himself and stumbling toward Rayen.

"There's something in the water that we continue to brush up against. I've been careful not to crash into it too often, but I worry that the longer we are out here, the more likely we will slam into something that will crush our hull."

Daniel nodded. They didn't want that, especially if there wasn't any way for him to Slide them to safety if necessary.

"Rocks?"

"I don't know. I haven't sailed these waters before."

"We could have waited for Carth."

Rayen glanced over to him. "I don't know how long she'll be gone. From what you tell me, this is important, and we needed to investigate."

Daniel took a deep breath. When he'd gone back into the city, he had searched for Carth, but she had been away. That wasn't uncommon. She was probably with Lucy. Each of them had their own purpose, like pieces on the Tsatsun board, and he wanted to fulfill his role.

"This is important." If Carth and Lucy were to end up on the island, they could be stuck the same way that Daniel very nearly had been. Then again, Lucy was far more capable at Sliding than he was; it was possible she wouldn't find the same issue with Sliding away.

"Rayen. Port side."

Daniel glanced up to the woman in the crow's nest. He didn't know Isabel very well, but with her short curly hair, dark skin and deep brown eyes, she was different than most of the women he had grown up around.

Daniel followed the direction that Isabel pointed, looking off to the left side of the ship, and saw a large island stretching out in the far distance. He frowned, focusing on where he had Slid.

Rayen glanced at him. "Is that it?"

"I think so."

"It doesn't look like there's anyone there," she said.

"No."

"So much for us needing everyone we brought with us."

Daniel smiled. He was relieved they didn't need the dozen Binders, though he was thankful Rayen had trusted him enough when he had told her what he'd encountered. If they were going to have to fight Ai'thol, they would need more than just a couple people.

"It's probably for the best. This way we can investigate."

"If these stones are sunk far offshore, it might not matter. It will be nearly impossible to find anything on the seabed."

"We have to look, though."

Rayen turned her attention back in front of her. "We have to look."

"They didn't sail into shore. They took smaller vessels."

"That's my plan, too, but I want to get to a place where I feel more comfortable leaving the ship. Besides, if something happens, how many of us do you think you can Slide away?"

"One or two, but that's only if we manage to break

through whatever barrier they have that prevents me from Sliding."

"Even more reason to be careful."

Rayen turned her attention back in front of her, and Daniel let her work, staying near the center of the ship, trying to keep his balance. Every so often, a wave would crash along the ship, sending a spray misting up, drenching him. His cloak shed water quickly, but he was still far wetter than he wanted to be. When sailing, it felt as if he were drenched all the time. He didn't understand how Rayen and the others seemed completely unbothered by it, but he did understand why so many sailors and smugglers he'd come across over the years preferred to be shirtless. It was easier to dry that way.

After a while, Rayen whistled, and Tori hurried over from where she had been working lines near the mast. Rayen handed her the wheel, whispering something to her before turning to Daniel. "Let's grab the dinghy and take a few of us."

He made his way to the back of the ship, climbing into the dinghy, and Rayen, Isabel and Beatrice joined him. Beatrice had bright red hair, a freckled face, and strangely silver eyes. She carried two swords at either side, both slender blades, and there was something dangerous about the way she moved. Daniel had spent very little time talking to her, but *not* because she intimidated him. Many of the women who worked with Rayen were capable fighters.

Once they hit the water, the spray continued to splash up over the edge of the boat. Daniel gripped the railing, and rather than using an oar, Rayen pushed off with her shadows, sending them streaking through the water, moving far more quickly than they could were they under sail or oar.

He tapped her on the arm as they approached. "We don't want to get too close. I don't know where the boundary might be."

"How far out were you when you were able to Slide away?"

Daniel shook his head. "I don't know. I was trying to stay out of view of the Ai'thol."

"If nothing else, we can reach the shore and you can start working your way out, searching for anything that might give you an idea of where the barrier is."

"What we really need to do is find one of those stones. We're going to have to study it."

"Possibly," Rayen said.

"Can you use your shadows?"

"It doesn't work like that."

"Why not? If you can probe the seabed, maybe you can find any irregularity."

"You do realize how incredibly massive the ocean is?"

Daniel nodded, sweeping his gaze around him. "We're not talking about the ocean itself. We're talking about just one part of it. And once we figure out where that barrier is, we can search around that line, trying to find where they would have placed the stones. And I know they have one in front of this beach, so we could use that to help us identify where it might be."

Rayen shook her head. "You're diving for it."

Daniel glanced over to Isabel and she shrugged. "I'm with Rayen," she said.

"Thanks. What about…?"

He trailed off before asking Beatrice. Turning his attention back in front of him, he focused on his ability to Slide. What they needed was to know where that threshold might be, and he pulled himself, moving barely more than an inch or two, enough that he felt confident he still could Slide.

As he Slid, he kept the shore in view, watching for a moment where he wouldn't be able to Slide again.

Rayen continued to push them forward, propelling them across the water much more slowly than before. Daniel stood, taking a step forward and back, Sliding with each one. At first, he wobbled, nearly falling into the ocean—much to Isabel's amusement—but the more he did it, the easier it became, and he sort of rocked in place, moving forward and back as he tested his ability to Slide.

And then he couldn't.

"Here."

Rayen glanced over her shoulder, and the boat came to a drifting stop before reversing direction. Daniel attempted to Slide, but again he couldn't.

Rayen pushed them slowly away from the shore again. Daniel continued to work on rocking forward and back, each time trying to get a sense of when he could reach for the ability to Slide again.

It still didn't come.

"Well?" Rayen asked.

"I…" He Slid. "Here."

She leaned over the edge of the boat, and darkness streamed away from her. Daniel watched, uncertain whether he'd be able to pick up on anything or not, but he didn't See anything of use.

Rayen turned the dinghy, and they drifted parallel to the shore, the shadows continuing to sweep out from her. He knew this was unlikely to provide any answers, but they needed to do something—anything—that might uncover what the Ai'thol had done here.

"Here." Rayen pointed, her eyes closed, shadows swirling around her. "Straight down. There's something large. It's irregularly shaped, and"—she tipped her head forward, placing her face almost up to the water—"it seems anchored." She opened her eyes and glanced over at Daniel. "Get going."

He peeled off his cloak, pulling off his boots next. Isabel sat back, arms crossed over her chest, a hint of a smile on her face. "What is it?"

"I'm hoping you'll take off more."

Beatrice snorted, and Daniel felt a flush working through him. He pulled his shirt off, and Isabel whistled.

"The pants are staying on."

"You'll have to take them off later. You'll be too wet," Isabel said. She reached forward as if to grab his pants. "I'm happy to give you a hand."

Daniel shot Rayen a look. "Can you help?"

"She's right. We don't want you to suffer needlessly on board the ship once you grab this." She grabbed his pants, giving them a sharp jerk.

Pulling away, he jumped into the water, bobbing in place for a moment as he took in a deep breath. "I'll be fine. Now can you tell me where I'm supposed to go?"

"I'll tell him—"

Rayen cut Isabel off. "Straight down. I can't tell how deep it is here, but it's pretty deep. You're going to have to hold your breath for a while."

"You know, it might be better for you to do this."

"It might, but seeing as how you brought us out here, I figured you would be the one who would take the swim. If you can't do it, I'll give it a try."

Daniel glared at her for a moment before plunging beneath the surface of the water. He swam straight down, kicking. After taking a few strokes, he could already feel the pressure of the water as it threatened to squeeze the remaining air out of his lungs. He hadn't been kidding when he'd suggested that Rayen might be the better of the two of them to do this. With her ability with the shadows, she could propel herself through the water far faster.

His hand struck the seabed.

It was soft, mucky, and not nearly as deep as he had expected.

He crawled along the seabed, searching for anything that might be off. The one advantage he might have over Rayen was his enhanced Sight, and with it, he tried to peer through the darkness, but he saw only gradations of gray.

The water was calmer here. An occasional fish swam past him, and other creatures were on the seabed, but he tried to ignore anything else. There were much larger creatures in the ocean, and he dreaded the possibility of coming across anything that might keep him down here.

A slightly darker item caught his attention.

Daniel kicked toward it and grabbed it. It was smooth,

and he wrapped his hands around it, trying to pry it free. Unfortunately, it was also heavy.

He wasn't going to be able to carry it out of the water.

He planted his feet on either side of the stone, wrapping his hands around it, digging deep beneath the rock. When he had a solid grip, he kicked, streaking toward the surface.

The rock started to slip out of his hands, and Daniel tried to grab it, but he wasn't able to hold on. It tumbled from him and plunged back to the seabed.

He wasn't going to be able to swim his way back to the dinghy.

Making his way back to the surface of the water, he popped his head out of the waves and looked around. There was a moment of panic when he feared that Rayen had taken the dinghy away, but he found them twenty feet from him. He waved, and she navigated the small vessel toward him.

"I found it, but it's heavy."

"You're a big, strong man," Isabel said. "I'm sure you can pull it out of the water."

"I can't get it to the boat. Do you have a rope?"

Rayen frowned at him. "How long do you need it to be?"

"I don't know. Forty or fifty feet." That was probably a little too long, but it would give him some extra length if he were to drift.

"We don't have any rope quite that long in here," Isabel said. "Now, back at my place is a different story."

Daniel shot her a look, which she ignored. "Do we

have any other way of helping me get back to shore if it comes down to it?"

"There's something I can try," Rayen said.

Daniel waited, feeling pressure all around him, and it took a moment for him to realize that she had wrapped a band of shadows around him.

"Go quickly. I don't know how long I'll be able to hold on to this."

Daniel took a deep breath and then plunged back under the water. He swam back the way he'd gone before, moving as quickly as he could. Now that he knew how deep the water was, he wasn't nearly as worried about holding his breath. He scanned around for the stone but didn't find it.

His hand sank into the muck, and he crawled along the seabed, feeling the way Rayen held on to him with her shadows. There was a certain resistance that made it hard for him to swim.

How long would she be able to hold on to this?

He continued to swim, trying to pull himself in the direction where he thought he had seen the stone before. At last, he made out the shadowed form of what he thought was the stone.

Daniel had to drag himself along the bottom of the ocean, the shadows making it more difficult. When he reached it, he wrapped his arms around the stone, and then he yanked on the shadows a couple times to get Rayen's attention. He clutched the stone and then kicked.

The stone began to slip from his grip much like it had before. He squeezed, wrapping the entirety of his body around the stone, afraid that if he lost it again, it would get away from him. How many times would he be able to try this?

In order to understand just what the Ai'thol did, he knew that he would try it again and again.

Pressure suddenly pulled on him, dragging him. His ears popped, and he burst free of the water. He gasped, sucking in a deep breath, squeezing his arms around the stone. The dinghy was near, and Rayen continued to pull him.

Arms grabbed him, wrapping around him and heaving him into the dinghy.

Once he was in, he released the stone. He leaned back on the railing, looking at it. It was a silvery black, though there seemed to be a pattern within it. It was mostly made of what appeared to be rock, though veins of metal ran through it. Even with a cloudy sky, the silver striations caught reflected sunlight.

"That's it?" Isabel asked.

"I don't know. This was what I found."

"How do we know if it's what we were looking for?" she asked.

"Let's take it back onto the ship, and if I can Slide onto the island, then it was it."

Rayen arched a brow. "What happens if you get trapped?"

"Then you bring the dinghy and rescue me."

"Maybe I'll bring the dinghy and the two of us can have some time before we head back," Isabel said.

Daniel met her brown-eyed gaze, shaking his head, not even certain how to answer. Isabel looked back at him and then started laughing.

Rayen steered the boat back toward the ship and motioned to the other Binders on board to raise the dinghy. As they did, she pulled the stone onto the ship, lifting it far more easily than Daniel had managed.

"See? I think you should have been the one to have gone after it."

"I wouldn't have been able to find it so easily."

"Even with your connection to the shadows? I think you could have used them to search for the stone."

Rayen cocked an eye at him. She watched him for a moment before turning away and heading back on board.

Daniel hopped onto the deck of the ship, chasing her.

"Why didn't you?"

"I don't like to swim."

"You don't like to *what*?"

Rayen paused, holding the stone in her arms as if it were nothing. He suspected she was using her shadow connection in order to do so, but seeing her cradling it so easily still left him at a loss. "As I said, I don't like to swim."

"But you're the captain of this ship!"

"And I stay on board the ship."

Daniel shook his head, watching as Rayen set the stone down next to her at the wheel, shooing Tori away. Rayen quickly turned the ship, pushing shadows out behind her. How much strength did she have? There had to be some limit to her abilities, though he hadn't seen it.

"Can you Slide to the island?" Rayen asked.

"We might need to be farther away before I try."

"Then try."

He looked over, realizing that she had propelled them

rapidly through the water, and they had to be quite a distance from where they had been before. The shadows were powerful, but he hadn't understood just how powerful they were when she was sailing. He made his way to the stern, looking back at the island, focusing on it.

Beatrice joined him, one hand on her sword. "I'll go with you if you want."

It would be good to have someone else with some fighting skill if there were any Ai'thol remaining. "Have you ever Slid before?"

"No. Is it painful?"

She didn't sound as if she were worried if it were, and he marveled at her calm. "It's not painful, but those who Slide for the first time often describe it as somewhat disorienting. I just wanted to warn you before we go."

"How long will it take?"

"Not long." He grabbed her arm, and she stiffened. "I have to have contact with you in order to Slide."

Beatrice nodded.

He stepped forward, moving in a Slide, and emerged on the shore of the island. He took a deep breath, noting a pungent aroma. It wasn't the same as what had been here before, and there were the remnants of the campsite along the shore. It was almost as if they hadn't cared about hiding the fact that they were here.

"That is odd," Beatrice said.

Daniel nodded. "I would've expected them to have removed any evidence of their presence. I don't know why they wouldn't have done so."

She glanced over at him, her silvery gaze locking eyes with him. "No. I meant the traveling. There was a fluttering of movement and a chorus of music. It stopped when we appeared here."

Daniel was scanning the shore, preparing to Slide back to the ship when he paused. "A what?"

"Movement. You told me there would be movement, and I suppose I should not have been surprised by it."

Daniel shook his head. "That's not it at all. What I'm asking about is the chorus of music you mentioned."

"Yes. It was soft, and it called to me. I suppose that was your doing, some way of holding me with you."

Daniel frowned. As one of the Elvraeth, he had aspects of each of the abilities of the Great Watcher, but his ability with Listening wasn't nearly as strong as others. Was Beatrice a Listener?

Even if she were, the fact that she heard music during the Slide surprised him. He had Slid hundreds of times during his life, and in none of them had he ever experienced what she described.

What would that mean?

It was something to ask someone with much more experience Sliding than himself. Rsiran might have answers, or even Lucy now that she was so skilled with Sliding.

"What did the music sound like?"

"It was a choir."

"Choir?"

"Many singers all joining together. You do have those where you're from, don't you?"

Daniel shook his head. "We don't. We have musicians. Minstrels."

Beatrice met his eyes. "In my land, we have the

Hallowed Choir. Three hundred of them in all, and their voices join together to make beautiful songs to the gods. Many wish to join the choir and sing, but very few are skilled enough to do so."

"And that's what you heard?"

"Not quite like that, but it was reminiscent of it. The sound is beautiful. The songs are meant to stir even the most reluctant of gods to turn their gaze upon our people and grant their favor."

"Maybe that's what it was," Daniel said.

"It was not your doing?"

He shook his head, debating whether he should say anything more, but Beatrice intrigued him. "I've never heard the choir you speak of before. When I Slide, I hear a whistling of wind and the sense of movement, but that's it."

"I heard no wind or whistling, but perhaps what you hear as whistling, I hear as a choir."

He shrugged. It was as good an explanation as any, and regardless, it probably didn't matter.

"Are you ready?"

She nodded. Daniel grabbed her arm and Slid her back. For a moment, he feared that the Slide would fail, and he felt an overwhelming sense of relief when they emerged once more on the deck of the ship.

"It appears you disrupted their work," Rayen said.

"It appears so."

"Let's return with this stone and—"

"Ship!"

Daniel glanced up to see Isabel once again in the crow's nest. She was pointing off to the south, and he turned, reaching the railing and staring out. He caught sight of sails in the far distance but didn't recognize the ship. That it was here, so close to the island, suggested that it was one of the Ai'thol's.

Daniel turned to Rayen. "What's your plan?"

She glanced down at the stone. "I think we must sail as quickly as we can."

"You don't intend to fight?"

"Normally when it comes to the Ai'thol, I relish the opportunity to confront them, to make them pay for everything they've done, but in this case…" She stared at the stone, nudging it with one boot before turning her gaze back to Daniel. "Unfortunately, I think it is far more critical that we return to Nyaesh and have an opportunity to study this stone. We need to know what they're planning."

"Is there anything I can do?"

"Don't bother me." She gripped the wheel, and they suddenly lurched forward. He moved away from her, reaching the railing, staring out over the water at the ship in the distance. As they raced along, he realized there was more than one ship. There were three, and each one seemed to be holding pace with them.

At least they weren't getting any closer, but how long could Rayen hold out? Would she reach a point where she grew fatigued and the ships overtook them?

8

DANIEL

It was late in the day, dusk settling in, and Daniel continued to stand at the railing, unwilling to move anywhere. He watched, noticing the ships ever so slowly moving closer to them. It was a subtle thing, but it happened gradually enough he doubted they would be able to outrun them.

He turned his attention to Rayen. She remained at the helm, but the usual stiffness to her spine was gone. She slumped forward slightly. He worried she wouldn't be able to hold out much longer.

"How far to Nyaesh?" he asked her.

"We still have quite a ways to go," she said.

Daniel glanced over to the water, looking outward. "We aren't going to outrun them, are we?"

"I intend to do my best," she said.

"I think it's time I do my best."

"And what is that?"

Daniel glanced around the deck of the ship. Ever since encountering the three ships, the Binders had been active, all of them staying above deck, working quickly. All told, there were probably a dozen people.

"If we can't outrun them, and we need to get the stone out of here, then you should let me Slide them away."

"Take the stone. The rest of us will—"

"I'm not taking the stone first. I want to save the people."

"We can handle the Ai'thol."

"I know you can, but three ships' worth?"

Rayen clenched her jaw. "Take the women who have been on duty longest."

"I need to go quickly. Otherwise you're going to be too far for me to return." Even if he took one at a time, he would have to Slide as quickly as he ever had in order to return to the same spot. That would require him to start at the bow and hope that he would return no farther than the stern. He'd have to move with a speed and a focus he wasn't sure he could manage.

For these women, women who had fought beside him, he would try.

He glanced down at the stone. It would be the hardest for him to Slide, so he would have to take that last.

"You're going to have to give the order," Daniel said.

"Of course." Rayen whistled, and Tori came running toward her, waiting as she whispered something into her ear. When she was done, Tori nodded, racing off.

Daniel started toward the bow, waiting. Two women appeared, neither of whom he knew all that well. Mandy was short and strong, wearing a single sword, whereas Leah carried two much like Beatrice. Leah was taller, coming up to Daniel's chin, and they both looked at him with suspicion.

"I'm going to Slide you to safety," he said.

"We aren't abandoning the others."

"Rayen agrees with this plan," Daniel said.

Mandy watched him, and something in the way she did made him think she wanted to hurt him. "I know what Rayen agrees with. That doesn't mean I agree with this plan."

Daniel glanced at the two women before flicking his gaze over to where Rayen remained at the helm. Was he going to have to fight with them to convince them to do what was needed?

In the distance, the ships were now close enough he could make out the logos fluttering on the sails.

"We need to stay ahead of the Ai'thol. This isn't about fighting them. Not this time. I know you are both capable fighters, but the longer we remain, the more likely it is they will overpower everyone on board this ship." When neither gave him any sign that they were in agreement, he shook his head. "There are three ships, and likely all of them are full of Ai'thol. We need to get moving before anything happens."

Mandy opened her mouth, and Daniel decided to simply Slide to them, grabbing both women and then Sliding them to Nyaesh. He released them and Slid back to the ship.

He was gone for no more than a heartbeat or two, and yet when he emerged, he did so near the stern. He staggered, almost thrown over the railing, catching himself and Sliding so that he ended up near Rayen.

"I thought you were going to take some people off the ship."

He nodded. "I am. I did. Mandy and Leah."

"They are safe?"

"They're safe."

"This is difficult for you?"

"Reaching a moving ship is difficult. If I mistime it, I could end up in the water, or even embedded in the deck of the ship." That was part of the reason he made certain to emerge a little above the deck, landing with a thump on board, and part of why he'd staggered so much when he had emerged.

"I could slow the ship," Rayen said.

"I don't need you to slow it. I need to be faster."

"I don't know how much longer I can hold this." Rayen looked over at him, meeting his gaze. It was a rare moment of honesty from her. She was a strong woman, and he knew she hated to admit to any weakness. The fact that she did meant she was very near the end of her abilities.

He needed to work quickly.

"Give me a few more minutes."

She took a deep breath, gripping the wheel, and nodded.

Daniel Slid to the bow, waiting for others to join him. Two more women, Isabel and a woman named Elaine, arrived. He said nothing, Sliding them rapidly to Nyaesh before Sliding back.

He thought he was as fast as he had been before, counting his heartbeats, but he emerged closer to the railing, practically falling onto it with the movement of the ship. Daniel caught himself, glancing over to the oncoming ships before turning his attention to where the other women approached. He Slid to the bow, waiting for two more. He grabbed them when they appeared, Sliding them, and returning as quickly as he could.

When he emerged, this time he slammed into the railing.

Daniel staggered, catching himself before he fell over and into the water.

It seemed as if he were going as fast each time, but it couldn't be true. If he were, he would end up in the same place.

The only way he would be able to keep this up would be to go one at a time. It would take more trips and more effort, but it was possible he would be able to keep from ending up in the water.

He grabbed the next Binder, Sliding her to Nyaesh before Sliding back. When he emerged, he was pleased to see that he was in the middle of the deck.

One after another he went, taking woman after woman away until it was only he and Rayen—and the stone.

The three ships were near.

"We're going to have to abandon the ship," he said.

"I know."

"Will Carth be angry?"

Rayen glanced over, frowning at him. "Carth doesn't care about the ships. If you know anything about her, you know that all she cares about is the Binders."

"Then what's the problem?"

"There is no problem."

The way she said it told him that she wasn't convinced.

Something slammed into the ship.

Rayen jerked the wheel, and her jaw clenched.

"What is it?"

"They mean to board us."

"They're still quite a ways away," Daniel said.

Rayen nodded toward the nearest ship. "It won't be long."

"Then it's time for us to go."

"What's your intention?"

"I intend to get you out of here."

"And leave the stone?"

Daniel glanced down at it. It still reflected the light, shimmering. After all the Sliding he had been doing to rescue the rest of the women from the ship, he didn't know if he had the strength needed to Slide both the stone and Rayen.

If he had to choose, it was an easy decision. Rescuing Rayen was far more important than bringing the stone with him. It was possible that he could return to the island, find another stone, and uncover what the Ai'thol were doing in that way. It was better that than to lose Rayen.

Could he bring them both?

He was already tired, and it was possible he didn't have enough strength to do so.

Rayen continued to squeeze the wheel, her knuckles white. She wouldn't say it, but he could tell she was nervous.

"What are you waiting for?" she asked without looking over at him.

"I'm trying to prepare myself."

"For what?"

"For taking you and the stone at the same time."

"Take the stone. Don't worry about me."

"I can't do that."

"You might not have a choice."

One of the other ships aimed something at their ship, and Daniel stared, caught up in trying to understand what was targeting them. Almost too late, he realized it was a massive ballista bolt. It crossed the distance between their ships far faster than he would have imagined possible. Another struck. Then another. All of them attached with rope, and they dragged their ship back.

Daniel grabbed Rayen, leaning down to lift the stone, but it was heavy.

"I'm going to need your help."

"With what?"

"Holding on to the stone."

Rayen cracked a half smile. "You're not strong enough to carry it?"

"I'm not strong enough to carry you and it."

"And I've told you that you don't need to carry me."

"And I've told you that I—"

He didn't have a chance to finish.

The ship started to heave.

Rayen released the wheel, scooping up the stone, holding it with swirls of shadow curving around her. She looked at him expectantly.

Taking her arm, he stepped into a Slide.

They didn't go anywhere.

"Daniel?" Rayen said.

"Give me a minute," he said.

"We have only a moment more."

He took another step. Something held him back.

It wasn't the same resistance as when he had been on the island. This seemed to come from something closer—the stone.

It would require a great heave of effort. At least he hadn't tried to Slide it first. If he had, he wouldn't have been strong enough to return for the others. He might not be strong enough to get it away.

He continued to try to pull, tearing himself across the distance, dragging himself toward Nyaesh, but they didn't move.

"They intend to capsize us." Rayen was far calmer than he felt.

Panic raced through him as he tried to Slide. Each attempt left him failing, and though he knew the solution was to take only himself and Rayen, there wouldn't be any point in having risked themselves if they didn't take the stone back with them.

He needed to do this.

Daniel screamed as he attempted to Slide.

With a tearing sensation, they began to move, but slowly. Painfully.

There was no whistling, and no choir. There were only the slow reverberations of the painful Slide.

Daniel held on to the focus of the Slide, worried that if he didn't, they would end up emerging someplace far from where he intended. There were reports of others who had ended up emerging places where they hadn't wanted to be, and he could easily envision some mistake with the Slide—especially one this difficult—pulling him out and leaving him someplace unsafe.

He screamed.

He tried to refrain from crying out, but couldn't. There was too much pain rolling through him from the effort involved in Sliding. Everything about him hurt. Arms and legs and even his insides all throbbed from the effort of the Slide.

And then they emerged, like drawing free from thick mud.

He staggered, stumbling forward and looking over at Rayen, who lay next to him. For a moment, he feared she wasn't moving, but then she rolled over, looking at him.

"You could have warned me that it would be so painful."

"It's not supposed to be."

He glanced down at the stone. He had made it, and the stone had come with him, but where were they?

It wasn't Nyaesh. The landscape around them was incredibly rocky, and he didn't see anyone moving. There was the sound of waves crashing against the shore nearby, but not so near as to be able to see them.

"Where did you bring us?" she asked.

"I don't know." Getting to his feet, Daniel had to brace himself, resting his hands on his thighs. He took a few gasping breaths, straining to calm himself. If he had to Slide again, he wasn't sure that he'd be able to. It had required every ounce of strength he'd possessed to make it this far, and going any further would be nearly impossible at this point.

"There's something familiar about it," Rayen said.

"You've been here before?"

She wasn't nearly as shaky as he was when she got to her feet, and she started to venture away. After taking a dozen or so steps, she paused, and shadows drifted away from her, rolling across the ground. Rayen's breath caught.

"What is it?" Daniel asked.

"I know where we are."

"And?"

She looked over at him. "I've never visited, not as an adult. And I thought it was destroyed."

"You thought where was destroyed?"

"Here. Ih."

9

DANIEL

Daniel looked around the landscape. It was unwelcoming. The rock was all black, likely volcanic, and rough under his boots. The air hung with a sulfuric stench, though the wind carried it away, whipping inland, bringing with it the smells of the sea. A gentle haze hung over everything, making it difficult to see clearly. When the wind picked up, it carried the haze away, leaving more of the landscape visible.

Had they Slid only a little ways inland?

They were lucky to be alive, if so.

"Are you sure this is Ih?" he asked, heading toward Rayen and joining her where she stood surveying the landscape.

"Look out there." She pointed, motioning toward the distant rocks.

Daniel frowned, trying to uncover anything he could, but nothing was clear. All he noticed was more of the rocks. "What am I supposed to be seeing?"

"This. All of it. This was once Ih."

"Once?"

She nodded, squeezing her hands into fists at her side. Rayen wore tension upon her like a cloak, mixing it with the shadows that swirled around her. "It wasn't always like this. It was supposedly a wondrous land, a place where my people were able to understand and master the connection to the shadows. Over time, something changed."

"What changed?"

"War. Ih battled with Lashasn, two nations that had once been separated."

"How long ago was this?"

"Centuries."

"It still looks like this?"

"The Lashasn are the precursors to the power that exists in Nyaesh."

"The Elder Stone?"

Rayen nodded. "The history of that time is not well known. There was so much destruction, so much devastation, that everything that mattered was lost. Eventually, both Ih and Lashasn fell, leaving only Ih-lash in its wake. Even that didn't last long."

"The two peoples merged?"

"There was an attempt to merge, but how can you merge two people who have never trusted each other? It wasn't possible. Instead of merging, there was nothing but more fighting. Rather than fighting openly, the fighting that took place after Ih-lash was founded ended up being on a smaller scale." She wandered away from him, pausing from time to time to lean down and touch the rocks. Every time she did, Daniel waited, uncertain what she was attempting to determine, but then she would stand again, making her way further along the rock. "This was the heart of Ih long ago."

"How can you tell?"

"Because it still steams," she said.

He frowned, realizing that the haze wasn't what he had thought. "This is from destruction caused by the Lashasn?"

She nodded. "Much of ancient Ih was destroyed, much like Lashasn was destroyed by my people." She turned to him, standing and wiping her hands on her pants.

"What if the Elder Stone is here?"

"We've searched for it, but we haven't been able to uncover it."

"Why do you think that is?"

"Carth has plenty of theories. It's possible that when Ih fell, they moved the stone. The people of that time were incredibly knowledgeable about their abilities, and more of them were shadow born than now."

She stared off into the distance, shadows stretching away from her, and Daniel wondered what she was detecting. Maybe it was nothing. Maybe this was only her way of exploring a place that had meaning to her and her people.

She turned back to him. "My ability is more potent here."

"How so?"

"I can stretch further away from myself than I normally can. I don't know how much of that has to do with this location, or perhaps it's simply that everything else has been burned away, leaving nothing but this blackened stone."

The mention of the stone drew his focus back to the rock he had Slid here. He headed back the way they'd come and found the stone resting where he had emerged from the Slide. It blended into the landscape, though the silver striations within it caught the light. He ran his hands along the surface of the stone. There seemed to be something metallic about it, though it wasn't entirely metal.

"We can't forget that," Rayen said as she joined him.

"Do you think they used something from these lands to help them make it?"

"I doubt the shadows would prevent anyone from Sliding."

"What if it isn't just shadows?" He studied the stone, noticing how similar it looked to much of the rock around here. His fingers traced along the silver streaking through it. It was almost as if he could detect something within that silver, though what was it?

"What else prevents you from Sliding?"

Daniel stood, taking a step back as he eyed the stone. "Me personally?"

"Is it different for each person who can Slide?"

"Some are more powerful than others. Rsiran isn't limited when Sliding. Neither is Lucy."

"What prevents you from Sliding?"

"There is a naturally occurring metal many within Elaeavn know of. We call it heartstone."

"I'm familiar with heartstone."

"Well, in sufficient quantities, it makes it difficult to Slide."

"This doesn't look to be heartstone."

Daniel studied the stone. Heartstone had a bluish hue to it, and this carried none of that. "No. I don't think it is heartstone, though I don't really know what it is."

"Do we need the entire stone to study it?"

"Why?"

"Seeing as how you struggled to carry us here, I wonder if we could take a smaller sample and you would have an easier time of returning us to Nyaesh."

"It's possible," Daniel said. But even if it were possible, there was value in taking the entirety of the stone. He needed to know just what the Ai'thol were intending with these stones, and if they only had a single one, and not even the entirety of it, it might not be possible to unravel the mystery.

"You don't want to try."

Daniel shook his head. "I think we need to bring all of it."

Rayen watched him for a moment before shrugging. "I will leave it to you."

"I'm not going to be able to Slide just yet."

"I didn't think you would."

"It takes a while for me to recover after using such energy."

"Of course."

"We could explore while we're still here."

Rayen glanced over at him. "Won't that preclude you from recuperating?"

"Not much. All I need to do is not use my ability for a

while. As long as I allow it to recover for a bit, I should be able to Slide us back to Nyaesh."

And now that he had managed to rescue Rayen from the ship, he could take her back to Nyaesh and return for the stone. But he didn't think Rayen would let him do that. There was a look on her face that warned him she wanted to be here.

"We can take whatever time is needed. Besides, I am curious about this place."

"Should we take the stone with us?"

"I think I can find it again, unless you're worried about someone else coming upon it?"

Daniel scanned the empty landscape. There weren't any birds or animals or any other signs of life. "Not terribly concerned."

"I doubt that we need to be concerned, but I will still conceal it." Rayen crouched in front of the stone, running her hands alongside it. As she did, shadows swirled, blending together, concealing the stone from him. It was subtle at first, but the longer she worked, the more difficult it became for him to make anything else out.

"That's impressive."

She shrugged. "And probably unnecessary, but I'd rather err on the side of caution."

"You think the Ai'thol can track us?"

"I honestly don't know what the Ai'thol are capable of."

There were some who had the ability to track those who could Slide, though it was a rare power. Rarer still was the ability to influence someone who could Slide. He wouldn't put it past the Ai'thol to have worked to ensure they had such capabilities, but they had seen no evidence of them having done so.

Rayen started off across the rock, moving quickly, almost as if drawn in a direction. Daniel followed, glancing back toward the stone as he went, but he didn't see where she had left it. When he caught up to Rayen, she was moving quickly along the rocky ground. Every so often she would pause, her gaze flicking around her, and then continue onward. With each pause, she changed her direction ever so subtly, enough that he had to wonder what she detected.

"What are you following?"

"I'm following the sense of the shadows."

"What do you sense?"

"It would be difficult to explain."

"It seems we have some time for you to try."

Rayen glanced over, grinning. "Perhaps we do. I am following what I can perceive of a density of shadows."

"A density?"

"Shadows exist around everything. Those who have abilities with the shadows can pick apart that connection and probe for greater access to the shadows. In this case, I can detect a greater connection to shadows."

"How can shadows exist around everything? What about sunlight?"

"The sun creates shadows. It is more difficult, but those with knowledge have the ability to use the shadows found even in bright sunlight."

She said nothing more as she continued onward, heading across the land. Daniel followed, silent, focusing on his ability to Slide. How long would it be before that capacity returned fully? Normally, it could take hours before his strength fully recovered, but in this case, he didn't want to be gone that long. The longer they were gone, the more likely it was that others within Nyaesh would begin to wonder whether something had happened to them. All of the women he had helped rescue would begin to raise the question of whether they had survived, and he wasn't thrilled with the idea of someone thinking to go after them. They had already lost one ship; they didn't need to lose another.

The expanse of rock continued to stretch before him. Everything about it was bleak, desolate, and despite the wind blowing through here, a persistent haze hung overtop everything. Daniel wished for another gust of wind, hoping that perhaps there might be something more that could carry the haze away, making it easier for him to see clearly, but it never came.

After walking for an hour or so, with little conversation between him and Rayen, they crested a rise. He looked out, noticing the ruins of what had to have been an ancient city far below. A river ran near the ruins, burbling gently. It reminded him of the river in Nyaesh, though it wasn't nearly as wide as that one, and it didn't move with quite as much speed.

"Is that it?" Daniel asked.

"That must be one of the ancient cities," Rayen whispered.

"How many cities were there in Ih?"

"Dozens. It was once a powerful land, bolstered by the strength of the shadow blessed along with those shadow born."

Daniel still marveled at the fact that there was such history here in a land that was so far removed from anything he had known. "We could go down there."

She shook her head. "It doesn't feel right."

"Why not?"

"The city is gone. It's been gone for years. Centuries. I'd prefer to leave the dead to my memories. I'd rather not disrupt their resting."

Daniel nodded. What had she hoped to encounter by coming here? Was it only to see this place, to realize that the remains of Ih were still here, or did she have another purpose?

"Would Carth have been here?"

"Carth has traveled extensively, even before I met her. It's possible that she has."

"What do you think she discovered?"

"It's hard to say what she might have encountered. Carth goes after an understanding of where she came from. She's the one who helped me understand the history of Ih and Lashasn."

She fell silent again, and Daniel didn't push. She seemed focused, determined, as if she wanted to have this moment of silence. Far be it from him to be the one to disrupt it.

Rayen stood there for long moments, and Daniel wandered along the ridgeline, looking down at the city. It had to have been impressive once upon a time, and even now there were remnants, towers that still stood, though the stone was blackened, giving evidence to what Rayen suggested about its destruction.

Was that understanding how she was detecting the

pools of shadows? Whatever it was that she picked up on was interesting and unique. He had no idea how she was able to detect the shadows, though she had no ability to Slide, so perhaps his inability to understand shouldn't surprise him.

"Daniel!"

He turned, sensing the urgency in her voice. "What is it?"

"There's something nearby." She looked around, tipping her head to the side. "I can feel the presence of something—and someone."

"Where?" He turned back toward where he thought the stone had been left, though he wasn't certain.

"I don't know."

"Your shadows don't reveal that to you?"

She shot him a withering look. "Does your ability to Slide allow you to know everyone around you?"

"No."

"We should get moving. If it's the Ai'thol, then we need to see if we can't grab the stone and return to Nyaesh. Do you have enough strength to do that?"

Daniel wasn't certain. It had been an hour, possibly two since they had arrived here. Would that have been enough for him to recover? Without trying, he wasn't sure he would know for certain.

"Now there's another," she said.

"You can detect two people?"

"It's possible there are more." Shadows swirled around her, and Daniel wished he had the same ability to detect others. "Dark night!" she hissed.

"What is it?"

She nodded behind them, back in the direction they had come from. “There are at least a dozen.”

That many meant the Ai’thol—they needed to go.

Daniel attempted to Slide, reaching for Rayen, but he could feel the struggle within him. His ability wasn’t fully returned.

“I’m not going to be of much use yet. I can’t even Slide a little,” he said.

“It took that much out of you?”

Daniel nodded. Perhaps he had expended himself far more than he had known. The effort had been intense, incredible, and he had felt just how much power had been involved in trying to tear himself away from the ship, dragging himself with the Slide. He should have known that with as painful as it had been, he would struggle to fully recover. Anytime he’d exerted himself like that before, he’d barely managed to recoup. It shouldn’t surprise him that this time would be no different.

“Then we must be prepared to fight.”

“If there are twelve or more Ai’thol, what makes you think we can fight?”

“We can manage.”

“Are you sure?”

“What would you have us do? Run and hide?” She looked all around her. “And where exactly would you have us go? Look around you.”

Daniel did, motioning to the remains of the city far below. “That’s where we can go.”

“We can’t go down there.”

“I think we have to.”

"That city deserves to be protected. It should not be defiled."

"Do you fear your ancestors would be angered by you coming here?"

Rayen glanced behind her, everything about her still tense and on edge. "I have been taught to respect my family. I was taught that we must treat them with the measure of respect they deserve for the contributions they made so we could live the way we do."

"That doesn't change anything. Going down there doesn't mean that you suddenly don't respect them."

Daniel didn't want to force her to do something she was uncomfortable with, but at the same time, he didn't want to get caught out here by the Ai'thol. There was no good place for them to hide, and he thought the only thing that would keep them generally protected would be going down into the city, where they could disappear among the towers.

A shout echoed behind them, and Daniel turned to see the Ai'thol in the distance. They stood outlined on the ridge, making their way toward them, though there was still time before they could get to them. He hoped they hadn't been spotted yet, though it wouldn't take long before that changed.

"Rayen. I'm going to go down there."

She let out a heavy sigh and finally nodded.

They hurried down into the city, Daniel glancing back behind him every so often, afraid that perhaps the Ai'thol had seen or heard them moving, but there was no sign of that. As far as he could tell, they remained unnoticed.

He would keep it that way as long as possible.

When they reached the outer buildings of the remains of the city, Rayen slowed, her gaze drifting all around her. Daniel grabbed her arm, dragging her with him. If only he could Slide. He hated that he was the reason they were stuck here, though surprisingly, Rayen didn't seem to mind. Rather, she appeared curious, wishing she could have more time to look around her, though Daniel didn't dare give her that time. Not until they were safe from the Ai'thol.

He pointed, motioning to one of the towers in the distance. That would be the most likely place to ensure their safety. Rayen followed, saying nothing, and Daniel began to worry about her. What would happen if it came down to fighting here? Would she view this as too sacred a location to do combat in if it were necessary?

He knew Rayen and didn't think she would, expecting her to be far more practical when it came to matters like that, but a part of him still worried.

They reached one of the towers, and he hid behind it. Rayen followed, staying close, but also remaining generally silent. Perhaps that was for the best. He didn't want or need her to say too much until they knew what the Ai'thol might do. Hiding here at least gave them the opportunity to take better stock of the situation.

When the nearest Ai'thol came into view, Daniel pointed.

Rayen nodded but said nothing more.

The Ai'thol made their way into the city, moving slowly, quietly, and yet with a determined step.

Did they know that they were here?

Daniel thought they had managed to stay ahead of the

Ai'thol, and had done so in a way that had kept the Ai'thol from realizing they were there, but perhaps they hadn't been as successful as he had thought.

He attempted to Slide, doing so with a single step, nothing more than that, and still couldn't.

Either they would have to hide here, or they would have to fight. The idea of hiding became less and less likely the longer they were here. Yet he didn't like their odds if they were forced to fight and there were as many Ai'thol as he suspected.

Rayen remained silent, and Daniel motioned. The nearest of the Ai'thol were almost within reach. He thought he could get to them, and if he could, maybe he could take one of them down. It would involve fighting, and he didn't know if he was up to it. Would the weakness he felt following the Slide that had brought him here overwhelm him in a way that would keep him from even being able to fight? He had been training, working with the sword, so he wasn't unskilled.

There was no chance for him to decide. One of the Ai'thol came around the corner, appearing in view, and Daniel unsheathed, cutting through the Ai'thol before the man had an opportunity to realize they were there and reveal their presence to others.

As he fell, his body bleeding out on the ground, Daniel looked over to Rayen. It seemed as if the sudden appearance of the Ai'thol had triggered something within her.

She looked over with a start, grabbing her own sword and nodding. "I'm ready."

"Good. I don't know what we might have to do, but we

should be prepared for the possibility that it will involve taking down every Ai'thol that comes in here."

"Like I said, I am ready."

Daniel decided not to push. If Rayen said she was ready, he believed she would be. They dragged the fallen Ai'thol back, keeping him out of sight so others wouldn't realize he had fallen, and they waited.

They didn't have to wait very long. Two Ai'thol appeared. When they did, they seemed surprised by the fact that Daniel and Rayen were there. Daniel launched himself forward, swinging his sword, and the Ai'thol started to flicker, his attempt at Sliding. But Daniel reacted, catching him before he could finish the Slide. If he had disappeared, the others would have converged.

With that one down, he glanced over to see that Rayen had managed to defeat the other Ai'thol.

They nodded to each other, and together they dragged the two fallen Ai'thol back, away from the edge, and away from the possibility of detection.

That was three. If Rayen had picked up on twelve, they still had quite a few to handle before they ensured their safety.

He peeked his head around the corner, noticing that three more Ai'thol converged. He jerked his head back, motioning for Rayen. Shadows began to drift away from her.

"There are four coming toward us."

"Four?" Daniel started to poke his head back around, but Rayen grabbed him, pulling him back into place. "Are you sure?"

She arched a brow at him. "Quite."

Even if they could handle four Ai'thol, it likely wouldn't be quiet. The attack would draw attention, and he had wanted to avoid any unnecessary attention in order to ensure they got out of here alive.

Fighting might not be safe.

The tower behind them might be their only protection.

Daniel nodded to Rayen, motioning for her to follow, and they disappeared into the darkness of the tower. From here, he thought he could find a place to hide, at least gather some time to determine their next step.

But that depended upon the tower having enough capacity to hide them.

Steps led down.

Down might trap them, but at the same time, once his ability to Slide returned, they wouldn't be trapped. All they needed was time in order to ensure their ongoing safety.

As he started down, Rayen grabbed his arm, frowning.

"We just need to buy ourselves some time," he whispered.

"And if we are forced to fight down here?"

"If we're forced to fight, then we fight."

She nodded, saying nothing more.

Daniel continued down into the dark. With his enhanced Sight, he didn't struggle as the daylight began to fade, disappearing into greater and greater shadows. He glanced over to Rayen, wondering if she would struggle, but saw darkness fading away from her.

"You're using the shadows?" he asked.

"There is some benefit to being shadow born."

"You can manipulate them in order to see clearly?"

"Sometimes. In places like this, pulling away the shadows doesn't necessarily make it lighter, but it does make it easier for me to see. At least I won't stumble down the stairs and fall to my death."

Daniel grinned, and they continued to make their way down. They reached a landing, and he was surprised to see that it was tiled. He was even more surprised to see that it remained completely intact. As they wandered, he paused, listening to see if the Ai'thol would follow, but there was no indication of that.

"I think that we—"

Something appeared in front of him.

Daniel darted forward, swinging his sword, prepared for whatever it was that might come toward them, but he swung toward nothing.

Which meant the Ai'thol had found them.

And if the Ai'thol had found them, they were Sliding, and it wouldn't be long before they appeared again.

Daniel darted forward, swinging his sword, racing into the darkness of this level. He had no idea what he would find down here, but he continued to race, glancing over to Rayen, who followed. Shadows pushed away from her, and the longer they were down here, the clearer the shadows became to him.

Everything ended in a section of wall.

Daniel paused, placing his hands on either side of it, spinning around to look backward. There was still no evidence of the Ai'thol having returned, but he knew they would come soon.

"This is an ancient temple," Rayen whispered.

"How do you know?"

"The design. The temples of Ih were always below ground, celebrating the darkness and the shadows."

"Then we're trapped here. I suppose we can fight our way out, but I'm still not strong enough to Slide us from here."

"There might be another way."

"What other way?"

Rayen ignored the question, stepping up to the wall, running her hands along it. As she did, shadows swirled away from her. They pressed into the wall, surging with a sense of power.

And then something clicked.

A massive panel along the wall slid away.

She nodded to him. "Come, Daniel. Let us enter a Temple of Ih."

10

DANIEL

Darkness swallowed Daniel as Rayen closed the door behind them. He stood in place, trying to let his eyes adjust, but still couldn't easily See through the darkness.

"All of this is amazing."

Daniel turned toward the sound of her voice but couldn't make her out in the darkness. "How can you see anything down here?"

"I have control over the shadows, and all of this is consumed by the shadows."

"What do you mean?"

"This is the temple. There is considerable power within the temple."

"Is this the power you've been detecting?"

"Possibly," she said. She had moved past him, and while he couldn't see her, he could follow the sound of her voice. Footsteps sounded over tile, muted and soft, but reverberating nonetheless. "All of this is tied to the shadows. It's amazing."

"I wish I could see it."

"Focus on what you can detect," she said.

Daniel smiled to himself. "I don't have any connection to the shadows, so I doubt I'm going to be able to detect the same things as you."

"You never know. It's possible all you need is time and an opportunity to have your eyes adjust to the shadows before you are able to see through the darkness."

More likely with the shadows all around him, he wouldn't be able to See anything. His ability with Sight wasn't nearly as strong as some, and when it came to the shadows, he didn't doubt something about them would prevent him from being able to easily peer through the darkness.

Still, he did as Rayen suggested, focusing on everything around him, trying to See if there was anything he could make out. He had a sense of size and enormity that came from the way her feet reverberated on the tile. Perhaps that was only his imagination.

Rayen touched his arm, guiding him deeper into the temple.

"They could Slide here," Daniel said.

"Are you able to Slide beyond shadows?"

"Not well. That's why I wondered if the stone used the power of shadows."

"That's what I thought. And this place is quite powerful with shadows."

"It's dark, but—"

"It's more than just dark. There's something of the shadows here. When you are aware of it, you realize it's almost a physical thing."

Daniel could envision her smiling. Gone was the

reluctance he had sensed when they had been outside the city. In its place was a sense of awe, and she was once again more like the woman he knew.

"It does feel like a physical thing to me, but it's not the kind of thing I can take advantage of," he said.

"I wouldn't expect you to be able to do that. That would involve you having the ability to control the shadows, and short of being born to the shadows, you would need to…"

"I would need to what?"

She took a few steps forward, her feet still echoing on the stone.

"I would need to what?"

"You would need to find the Elder Stone," she whispered.

"Why do I get the sense that something's wrong?"

"There's nothing wrong at all."

"Then why do I get a sense you're troubled?"

Rayen touched his arm, guiding him forward without answering. He followed, wondering if she knew of some way out. Even if there wasn't a way out, they could stay here, wait until his connection to his abilities had been replenished, and then they could Slide back to grab the stone and return to Nyaesh.

They paused, and a presence pressed upon him.

"What are you doing?" He twisted toward where he felt Rayen near him.

"I'm doing nothing."

"Where are we?"

"I think we have reached the heart of the temple."

"How do you know?"

"Because it draws me to it."

She moved away from him, and Daniel followed the sound of her footsteps, uncertain where she was going or what she was after. As he followed, the pressure he detected continued to build all around him. There were shades of darkness that were deeper and blacker nearby.

He took a step forward, toward the darker sections, wondering if perhaps he wasn't being drawn in some way toward the shadows and whatever it was that lay at the heart of the temple.

"Daniel?"

He paused, turning toward the sound of Rayen's voice, though it seemed to come from everywhere and all around him.

"What is it?"

"Where did you go?"

"I'm right here."

"You walked away from me, and I can no longer see where you went."

Daniel turned, but all he saw were increasing depths of shadows. Could he have somehow walked into the heart of the temple?

Doing so felt a bit like a violation. It would be no different than were someone to head into the hall housing the sacred crystals in Elaeavn, though he didn't know whether the temple held the Elder Stone.

The shadows continued to deepen around him. He tried turning away from them, but every time he took a step away, it seemed almost as if they were coming back in his direction.

"Rayen?"

Even to his ears, his voice was muted and quiet.

"Where are you?" Rayen's voice seemed to come from a great distance, almost as if she were disappearing along the hall, though he doubted she would have done that. Daniel turned toward that sound, trying to fixate on her, but couldn't determine where she had gone.

All he saw was shadows. They surrounded him, nearly overpowering him. He took a step in every direction, trying to get away from the darkness, but it followed him, trailing after him.

He needed to stay near Rayen so he'd know how to get out of here. Trapped as he was by the shadows and the darkness, he wasn't going to be able to find his way out very easily.

"Rayen?"

He called out her name again, hoping for some sign that she heard him, but there was no answer.

Worse, the shadows and darkness seemed to swirl even more densely around him. There was pressure from it, an awareness of that power, and everything he did seemed to draw them even closer to him.

Rather than continuing to try to move, Daniel stood in place. Even then, he felt as if the shadows came toward him, as if he were targeted. Their power pressed upon him, squeezing, growing in intensity.

"Rayen?"

His voice sounded muted, flat, and he worried that something intended to trap him here. A strange coldness worked its way through him.

Daniel cried out, but his voice didn't carry.

He pushed against the cold, trying to escape, but there

was no escape. He would be bound by the shadows. He would die here.

The realization sent tremors through him. He wasn't ready to die yet and wanted nothing more than to Slide away from here.

Could he Slide?

Rayen had suggested the temple and the shadows would prevent it, but maybe with him being inside, he wouldn't have the same difficulty. He needed more time to recover.

When he attempted to Slide, there was a strange shimmering, as if the shadows attempted to part around him but then retreated.

That had to be his imagination, didn't it?

Daniel tried again, taking a step, attempting to Slide.

It seemed as if he had a little more strength than he'd had before. He moved, the Slide carrying him forward barely more than a few steps. That was all he needed. He only wanted to Slide a short distance, to test whether it would even work. The fact he could Slide again reassured him.

He took another step, once again attempting to Slide.

This one carried him further.

With each Slide, there came a shimmering quality to the air around him, a lightening. It retreated the moment he emerged, once again surrounded by shadows.

"Rayen!"

He waited, listening, but she didn't answer.

He attempted another Slide, and the shadows separated.

When he emerged, the shadows congealed around him once again, making it so he could see nothing.

"Daniel?"

It was Rayen's voice. It was muted and soft, but it was there.

"Rayen?"

The shadows began to dissipate, pushing away from him, and he watched for a moment, prepared for the possibility that he might need to Slide. And then the darkness around him faded, and Rayen appeared before him. She grabbed him by the arm, pulling him back, saying nothing. As they backed away, Daniel could finally make something out. The darkness that had existed within the temple seemed to fade. Not entirely, but enough that he could see Rayen.

"What happened to you?" she asked.

"I don't know. I got lost in the darkness."

"How?"

"I don't know."

"This is strange," she said. "Do you remember me talking about a density of shadows?"

"You said that you were able to detect a density here."

"I think what I was detecting comes from here. The temple."

"What does that mean?"

"Normally it simply means a greater density of shadows, but in this case, it seems to be something more. I've never been to a Temple of Ih, so I wasn't entirely certain, but a concentration of shadows seems to have been placed here by the people who lived here before."

"How were they able to place a concentration of shadows?"

She shook her head. It surprised him that he could make that out within the darkness, but it was increasingly clear. "I don't know. Somehow, you were drawn toward that clustering of shadows, too. This temple is quite a bit larger than I expected, and I nearly lost you."

"I was able to Slide."

"Within the shadows?"

Daniel nodded. "I don't know that they were trying to hold me. I was trying to find you and attempted to Slide."

"Do you think you can Slide us back to the stone?"

"I don't know." Even if he could, he still wasn't sure if he was strong enough to Slide them back to Nyaesh with the stone. It might be easier for them to leave it and return, to come back with someone who might be stronger than he.

That meant coming with Lucy.

Would she agree?

"I can take just you," he said.

"Then we can wait."

"I don't know how much longer we can wait. The longer we're gone, the more likely the others will worry that something happened to us."

"I hadn't considered that. I suspect many of them think we're already lost."

"Or they think you decided to attack the Ai'thol on your own," he said, smiling but not knowing whether she could see it.

"Maybe. It wouldn't be the first time."

"It wouldn't?"

She shrugged. "It's not as if I haven't fought the Ai'thol before. Before I knew better, I was unmindful of the possibility that something might happen to me."

He could see Rayen being reckless. "Are you ready?"

"Why don't we Slide from here, back to the edge of the city, and take a look?"

"If they find us…"

"Do you think you can take more than one Slide?"

Surprisingly, Daniel did. The longer he was here, the more refreshed he felt. It was as if being in the darkness helped him. "I should be able to. As long as we don't need to carry the stone, then…"

"Let's at least make sure that the Ai'thol haven't gone after it."

Daniel took her hand and Slid.

He emerged at the edge of the ridgeline, looking down upon the darkness that was the remnants of the city. There wasn't much there. As he stared down into the city, he saw no sign of the Ai'thol.

Now that he had been within the temple, the sensation that had called to him within the temple was far more noticeable. Could it be that his time within the temple itself had given him some connection to it?

"I don't see any of the Ai'thol," he said.

"I don't either," Rayen said.

He turned, looking away from the remains of the city, staring back across the bleak rocky landscape. In the distance, the steam continued to rise up off the ground, though it wasn't nearly as thick as it had seemed before. Had the wind picked up while they were within the temple?

"How long were we down there?" he asked.

"I don't know. I lost track of time."

"Do you think they will have discovered the temple?"

There was power there, stored by people who had lived centuries before, and they didn't deserve for their memory to be defiled by the Ai'thol.

"Even if they discovered the temple, they would need some control over the shadows in order to open that section of wall," she said.

"What if they have managed to find some way to do that?"

"Carth has been working to ensure that the Ai'thol don't uncover the key to the shadows."

"We've already seen that the key to the Elder Stones the Ai'thol are after may be different than what we assumed," he said.

A troubled look fell across her face. "It's possible."

"Let's return to Nyaesh, reassure the others that we're not dead or captured, and then we can figure out what else we need to do about this."

"Once Carth learns about our visit here, I doubt she'll intend to do anything."

"You don't think she would want to protect the temple?"

"I don't know that it's a matter of her wanting to, but it might be more of her ability to do so."

"I don't want to be there when you question Carth's ability to do anything."

Rayen shook her head, a grin spreading across her face. "I wouldn't be so foolish as to do that."

"You already did."

"That was before."

"Before what?"

"Before Carth was rejuvenated. All of this seemed to have changed her. Before, she was fading, but now..." Rayen turned her attention back to the remains of the city. "I don't know how to explain it other than after everything that's happened, she seems to be more alive."

"She *was* trying to fake her own death for quite some time."

"Don't remind me."

"You're just mad because she succeeded."

"None of us wanted Carth gone. She has been too valuable as both a friend and a mentor, but..."

"But what?"

"But it shows a certain lack of trust that she was unwilling to reveal to us what she was planning."

"I don't know you and Carth all that well." Rayen arched a brow at him. "Certainly not as well as you know each other. I've only been around you for a few months. But you can't let something like that get in the way. Carth has been playing a different game, and it's one I'm not sure that anyone other than the leader of the Ai'thol will know."

"Olandar Fahr. We should use his name."

Daniel stared toward the distant temple. "And he's after Elder Stones. Has Carth never shared with you how many Elder Stones she thinks there are?"

"We talked about it once, but it was in vague terms."

"By that, she doesn't know."

"I think she has a general idea, but whether she knows

exactly is something else entirely. And you know Carth. She won't admit to ignorance."

"She will if it suits her goals."

"There is that."

"We should see if we can't get back. I can try to carry the stone."

"I thought you were too weakened to do so."

"The longer we're here, the better I feel."

"Maybe your time in the temple has rejuvenated you."

Daniel shrugged. "Maybe. It was terrifying, so why not rejuvenating as well?"

"What was terrifying about it?"

"I felt as if the shadows were trying to swallow me."

"The shadows would not swallow you. They aren't alive."

He scanned the horizon before turning his attention back to the city. Within the city, he saw the remnants of the tower, with the temple deep beneath it. He was thankful they had been able to Slide free; if he hadn't, they might've been forced to fight their way out.

"They might not be alive, but when I was there, it felt as if they were."

Rayen looked at him, frowning while biting her lip.

Daniel turned away from the intensity of her scrutiny, grabbing her arm and Sliding her back toward the stone. The landscape looked just as bleak as it had when they first arrived. The rocks carried that hazy energy to them that seemed to drift with heat and the remnants of fire, though the fire would have been centuries ago. In the distance, the sound of waves crashing along the shore caught his attention.

Rayen waved her hand, and the shadows surrounding the stone disappeared. Once again, the veins of silver streaking within the stone caught the light. She easily hoisted it.

"If this fails, I want you to drop the stone and we'll leave it behind."

"If this fails, I would like to conceal it before we do that."

He took a deep breath, readying himself. Attempting to Slide with the stone made him nervous. The last time had been incredibly painful, and though his strength was returning, there remained the distinct possibility he wouldn't be strong enough to overpower the resistance from the stone.

The more he thought about it, the more certain he was that they needed to study and analyze the stone, if only so that they could ensure the Ai'thol didn't have some way of controlling those who could Slide. He didn't want to be caught again, and he certainly didn't want anything to happen to Lucy. They would use her, the same way they had attempted to use her once before.

"Are you ready?" she asked.

"As ready as I can be."

"Take your time."

Daniel glanced over at her. "Don't worry."

"What is that supposed to mean?"

"What it means is that if this Slide is anything like the last one, it will be slow, and possibly painful."

"Painful?"

"Not for you, but for me."

"Good."

"Good?"

Rayen waved her hand. "I don't mean it's good that it's painful, I just mean that—"

Daniel laughed softly, taking another deep breath. "You don't have to explain."

With that, he took a step, beginning to Slide.

It happened much like the last time. They moved slowly at first, though this time there wasn't nearly as much resistance as he had felt before. He was delayed, as if the stone were trying to hold him back. He had to compensate for it and drew upon more and more strength, surging power through him, forcing himself forward. If he didn't Slide completely, they could end up in some other place he didn't intend.

He wanted to reach Nyaesh and the others. He wanted to be able to speak with Carth about the stone and to have someone analyze it. And he wanted to get back, to rest, and to have a chance to continue to train for the Ai'thol.

He forced himself forward, tearing through the Slide.

As he went, sound rang around him. It seemed musical, like voices all singing together, something he hadn't heard before.

Always before, there had been the whistling of wind, the sense of movement. While there was some sense of movement now, it wasn't as profound as what he was accustomed to. It came gradually, without the same pain as when he'd attempted to Slide them free of the ship.

And then they emerged.

Daniel blinked, steadying himself as he looked around, half afraid he had not managed to make it all the way to Nyaesh. The city spread into view, the river behind him filled with ships making their way along it, and the distinct odors of Nyaesh—that of ash from the A'ras working with their magic, mixed with a metallic odor he had never fully understood—hung over everything.

Daniel let out a shaky breath. "We're back."

"I get the sense you weren't sure that it would work."

Daniel glanced over at Rayen. "Not entirely, but it doesn't matter. We're back."

She glanced down at the stone. "Now we must understand what the Ai'thol have discovered and why it was so important for them to chase after you."

"They weren't chasing after me. They were chasing after the stone."

"Then we must understand why the stone is so important."

"Will Carth know something?"

"If she doesn't, then we need to find someone who does."

Daniel looked out at the river. "You go ahead. I'm going to stay here for just a few moments and gather myself."

"Are you sure?"

He took a deep breath. "I'm exhausted, and I just need to rest for a minute. Besides, now that we're back in Nyaesh, we aren't in danger like we were."

"There's always danger, Daniel Elvraeth."

"I know, but at least here, there's a certain relative safety."

Rayen regarded him for a moment before starting off. He watched her go, marveling at the way the shadows swirled around her, much darker than he remembered having seen before. There was something about the shadows that seemed to call to him, though maybe that was his imagination. Or maybe it was the fact that he found Rayen appealing. The nature of her control and her power attracted him.

He pushed away those thoughts. He was committed to Lucy, though she had no real interest in him. He would wait until the time when she did, even if it took months. Possibly years.

Was he willing to wait that long?

He had left the city for Lucy, but he had remained away from the city for himself. The longer he was gone and the more he saw of the world, the more uncertain he was about what he wanted.

Maybe Lucy wasn't what he wanted, but if not, what *did* he want?

He took a deep breath, turning away from the city, staring down at the river. He hadn't been lying to Rayen when he'd said he wanted to stand here and look out at the water, to get a sense for the movement along the shores. There was something peaceful about it, and what he needed after everything that had just happened was a sense of peace.

If nothing else, he would take this moment, find that peace. It wouldn't last for long. Soon enough, he would be thrust back into fighting the Ai'thol.

11

LUCY

WAVES CRASHED NEARBY, AND LUCY GAZED UP THE SHEER rock wall, looking to see if there was any way for her to know what was out there. She had been exploring, searching along the coastline, looking for answers, and more than that, looking for a place of safety.

So far, the women had remained in this empty village, a place Lucy had happened upon in her search with Carth. It was the place she had brought them, thinking they might be safe here, but she didn't want anything more to happen to them and so was looking for other places of safety.

"How long will you be gone?"

She looked over to the woman. She had dark hair cut in a jagged and severe manner. A round face with wide eyes that were a pale green. Thin lips pressed together in a questioning line. Lucy smiled, trying to exude a sense of comfort and confidence, knowing most of these women needed that from her.

"I shouldn't be gone long," she said to Marcy. "Besides, you have each other."

"Most of us don't know each other," Marcy said.

"This is an opportunity for you to get to know each other."

"As much as we want to get to know each other—and we do—especially as we have shared experiences that are important, we need you around us, Lucy."

She patted Marcy on the shoulder. Many of the women were like Marcy, and given everything they had suffered, it wasn't surprising. Some had taken a considerable amount of time to recuperate, and though Carth had wanted Lucy to remain with her, to continue working with the C'than, she had felt compelled to spend as much time as she could trying to find a way to heal these women.

They had refused to allow her to take them to Elaeavn. That surprised her, especially as some of these women came from Elaeavn. She didn't know how many, but she had recognized some of them, and the longer she spent with them, the more uncertain she was as to why they wouldn't want to return to the city.

There had to be more to it, and yet, she didn't have the opportunity to stay here long enough to get to the bottom of it. She wanted to better understand these women, but striking that balance was difficult for her. It was a balance between what she wanted to do, what she wanted to understand, and the C'than and what they wanted of her.

Unfortunately, the more time Lucy spent away from Ras and the C'than, the harder it was for her to return.

Eventually, she had to wonder if staying with the C'than was even going to be possible.

And yet, she felt obligated to work with these women. They were here because of her, and she felt as if they needed her.

"I won't be gone long."

"Where are you going off to this time?"

She had hesitated to tell them she was working with the C'than, not sure how they would react. Many of them knew they had been captured by the C'than, and though she had tried to tell them they they had been captured by a splinter group, the idea that Lucy might be working with the C'than left many of them troubled.

If the situations were reversed, she probably would've felt the same way, and the more she thought about it, the more certain she was that for now, the best course of action was not sharing with the others what had happened.

"I'm still looking for a place we can be safe."

"Why not here?"

Lucy looked up along the rocky shoreline, staring up the sheer cliff's edge. From here, it was little more than a Slide to bring her back up there, and yet there were stairs worked into the rock wall that led down here. That was how Marcy had gotten down. Lucy had been surprised to find the other woman here. There was something about Marcy that suggested she came here regularly, looking for answers.

"I don't know how safe this place is."

"It's been safe enough so far, and as far as we can tell,

no one has come by here. Every so often, we find ships moving past the shore, but nothing more."

"No one has traveled nearby?"

"Why would they?"

"We're only a few days from Asador."

It seemed impossible to believe that. If she went by ground, she could reach Asador in only a few days' time. This wasn't a bad place. There were buildings here, many of them run-down, but in the time they'd been here, they had already begun to repair them, fixing broken windows and generally preparing to remain.

This wasn't the kind of place Lucy thought would be safe. Here they were isolated, and in her mind, that wasn't a good thing. But perhaps after what had happened to these women, isolation wasn't necessarily a negative to them.

She didn't know how she would feel if the situations were reversed. If she had to be isolated like this, what would she do?

Then again, she had been isolated in Elaeavn her entire life, and the longer she had spent here, the more she felt as if she understood what that isolation was like.

It was possible that the reason the women from Elaeavn didn't mind this place was because they were so familiar with isolation. Not all the women were from Elaeavn, and those who were not were the most vocal about not returning to their homelands.

She looked over at Marcy. "Where is home for you?"

"Nowhere now."

"Why?"

Marcy touched the back of her head, the same way

that most of them did. It was their way of reminding themselves of the implants they had obtained. Lucy understood that all too well, having done the same thing herself, and it was only now that she found she didn't need to touch the back of her head so often. She still had headaches, though they were less frequent than they once had been. Every so often, she would wake with a pounding headache, almost as if her body were trying to reject the implant, but for the most part she was able to ignore that sensation, and to pretend as if it had never been there.

"Before all of this happened. Where was home?"

Some of the women had been more reserved about their answers, and Lucy realized she hadn't spoken much to Marcy about what was home for her, and now was as good a time as any to get a better understanding of the woman and what she had been like before she had come here.

"I was from a city called Cort."

"I'm not familiar with it."

"Not many from Elaeavn are. Then again, there aren't many people from Elaeavn who leave, are there?"

"Your parents or your grandparents?"

Marcy smiled sadly. "My grandparents. My mother was pleased I had such bright green eyes."

As far as Lucy knew, abilities faded over time after being away from Elaeavn. No one had ever been able to explain why that was, but it was part of the reason the old punishment of exile mattered so much. It meant that people were away from the influence of the Great Watcher, but also that in time, their abilities would diminish. Perhaps not theirs, but those that they might be able to hand down to their children. It would eventually fade to the point where there was almost nothing left.

What must that be like?

So many people had been exiled over the years, and Lucy had a hard time understanding why. Some of the punishments were for very strange reasons, and the more she had learned about the exiles, the more she regretted what her people had done, hating the influence they had.

"Did you have much in the way of abilities before all this?"

"I…" Marcy squeezed her eyes shut and took a deep breath. "I had some ability. Nothing like what my parents say I would've had had we never had been forced from Elaeavn, but it was different than anyone else."

"What could you do?"

"I had the ability to understand someone's thoughts."

"Reading," Lucy said. She tapped her head. "My implant augmented my ability to Read. I got to the point where it's almost too much. Have you noticed anything like that?"

Marcy shook her head. "Nothing like that."

"Then it's unlikely to change you that way." In her case, the shift in her ability to Read had been rapid, almost instantaneous. She remembered awakening with that ability, the way the voices had screamed inside of her mind, making it so she had a difficult time trying to exclude them. With as much as she heard, she could think of nothing else, and it was only through practice that she had begun to ignore those voices and find her own.

"Some of us wonder what abilities we might get."

"It's possible you won't obtain anything," Lucy said.

"Why not?"

"Because they were experimenting," she said. "They didn't fully understand the nature of the augmentation."

"Why would they do that?"

Lucy breathed out heavily. "I don't know. There have been adversaries my people have faced over the years. We called them Forgers, but they are known by another name. They have augmentations, but theirs are different. They involve a massive scar somewhere along their face where the metal is implanted."

"We know them. Many of them have incredible abilities, to the point where we thought they were from Elaeavn. My parents claimed they were not."

"As far as I know, they aren't from Elaeavn, but that's not to say that they don't have similar powers."

The Architect certainly had been from Elaeavn, or at least he had descended from there. His abilities were far too much like her own, and with his augmentations, he had been given gifts that made it seem almost as if he were one of the Elvraeth, and yet his abilities were even more than what the Elvraeth possessed.

Lucy had changed in the same way. With her augmentations, she couldn't help but wonder if perhaps she was more powerful than any of the Elvraeth. Was there any natural way for someone to have these abilities?

It was something she wasn't sure even mattered.

Now that she had stayed out of the city, she didn't think she would ever come to know that place again.

"The Forgers, what we now know are called the Ai'thol, have been using augmentations for many years.

This is the first time I've ever heard of the C'than using them."

"But it's different, isn't it?"

Lucy touched the back of her head, closing her eyes. She could practically hear the voices all around her from the camp up above, and yet they were muted. It took a concerted effort on her part to try to understand more about these women. With her ability to Read, something had changed, almost as if the implant made it difficult for her to reach into their thoughts. She wondered if the metal somehow interfered with her Reading.

"It is different. I've been trying to understand it."

"What's to understand? They have perfected what the Ai'thol started."

"I'm not quite convinced that's the case."

"If you say so."

Lucy studied Marcy for a little longer. "What else have you noticed since you had the augmentation placed?"

"I haven't noticed much of anything."

She fell into silence and Lucy didn't interrupt for a long while, simply listening to the sound of the waves. Eventually, she turned to the other woman. "Did you come down here just to stare at the water?"

A flush worked over Marcy's face.

"What is it?"

"I didn't exactly wander down here."

"How did you end up here?"

"I... I don't know."

Lucy frowned, watching the other woman. "You don't know?"

Marcy glanced back up the sheer face of rock. "I

found myself down here. I don't really know what happened or how, but I was walking through the village, and then I was here. I was thinking of the water, thinking about how relaxing it sounded, and wondering what it looked like from down here, and then…"

Lucy started to smile. "That's called Sliding."

"Sliding?"

Lucy nodded. "That's how I traveled. And I was able to do it even before my augmentation, but since then, my connection to Sliding has been greater, and I don't have nearly the same limitations as I had before."

"What sort of limitations?"

"Before, I had a difficult time carrying many people with me, and now… I don't seem to be limited with carrying others. More than that, I have a way of Sliding where I couldn't have before."

"What is it?"

"It's complicated, but you mentioned knowing things. I have that same ability, and I have been able to use that and the people I know to latch on to their minds to allow me to Slide with them."

"That's an amazing ability."

"I suppose it is," she said. "Still, it's unusual."

"Can you teach me how to Slide?"

"I can try, but I'm not sure how effective it will be. I've never had to teach someone else. More than that, there is something about Sliding that you need to figure out on your own. I guess you have discovered it on your own, haven't you?"

"I suppose so."

"I can see if I can help you a little bit, but I don't know if it will be all that effective for you. I can try, though."

Lucy had no idea whether or not it would even matter, no idea whether she could teach someone to Slide the way she could, but having an instructor would be beneficial to Marcy.

"You've already realized the first necessary part of it."

"What part is that?"

"Knowing where you're going to go. I find it easier to have been there before, but there are tricks around that. There is some danger in not knowing where you're going, and from what I have heard, some people have ended up in dangerous situations if they don't know where they're traveling, and so I would caution you against using this ability if you're not fully competent with it."

"What might happen?"

"It depends on where you Slide. If you were to Slide out to the middle of the ocean, you could end up drowning because you weren't able to return. If you were to Slide into the middle of this rock wall, you might be trapped, suffocated by stone. If you Slid to the top of a tower and the—"

"I get the idea," Marcy said, shivering.

Lucy shook her head. "I'm sorry, Marcy. I wasn't trying to scare you. I was trying to help you understand the nature of your ability, and… I guess I wasn't doing a good job of it."

"You are doing a good job of making sure I don't want to use it."

"That wasn't my point at all, but I do think it's necessary you use it intentionally, and be careful when you do.

You shouldn't use your ability without knowing how to do so in a way that allows you control."

"Which means?"

"Which means practicing."

Lucy looked up the rock wall, and a realization came to her. If Marcy was developing this ability, then others might be as well, and she would need to work with these women. Though she had thought she wanted to find safety for them, perhaps safety was in mastering the gifts they had been given, the augmentations they now had, and being prepared for the possibility that they might face dangers. Safety came from understanding themselves.

Hadn't that been the case for her? After her augmentation, it wasn't until she had mastered the nature of it that she had truly felt as if she were in control. The Sliding had been easy, but mastering her control over Reading, preventing herself from being overwhelmed by all of the thoughts, had been the biggest challenge.

It would be the same for these women.

Perhaps that was why some of them didn't want to return to their homes. Isolating them here was safer for them in a way.

And some of them might be Readers, their minds filled with other people's thoughts to the point where it was difficult to ignore them.

Lucy knew all too well how hard that was and how much she'd suffered when it had happened to her.

"I think I need to work with you and the others. I think I need to help you find your abilities."

A relief swept across Marcy's face. "You would do that?"

Lucy swore to herself. Could she really have not thought about that first? That should have been the first order of business for her, the first thing she had considered doing. The fact that she had needed Marcy to prod her was shameful.

"I will do that. I'm sorry I didn't think about it sooner."

"You don't need to be sorry."

Lucy smiled sadly, shaking her head. "Unfortunately, I think I do. Anyway, how about I get you back to the village and we can begin?"

She reached for Marcy, and the other woman hesitantly reached for her. Lucy held out her arm, and she focused on the village.

"The first step that I do when Sliding someplace is think about where I want to end up," she started.

Marcy nodded, and Lucy realized just how much this meant to her. She should have known that before.

12

LUCY

Wind whistled around her, and Lucy stood on the rocky shoreline, staring out at the water. She wondered if there might be something she could determine from here, but the longer she was here, the more uncertain she was that she would find anything. There was movement behind her, and she felt it, almost as much as she heard it when she was Reading.

She tried to Read these women, using her ability as much as she could, but there was nothing to them that she could uncover, despite every attempt on her part to find answers.

More and more, she suspected the key was tied to the nature of the augmentation. There was something about the metal implant that made it so she didn't Read them as well as she should.

It hadn't been the same way with the Architect, but then he didn't have the same type of augmentation, did he?

She needed to be getting back to the C'than. She'd

been gone for the better part of the day, and in that time, she had been working with these women, trying to help them find answers for themselves, trying to help them understand their abilities. She hadn't been able to help them as much as she'd hoped. Marcy was easy, but she had already demonstrated some capacity to Slide. She hadn't been able to gain control over it yet, but Lucy suspected it was only a matter of time. She remembered her own lack of control the first time she had managed to Slide, and it had only been a matter of time before she had improved.

The same thing had to be said for the others, but she wasn't sure what abilities they had.

She closed her eyes, trying to See, but her mastery of the visions was minimal at best. When she focused on them, they came to her, a flurry of imagery, but in none of them did she have any idea of what was out there or how she could grasp it.

She had abandoned that ability, knowing there wasn't much she would be able to use it for without any real control.

The only problem was that she thought it was perhaps the most potent of her powers. If she could master it, she might be able to better understand what Olandar Fahr was up to and figure out some way of stopping him. He likely had the ability to See things others could not. With that ability, he was far more formidable than Lucy, and far more formidable than the others working with her.

She sighed, pushing those visions away, ignoring them, and turning back to the women.

"I know there's something there," Teresa said. She was a heavyset woman, probably five years younger than

Lucy, and had pale green eyes. She came from the city in the south called Hej, a place Lucy had never visited. She tried to Read the woman but wasn't able to uncover anything from her thoughts. If only she could, she might be able to know how to find the city from her.

"You have to keep focusing."

As far as she could tell, Teresa had the ability to Read, though it was weak and uncontrolled. Given the paleness of her eyes, she'd likely had no abilities prior to any of this happening, but the fact that she had green eyes at all suggested she was touched by the Great Watcher, however faintly.

Had she grown up in Elaeavn, it was possible she would've had far more abilities. It was when Teresa had admitted she had detected someone's emotions that Lucy had realized the nature of her ability. It was difficult for her to try to teach someone how to Read. In Elaeavn, people knew they could Read from birth, and it took no time for most to know the nature of it and what to do with it, but then again, in Elaeavn, most people who could Read were prevented from doing so. Everyone had the ability to shut off their minds, to wall them away, and only the most powerful of Readers were able to penetrate those barriers.

"How, though?"

"You have to think about the strange nature of the thoughts you're encountering," Lucy said. She squeezed her eyes shut, thinking about what she had experienced when she had first awoken with the implant. The voices had been there, screaming in her mind. It would have to be something similar for Teresa; whether or not they were screaming, the voices would definitely be present. "Focus on what you hear. If it feels unusual, it probably is."

"How am I supposed to hear anything?"

"I'll admit it's muted here. I could bring you someplace else—"

"No," Teresa said quickly, shaking her head.

Like so many others, Teresa was nervous about leaving the village. Many of these women had been tormented, and the village was a place of safety, a place where they didn't have to fear what might happen to them. She would protect them.

"It's going to be difficult here. It's difficult for me here, so what you have to do is focus on what you can detect, and trust that it's there. Hold on to it. If you find something unusual, use that, let yourself be drawn to it, knowing that strangeness is real."

Teresa nodded, and she looked at Eve, a slender woman who stood next to her. Lucy knew very little about Eve other than that she had a hard edge to her. One of the first women Lucy had rescued from Nyaesh, she had been malnourished and near death, but time had been good to her, and she had begun to recuperate. Lucy suspected Eve would fully recover. The only thing Lucy didn't know was how much of Eve's hard edge was new and how much had been there before.

It probably didn't matter anyway. The edge was helpful, at least when it came to trying to be prepared for various challenges they might face.

"I haven't demonstrated anything," Eve said.

Lucy looked over at her. Eve was from Thyr, though she had a sense she had been somewhere else before that.

Eve didn't want to talk about it, and yet Lucy wondered if the other woman needed to talk.

"It's possible that you won't," she said.

"You keep saying that, but half of these women have abilities now, Lucy," Eve said.

Lucy nodded. "Half of them do, which means half of them don't. You might be in the other half. I know you want an ability..." Eve did, but she didn't know why. Perhaps it was only so she wouldn't feel helpless. If so, it was an emotion Lucy understood. It was better to have some ability, even if it was one she didn't fully understand, than to be completely powerless. Most of these women had suffered enough and had no interest in going through something like that again. They feared the C'than would return, bringing their torment with them, which meant these women were constantly on edge.

Lucy had hoped getting them away from that experience and letting them know she would do everything in her not inconsiderable power to protect them would give them a chance to relax, but not all of them had done so.

Then again, she understood. They had been through so much, and had suffered so much, that it might be difficult—almost impossible—to fully relax.

"I refuse to believe I don't have anything." Eve crossed her arms over her chest, meeting Lucy's eyes.

Lucy nodded. "Then we will keep looking." It was possible that continuing to look would be a waste of her time, but if Eve needed something, even if it was to make herself feel better, who was Lucy to refuse? Besides, it didn't hurt her to continue to work with the other woman to help her dig for other abilities. It was possible she had something Lucy had no way of detecting. As most of these women were either from Elaeavn or directly descended from those who were, Lucy suspected that her ability, whatever it might be, came from one of the Elaeavn abilities, which gave her an opportunity to better understand what she might need to do to help them. Yet the more time she spent with them, the more she wondered whether or not there was anything she could do to help them at all.

In the case of Eve, the woman was stubborn, but it was a stubbornness she thought she could help, and she decided it would be beneficial to do so, if only so that Eve might gain a better understanding of her own abilities.

"We've tried Sight, Reading, and we even tried Listening. So far, we haven't found anything that matches with your skill set, but that's not to say that we won't."

Eve nodded as if there were no other choice but that.

"It's possible you have one of the more unusual abilities."

"Unusual how?"

She glanced over to Marcy. While Lucy remained in the village, Marcy stayed with her, almost as if the other woman thought she could learn something from Lucy simply by watching her. She didn't remember what it had taken for her to learn how to Slide, and she could see the desire burning on Marcy's face to have some control over that ability, regardless of whether there was anything Lucy might be able to teach her by observation.

"Take Marcy. She's able to Slide. That's not one of the typical abilities the people of Elaeavn have."

"It's not?" Marcy asked.

Lucy shook her head. "Sliding is different. We view things like Reading and Sight and Listening as the gifts the Great Watcher gave our people, but there are other abilities. I've got the ability to Slide, and that's not considered one of the Great Watcher–given abilities."

"Why not?"

"To be honest, I'm not entirely sure. It comes from somewhere else, though I don't really know." All she knew was there was a belief that Sliding was something else. Then again, there was a connection to lorcith, which was also viewed to be something separate.

What if Eve had the ability to use lorcith? It would be something different—and useful. She had been around enough people who had the ability to control lorcith, so she could see how beneficial something like that would be.

Did she have anything on her that might help?

Lucy raised her hand. "Wait a minute. I'll be right back."

"Where are you—"

Lucy Slid, emerging near Ilphaesn Mountain. It was easy enough for her to do now, and she held herself there, hesitating, looking for something in the mountain. She Slid inside the mine and found a collection of metal that had been freshly mined, grabbing two lumps of it. She hoped the mining guild wouldn't mind, but then, they wouldn't even know she'd been here.

Lucy Slid, returning to the village. She held the pieces of metal out to Eve.

"What do you feel?"

"Annoyed that you left."

"But I returned."

"You still left," she said.

Lucy chuckled. "Fine. You can be annoyed, but what do you feel?" She continued to hold out the pieces of metal for Eve. She wondered whether the other woman would notice anything at all.

Eve stared at them, and then she took one of the hunks of metal, holding it in her hand. "Am I supposed to be impressed by this?"

"I don't know if you should be impressed, but I wondered if you might detect something from it."

"What should I detect?"

"I don't know. If you have some connection to the metal, you might be able to know how to find it, or perhaps you would have a way of controlling it."

"Controlling the metal?"

Lucy nodded. "There are some who can control it. They use it in their fighting, and to do other things as well."

Eve held on to it, twisting the hunk of lorcith from side to side, staring at it. "I… I don't feel anything."

"Well, you can keep trying," she said.

The other woman frowned, and she stuffed the piece of lorcith in her pocket. Lucy was about to argue, but if Eve was going to find some way of connecting to it, then having it on her would be beneficial. The longer she had to work with lorcith, the more likely it was that she would find some way of connecting to it, and Lucy hoped she did.

"I'll be back in the morning," she said.

"You're leaving again," she said.

"Like I said, I have—"

"Responsibilities. We've heard you."

Lucy glanced at the women around her. Most of them had seemed as if they understood why she was leaving, even though she hadn't given them the explanation. She hadn't told him that she was going to C'than, but she had said she had other responsibilities to take care of, and the fact that she was able to return as easily as she was shouldn't have been a problem for them. But there were some, like Eve, who made it a problem. Lucy worried there were more than she realized. She didn't want the woman angry at her, but the longer she spent away, the more likely it was they would end up displeased.

"I could stay, if you think it will help."

"Don't stay on our behalf," she said, then turned away.

She walked back toward the village, and Lucy was of half a mind to race after, to say something, but she didn't know what she could do to get through to Eve.

"Don't mind her," Marcy said, looking back at Eve. "She's upset she doesn't have any abilities."

"We don't know that she doesn't," Lucy said. "All we know is she hasn't discovered what they are."

"Right. So don't mind her."

Lucy breathed out in a frustrated sigh. She wanted to help *all* these women, which meant she would have to help them find a way to move past the torment they had experienced. If that was a matter of them understanding their abilities, she wanted to be a part of that, as well.

How was she going to do that if she was gone all the time?

And yet, the more she was gone, the more she felt as if she were abandoning the C'than.

How was she supposed to do both?

The easy answer would be to find some way to merge the two, but Lucy didn't think she could bring these women to the tower. If she did, there would be a different sort of rebellion, and given what they had gone through already, she didn't want to expose them to the C'than again.

"I really will be back tomorrow."

"Most of us know," Marcy said.

"Most?"

"Well, we understand you've been returning. I think some people worry there will come a time when you won't return, and that if that happens, we will be stuck here."

"But you won't be captured. And you will have each other."

"We don't know each other," Marcy said.

Lucy thought she could do something about that. Perhaps not yet, but if nothing else, it was an aspect of the village she thought could be corrected. If these women had a better sense of each other, who they were and what they had gone through, maybe that would bring them together in a way she had failed to do so far.

"That's something I need to help you with again tomorrow."

13

HAERN

HAERN *PUSHED* OFF, USING HIS CONNECTION TO LORCITH TO soar overhead, traveling through the forest and weaving between trees. He *pushed* and *pulled* on his connection to lorcith, forcing his mind to focus, wanting nothing more than to be able to draw the metal in a way that allowed him to make steady progress as he moved. Every so often, he thought he caught a glimmer of movement within the trees, but then it disappeared.

After traveling for a while, barely managing to keep from scratching himself with branches, he paused, leaning on one of the nearby trees. His breathing was ragged, and the effort of *pushing* like this more difficult than he would have expected. It took just as much energy as running, especially as he tried to navigate between the trees, twisting and contorting his body in a way that allowed him to stay unharmed.

Movement caught his attention, and he spun. A dart whistled past, striking the tree where he'd been resting, and Haern swore under his breath, *pushing* off once more and moving.

Galen was somewhere near.

The other man had promised to challenge him, and so far, he had managed to do so with some modicum of success. Not only had Haern been forced to gather a better connection to lorcith—something that had prompted his return to the mines over the last few weeks to ensure he continued to understand that connection—but he had required Haern to practice with much more intensity than before.

He checked his pouch while moving to ensure he had the necessary supplies on him.

There was another lesson Galen had taught him. *Always be aware of what supplies you have on hand.* It was far too easy to lose supplies with an unfortunate stumble, and then he would end up not only at risk of injury but lacking the gear he might need.

He needed to become less reliant on his connection to lorcith, but he also needed to use his connection to the metal in a way that would allow him to move.

The lorcith in the coins he used now was *far* less than what he had used before. It was less than a quarter of the total composition of the coin, a small hint of an alloy, and despite that, Haern still managed to employ it the same as he had before. Part of that came from his training, but part of it came from time spent around the metal. Eventually he hoped to get to the point where he wouldn't need much lorcith. Anything that made it so the Forgers couldn't track him easily was valuable to him.

No other movement came, and he slowed. The edge of the Aisl forest was near. The humming sensation from the lorcith rods called to him, the metal imbued with a certain magic energy that created a barrier. Attuned to the lorcith as he was, he could feel it more rapidly than he had before.

A flicker of movement caught his attention.

Haern *pushed* off, barely avoiding another dart that streaked his way.

If one of them hit him, not only would it hurt, but whatever toxin Galen had added to the dart would likely incapacitate him for an extended period of time. It was unlikely Galen used anything that would do more than that. He didn't *think* Galen had any intention of forcing him to try to overcome a poison, but he couldn't be entirely certain. It was possible that Galen would use something that would require him to somehow survive. It was the way that the other man had learned, though he claimed he wouldn't try the same technique on Haern.

Another dart whistled toward him.

Rather than *pushing* off, Haern sent a knife streaking toward the dart, trying to catch it in the air. He managed to collide with the dart, but as he spun, Galen was there, a dart jabbed into his belly.

Haern's breathing quickened, and he found his body didn't move.

"What was your mistake?"

He swallowed, trying to open his mouth, but it didn't work.

"Right. You won't be able to say anything at this point.

Let it work through you. Don't fight it. It won't linger all that long, and you should be thankful I didn't choose to use anything more painful." Galen withdrew the dart, taking a step back and twisting something within his pouch. Likely reloading the dart, preparing for the next time he would catch Haern. It wasn't the first time he'd managed to do so, and it wasn't going to be the last. "As you can't talk, let me tell you what you did wrong. You thought to counter."

Haern's mouth could move, and he licked his lips. Whatever poison Galen had used was already beginning to wear off. "I. Didn't try. To counter."

"No?" Galen took a few steps away, crouching down and plucking the lorcith knife off the forest floor. "What's this, then?"

Haern *pulled* on the knife, drawing it back toward him. Poisoned as he was, his body might not respond the way it should, but his connection to the metal remained. There were certain toxins that could incapacitate that, but so far Galen had not chosen to use them. He was thankful for that, though he suspected he needed to learn to fight without his connection to his abilities. If they failed him, what would he do?

Which was the exact point Galen was trying to make with him. He wanted Haern to be prepared for the possibility that his enhanced Sight and his connection to lorcith might one day fail. If they did, he still had to be prepared for fighting. If he could avoid poisoning, he could stay safe.

"Good. At least you didn't give up on fighting entirely."

"Should I attack you?"

"If you think you can."

Haern sent the knife streaking toward Galen, and the other man twisted out of the way, easily avoiding it. Despite his age, Galen still had an agility that Haern marveled at. He had been rusty when they had first begun training, but the longer Haern trained, the better Galen's skills became. It was as if both of them benefited.

Then again, Galen's skills were more a reassertion of existing abilities, whereas Haern needed to develop them in the first place. Learning was slow, and he didn't know all the ways he could use his abilities. Without his father to learn from, he might never know the full capacity of someone with a connection to lorcith. It was more than the ability to forge metal, to hear it singing, and to send it streaking away from him. There had to be more to it.

"You continue to rely on lorcith, though you've grown stronger with it. I'll give you that. It's something your father depended on far too much as well. One of the advantages I had in my exile was that I learned I couldn't rely upon my abilities all the time. Perhaps you should be exiled in order to understand the same thing."

"Do you think I need to be exiled in order to recognize that?"

"If you fail to consider alternatives, I do."

"My connection to lorcith makes me stronger."

"Your connection to lorcith makes you dependent upon the metal. I thought you might be easier to work with, as having only Sight isn't always an asset. I would have thought you would be easier to educate, but..."

The poisoning had nearly worn off, and Haern took a step back. His legs were shaky and weak, but even that was beginning to fade. In time, the weakness would dissipate completely, allowing him to stand. Even if he couldn't, his connection to lorcith was such that he thought that he could *push* himself through the forest and return home.

"Do you still think to hunt the Forgers?" Galen asked.

"I told you that I would talk with you before I did anything."

"That's not a no."

"It's not." Haern checked his knives, slipping them back into the sheaths. Whereas the coins might contain a smaller percentage of lorcith, the knives were made entirely of it. It was something he would have to remedy eventually, but he had been focused so much on training that he hadn't taken the time. If he was going to hunt Forgers, having lorcith blades put him at a disadvantage. He needed something they couldn't stop, and whether that was some alloy he might make or something else he could do, he had yet to determine.

If only he had his father's ability with other metals.

"There you go again."

"There I go doing what?"

"Looking at your knives as if you wish to seduce them. They're tools. The sooner you understand that, the more likely you will be able to use them in the manner they were meant to be used."

"Like you with your darts?"

"Exactly like that. I understand the darts are tools,

much as I understand that without them, I am not helpless."

"You're still diminished."

"Perhaps, but that doesn't mean I'm unable to defend myself." Galen looked around the forest, and he nodded. Two men who Haern hadn't seen hiding through the trees suddenly appeared.

How had these men hidden?

Both carried long swords, reminding him of the men who patrolled the water's edge.

Sellswords.

They unsheathed their blades.

"Galen?"

"I warned you that I would push you. It's time to remove your crutch."

"Remove my what?"

Galen flicked a dart at Haern, and it stuck into his shoulder. He winced and blinked as everything began to dim.

His Sight faded.

He attempted to connect to lorcith, but even that ability was absent.

Galen took a few steps back and nodded toward a nearby tree. Haern jerked his head around quickly and realized a sword rested alongside the tree.

"It's time I push you a little harder. My friends here will offer you a different type of instruction than what I might be able to provide."

The two sellswords approached, and Haern jumped back, thankful that his agility and strength were still there. He reached the base of the tree, grabbing the sword—simple steel, he realized, probably why he hadn't noticed it before—before bringing the blade around. The two men stood far enough apart that neither would interfere with the other's movements. They appeared comfortable, practiced in the way they approached, and unconcerned that he had a sword of his own.

Maybe this was nothing more than another attempt at practice. He glanced at the blades, wishing for his normal Sight, and hating that he couldn't tell with any certainty whether the blades were dull or sharp.

One of the blades whistled toward him, and he managed to swing his sword around barely in time, blocking.

Definitely sharp.

What was Galen thinking having him battle *two* sellswords? What could he learn from doing so?

He spun the blade around, trying to force them to keep distant. He needed to buy enough time for whatever poison Galen had used on him to wear off, though he didn't know how long that would take. If it was a long-lasting poison, he would have to deal with this without his abilities.

One of the sellswords continue to press, and Haern tried to spin away but wasn't fast enough. The sword crashed down toward him, and he resisted, pushing away, but he didn't do so in time. As the sword swung closer and closer, he braced for an impact that never came.

The sellsword stood over him, sword angled down and ready to strike, but he didn't complete the movement.

Haern swallowed, and Galen stepped between them. "Meet your new swordmasters."

"What?" he asked, looking from one man to the other.

"This is Timothy Narl," Galen said, motioning to the man holding the sword just over Haern. "And this is Charen Ohls. As you probably have surmised, they are both Neelish sellswords. I will leave you to their tutelage."

Galen turned, and Haern wanted to go after him, but the other man continued onward, leaving him stranded alone with these two sellswords, feeling as if he were trapped. And he *was* trapped. He knew nothing about these men other than that they were here at the urging of Galen.

"Get up," Timothy said.

Haern crawled to his feet quickly, still holding on to the sword. The other man, Charen, stood off to the side, having sheathed his sword at some point. When had he done that? As far as Haern knew, both men had had their swords unsheathed before.

"Have you ever fought with a sword before?" Timothy asked.

Haern shook his head. "Not much."

The sellsword glared at him. "Not much?"

He swung the sword, sweeping it toward Haern, and he brought his sword up to block. The effect of the attack was jarring, sending his arms quivering. He barely managed to hold out as the sellsword struck, and he was thankful he hadn't been injured any more than he already had.

"Your posture is terrible."

"My posture?"

Timothy accentuated the comment by slamming his sword into Haern again. Each strike left him shaking.

"You must grip the sword so that you won't lose it. Hold it as if you mean it."

"How so?"

The other man swung again, connecting with Haern's sword. "Like this."

He twisted his hands, bringing them around so that Haern could see how he held it. He shifted his grip, and Timothy attacked again, striking at him with the sword with a sharp, jarring motion.

Haern nearly dropped the sword, but he had the sense that if he did, Timothy's wrath would be much greater. He didn't dare let the sword fall, much like he didn't dare lower his guard around a man like this. Rather, he needed to be cautious, assertive, and he needed to ensure he didn't anger them in any way.

"If you have no experience with the sword, you must learn to defend."

He swung the sword around, and Haern braced for another attack, but it didn't come. Instead, he brought the sword around, and Charen unsheathed quickly, blocking the blow. The two of them twisted, stepping from place to place in what almost appeared to be a dance. As he watched, the only thing Haern could think of was that his father had never needed to learn to fight like that. Why should he?

But then, if he didn't, it was likely he would end up in a situation where he wasn't prepared. Galen had proven how easy it was to incapacitate him, and when it came to facing and defeating Forgers, he needed every bit of opportunity he had. If he failed at this, then his father would be lost.

The men continued their movements, and Haern found himself following Charen as he blocked, knowing that if nothing else, that was the movement he needed to master. There was no obvious skill to it. It seemed as if Charen knew where to bring his sword, sweeping around and blocking blow after blow as if the other man were alerting him of what he was going to do with each attack.

How was he supposed to anticipate a fighting style like that?

Maybe it wouldn't be important. At this point, all that mattered was that he had to come up with some method of blocking an attack.

All of a sudden, Timothy spun toward Haern, and he raised his sword, preparing for the inevitable crashing of the blade. When it came, Haern struggled to maintain his grip on the sword. As long as he could hold it, he could withstand the force of the attack.

Timothy continued to swing at him, sweeping his blade in one attack after another, each of them as brutal and rapid as the blows he had struck Charen.

As he defended, blocking each blow, Haern realized that wasn't entirely true. The blows were similar, but they weren't nearly as rapid as what Timothy had directed at Charen. There was more of a fluidity to that attack. This was slower, for his benefit. He was giving Haern an opportunity to defend, but it didn't even matter. He wasn't quick enough to block the other man.

Timothy's sword slipped through, catching Haern on the arm.

"There's no doubt that you need to do more, but the question is whether you *can* do more."

"You won't work with me?"

For some reason, that bothered him. It shouldn't. He didn't necessarily care if they worked with him. All he cared about was continuing to train, but if they refused to teach him, how would he be able to improve? This was what Galen wanted for him. He wanted to ensure he obtained the necessary skills so he could fight, resist, and learn to handle the Forgers in another way. If they weren't willing to work with him, what other options did he have?

Then again, did Galen know how to fight with the sword?

As far as he knew, Galen didn't have any experience with sword fighting. He was an assassin who used poisons and darts, nothing more than that. Why should he have to learn something that Galen didn't find necessary to know himself?

"Go. I'll find another way to learn."

The two men glanced at each other before disappearing. It happened quickly, almost as if they were Sliding; they faded, slipping away before he could react. Haern watched them for a moment before racing after them, but they were gone, disappeared somewhere beyond where he could find them.

He tested his connection to lorcith but found it was still missing. Whatever poison Galen had used on him persisted. He would need to walk through the forest to get back.

It took the better part of a day to reach the heart of the Aisl forest. He encountered nothing and no one during the journey, certainly nothing that would tell him where the Neelish sellswords had disappeared. With them gone, he had thought he might come across Galen, but even he was absent. By the time he reached the heart of the Aisl, he was frustrated and angry.

He stormed through the trees, unsurprised to find Galen waiting for him. "You left me with them?"

"I anticipated you would spend longer working with them."

"You anticipated?"

"I cannot help it that you failed so quickly."

"I didn't fail quickly."

"Then you succeeded? You're still working with them?" He glanced beyond Haern, looking toward the forest. "Interesting, as I don't see it."

"That's enough," Haern said.

"I imagine they said the same to you."

"Galen—"

"Would you have me say something else?"

"I've never even seen you work with a sword. Why would you have me do it when you can't?"

"What makes you think I cannot?"

"Oh, so you can? I just haven't seen it before?"

"Do you believe you know me so well as to know every fighting style I'm capable of?"

There was a hardness to his voice that took Haern aback, and something deep inside of him cautioned him to be careful what he said next. He might anger Galen even more, and that wasn't something he wanted to do. Galen had offered him an opportunity, and he needed to continue his studies with him to prepare to confront the Forgers. But irritation overwhelmed his reason.

"I think that if you could use a sword, I would have seen it by now."

Galen cocked his head, studying him for a moment before throwing back his cloak, revealing a sword sheathed beneath. He quickly withdrew it, bringing it around. Haern had barely a moment to react, blocking. Galen darted forward, swinging his sword in one attack after another, each one striking with rapid intensity, reminding him of the way the sellswords had fought, though Galen was perhaps even faster than the sellswords. There was a precision to his movements.

The sword swept through Haern's ability to defend, catching him on the leg, and Haern dropped, pain shooting through him. As he knelt, looking up at Galen, gripping his sword helplessly, Galen stood over him and casually sheathed his sword.

"Don't make assumptions."

"If you can fight like that, why use your darts and poison?"

"Not everything is as easy as you would like it to be, Haern. And as I've told you, there are many ways to fight. If you continue to work with me, I will ensure that you are capable of fighting in as many ways as possible. And I will help you become less reliant on your Great Watcher–given abilities. If you choose otherwise, I can make no such promises. Perhaps that is as you would like it."

"That's not—"

"Do you want to learn? Do you want to train? Or would you like to remain easy for the Forgers to defeat?"

"I'll keep training."

Galen nodded. "Good. Now, go on to Darren and see if he can't heal those two injuries."

Galen nodded. "Why do you need me to work with the Neelish sellswords if you're such a skilled swordmaster?"

Galen paused, his brow furrowing as he considered Haern. "Who do you think taught me?"

Darren grunted as he grabbed Haern's arm, running his fingers along either side of the cut. It was deep, and though it had stopped bleeding, Haern was forced to look away from it, not wanting to see the muscles revealed beneath the bite of the blade. A wound like that could be fatal without someone like Darren to Heal it. Thankfully, he didn't have to worry about that.

Then again, outside of the city, there weren't Healers like Darren. He was unique—at least, somewhat unique. There was another like him, though Haern didn't know the old Healer Della as well as his father did.

"There was a time when swords were forbidden within Elaeavn," Darren said, the Healing washing through Haern.

"I know."

"Sometimes I wonder if that might not have been a better time."

"You realize that time involved the Elvraeth having complete control over the city," Haern said, bringing his gaze back around to Darren. Darren had pale green eyes, which startled him each time he saw them, mostly because he was such a powerful Healer.

"I'm not saying that the Elvraeth rule was a better time. All I'm getting at is that weapons like this," he said, tapping him on the arm, "are unfortunate. I've seen far too many people suffer because of such injuries. I would try to protect as many as I can."

"I'd like to protect as many as I could, too, but with the Forgers—"

"Don't go into the Forgers with me," Darren said, a little more sharply than necessary. The heat in his voice

14

HAERN

HAERN KEPT HIS ARM PRESSED UP AGAINST HIS BOD holding it close. It still throbbed, but less than it had. Th healing Darren had used on him left him feeling col awash with his Healing magic, and while Haern tried t ignore it, much like he tried to ignore the pain in his ar he succeeded with neither.

"A training accident?" Darren asked, standing fro where he'd been crouched next to Haern's leg.

Haern looked past the Healer. He was friendly wi Darren, having known him nearly his entire life, but late there had been a distance between them. He'd come Darren far too often looking for help and Healing. wished it weren't necessary, but unfortunately it seem to be. Too often he had to have something restored, a rarely was he able to offer the right sort of explanation to what had happened. Each time it was a training ac dent, but some accidents weren't quite accidents, when it came to training with Galen.

"He has me learning to handle a sword."

surprised Haern. Darren took a deep breath, shaking his head. "I've heard enough about the Forgers. They might have left us alone—"

"Except for the fact that my father went after them. That's what you mean, isn't it?"

"There's something to be said about that," Darren said.

"My father isn't to blame for the Forgers continuing to attack the Aisl and Elaeavn."

"We won't know, now will we?"

"I've traveled out of the city. I've seen the way the Forgers are willing to attack, to hurt other people. I understand just what they do." Haern took a deep breath, struggling to remove the image of the Forgers in the last city from his mind, but he couldn't shake it. They had overpowered him, and had Galen not arrived, he might have fallen, cut down by them. He had no idea what the Forgers did to others in that city or how much the people there suffered. Maybe it was no different than how his people had suffered under the Elvraeth. In both cases, there was a certain tyranny. "The Forgers would have come regardless of what we might have done," he said.

Haern got up, pulling his arm away from Darren. The Healing continued to leave him cool, some of his energy waning, but that was the price of Healing. It took energy from the person who was Healed, forcing them to use their own abilities to recover, though this was a relatively minor injury in the scheme of things.

He scanned the inside of Darren's home. A small fireplace crackled softly, the heat radiating into the room. It was a welcome heat after Healing such as he had gone through. Without the fireplace, the chill of the Healing might be more than he could tolerate. Some who suffered from more serious injuries would be even colder, and he was thankful he didn't have to know what that felt like. At least not yet. Within the fireplace, a pot boiled, casting off a hint of spiced steam he suspected was some medicinal Darren preferred. Galen would have known, but he had returned to Elaeavn, back to the Floating Palace, and back to his comforts.

"Are we done?" he asked.

Darren frowned at him. "You don't need to be angry about this."

"I'm not angry. There's just so much for me to do."

"Is this all about your father?"

"This is about the Forgers, not just about my father."

"And once you're done training, what is it you intend to do?"

Haern shook his head. "I don't know."

"Will there be an end to your training?"

"I don't know."

"I hope you can find a measure of peace your father never managed. It's unfortunate he wasn't able to relax and enjoy the comforts of the forest he helped the guilds establish."

"I think he would claim that he managed to enjoy those things."

"He might make that claim, but did he really?"

Haern scanned the inside of the home again, his gaze lingering on the row of jars near the door. In them were various medicinals. Some were herbs that could be used for healing. Many of them were names that Haern had learned, names of items that had much benefit, whereas others were things he didn't know, and perhaps never would. He had trained with Galen, learning about both healing and harming medicines, and unfortunately, he had more use for the latter.

"We'll never know."

"Good luck, Haern. You know that I'm here if you need me."

Haern nodded. "I know. And I thank you."

They met each other's eyes for a moment before he turned away. It was unfortunate that there remained an awkwardness between them. There shouldn't be, not between men who had been friends, and yet there was. Darren was content remaining within the Aisl, Healing, comfortable with his life and the lot the Great Watcher had given him. Haern no longer believed he could sit back and observe as he once had. Would it be so awkward if he and Lucy came back together? His friend had changed even more than Haern had.

Maybe that was what he should have been spending his time doing. There were still people within Elaeavn who could Slide him to Lucy, and once Lucy learned Rsiran was missing again, wouldn't she help?

Maybe she wouldn't—or couldn't. Considering what she had been through, it was possible that she needed to continue working with Carth in order to fully understand what she needed to know.

The challenge would be in finding her. They had left Asador, and now he didn't know where to locate his friend. With Lucy's ability to Slide now augmented by the lorcith alloy, he might not be able to find her. It would be easy for her to disappear, to go someplace she couldn't be tracked. Which was a shame. Lucy could be a valuable ally—and an asset—in confronting the Forgers.

As he stepped back into the clearing at the heart of the Aisl, he shook his head. Could he really be thinking like that? Could he really be viewing his friend—a woman he'd known for years—as simply an asset?

Maybe he had changed more than he realized.

He paused in the center of the clearing. The forest forge took up most of the space in the center, smoke billowing from the chimney telling him that the forge was active. Likely that meant his grandfather. Though he had a forge in Elaeavn—the Lareth family forge—he often preferred to use the one here, wanting to be connected to the Aisl. Since Rsiran's disappearance, he had spent even more time here. It was as if his grandfather wanted to keep the tradition of the forest forge operating. More than that, though, his grandfather had an ability with lorcith that, while not as strong as Rsiran's, still had significant potential.

Stepping inside the forge, he was greeted by a familiar heat. The steady tapping of the hammer on metal alerted him of his grandfather's work, and he paused for a moment, listening for the sense and sound of lorcith, but there was none. Either his grandfather wasn't using the metal, or there was simply too much lorcith all around. After his time in the lorcith mines over the last few weeks, though, he was more attuned to lorcith than ever before.

He stood back, watching his grandfather work. He had a steady and rhythmic movement, each blow made with precision, and Haern wondered what his grandfather was creating. He stepped closer and realized that it was a long slender bar, and while it wasn't made from lorcith, he didn't know what material it was.

"Are you going to watch, or will you join me?"

Haern stepped up to the forge, joining his grandfather. "What are you working at?"

His grandfather paused, hammer in midswing, and glanced over at Haern, a hint of a smile on his face. "Have you been away from the forge so long that you don't recognize a crafting?"

"I don't think so, but in this shape, you could make many things."

"Indeed. But what do you think a shape like this likely represents?"

"I don't know."

His grandfather stared at him for a moment before flicking his gaze to the sword Haern held. He'd carried it from Darren's shop but had forgotten about it. "You don't know, yet you carry something similar?"

"You're making a sword?"

His grandfather began to hammer again, the movements steady and regular. Each blow struck the metal, thinning it slightly. "Don't say it as if you're so surprised."

"It's just that I know how you feel about swords." His grandfather felt much the same way as most of the older generation did, those who had lived in the time when the Elvraeth had forbidden the use of swords.

"Times—and people—change, Haern."

"I know they do, Grandfather, it's just..."

"Are you going to help me, or do you intend to just stand there?"

Haern nodded and carried the sword over to the side

of the room, where he set it down. There was a table with other items, and he placed the sword amongst them, though most were far more nicely made than his sword. This didn't appear to be one of his father's creations, or that of anyone from the guild.

Returning to the forge, he grabbed a leather apron, tying it on, and slipped on the leather gloves to match before picking up the tongs and helping his grandfather as he hammered. His role was to move the metal, carrying it over to the heat, and he had done it enough over the years to know how he could best assist his grandfather, though it had been quite a while since he had spent much time forging.

As they worked in relative silence, nothing more than the steady hammering of metal, Haern fell back into the rhythm of it. It was something he knew, though not as well as others in his family. His father was far more comfortable working at the forge, but then again, his grandfather was more comfortable than either of them.

The blade began to emerge. His grandfather had a practiced stroke to his hammering, each blow perfectly placed, drawing out the length of the blade, flattening it, turning it into a slender and curved blade. Haern focused on the metal, trying to determine what it was.

"It's not steel," he said.

"No," his grandfather answered. He continued hammering, and Haern turned it before bringing it back to the forge to heat.

"And it's not lorcith, either."

His grandfather glanced up at him. "Are you certain?"

Haern frowned, focusing on the blade. Lorcith was

notoriously difficult to work with, and it required someone with patience and an understanding of the metal in order to form it into the various shapes it could take. It could be forced, but lorcith worked better if you worked with it. That was something his father had taught him, and Haern had taken it to heart. Forcing lorcith became difficult, and the more someone tried to force it, the more likely it was that the forging would fail. Working with it allowed the forging to happen more naturally, and each piecing that emerged came out stronger for it.

As he focused, he didn't pick up on anything within it that suggested the blade was lorcith.

He glanced over at his grandfather. "I don't think it is lorcith."

"Your father would be disappointed."

"Why? Is it?"

"There's lorcith in this."

As his grandfather continued to hammer, Haern worked on connecting to the metal, searching for anything within it that would reveal the lorcith. If it was there, it wasn't obvious.

There was other lorcith around him. The knives he had made. The part-lorcith coins he had in his pouch. There were even lumps of lorcith in the forge. All of those drew his attention the way lorcith always did. This did not.

Could he *push* away the sense of lorcith all around him?

There was a lot of competition for his attention, and unlike in the lorcith mines, it wouldn't be easy for him to ignore that sense here.

Still he tried.

It required that he *push* away the sense of the lorcith closest to him, and as he did, he was able to ignore the knives sheathed at his side along with the lump of lorcith in the room. That left the coins. They were smaller, and he tried to ignore them, *pushing* away his awareness of them.

When that was done, he focused, attempting to maintain a connection to the lorcith, trying to understand whether the sword his grandfather was making had any lorcith in it, and came up empty.

If there was lorcith in the blade, it had to be a negligible amount, less even than what was in the coins. A blade like this would be useful, but only if he could connect to it.

He continued to focus, searching for the stirrings of metal.

It was faint. Little more than a tracing.

Striations of lorcith traced along the blade, and he marveled. It wasn't an alloy so much as a filament of lorcith worked within the rest of the metal.

He focused on that filament, connecting to it.

"Would you stop that?"

"Stop what?"

"You're going to draw it out," his grandfather said.

"You can tell what I'm doing?"

"Of course."

"It's so *small*. It's almost as if it's not even there."

"Which is exactly how I was instructed to make it."

"Who wants a sword like this?"

His grandfather continued to hammer, working on the

blade without answering. It was incredibly shaped, slender but curved, and now that Haern was aware of the lorcith in it, he could practically hear it humming. It was soft, like a stirring on the breeze, little more than a faint voice. Nothing more than a murmuring, really.

His grandfather carried the blade over to the quenching basin, stuffing it in there and leaving it. When he was done, he turned to Haern.

"Who is that for?"

"You, now that you can pick up on the lorcith."

"Me?"

"Your mentor thought you might need a blade and suggested I put in the smallest amount of lorcith I could. This is about as small a quantity as I've ever worked with."

"How much was it?"

"No more than a strand of your mother's hair."

He had thought he sensed a striation, but it would have been less than that. It would have been so negligible that it shouldn't even be detected, and yet now that he was aware of it, he could feel it easily.

Galen had wanted that for him?

And here he had thought Galen didn't want him to use his connection to lorcith. That hadn't been the case at all. Galen had wanted him to learn to control it—not depend upon it, but be able to work with it.

If he had a sword like this—and one that he could actually use—it was possible even the Forgers wouldn't be able to overpower his connection.

Haern went over to the quenching basin, carefully lifting the blade. It needed a hilt and a guard, and then it would be complete. He suspected there weren't too many within the smith guild who could forge it any better, not out of the metal like this. Perhaps if it had been made entirely with lorcith, it could have been *pushed* and *pulled* into whatever shape was needed. He'd seen some of the sculptures his father had made and knew that with the right touch, there was incredible power to that connection, but using an actual forging technique, the techniques taught to generations of Lareth smiths, he thought his grandfather had done about as well as anyone could have.

"How did you get the strand of lorcith within it?"

"Carefully. Slowly. It required folding metal in a specific way. And then it required caution hammering it."

"I don't know if even my father would have been able to do this."

"Your father is a skilled blacksmith, Haern. He was the guildlord for a time."

"He might have been the guildlord, but he also depended upon his connection to the metal."

His grandfather nodded. "That he did. There are some techniques us old ones still remember."

"You're not that old."

"No? There are days I feel it. Most of the time it's when my bones ache when the rain is coming, and occasionally it's when I sleep wrong." He laughed to himself. "I know I'm getting old when I wake up sore from sleep."

"What about working at the forge?"

"Ah," he said, waving his hand. "That's never bothered me. My body has known that work my entire life. Ever since I was barely able to walk, I've been holding a hammer and working at a forge. No, this is more about the rest of me that's breaking down. My ability to continue to hold a hammer, to beat at metal, hasn't changed."

"It's a beautiful blade."

"Good. I will be proud for you to take something of mine with you."

"I'm still learning to use a sword."

His grandfather watched him for a moment, finally setting his hammer down near the anvil. "I wish it weren't necessary."

"Not you too."

"Not me with what?"

"It seems more and more people are trying to convince me that it's unnecessary for me to train the way I have been."

"I wouldn't convince you of that at all. I think you need to continue your efforts. If anyone will be able to bring Rsiran back, it will be you."

"I'm not sure that's true."

"Sometimes it takes having a person care about you to believe something is possible."

"Are you saying you believe I can do this?"

"I wouldn't have made you the sword if I didn't believe it, but that's not it. I'm saying that your belief in your father and the fact that he still lives is what is important. Others might think he's gone, but you hold out hope. I share it with you, but I am in no condition to go after him."

"There are times when I'm not sure I'm in any condition to go after him."

"And yet, despite feeling that way, still you work. You train. You will attempt to do what you can. That is valuable."

Haern took a deep breath. Everything he'd been doing had been on behalf of his father, and though he didn't know if he would succeed in finding him, he was determined to attempt it.

"Are you going to help me sharpen it now?"

"I thought you were making the sword for me."

"Don't be like that," his grandfather said.

"Like what?"

"Lazy. The hard work is done."

"I've sharpened a few blades in my day. I know the hard work isn't done quite yet."

His grandfather smiled at him. He was a focused man, and his smile was barely more than a curve of his lips, but it spread to his eyes, making them twinkle. "Perhaps not, but as I'm an old man, I think having a young man like yourself doing some of the hard work is most appropriate, don't you?"

"Now you're going to try to guilt me?"

"Isn't it working?"

Haern chuckled, taking the blade over to the grinder. "Not entirely."

His grandfather pulled a stool out from the bench, taking a seat and watching him. "And yet, here you are. Doing the hard work."

"I thought you said this wasn't the hard work."

"And you said you knew the hard work wasn't done. Get to it. You're going to need that blade in your studies, I think."

As Haern began to grind the blade, bringing it to a sharpened edge, he feared his grandfather was right. If it worked as his grandfather intended, maybe he could find a way to use small amounts of lorcith in his knives. Maybe he wouldn't have to be dependent on his abilities, but could still have access to them.

He glanced over at the forge. It meant he would need to get back to work. And it was the kind of work he thought his father would approve of.

15

HAERN

The wind whipped around him, and Haern clutched his cloak around him tightly. There was a strange fragrance to the air that he didn't recognize, though considering how far from home he had traveled, that wasn't entirely surprising. He gripped the hilt of his sword. There wasn't much in the way of decoration on the hilt, but that was the way he liked it. He had made it simply and designed for his grip in particular. His grandfather had helped him with that, ensuring he knew just how to fine-tune the grip so that it was specific for his hand. They had used the smallest amount of lorcith, little more than a grain of sand, embedding it into the end of the hilt. Surprisingly, doing that added a certain balance to the sword.

He kept his focus on the blade, using his connection to lorcith to maintain it. Now that he was better connected to the lorcith within the blade, he found he could reach it easily and quickly.

"What do you See?" Galen asked.

He glanced over at the other man. They were crouched on a rooftop, and this time it was a firmer support, nothing like the thatched roof they had stood on before. This was slate, and while it was dry, there was still something almost slick about it. It was as if there was moisture in the air that clung to the slate, making it so that he would lose his footing if he weren't careful.

"I don't See anything," Haern said. They'd been sitting there motionless for the better part of an hour. Thoren had left them in this city to the east of Elaeavn with a promise to return at a specific time. If they weren't there, he would return to Elaeavn, waiting before coming back later.

They had only a few windows of opportunity before he stopped returning.

In that way, Galen wanted to ensure that they didn't put Thoren at risk, though Haern wasn't sure whether this was the right plan.

"I don't either, which tells me that either there's nothing here, or they don't want us to detect anything."

"You think they know we've come?"

"Have you made the mistake of bringing too much lorcith with you?"

"Only the sword."

"Only the sword?"

"I have a few filament coins as well, but you told me to bring those."

"Of course I did. We need to know whether it's effective."

Haern was still surprised Galen was willing to attempt this. He had agreed to risk themselves, searching for an opportunity to confront some of the Forgers and test whether the threads of lorcith within both the sword and the coin, along with the two new knives Haern carried, would be effective against them.

The real test would be up to Haern. Galen was here for support, and mostly to ensure he didn't get in over his head.

If this worked, Haern held out hope he could get back to his search, hunting the Forgers, looking for anything that would give him an idea about where they had taken his father. He was growing tired of sitting and waiting, tired of doing nothing, knowing his father suffered through his inactivity.

That was, if he still lived.

Haern tried to ignore that possibility. He might be one of the few who still believed his father lived. While he hadn't spoken with his mother about it, he had grown increasingly certain that even she doubted Rsiran was alive. And if she gave up hope, there might not be any hope remaining for anyone.

"Maybe we'll be returning to the Aisl without testing this," Haern said.

"You're disappointed."

"Of course I'm disappointed. I need to know if they'll be able to use these against me or not."

It was more than that, though. He'd been training with the sword, working with his two swordmasters after Galen's urging, and believed he'd gained in skill, but didn't know with any certainty if he would be able to withstand an attack. He suspected he could handle the Forgers, especially if they weren't able to pick up on the lorcith within his knives. That had been his downfall before. Always before they had known about the lorcith and the blades, and if he could hide the fact there was any metal within his weapons that he was able to control, then he might be able to overpower them.

"I think you will get your opportunity." Galen nodded down the street.

Haern turned, noticing a flickering sort of movement.

Sliding.

That indicated a Forger. It had to.

He followed the figure as they Slid along the street, moving off into the shadows.

"I'm going to follow," he said.

"Be careful."

Haern grabbed a handful of the coins and *pushed* one of them away. When it landed softly on the ground, he used that to *push* off, soaring above the street. He sent another coin flying, *pushing* off on that as well. As he moved along the street, he drew the coins back to him. He refused to leave any behind, not wanting the Forgers to detect how he'd followed them. It was possible they wouldn't know, but it was equally possible they would discern the way he used the coins, and with their connection to lorcith, they might be able to uncover *how* he had used them. He wouldn't put it past them to study the technique, decide if it was something they could replicate, and find some way of stopping him.

When he reached the end of the street where the Forger had disappeared, he rested on a nearby rooftop. He looked down, searching for movement along the street, but there was nothing.

That wasn't how he was going to detect the Forger. He needed to focus on lorcith.

He strained, letting his awareness of the metal stretch out from him. There was no sense of lorcith anywhere else but with him.

That wasn't quite true. A trace amount existed down the street, back the direction he'd come. Galen must have taken one of his coins.

Sneaky. Then again, with Galen holding on to one of his coins, Haern had a way of tracking him if anything happened to him. Not that anything was likely to happen to Galen. If anything, Haern would be the one captured.

He waited, searching for movement, and after a while, he noticed a flickering farther down the street.

Without pausing too long, he *pushed* off, soaring above the street. There came a steady thump with each coin as it sank into the ground when he *pushed* it, though he didn't know if he could slow it while maintaining his momentum. The noise would hopefully be overlooked, especially as he wouldn't be moving along the street itself but high above it.

The Forger turned, and this time, Haern was able to follow him. He reached a central square, with a three-story building rising nearby. There was more of a crowd here. From his position overhead, the sounds of the city drifted to his ears, and Haern knew he couldn't hesitate.

He dropped to the ground in front of the Forger.

The man looked at him, cocking his head to the side. "What is—"

Haern pushed on his knives, sending them streaking.

It took more effort using his knives in this way than it

did when they had more lorcith within them, but even with this faint amount of lorcith, he had control over them. It was enough.

He felt resistance against the knives but pushed harder and overcame it, sending the knives stabbing into either shoulder of the Forger.

The man cried out.

Others on the street turned in his direction, and Haern darted forward, grabbing the Forger, dropping a coin, and *pushing* off.

It carried them to the nearest rooftop. When he was there, he recovered the coin and threw the Forger back.

"You made a mistake."

The Forger had a strange accent to his words. Brown eyes glowered, and he reached for the knives in his shoulders, wincing as he did. Haern didn't give him the opportunity to grab them; he *pushed* him back, sending him staggering.

"You and I are going to talk."

He tried to suppress the elation he felt. The filament of lorcith worked. The Forger had managed to slow the knives a little, but not much. If he could get the jump on them, maybe he could finally get information about his father. Maybe he could finally begin to actually *find* his father.

"What sort of talk?" the Forger asked.

Haern hated how calm he sounded. It was almost as if…

Haern spun around, keeping his pressure on the knives, holding the Forger back against the roof, wondering if another Forger might come. They came in pairs and trios, so it was likely that he wasn't alone.

"Where's your partner?"

"Partner? What makes you think I have a partner?"

Haern glanced back, glaring at him. "You always have partners."

"You know us so well as to know how we travel?"

"Yes."

The Forger smiled darkly. "Interesting."

Pressure built within his mind, and almost too late, Haern slammed his mental barriers into place, locking onto the image of lorcith as his father had taught him.

"You resemble him."

"What's that?"

"Him. Your father."

Haern turned his attention back to the Forger, trying to resist the urge to tremble. He had gotten into Haern's thoughts.

It was another mistake he'd made. Many of the Forgers were skilled Readers, having stolen that ability as well. It was much the same as what had happened with Lucy when she had been augmented with the metal.

Even with his mental barriers in place, it was possible Haern wasn't strong enough to withstand this Forger digging into his thoughts. Did the other Forger know he was here?

Worse, could this Forger have sent out a call for help?

The Forger stared at him.

"Where is your other friend?"

"Friend?"

"You're right. I doubt that you're friends. Where is

your other Forger?"

The man grinned more widely. "You continue to make the mistake that we are all Forgers."

"Forger. Ai'thol. All of it is the same to me."

"And yet, it's not all the same to me."

The Forger took a step toward him, and Haern *pushed*.

There was a shimmer of movement. Haern quickly *pulled* on the knives, drawing them back at the same time as the Forger Slid away.

He breathed out heavily.

Now they knew he was here.

Worse, they would know he was using lorcith in a way they couldn't detect, unless they believed he had control over another metal. That was possible. His father had power over other metals, while Haern didn't have that same connection—yet.

Using one of the coins, he *pushed* off, making his way back to the street, heading toward Galen. As he did, he realized the sense of the other man was absent.

Could something have happened to Galen?

Galen was far too skilled for anything to have befallen him. He would have been ready, prepared in a way that even Haern was not, and he would have managed to avoid any sort of attack.

What Haern needed to do was find where Galen had gone.

He reached the rooftop where he'd left Galen. There was no sign of the man.

With the lorcith coin, he could draw upon that connection and search for him, but he would need to work quickly. Galen didn't have any way of traveling, and it was too soon for Thoren to have returned for them. Unless something had happened to Galen, he wouldn't be all that far.

Haern focused on the sense of lorcith.

First he pushed away the sense of the sword, then the knives, and finally the coins he had on him. It left him with an emptiness.

He listened.

If the lorcith coin was anywhere nearby, he would be able to find it.

There was something at the far end of the city.

It was faint, and Haern wasn't even sure if he was detecting it correctly or not, but as it was the only thing he could pick up on, he had to search.

Pushing off down the street, he made his way as quickly as possible, recovering the coins as he went. He kept a certain height as he traveled, trying to stay high overhead, not wanting to be seen by anyone on the street below. The only thing that might be spotted would be the coin as he recovered it, drawing it back to him, but that was a chance he was willing to take. It was late enough the streets were mostly empty, and anyone who might be out here was likely half intoxicated, so they would question what they saw anyway.

As he neared, he slowed, focusing on the sense of lorcith, searching to see if it was the coin he'd created.

It was there. And it was his coin.

He came to rest on a stout two-story building. Two windows on the front of the building glowed softly. There was no movement around otherwise. He dropped onto the roof, trying to slow his descent, but with so little lorcith in these coins, control wasn't something he had in great quantities. It was hard enough for him to simply *push* off, as that took incredible strength. Control was the next piece, and it was one he hadn't yet mastered.

Haern made his way to the back of the building, looking around. It was a walled garden around the home, and he detected nothing else that suggested there might be more lorcith here, though the fact that he sensed anything at all reassured him. The coin had a certain signature to it, letting him know it was *his* coin.

He searched around the outside of the building to see whether anyone else moved. Finding nothing, he dropped another coin to the ground and *pushed* off, lowering himself back into the garden.

Fragrance from flowers lining a path caught his attention, and he ignored it, plucking the coin off the ground. A trail around the home suggested that it had been patrolled before, but there was no evidence of a patrol now.

He reached the door.

It was locked.

Taking one of his knives, he twisted it in the lock until it popped open. His attempt wasn't as skillful as what his mother or Uncle Brusus would have been able to do, but it worked. The entryway was darkened, and he paused for a moment to let his eyes adjust. When he did, he Saw faint shadows and crept forward, pausing at each open door to glance inside the rooms. This was nothing more than a home—and empty. It was odd that he would detect the coin Galen had on him here.

His whole body remained on edge. Not only was

Galen missing, but with the Forgers in the city aware of him, it wouldn't be long before they detected where he'd gone and came after him. If they used their ability to Read him, they would be able to find him far too easily.

As far as he knew, Reading was similar to following lorcith. It was likely they would be able to track a certain signature the same way he could track lorcith he'd had a hand in forging—the same way that he was now tracking Galen.

The sense of lorcith was above him.

Haern found a staircase in the middle of the home and took the stairs two at a time, moving as softly and quietly as he could. It was times like these when he wished he had the ability to Slide.

When he reached the upper level, he paused. There had been light in two of the windows, and now that he was on this level, he could see movement shimmering under closed doors.

The lower level had been empty. This level was not.

He needed to be careful.

Holding on to his knives, he was ready to *push* them if necessary.

Reaching the first door, Haern paused, pressing his hand upon the door, focusing on the sense of lorcith.

It wasn't there.

He moved on, staying pressed up against a nearby wall, keeping his back flat against it as he went, searching for signs of any movement. When he reached the next door, he pressed his hand against it, focusing. As before, there was no sense of anything behind the door.

He paused. Was the lorcith still here?

It had to be.

How had Galen managed to get here so quickly? He wouldn't have been able to travel the same way as Haern, and without any way of Sliding...

Unless he hadn't Slid himself.

This didn't look to be some sort of Forger stronghold, but there should be no way Galen had reached this part of the city on his own.

It might be a mistake for him to come like this, but he wasn't about to leave Galen behind. Were the situations reversed, Galen would have come for him. He'd done so before.

Stalking forward, keeping his steps as quiet as possible, wishing he were a Listener, he reached the next door.

He pressed his hand on the door, focusing on lorcith.

The sense of it reverberated from the other side of the door.

Haern checked the door.

Locked.

Taking one of his knives, he tried to pry it into the door, but it seemed to be bolted from the other side.

What were his options?

He studied the layout, realizing he might not be able to get to it from this side. But what if he came at it from the other?

Haern hurried back down the stairs, back outside, and *pushed* off on one of his coins to reach the rooftop. Once there, he traced the layout on the inside, reaching the point where he thought the room was.

Looking down over the roof, he saw a light glowing in the window. From here, he could reach it, but it would take a different sort of approach. He would have to suspend himself in the air.

It required control.

Did he have that kind of control?

To reach Galen, he would need it.

Haern dropped the coin, lowering himself to the ground. He was in front of the house, facing the street, but a massive stone wall surrounded the entirety of the house, giving a certain privacy on this level. That privacy would disappear the moment he hovered in the air.

Taking a deep breath, he *pushed*.

He did so slowly at first, *pushing* carefully as he sent himself higher and higher into the air.

He reached the bottom of the window.

As he continued to *push*, he grabbed the windowsill and then reached for the windows, pulling on one of them to see if it would open.

It did.

Next would be the hardest part. His strength was waning, and he would need to act quickly. If he didn't, he would fall back to the earth.

He rolled into the window, *pulling* the coin back to him. He crashed with more noise than he wanted, coming quickly to his feet, grabbing his knives and pointing them outward.

There was no one here.

How was that possible?

He focused on the lorcith, and the sense of the coin was still here.

Haern looked around. The door on the other side would lead out into the hallway. It was bolted, but for how much longer? He'd made considerable noise crashing into the room, and he worried that whoever was guarding the house would come and investigate what had happened.

There was another door, and he turned to that one.

It would lead to the room adjacent, but he didn't think that was where he'd detected the lorcith. Instead, it seemed to come from a large trunk along the wall.

The trunk was locked, and he tried to pry his knife into the lock, but it wouldn't open. Unsheathing the sword, he slipped it into the lock and tried it. With a scream, the lock snapped at the same time as the wood cracked.

If someone wasn't aware that he was here already, they would be now.

Haern flipped open the lid.

Inside, he expected to see Galen and was prepared to grab him and return to where Thoren would meet them and Slide them back to the Aisl.

Only Galen wasn't inside.

His cloak was.

Haern grabbed the cloak, clutching it in his hands, staring at it. What had happened to Galen?

Something thudded against the door.

He needed to get out of here before whoever was on the other side of that door came crashing inside, but if he left, he would miss out on the opportunity to find out what happened to Galen.

A thought occurred to him, and it was one that should have come sooner.

Why would the door be locked from this side?

16

HAERN

SOMETHING THUDDED AGAINST THE DOOR AGAIN, AND Haern grabbed Galen's cloak, squeezing it in his hands, turning back toward the window. He wasn't going to go out the door; then again, if this were Forgers, they would have just Slid into the room. The fact that someone was trying to open the door suggested this was something else.

The realization that someone had locked the door from this side troubled him.

As he turned, he came face-to-face with a Forger.

This was a different Forger than the one he'd encountered in the street. He had a youthful face, and the scar working along his chin looked to be fresh and still healing.

The man glared at him.

"Where did you come from?" he asked.

"How do you have this?" And why was it here? Could Galen have managed to get away?

Great Watcher. Could he have made a mistake?

He'd been following the coin in Galen's pocket, but what if he'd lost his cloak while escaping the Forgers?

Haern *pushed* on his knives.

They crashed into the Forger, catching him in the stomach, and Haern pinned him to the ground. He lunged forward, landing on top of the other man, withdrawing the knives and shoving them into his shoulders. The man screamed until Haern clamped his hand over his mouth, silencing him.

"We're going to talk."

"You won't get anything out of me."

"Probably not, but it seems your friends aren't going to be able to break down the door, and until someone else Slides in here, I think you and I have a chance to chat. Where did you get this cloak?"

"It doesn't matter."

"It matters to me."

"Some fool thought to hunt the people of the city."

"He wasn't hunting the people of the city."

"And what was he doing? He carried poisons with him. He's a man we know all too well."

"How do you know him?"

"Galen," the man spat. "He's been hunting the Ai'thol."

Haern blinked. Galen had been hunting the Ai'thol? As far as he knew, Galen had remained in the city, working to train him, but could that not be the complete truth? Galen certainly had far more skill than Haern at using his abilities. Maybe he'd been working the streets, trying to find answers to what happened with Rsiran. If so, everything he'd said to Galen would be wrong. Galen hadn't given up on Haern's father. He had done things his own way.

"Where is he?"

"Did he hunt you, too?"

"Yes."

"Then you should know he will face Ai'thol punishment. As will you for breaking into this place."

"I don't intend to face Ai'thol punishment."

"And yet you have presented yourself for it."

"All I've done is come for answers."

"There will be no answers. Nothing but the Council."

"The Council?"

The man glared at him, his gaze darting past before flickering back to Haern's face.

The pounding on the door had eased, and still Haern worried that he didn't have much time remaining. If they managed to break down the door—or if another Forger suddenly appeared—he would need to be ready.

"Where is he?"

"I've already told you that he will face the Ai'thol punishment."

"And I don't mean Galen. Where is Rsiran Lareth?"

The man glared up at him for a moment before his gaze changed, amusement sparkling on his face. "Interesting. You would go after Lareth?" He cocked his head to the side, and Haern reacted, slamming his barriers into place. He hoped that he did so before the other man managed to start filtering through his thoughts. He tried to solidify the mental barriers with lorcith, using the technique his father had taught him.

He waited. If this Forger had managed to Read him the same way the other one had, then he would know.

No spark of recognition crossed the man's face.

"Where is Lareth?" he asked.

"He has been granted a great honor."

"And what honor is that?"

"He gets to speak with the Great One."

"And who is the Great One?"

The Forger smiled. "Unfortunately, I cannot speak his name. To do so would be a violation."

Movement on the other side of the door drew his attention, and Haern glanced back.

The Forger trapped beneath him tried to Slide; Haern could feel it.

The Slide failed.

How?

Could it be the knives?

If so, they would have prevented the other Forger from Sliding as well, but that hadn't seemed to be the case.

Maybe he wasn't able to Slide with Haern sitting on him, or maybe he didn't have as much ability with Sliding. With the freshness of the scar, it seemed as if this Forger wasn't nearly as established as some of the others, so perhaps that was it.

Something flickered around him again, and Haern glanced up almost too late.

Another Forger had appeared.

The same one Haern had attacked.

Blood stained his jacket where Haern's knives had pierced his shoulders, but he moved as if unharmed. Could he have found a Healer?

Haern jumped to his feet, *pushing* off on the knives and spinning around, unsheathing his sword. He flicked it around, catching the other Forger on the arm, carving through skin and bone.

The Forger jerked his hand back, away from Haern. Blood poured from the wound, but the man gave no indication that he suffered ill effects from the attack.

"Why are you here?" the now injured Forger asked.

"He's here to find information about Lareth," the younger Forger said. "Why would he think we have information about Lareth?"

"Because Lareth is his father," the injured Forger said, clutching his arm to his chest.

The younger Forger backed toward the window, preventing Haern from heading out the only way he could. Two Forgers blocking his path would make it difficult for him to escape, but not entirely impossible. He'd already harmed both of them, and with the knives and his connection to the lorcith within them, perhaps he could *push* through anything they might be able to do.

"He would make a great prize."

"Stop talking about me as if I'm not here," Haern said.

"He would," the other Forger said.

He still didn't know what happened to Galen but was increasingly convinced that the former assassin had managed to escape. Following him here, following the cloak and the coin, had been a mistake.

And somehow he had to get out of here, return to that place along the street, and do so by the time Thoren reached them. If he didn't, the next window wouldn't be until considerably later, which meant Haern would be trapped in the city, possibly for a long time.

"He's not said to have the same abilities as the elder Lareth."

"If he did, he would have Traveled, and yet he remains here. Look at the uncertainty on his face," the older of the two Forgers said.

"Shall we?"

The two Forgers converged.

Haern *pushed* on the knives, trying to send them in opposite directions, but splitting his focus in such a way was difficult, almost more than he could manage. He felt some resistance to the lorcith within the blades, enough that they lost the momentum they had had.

The Forgers had discovered that they could overpower his connection to the knives.

He jumped forward, swinging the sword. In the confines of this small room, there wasn't much space for him to use the sword as he had been trained to.

As he swung the blade, pressure pushed against it.

Haern continued to fight, using both his physical strength and his connection to lorcith, forcing the blade down. It carved into the side of the younger of the two Forgers, and the man crumpled.

Haern spun around, turning to the remaining Forger.

"Perhaps you aren't as weak as we were led to believe."

The man flickered and disappeared in a Slide.

Haern glanced down at the fallen Forger, listened to the sounds of pounding on the other side of the door, and jumped toward the window.

As he cleared the window, he *pushed* down on one of

the coins and then off, soaring back into the air, over the street. He *pushed* and *pulled* on coins, using them to travel into the city, back the way he had come, hoping he would get there in time to track down Galen.

He hated that he was running again. It seemed as if every time he tried to bring the fight to the Forgers, something happened and he lost. This time was supposed to have been different. This time was supposed to have allowed him to use the filaments of lorcith within the knives and the sword to overpower them, but even that hadn't been enough.

How was he going to overcome them?

More than that, how was he going to be able to rescue his father?

He had some information, but not enough.

He slowed when he reached the place where he'd left Galen the first time. He searched for signs of movement, but there was none. He hesitated, scanning the street, afraid that one of the Forgers would return. When he did, there would likely be more. It wouldn't take long for them to get reinforcements as they were able to Slide. His own ability to recover and escape was much more limited, something that the Forgers now knew about him.

There was no movement.

Could he have been wrong? Could Galen not have escaped?

He didn't think so. With the cloak, he believed Galen had managed to get away. But he wouldn't have gone far, knowing this was where Haern would return to meet up.

Movement at the end of the street caught his attention.

It was a flickering sort of movement.

Sliding.

Great Watcher.

There were at least three distinct people Sliding down the street, and as he turned his attention in the other direction, he saw more.

Too many.

Worse, they were going to trap him in between them. The moment they got here, he wouldn't be able to fight. Which meant he would be captured.

A hissing noise caught his attention, and he jerked his head around, staring down into an alleyway across the street.

Galen stood there, crouched in the shadows, looking up at him.

He breathed out a sigh of relief. Galen was here, which meant he wouldn't have to face this alone. But as he watched the street, witnessing the various Forgers making their way down here, he counted almost a dozen. That was too many for the two of them to take on. It would have been too many for his father to take on.

And it felt as if he were trapped here.

He wasn't about to stay trapped. He *pushed* off on a coin, sending himself streaking across the street, and came to land near Galen. He *pulled* on the coin, summoning it back. The other man looked over, frowning at the cloak.

"Where did you find that?"

"I tracked it."

"You tracked it?"

Haern slipped his hand into the pocket of the cloak

and pulled out a coin, holding it up before stuffing it back into Galen's pocket. "I tracked it."

"Did you place that there?"

Haern frowned, shaking his head. "I thought you put it there so I could follow you if anything happened."

"I wouldn't have kept lorcith on me. Not here and not with what we were doing."

He frowned. Who had done it, then?

"Well, I got your cloak back for you."

"I suppose I should thank you, but I can always get another cloak—and a coin."

"I counted a dozen different Forgers making their way toward us."

"Unfortunately they appear to be converging on this location," he said.

"I think they have converged on this location because of me."

"What did you do?"

"I killed one of them." Galen arched a brow at him at that. "The other got away. And I came back here looking for you."

"You should have left me."

"I wasn't going to leave you here."

"It's easier for one person to get away than for two."

"Thoren should be here soon."

"And we will involve someone else who shouldn't have any part in this."

"You've been hunting them, haven't you?"

Galen glanced over at him. "I've been what?"

"When I caught up to the first Forger, he knew about you. He said that you've been hunting the Forgers."

Galen smiled darkly. "He said that, did he? I suppose that should be taken as a positive step."

"It's true?"

"You can't believe you were the only one who's been looking for information about your father."

"Well, actually…"

"I've been willing to work with you, to train you, knowing others need to engage in this battle, but you haven't been ready. I wasn't willing to bring you in until you were. That was a commitment I made to your mother."

"You promised my mother?"

"She asked me to do everything I could to get your father back. I told her that would involve training you to the fullest extent that I was capable of doing."

"And now?"

"And now we need to escape."

"I don't know if two of us can take on a dozen Forgers."

"Neither do I. Which is why you are going to run, and I'm going to draw them to me."

"No—"

"I'm not going to sacrifice you, Haern. And besides, I have much more experience facing men like this than you do."

"I'm not going to return to Elaeavn and tell Cael that you were willing to die so I could get away."

"Who said anything about dying?"

He grabbed the cloak, wrapped it around his shoulders, and began to prepare darts. Galen worked far more rapidly than Haern would ever have expected him to be able to do, and within a minute or two, he had two dozen darts prepared. Most of them were likely filled with deadly poisons that Galen had only begun to teach him about.

"Head north. Get out of the city. Return to Elaeavn. I will send Thoren your way if he comes. Otherwise, you need to use your lorcith ability to travel as quickly as you can."

"Galen—"

"Go!"

17

RYN

ONCE AGAIN, THE AIR HUNG WITH THE STRANGE STENCH OF fire, though it was more like a memory of fire, as if it had been here long ago. The landscape was different—mostly rolling hills and the occasional tree. The landscape had been different in each place that Olandar Fahr took her, traveling from place to place, motioning her to silence the moment they stepped free.

Ryn had taken to remaining as quiet as possible, afraid of doing or saying something that would anger him, but despite his concerns, she had seen nothing she thought worrisome. Whatever threat he feared they would encounter had not come to fruition.

This place was both the same as and different than so many others.

It was the same in that she saw no movement around her, and though there was a sense of fire, there was nothing else.

It was almost as if he were taking her to places he

knew would be empty, but if he wanted her to help him observe, why take her to locations like that?

He stared outward, and Ryn followed the direction of his gaze, trying to understand what drew Olandar Fahr's attention. As far as she could tell, there was nothing there. The more she stared, the more certain she was there had to be something she could find, only somehow she missed it.

Observe. That was what Olandar Fahr wanted from her, and yet as Ryn strained, trying to observe, she found nothing.

She thought back to the time he had shown her the game board, moving pieces along the side. He had wanted her to watch the game unfolding. As she tried to watch it now, she wasn't able to find anything helpful.

In the distance, a pile of rubble was more distinct than anything else.

As she stared at it, she realized it wasn't just a pile of rubble but the remains of what must once have been a city. The debris was extensive, and with a soft gasp, she was reminded of Vuahlu when Lareth had come and destroyed it.

Now that she had made that association, she continued to study the remains, searching for anything within them that might help her discern whether there was anything more for her to uncover there. The longer she looked, the less certain she was she would be able to find anything. There was no movement, nothing to suggest anyone still remained here. No animals moved, and there were no birds in the sky. Everything had a look of desolation to it.

Was this what Lareth wanted?

When he had come to the village, destroying her people, she had been lucky to have escaped, but his actions hadn't even been necessary. The village would have been destroyed regardless as the volcano erupted.

Or would it?

The strange stench of fire took on a different meaning to her. Could he have controlled the volcano? Something like that seemed almost impossible for her to believe, but then again, the nature of his power was also impossible for her to fully grasp. He was known to be incredibly powerful, and it was the sort of thing she could imagine him somehow replicating.

Her gaze drifted from the debris, looking to the mountainous areas around it. Could there be a volcano here?

The longer she stared, directing her attention away from the rubble, the more she thought the answer was just at the edge of her understanding.

This was what Olandar Fahr wanted from her. She didn't have to know how to play the game to observe the moves. In this case, it wasn't so much about knowing what Lareth had been after as it was to be able to recognize the move.

More than anything, she suspected that Olandar Fahr already knew something had happened here.

Why bring her here, then?

It was his way of testing her, of trying to determine how much she might be able to observe, and perhaps his way of trying to find out if she would be useful to him.

Ryn needed to be useful.

She swept her gaze around everything one more time, and Olandar Fahr took her arm, and they traveled.

When they stopped, they did so once again near a sandy beach. Each time they traveled, they returned to a similar sandy beach, and she couldn't help but wonder if there was some reason behind it, as if Olandar Fahr was somehow reassured by visiting this place. The steady sound of the waves lapping at the shore was a welcome respite from the silence that had enveloped her in the other place. The air had the salty odor of the seawater, and seagulls circled overhead, cawing every so often.

She let out a relieved sigh.

"Did you observe anything?"

It was the same question he'd asked each time they had visited another location, and each time, Ryn felt guilty at not being able to offer him anything. This time, though, she thought she might have some answer, even if it wasn't one that would be of much use to him.

"Did Lareth do that?"

He turned to her, cocking a brow. "Why would you ask that?"

"Only that it reminded me of what happened to my own village."

"You blame Lareth for what happened?"

Ryn closed her eyes, and when she did, it was easy enough for her to think back to when Vuahlu had been destroyed, the way hunks of metal had seemed to fly toward the village, controlled by someone with power she didn't grasp. Homes had been torn apart, people crushed. Her mother. Dab. So many others whose names continued to roll through her mind when she closed her eyes and allowed herself to think back to that day. For the most part, she tried not to think about it, fearing that if she were to dwell on what had happened, she would get lost in the torment of that time. She needed to move on. If nothing else, her time working with Olandar Fahr had taught her there was a benefit in moving forward.

"I don't know if he was," she whispered. "It's just…"

Ryn opened her eyes, staring out at the water. She let the soothing waves relax her, thankful that Olandar Fahr had chosen this place. Had he known it would soothe her after everything they had seen?

Perhaps he needed the same relaxation, some way of finding peace in between what they encountered. If so, Ryn completely understood.

"The village was destroyed, and seeing it like that reminded me of what happened to my village."

"How so?"

"It was the way the buildings were crushed. That, and the fire."

"Tell me about what happened in your village," he said.

"I *have* told you," she said.

"And yet, despite everything we've been through together, I don't know that I fully understand."

Ryn clenched her jaw and swallowed. "It's hard to think about."

"Until we can let go of the past, we can't move forward."

She glanced over at him. "I don't know that I can let go of it."

Olandar Fahr stared at her, and there was a strange

fluttering in the back of her mind. When it retreated, he took her arm, and they traveled.

The suddenness of it was jarring, and she was prepared for the possibility that they would step free from the traveling in another place much like the others, and yet this time was different.

She looked around her.

"Vuahlu?" she whispered.

Olandar Fahr stared up at the distant mountain. "Is that Maunial?"

Why would he bring her here, knowing how hard it was for her?

Still, her gaze drifted toward the mountaintop, and the familiar sight of the volcano belching smoke and steam drew her gaze. She had seen it so often over the years that she recognized it easily. It was still powerful, and the mountain gave a sense of fear that trembled through her, a sense of uncertainty, and the longer she stared at it, the more she wondered whether there was anything she might be able to understand by coming here. He seemed to believe she could, yet Ryn wasn't sure if there were any answers here.

"It is," she whispered.

"Do you fear it?"

"It destroyed everything," she said.

"Did it, or did he?"

Ryn tore her attention off the distant sight of the volcano and focused instead on the remnants of the village. There wasn't much she could determine now, and the longer she stared at it, the harder it was for her to know if she could even recognize what had once been here. Buildings were crumbled, and lava had flowed, destroying what little had remained. The faces of the dead still stared up at her in her mind. As she pushed that out, she found nothing remaining that would make her feel the devastation that once had been here.

Surprisingly, there was nothing left of the village that was even familiar to her. The debris was difficult to piece together, to the point that she couldn't even tell there had once been a village here. Where the lava had flowed, there were now pools of dark stone.

Ryn looked around the village—or what had once been the village. It was strange coming back here. Seeing what had been here and was now lost filled her with anger again. Anger at Lareth. Anger at losing the last of her family. Anger that she would never know the same kind of home she once had.

"What do you observe?"

She turned back to Olandar Fahr, shaking her head. "I know what happened here. I was there the day he came and took everything from me."

Something in his eyes softened, and she felt guilt at how she had snapped at him.

"I know you were. What else do you observe?"

She breathed out, trying to ignore the tension within her but finding it difficult. "Other than the fact that Lareth destroyed everything here?"

"Did he?"

"Almost everything. Is that what you want me to say?"

Olandar Fahr watched her with a furrowed brow. "I want you to think about what happened. You hold anger within you, but that anger does you no good."

"I hold anger because of what he did."

"You survived."

"I did."

"Do you feel guilty that you survived and so many others did not?"

She turned away. Perhaps that *was* the source of her anger. She had lived when so many others had died. And then Maunial had claimed the rest, destroying what was left of Vuahlu until nothing remained.

How could she feel anything but guilt?

And anger.

There was so much anger, but Olandar Fahr was right —that anger didn't serve her at all.

And the more she thought about it, the less certain she was that she could observe anything of use. How could she move beyond what had happened to her and those she cared about?

"You shouldn't feel guilty about what happened, but you should also begin to understand that not everything you see is what you believe."

"I saw Lareth," she said.

She turned back, anger flashing through her, and she wasn't sure whether she should allow herself such rage around Olandar Fahr, especially as all he wanted from her was to observe. She should do as he asked, see if there was anything she might be able to detect.

It was too hard for her to let go of what had happened —but the longer she was here, the more she realized he was right. She had needed to return.

"Perhaps you did," Olandar Fahr said.

"I did see him."

"I said that perhaps you did."

"What happens if I didn't?"

"Then your anger may be misplaced."

She glared at him. "You don't care for him."

He turned toward the distant sight of Maunial. "I can't care for someone who has harmed so many that I care for."

"Why?"

"Why what?"

"Why has he harmed so many of your Ai'thol?"

Olandar Fahr held her gaze for a long moment. "Lareth is acting the way he believes he must, and I act the way I must."

The comment surprised her. It almost seemed as if Olandar Fahr didn't hate Lareth. When she had first met Olandar Fahr, she had believed he felt the same way that she did, but perhaps he did not.

"Why does he do it?"

"He was wrong," he said.

"Why don't you stop him?"

"What makes you think I haven't?"

Her breath caught and she turned back to him. "You have him?"

"Did I say that?"

"You said you stopped him."

"Is that the same as having captured him?"

"I suppose not."

"Besides, even if I had captured him, I wouldn't give him to you."

"Why? Don't you want me to get the vengeance I deserve?"

"This isn't about vengeance. This is about what is needed."

"And what's needed?"

He paused, his gaze sweeping all around them again. There was a weight to the way he looked at everything, an intensity that she wasn't sure she fully understood. "Have I told you about one of my abilities?"

She held his gaze for a long moment. "You have many abilities."

That was one of the things she had been aware of ever since coming to serve Olandar Fahr. Not only could he travel the way he did, but he was powerful in many ways. There were other things he was able to do, things others were not capable of.

"I have many abilities, but one in particular is the most important of them all."

"What is that?"

"I can see possibilities."

"Because of your game?"

He smiled placatingly. "Something like that. Because of these possibilities, I'm aware that I still need Lareth."

"Why?"

"Because he hasn't finished his task yet."

"What task is that?"

Olandar Fahr turned away from her, sweeping his gaze all around before settling back on her. "Stopping a greater destruction."

"Why do you think he would do this?"

"Because he will have no other choice."

18

DANIEL

DANIEL EYED THE SHIP MOVING ALONG THE RIVER'S EDGE. IT was small compared to so many that he'd seen here, and narrow of body, something he'd come to learn indicated a certain speed to the vessel. A dozen oars jutted out on one side of the ship, a matching set likely found on the other side, and they swept along the river quickly. He stared, searching for anything that might pose a danger to them, but there was nothing.

He had to be careful. In Nyaesh, ships moved through the port frequently. It was a busy city, nearly as busy as places like Asador, and Daniel had come to know that with such a volume of ships passing through, they needed to observe them carefully.

Behind the narrow and sleek vessel came another. It was further along the river, though wider of body, and massive sails billowed out, catching the breeze. He marveled that such a ship could even make its way along this river, though even this ship wasn't the largest he'd seen. There were some easily twice that size, though they would have a more difficult time navigating along the river. They required Carth and her particular brand of magic in order to make their way along the waterway.

A slight shimmering caught his attention, and Daniel glanced over to see Lucy appear on the rocky shore nearby. She watched him, ignoring the ships completely. Her golden hair was braided and tied, having grown much longer over the months they'd been away from Elaeavn. Her deep green eyes caught the light, and there was a look of concern on her face.

"What is it?" he asked.

"Why must it be something?"

He turned away from Lucy, not even bothering to shield his thoughts from her. She was far too powerful for him, and besides, she already knew that he came out here to get away from everything within Nyaesh.

Still, there were limits to how much he could escape. He had chosen this, and it wasn't as if he wanted to do something different. Far from it. He understood the need to continue his training, to continue improving as he worked with the others, learning not only to control his abilities better, but to hone his mind.

"You've been gone long enough that there's likely a reason for your visit."

Lucy sighed. For a moment, Daniel thought she might reveal something more, but she bit it back. "Carth has plenty of people fully capable of recording everything moving through here. Do you think it necessary for you to do so as well?"

It wasn't a matter of his capability. Then again, it wasn't a matter of him coming out here to take inventory of the ships. After the attack, he wanted to keep watch on the Ai'thol.

Lucy would know that, much like Lucy would know most things about him.

It left him feeling raw. Exposed. Surprisingly, he didn't necessarily mind. She already knew how he felt about her, and that she was the reason he was here in the first place, though that had never been a secret. While she might have been the reason he had come, she wasn't the reason he had stayed. She needed to know that, too.

"You remain troubled," Lucy said.

"You know what I'm thinking."

"Just because I can Read you doesn't mean that I want to do so. There are times when having a conversation is more valuable."

He turned to her and smiled. It was for his benefit, but he still appreciated her offering to have a conversation with him, knowing it would be unnecessary for her.

"I'm troubled by the Ai'thol."

"I believe Carthenne remains troubled by them as well."

"Carth has dealt with them for most of her life." Daniel didn't know quite how old Carth was but knew that she'd been fighting the Ai'thol for the better part of twenty years or more. Even if she was in her forties, she was still formidable. "She at least knows what she's dealing with when it comes to facing the Ai'thol."

"We know what we're facing."

Daniel turned to her, meeting Lucy's gaze. The light shimmered across her deep green eyes, giving them something of a metallic sheen. "We don't fully know what we have to face. That's part of the problem. Not only don't we know what they're after, but we don't know how to stop them."

Only that wasn't entirely true. They knew exactly what the Ai'thol were after. They wanted access to the Elder Stones, and once they gained that access, they would use it to claim that power and twist it. He didn't know if that meant they intended to try to rule, but it seemed a reasonable assumption.

"Why watch the shores of the river?" Lucy asked.

Daniel turned his focus back to the river. It was a fast-moving water, and eddies of current swirled around, creating whitecaps. The far shore was distant enough that it looked little more than a smear of land. The gray sky fit his mood, and the gusting of the wind carried the now familiar scent of Nyaesh to him. Despite that, all of this was foreign to him. He would rather be anywhere but here, and with his ability to Slide, it wouldn't be difficult for him to be anywhere else.

"You wouldn't understand," he said.

She rested her hand on his arm. Where she touched him, his skin tingled, leaving him to wonder if she was using some new element of her abilities. Lucy had always been strong, even before the augmentation had taken hold. Then again, her abilities had always been Reading along with a weak ability to Slide, nothing like what she now could do. If she wanted, she could control him. That was one aspect he didn't understand. He might be Elvraeth, gifted with aspects of each of the abilities, but he had nothing like that.

"You don't trust me to understand?"

"It's not about trusting you, Lucy."

He turned away, heading up the shore. The ground sloped down toward the water before dropping off into it. He'd never attempted to swim here, the current far too fast for him to even contemplate it, but he'd seen others out in the water, making their way downstream. Most of them were older children, and they would jump from the rocks, dropping to the water, but the current carried them downstream. He couldn't imagine being a strong enough swimmer to do that. After what he'd experienced with the Ai'thol, though, he now knew he could Slide free of the water if it came to it.

Lucy followed him, staying a step behind him, and he felt no intrusion into his thoughts. Maybe she wasn't attempting to Read him, though these days he wasn't sure if he would even be aware of it. In Elaeavn, he had grown accustomed to holding his mental barriers in place, using anything he could to prevent anyone from Reading him, but Lucy had such a subtle touch when she wanted to that he might not even know what she was doing. Daniel trusted that she wouldn't. She'd told him he'd know when she was Reading him, though he still wasn't sure if that was entirely true.

At the top of the slope, he paused. In the distance, the city of Nyaesh rose into view. It stretched from a gently sloping hillside where the palace loomed above everything else, the tattered remains of the wall that had once surrounded the palace nothing more than a blackened line leading through the city, evidence of what had once been there. Buildings arranged in orderly lines along the roads stretched down toward the shore, and a dozen or more ships were docked there while trading in the north. It was midday, and the city was awash with activity. People moved along the streets, only visible from his vantage because of his enhanced eyesight. A subtle sense of energy covered everything, power that emanated from Nyaesh. It was the power of the flame, the same power Carth could summon. Despite the attack, the A'ras remained powerful and the Elder Stone was still held within the city.

Lucy rested her hand on his arm again, and he turned to meet her eyes. She smiled at him, a smile that reminded him of when they had been in Elaeavn, a time when he had pursued her more aggressively. But then, when hadn't he pursued her more aggressively?

"You could return," she said.

"So could you."

She turned away from him. "I'm not sure that I can. Besides, there are other things I'm responsible for now."

He waited, hoping she'd share more, but she didn't. That wasn't uncommon. Not only was Lucy frequently absent, but when she was around, she didn't share with him what she'd been doing.

"Do you know what Carth intends to do?" he asked.

"She and I haven't had much opportunity to talk about her plans."

There was something more in that than what she stated, but Daniel didn't push to try and understand. "I think she's trying to find another Elder Stone before the Ai'thol do."

"That's what I can tell, as well."

Daniel glanced over at her. She seemed troubled—

could it be annoyed?—that Carth would be able to hide something from her. "She poses a challenge to you."

"Of course she does."

"But it upsets you."

"Now who's Reading the other?"

"I don't need to Read you to know." He watched her, but her expression remained neutral. "Maybe it's time for me to return."

She nodded, and he stepped into a Slide.

When he Slid, it happened quickly, with a flutter of movement along with a swirl of translucent colors. As she usually did, at least since having the augmentation placed, Lucy arrived before him, so that she was there when he stepped out of the Slide.

They emerged in the courtyard with trees growing all around them. It was an enormous courtyard, and had the palace wall still been here, it might have been even more impressive. As it was, it seemed lessened somehow by the absence of the wall. All that remained of it was the broken debris, a gouge in the ground from the destruction caused by the Ai'thol.

Daniel turned toward the palace. Had the wall still been here, he doubted he would have been able to Slide here in the first place. There was something about the wall that supposedly prevented Sliding, though he didn't know what that was. Carth wasn't eager to share either, though Daniel suspected some of it had to do with the Elder Stone she'd moved here.

When he reached the palace, he made his way up the stairs. He'd been here often enough that there was a certain familiarity to it, though Lucy still hesitated. He wondered how much of that was because she hadn't grown up within the palace in Elaeavn the way Daniel had. It was something she didn't talk much about, and he didn't have any desire to put her on edge, not wanting to upset her.

The palace in Nyaesh wasn't nearly as nice as the one in Elaeavn, though there was still a certain amount of formality to it. Paneled walls ran the length of the hallway, gleaming with brightly stained wood. The carpet ran down the hall and into each of the rooms. Portraits hung along the walls, and though they appeared to be exquisitely made, Daniel didn't know who they represented and hadn't taken the opportunity to try to understand.

They reached a staircase at the back of the hallway, making their way up. It spiraled around, the stone covered with a thin runner of carpet, unable to conceal the fact that this had once been a much stouter fortification, and a remnant from a time before. At the top of the stairs, Daniel hurried toward the main room.

Inside, a table occupied much of the center of the room. There had been a time when it had served as the throne room, but since Carth's arrival in Nyaesh, that had changed, and now it was little more than a gaming station. Carth sat on one side of the table, and Rayen sat across from her. A Tsatsun board rested in between them, the pieces arranged outward. Even from a quick glance, it was obvious to Daniel that Carth was in complete control.

He crouched behind Rayen, looking at the game board. "You should move the Ranger over to here."

"Do you want to play?"

He grinned. "I'd do better than you."

She laughed softly, staring at the board for a moment before shaking her head. "That move would trap me here."

"Only for a moment. Then you can claim three of her pieces." Daniel pointed to the three pieces he thought Rayen could claim by playing it that way, and she frowned to herself. It would take several moves, but that was the point of Tsatsun. It was a game of strategy, one where maneuvering the pieces in specific patterns allowed for the player to push the piece called the Stone across the board. One advantage of having spent so much time in Nyaesh was that he had improved at the game. He still wasn't much of a challenge for Carth, but eventually he hoped he could grow more skilled.

"I see it," Rayen said.

"No teaming up," Carth said from the other side. She flicked her eyes up to Rayen for a moment before looking back down at the board.

"Are you afraid the two of us will beat you?" Rayen asked.

"The two of you?" She shook her head. "Not yet. You get closer, but neither of you is quite ready."

Daniel tried not to be irritated by the comment, regardless of how true it might be. He wasn't able to challenge Carth yet. No one he'd met was really able to pose much of a challenge for her.

"There is something to be said about learning to play the game yourself. You begin to understand your own strengths and weaknesses."

"And what if we're stronger together?" Daniel asked.

Carth paused, sitting up and clasping her hands in her lap. "If you think so—but what happens if you are isolated and you have become dependent upon others to strategize?"

"And what happens if we aren't able to create the appropriate strategy because we are depending only on our own abilities?" He studied her, wondering how she might react.

Carth surprised him by chuckling. "A valid point. If you would prefer to work together, feel free."

"And what if we want to work with you?" Rayen asked.

"When it comes to Tsatsun, I play alone."

"Do you need to play alone?" Lucy stood off to the side, her hands clasped in front of her and her head cocked to one side. It was tilted in such a way that Daniel wondered if she were Listening, though what else could she hear? More likely she was trying to Read something about Carth.

"I don't need to play alone, but I enjoy it. And until you manage to defeat me, there's no challenge in joining."

Daniel pulled a chair over and took a seat in front of the board. This was one of the fanciest Tsatsun boards he'd ever seen, though admittedly he hadn't seen all that many. The board itself was black and white checkered, each square cut individually from marble. Cheaper boards were painted, and some of them faded over time, or the paint became scratched, making it obvious that moves had been made over the years. Even the game pieces were carved from marble. Many of them were incredibly exquisite carvings, far nicer than any he had played with prior to coming to Nyaesh. It was a board Carth had commissioned when they had overpowered the Ai'thol, and it had taken a while for the complete set to arrive.

Only in the last week had the final piece come. Fittingly, the Stone was the last one carved. Prior to that, they had used less well-made pieces. He still wondered why she would have gone to the effort of having this board made, questioning if she intended to bring it with them when they traveled.

Rayen made the move Daniel had suggested, and Carth quickly followed. She sat back, her gaze darting from Daniel to Rayen before turning her attention back to the game board. As far as Daniel knew, Carth worked through hundreds of possibilities. It seemed impossible that she could account for so many variations of what they might do, but that was what she claimed. Often times, she knew after a single move how the game would end, something he still marveled at. How was he ever to defeat her if she could anticipate every move he might make?

It wasn't as if Tsatsun had an unlimited number of moves, though with the number of pieces in play, over fifty in all, the variations were incredibly complex. He'd read several of Carth's books on Tsatsun, and while they had helped him understand strategy and anticipation, many of them seemed to require straight memorization, forcing him to try to recall each movement as it was made, predicting the odds of other moves that might follow.

As far as Carth was concerned, Tsatsun was how she trained for battle. She viewed everything in relation to the game, and though there was something to be said for that, he had seen how not everything could be interpreted in such a way.

Rayen reached for one of the Wardens, pieces that were relatively important, and he grabbed her wrist before she could make the move. He feared letting her complete it, worried that if she did, they would end up sacrificing another of their more important pieces.

"Not that one," he said.

Carth glanced up at him, a hint of a smile on her mouth.

"Why not? This move would allow me to place this piece," she said, motioning to one of the Archers, "near the Stone. Once we have that, then we can begin to push it."

"You'll never get the Archer quite close enough to the Stone." Daniel could see the way it would play out. The Stone might be there, but the moment she placed the Archer where she intended, the rest of the game would fall apart quite quickly. It had more to do with how the pieces would come together, requiring that they sacrifice piece after piece in order to maintain the Archer's position near the Stone. All the while Carth would be able to arrange her pieces on the other side. They wouldn't be able to do anything other than defend.

As he studied the board, there was another possibility. It involved a sacrifice, but the payoff was significant—if it played out the way he needed it to. He envisioned a dozen different possibilities based on that one move, and in more than half of them, he could see them gaining an advantage, however slight. When it came to playing Tsatsun with Carth, any advantage was better than none.

He reached for the piece and started to move it when he caught himself.

That wasn't the right move, either.

As he studied Carth's board, he realized she was playing cautiously, but it was all an act. It might appear she was moving her pieces more defensively, but the more he stared at the board, the clearer it became that those pieces weren't defensive at all. They were subtly moving in an advantage, pressing an attack, and he saw the way she anticipated using them.

Could he make her think they would continue along the same pathway?

He shifted, moving the Troop off to the side.

"Well, that was a wasted move," Rayen said.

"I'm sorry."

He reached under the table, tapping her on the leg, trying to signal to her. Rayen showed no sign that she noticed, not that he'd anticipated that she would. She was incredibly talented at hiding emotion.

Carth made her move, approaching the Stone—further proof that she was attempting a subtly aggressive approach. He was impressed by the way she played. How could he not be, especially in the way that she was maneuvering?

"Since you decided to make a stupid move the last time, why don't you go ahead and make another one?" Rayen said.

Daniel smiled to himself. She understood what he was getting at, though that didn't surprise him. What would surprise him would be if she managed to know exactly what he was doing. Rayen had some skill with Tsatsun, enough that she often beat him while playing, but something Carth had once said about Rayen stuck in his mind. She didn't have much creativity.

He didn't know if that was true or not. When he played Rayen, she seemed creative enough, but sometimes having a rigid mindset helped. Using that more deliberate, more regimented approach could be helpful in ensuring that any move they made would be successful.

What he wanted was to play together, to work together, but somehow they would have to be able to communicate. Unless Carth were somewhere else, he didn't have any way of communicating to Rayen.

But Lucy might.

He already knew that Lucy could Read him. She could also Read Rayen, and in doing so, it was possible that Lucy would be able to serve as the go-between, the key for the two of them playing together while Carth sat in front of them.

It would involve them letting Lucy Push them while playing, and he didn't love that idea, not caring for the possibility of being out of control of his body, but as far as he knew, it didn't hurt when Lucy Pushed someone. It was merely a lack of control.

A lack of control was not something to be taken lightly, but he believed that in this case, if they could prove this could work, then there would be other ways to use it.

He focused on Lucy, trying to get her attention, and didn't know if he was even successful. Maybe this was a useless idea and a mistake in general, but in order to play as a team—to truly play as a team—he and Rayen needed some way of working together.

It depended upon Lucy knowing what he wanted.

At first, there was no indication that she did.

Until he reached for a piece, but it wasn't him doing the reaching.

Daniel resisted the urge to smile to himself. If he did, Carth would realize something was up. Instead, he let Lucy make the move, holding on to the piece, getting a sense of what Rayen was thinking.

He understood where she was going with it.

It wasn't a bad move, but there was danger in it, and as he saw what she was intending, he began to pull away, guiding a different way.

In this case, he was in control, and he could feel Lucy's presence, little more than an awareness in the back of his mind, though perhaps that was intentional. It was possible —even probable—that she wanted him to know she was there.

He moved slowly, giving Lucy a chance to communicate to Rayen, and then he felt his piece moving again, once more without his control over it.

Interesting. That maneuver might work, and as he studied the board, he realized the way she intended to play it would be effective, perhaps even more effective than what he would have tried.

He let the piece move, and as he did, he smiled.

The approach was going to work.

Carth made her move, continuing her aggressive stance, and he prepared for the next play, but as he did, Carth reached across the table, grabbing his wrist.

"It's not going to work."

"What's not going to work?"

"Your intention here."

"What intention?"

Carth smiled, looking at the way he was using the piece, and she winked at him.

He frowned. Could she have known?

How, though?

He set the pieces down, glancing at Rayen.

"Can you Read us?" he asked Carth.

She winked again.

Great Watcher! If Carth could Read them—and since she'd been close to the sacred crystals in Elaeavn, it was possible that she could—then they wouldn't be able to outmaneuver her.

"I think you have the right idea," she said, glancing from him to Rayen before nodding to Lucy. "The only problem is, it's far too obvious what you are doing. Find a way to make it work where it can't be observed, and then we will see how this plays out."

"We didn't finish the game," Daniel said.

Carth made a series of moves, sliding her piece across the board and then moving theirs. Each move that she made was one Daniel most likely would have chosen, and he realized that she had known the moment he'd sat down how to defeat him.

She really was a master of Tsatsun.

"I think you have come across the possible solution," Carth said aloud, as if answering what he hadn't asked.

"What if it doesn't work?"

"As with any strategy, we must be prepared for all possibilities."

"What if something happens to one of us?" he said.

"As I said, we need to be prepared for all possibilities."

Carth got up, glancing at the table one last time before

making her way out of the room. Daniel stared at the board for a long moment, struggling with what had just happened, realizing that they had been outmaneuvered. And despite that, he had still learned something.

"Did you know?" he asked Rayen.

"Know what?"

"Did you know that Carth can Read us?"

"She's always seemed to know what's happening."

"Did you know?" Daniel asked, twisting to look at Lucy.

She frowned, seeming more nervous than she had been before.

"No, and I'm troubled that I didn't."

"It's Carth," Rayen said. "She has managed to keep many things from many people. It's all part of her game."

"I don't like being a piece in someone else's game," Lucy said.

"To Carth, I think we're all pieces. We just have to learn our role."

19

DANIEL

THE STONE RESTED ON THE GROUND OUT IN THE BRIGHT sunlight. Daniel crouched in front of it, staring at the silver veins running through it, thinking they had to be critical to understanding what the Ai'thol had wanted out of this stone. Maybe if he had Rsiran's connection to metal, it wouldn't be so difficult to figure it out. Even Haern might be better. Though his connection wasn't as potent as his father's, Haern's knowledge of metal was still far beyond Daniel's.

"Do you detect anything?" Carth asked.

He shook his head, looking up to see her staring at the ground. Other stones were arranged around it, almost as if she intended to play some massive game of Tsatsun. She had placed the stone they had dragged from the bottom of the sea outside the wall—at least, the remnants of the wall. He still didn't understand why, though Carth often had various reasons for things.

"There isn't anything that calls to me. I've wondered about the darker stone."

"And why have you wondered about that?" Carth asked.

"Well, since we were attacked on Ih, I questioned if they could have used something in that stone to do sort of the same as what they had done here."

Daniel turned. In the distance, the city rose up. It was almost as if Carth feared having the stone too close to Nyaesh, though the fact that it was something of the Ai'thol meant that caution was appropriate.

"It's possible they would try something similar," Carth said.

Daniel studied Carth for a moment. He had been wanting to ask a question ever since they had returned, but he had hesitated. Something about what Rayen had said left him troubled, and now that it was just him and Carth, he thought it was an appropriate time to ask.

"Rayen said that she had never been to Ih before."

"She had not."

"Did you keep her from it?"

Carth looked up slowly, meeting his gaze. As there usually was, there seemed to be a hint of shadows swirling around her eyes, making them even darker than he knew them to be. Heat radiated off her, her connection to the A'ras—or Lashasn, he realized. "Do you think I would keep Rayen from something important to her?"

"If it meant you were protecting the Elder Stone, I think you would."

Carth smiled slightly. "I would."

"So *were* you keeping her from it?"

"Ih is unique. It does not require someone to protect it actively the way other places do. It is naturally protected, hidden, the land itself concealing it from outside eyes."

"How?"

"When you were there, did anything feel off?"

Daniel stared for a moment. "Not until we were within the walls of the temple."

Carth frowned. "Yes. About that."

"About what?"

"There is great power found within those ancient temples. The people of Ih understood the shadows better than anyone else, and they knew there was power to be found by concentrating the shadows."

"Rayen called it a"—what had she called it?—"something like that, but we were trying to escape from the Ai'thol, so we were willing to do whatever it took to ensure our safety."

"She tells me you got lost in the shadows."

"I did."

"Describe what you experienced."

"Why?"

"Consider me curious."

Daniel watched her, squinting against the sunlight reflected off the stone he'd collected from the bottom of the ocean. "Why are you curious?"

"As I've told you, there is great power to be found within the temples."

"Are you worried that something happened to me?"

"Yes."

Daniel smiled to himself. "I've been fine."

It had been several days since their return, and other than the brief game of Tsatsun, Carth had been out of the city, though neither she nor Lucy would say where they had gone. Then again, it didn't matter to him that Carth was out of the city. The time alone had given him an opportunity to continue to recuperate. He had played Tsatsun with Rayen, managing to get in more games than they had over the last few months. Most of them, Daniel won. Occasionally, Rayen would come up with a maneuver that surprised him, and when she did, he found himself rooting for her, wanting her to defeat him.

If only Lucy had been around, they could have worked on practicing together, trying to coordinate their attack the way they had attempted with Carth. If they could find some way of doing so more effectively, then perhaps they could use that. It seemed to him there was something important in doing that, and if he could uncover the secret to communicating without anyone else being aware, it would be valuable in the coming war with the Ai'thol.

"Fine?"

"I'm not injured, if that's what you worry about."

"The fact that you managed to return to the city tells me that you are fine. What I do question is how you feel."

"Like I said, I feel—"

"Fine. And what I'm asking is whether you've noticed anything different."

He met her gaze, once again noticing the shadows swirling within her eyes and averting his own. He stared at the stone, wanting to determine what the Ai'thol had done, how they had used the stone, but could come up with nothing. "I don't feel any different. Why do you keep pushing this?"

"The temple is powerful."

"You keep saying that, but I've told you over and over again that I feel fine."

He met her gaze, wondering why she would be so focused on that, and a thought came to him.

"It's not just the temple, is it?"

Carth met his eyes. "No."

"The Elder Stone?"

"Shadows are different than other abilities. You can't simply confine them within a crystal or house them inside a flame. They must be concentrated. Collected. The ancient temples did that, and in doing so, they created power. Or perhaps a better way to describe it would be to say they concentrated power."

"You credit the ancient people rather than some ancient elder?"

"I don't know who to credit. In the case of the crystals from your homeland, it seems to me they were a storehouse of a certain type of power. The same could be said about the stone in Asador. Even here, the concentrated power is something that can be moved, augmented if necessary, and can give those who touch it a connection to the Lashasn and flame. There are other Elder Stones that are similar, though they are often difficult to reach."

"And the shadows?"

"The shadows are different. It's possible that the ancient people of Ih merely built the structure around natural concentrations of shadows, and given the age of those places, we may never know."

"That's why I was lost in the shadows?"

"You were lost in something greater than just the

shadows. I suspect you were lost in the power of the Elder Stone."

If that was the Elder Stone, what did it mean that he was lost within it? That power had swirled around him, pressing upon him. Flowing into him.

"That's why you wanted to know how I feel."

Carth nodded. "When you hold one of the Elder Stones, something changes."

"Not always."

"No?"

"I was near enough the Elder Stone for Lashasn. So was Lucy."

Carth smiled. "That is because I protected you."

That was probably for the best. Had she not, what would have happened to him?

"Some who hold one of the sacred crystals never experience change," he said.

Carth smiled. "Only because they don't know how to force the power."

"Force it?"

"Do you believe only certain people are destined to hold one of the crystals from your homeland?"

"We have presented many people with the opportunity to hold one of the crystals." In the years since Rsiran Lareth had gained a level of control over the crystals, anyone who wanted to handle one was given the opportunity. Always before, it had been a ceremony reserved for the Elvraeth.

"Having the opportunity to hold one of the crystals is very different from using one of the crystals. It's the same with any of the other Elder Stones. Most of the time, you simply need to know how to utilize the power stored within it. Once you do, you will find that it changes something about you."

"The same way as when you held the Wisdom Stone?"

"Unfortunately, it seems that when I held that stone, the effect was temporary."

"Why?"

"I don't know. As much as I would have wanted that ability to remain, it has faded."

Daniel stared at Carth for a moment. From what he knew, she had gained knowledge and abilities after holding that stone. Having access to it would allow them the chance to defeat the Ai'thol. Why wouldn't she utilize that power if it would allow them victory?

Unless she had seen something while using the stone that told her otherwise.

"And you think my presence in the temple has changed something about me?"

"I don't know. Which is why I question."

"When I was there, when I got lost in the shadows, all I felt was the shadows swirling around me. I couldn't see anything. I couldn't hear anything other than the sound of my own voice, and that was muted. Rayen was lost to me."

"I'm sure that made you uncomfortable."

Daniel remembered the terror he had felt at the idea that he was trapped within the shadows. That had all gone away when he had discovered he could still Slide, but that didn't change the fact he had been terrified while there.

"I'm not sure that uncomfortable is quite the right word."

"And yet you escaped."

"I was able to Slide away."

"Despite the fact that the shadows can contain someone who can Slide."

"I don't know how else to describe it. Why is this important?"

"I don't know. I'm still trying to understand myself, though something about this leaves me troubled."

"Why?"

"As I said, not everyone can reach Ih. The land itself is practically designed to ensure outsiders don't reach it, and yet not only did you reach it, you managed to Slide away from it. That tells me that something changed for you."

Daniel met Carth's eyes for a moment before looking down at the stone. "I don't know what to say."

"I'm not asking you to know what to say, but I am trying to understand."

When he had been within the temple, when the sense of the shadows had struck him, he had felt a chill that tore through him. But since then, nothing had been different for him. Whatever Carth was alluding to hadn't been his experience. While he might have been in the presence of an Elder Stone, it hadn't changed anything about him. It was much like when he had been in the presence of the crystals. Nothing had changed for him then either.

"What about the Ai'thol that were there?"

Carth frowned. "I'm not sure about that, either." She looked down at the stone, her brow furrowed. There was something she wasn't telling him. "Why don't you tell me if you detect anything about this stone?"

"I don't. We could go to Haern or Rsiran or…" He

shrugged. "Anyone from the guilds, I suspect. See what they know about it."

"To begin with, this isn't lorcith, so they would be unlikely to have any connection to it."

"Then why are you asking me?"

"You have been around it longer."

Daniel looked at her for a moment and then started laughing. "That's it?"

She shrugged. "Should there be more?"

"I don't know, it just seems to me that isn't much of a reason."

"On the contrary, sometimes having exposure to something gives you a greater understanding of it."

"I don't know anything about it. And why do you have these other stones around it?"

"Because each of these were found around that island."

Daniel tensed, standing upright and staring. "What?"

Carth nodded to him. "Try Sliding."

Daniel frowned. He started to Slide but wasn't able to go more than a step or two. The ring of stones all around him prevented him. And here he'd thought this was some sort of strange Tsatsun board.

"How did you manage to collect all these stones?"

"After we discovered the island where you were trapped, we went looking."

"We?"

"Lucy and I."

Daniel wondered how much it bothered Rayen to be excluded from things like this nowadays, though there might not have been anything Rayen would've been able to do. While she might have helped find the stone, she wouldn't have been able to pull it out.

But then, Daniel had almost not managed to pull it out. He had only been able to do so because Rayen had helped.

"This is all of them?"

He studied the stones with renewed interest. None of them looked the same as the first, which surprised him. He would've expected all the stones to be the same, and the fact that they were all different troubled him.

"These are the stones we uncovered at the bottom of the sea. There were others, but none of them seemed to be important. I question whether this was a test."

"A test?"

"I think the Ai'thol—or whoever they were—knew you were searching for them."

"They were Ai'thol." Carth only nodded, looking at the stones circling him. "How would they have known?"

"They know we're after them."

Daniel crouched near the stone nearest him. It was a light shade of brown and quite a bit smaller than the one he had grabbed. It would've been so much easier for him to have taken this one from the bottom of the sea. "Are they all hard to Slide with?"

"Lucy tells me they are quite difficult."

"But she managed to do it."

"Not without considerable effort."

"Does the order matter?" he asked.

"I don't know. I'm hoping you can help me determine that."

"These are in the order they were discovered?"

Carth nodded. "Where you're standing represents the island. As you look at the stone you brought, they should be arranged in a similar fashion. We were quite particular with how we placed them."

"Why so far outside of the city?"

"Without knowing what these stones might do, I didn't want them too close to Nyaesh."

"You didn't want them too close to the Elder Stone."

Carth smiled tightly. "No."

"If there's no way of Sliding to them, then it wouldn't matter."

"It always matters. I can't know what was intended with the stones, and until we do, I'm unwilling to place them anywhere near something of value. Just because we don't have the ability to Slide beyond them doesn't mean that the others don't. And if they have that ability, it is possible that they would use it to prevent others from getting where they want."

"You think they're plotting to have us bring the stones someplace to study?"

"I think it's a possibility."

Daniel lifted one of the stones nearest him. It was grayish, and much like the one he had grabbed, it had metal that seemed to work through it, though this was more of a copper color. He moved it and replaced it with the brown one. When he took his place back in the center of the circle, he attempted to Slide.

He wasn't able to move.

"Does it make a difference?" Carth asked.

Daniel shook his head. "Not that I can tell. I'm not able to Slide anywhere."

Carth grabbed one of the stones, lifting it far more easily than he did. She moved several stones, taking them around the circle, replacing them. She nodded to Daniel when she was done.

He focused, attempting to Slide—and failed.

It probably didn't matter which order the stones were placed in. There was something about the stones themselves that made Sliding difficult.

"If the order doesn't matter, then why have an assortment of different stones?"

"I suspect that it's to defend against people who might have overcome the various restrictions." She crouched next to one of the stones, running her hand along it. Daniel joined her, looking down at the stone, noting a bluish hue within it.

"That's heartstone."

She nodded. "I suspect it is. Heartstone is effective to prevent most of your kind from Sliding. Rsiran has proven that it doesn't work on everyone."

"And these others?"

"The others are all various metals. I am curious which metals they might be, but at the same time, I'm hesitant to bring these samples anywhere of importance."

"What if we bring someone here?"

"And who would you bring here?"

"Well, probably Rsiran, especially as we know that he has such an ability with metals."

"I doubt Rsiran would be able to take the time to work with these."

"Haern?"

"Is he skilled with metals?"

"I don't know him well enough to answer." Probably not, he had to admit. What he knew about Haern suggested he hadn't spent much time around the forge the way his father had.

"You know more than you let on."

Daniel watched her. "How long have you been able to Read others?"

Carth tipped her head to the side. "Is that what I can do?"

"You're not Reading me?"

She grunted. "Where you see an ability, I see knowing the way you think. Predicting patterns. Anticipating changes. Understanding irregularity. You can do the same, but you need to continue to practice."

"You've been around the crystals before."

"Several times. The first long enough ago that were it to change me, it would have done so by now."

"What was it like?" When she frowned at him, he went on. "The attack back then. Lareth. What was it like?"

"Why do you care?"

"My father never cared for Lareth. He blames him for much of what's changed."

"And now you question his opinion?" Daniel nodded. Carth crouched to the ground, lifting a stone, rolling it from hand to hand before setting it back down. "We blamed the Hjan then and thought they served the Ai'thol, and perhaps they did."

"You don't know?"

"The man who attacked then—Danis—was far too arrogant to have taken orders from anyone. If he did, then it's possible he believed he was in control. Perhaps

Olandar Fahr allowed him to believe that, if only to ensure his compliance."

"How well do you know Olandar Fahr?"

"Not well at all."

"But you've seen him?"

"A few times. Had I known then what I know now, I would have made a greater effort to kill him."

"Would you have been able to do so?"

Carth shook her head slowly. "I don't know."

Daniel walked outside of the ring of the stones, attempting to Slide, thankful that he was able to do so. "What happened with Danis?"

"I held him captive."

"You held him, as in you no longer do?"

"As in he no longer lives."

"What happened?"

"The Ai'thol."

"They killed him?"

"I'm not sure if they were trying to rescue him or whether killing him was the goal, but they came after him. I lost fifteen Binders, women who were incredibly skilled and highly trained. All of them had been guarding Danis, and all of them lost their lives that night."

"Are you sure Danis is dead?"

"Quite sure."

"How?"

"I saw the body." Carth frowned at him, getting to her feet and looking back down at the ground, studying the stones for a moment before turning her attention back in the direction of Nyaesh. "Are you questioning because you wonder if the Ai'thol were able to disguise their intentions from me?"

"I just don't know when it comes to the Ai'thol."

"Then you are making progress."

"I am?"

"That was one of my first considerations."

"What was?"

"That they faked his death. I didn't know how high within the Ai'thol Danis sat. He sat at the head of Venass, then a place of much power, and he led the Hjan. Such a position was one that I believed to be incredibly important. And now, I wonder how much of that was simply another move in a much greater series of plays."

"But they didn't succeed."

"I'm not so certain."

"But the crystals were secured by Rsiran—and you."

"They were secured, but they were moved. It proved the crystals *could* be moved. I wonder if perhaps their movement was some part of a grander scheme."

Daniel frowned. If it were part of a larger plot, it would have been one that had taken place over decades. Who was able to plan that far out?

If this Olandar Fahr was that capable, then he was someone to fear.

"What next?" he asked Carth.

"Now we try to understand the stones. We must get ahead of what the Ai'thol intend. Only then can we find ourselves safe. Doing so means you must return to Elaeavn for answers."

Daniel stared at the collection of stones for a moment. Even if he could Slide one of the stones to his homeland, doing so did pose a risk. Anything of the Ai'thol could be dangerous, and he wasn't willing to do invite danger to his home, much the same way Carth wasn't willing to bring the stones into Nyaesh. He thought he understood her reasoning and agreed that it was sound.

"I think the stone should stay here. I could bring someone here." Daniel stared at the stones for a moment before looking up at Carth. "That might be the only way."

"Who will you ask?"

He frowned. Rsiran Lareth might be the only person who could help them, though would he trust Daniel enough to come with him?

"Unfortunately, I think I have to ask Rsiran Lareth."

Though he'd helped save the man, he dreaded going to him for help.

20

LUCY

"How is it supposed to help me understand the C'than?" she asked, staring at the empty room. Ras stood in front of her, the flowing robes he wore seeming to glow. Something about him left her with a strange feeling, almost as if he did glow, and the longer she watched him, the more she wondered whether that was some part of his ability or whether there was something else to it.

For his part, Ras never said. Then again, she should have known better than to expect him to explain himself to her. He stood watching her, and there was almost a hint of amusement in the way he did.

"Who is to say you were going to understand the C'than by being here?"

Lucy looked around the inside of the room. It was empty other than her and Ras, though she sensed something here she couldn't quite see. There were no decorations along the wall, no sculptures, and in the days she'd been in the tower, she hadn't seen anything that would help her guess who else might be there.

Lucy turned to face him. "Why am I here otherwise?"

There was so much more for her to be doing, not the least of which was to work with the women in the village, trying to find some way of keeping them organized, keeping them together. The more she was away from them, the more she felt as if she were overlooking some aspect of care she was supposed to be providing to them. They needed her to help ensure they were safe, and though she could Slide back to them, her time here seemed to prevent her from doing that. Unfortunately, she didn't feel as if she could give either side short shrift. She had to ensure she was giving both the necessary time, and if she didn't, then she would fail. In this case, she very much feared failing.

"Why are you here, Lucy Elvraeth?"

"I'm here because Carth wanted me to be here," she said.

"If that's the only reason, then you should disappear once again, the same way you have been every day."

She looked at him with a neutral expression. "Have I?"

"Do you think you could Travel without my knowing?"

Lucy had, but that was beside the point. She had Slid away each day thinking Ras wouldn't know, but perhaps that had been her mistake.

"I thought I might be able to," she said.

"I understand what you thought, but nothing happens on this island without my knowing."

Lucy looked around her but wasn't shown anything that offered any insight. Inside this room, there was nothing, no way of her knowing anything else around her.

There had to be something, though.

The longer she was here, the more certain she was Ras had something in mind for her to learn, and yet she also had it in her mind that she had to work through what it was, and that he would not reveal it to her easily.

"How much control do you have over the island?"

"It's not a matter of control." Ras turned his back to her.

"It sounds to me as if it's a matter of control."

He stepped out of the room, turning toward the door. "I think you must reflect upon what you want before you decide what you will do."

"What's that supposed to mean?"

"It's time for you to decide how much of the C'than you want to understand."

"I came here, didn't I?"

"You did, and yet, you aren't here."

Lucy didn't know how to answer, but it wasn't that he was wrong. She had been distracted ever since arriving, wanting nothing more than to continue to work with the other women, and now she felt as if she understood what she needed to do with them. Even in that, she wasn't sure she was giving either side the necessary attention.

It felt as if she were trying to do too much, and yet how could she not?

Maybe that was a lesson that Carth wanted her to learn. Perhaps she wanted Lucy to understand what she wanted to do with herself and how she was going to work in the world. It was possible Carth wanted Lucy to ultimately decide to serve the C'than, and yet, more than ever, Lucy didn't think she could do that. She thought she needed to be a part of what was taking place. Even though she might not be the best equipped for such a conflict, she still felt as if she needed to have some role in it.

Ras closed the door, and it began to glow.

As it did, Lucy reached for it, suddenly nervous about his intentions.

She couldn't touch the door.

Her breath caught.

What was he doing?

She focused on the door, thinking about what she might need to do. She tried to Slide, but there was no way to get beyond what she detected.

He had trapped her here.

She tried again, but once more, her attempt to Slide beyond the door failed.

What was he doing to her? Why would he hold her here like this?

Lucy tried to Slide again, focusing on the other side of the door, nothing further than that, but it wasn't the distance that posed the challenge to her. It was simply Sliding.

Could she find something to anchor onto?

When it came to Sliding using her ability to anchor, she thought she could hold on to her awareness of Daniel, and she searched for his thoughts, looking to see if anything about them would help her know where to find him, but there was nothing.

She tried again, shifting the focus, thinking about where she might uncover him, and once again, there was nothing there.

It was the first time that trying to connect to Daniel Elvraeth had failed her.

Not only had Ras separated her from her ability to Slide, but he had removed her ability to reach for someone to anchor to, and in doing so, he had trapped her here, holding her in a way that she hadn't been imprisoned before.

She shivered.

The longer she stayed, the more she would be betraying the women of the village. Depending on how long Ras decided to hold her, it was possible she wouldn't be able to escape, and if so, she would end up permanently trapped here, unable to reach the people she had promised to help.

Lucy began to pace.

All this brought her back to the time when she'd been imprisoned by the Architect, his goal to hold her, to force her to serve him.

She would not suffer the same fate again.

She got to choose, didn't she?

This wasn't about Ras; this wasn't about Carth. This was about Lucy.

And she was not going to be held in some prison simply because they thought this was the best way for her to learn.

Anger continued to build, and she steadied her breathing.

Her augmentations hadn't prevented her from reaching thoughts before, and even now, she was certain she would be able to get free of this place.

Even though Ras had whenever ability he had—something she suspected to be similar to Carth's—nothing would prevent her from escaping.

She was determined to get free, and in order to do so, she would have to Slide.

Or would she?

He had sealed her in the room and kept her from her abilities, but she hadn't tried the most obvious thing.

Making her way over to the door, she paused with her hand in front of it, worried about the heat radiating off it. Yet when she reached for the handle, she found that it was not intolerable.

Twisting the handle, the door came open.

Lucy focused, and Daniel's thoughts came drifting back to her. They were distant, and she listened to them for a moment, knowing she could Slide to him if it were necessary. But she was no longer trapped.

Then again, had she ever been trapped?

She stormed through the halls, looking for Ras. She wasn't going to stay here for long.

She reached a staircase she knew led down to the main level of the tower, and from there, she would be able to walk out if she wanted. But since she was able to Slide again, she didn't have to use conventional methods.

Going up the stairs would take her to the library, where Ras might be, but she wanted to find him more rapidly. He had always prevented her from Reading him, but in her anger, she focused on his mind.

There were aspects to it she thought she could uncover, and the longer she focused, the more certain she was she could dig into his thoughts. She found him.

There was amusement within him.

All of this was a game to him.

She dug, borrowing his knowledge, and forced her way deeper into his mind.

If he was going to play a game with her, then she was going to be prepared for the next time. She wasn't going to allow herself to be trapped by him, nor was she going to allow him to torment her with games like this.

She had come here to learn, and if it took her Reading Ras in order to learn, then so be it.

Perhaps that was the lesson he wanted to teach her. She had to use her abilities, regardless of how invasive they might be to others, to gain the understanding she needed to ensure the people she wanted to provide care for had what they needed.

As she dug, she found barriers. Lucy continued to try to push, but the more she did, the more barriers she reached, and ultimately, she could go no further.

It was almost as if Ras had allowed her in, but only so far; beyond that, she wouldn't be able to find him.

Holding on to her connection to his mind, she Slid.

She emerged in a room.

It was a nicely appointed room, a comfortable-looking bed along one wall, a table against another. A wardrobe rested along a third, and next to the wardrobe was a low doorway.

Ras stood at the doorway, watching her.

"I wondered how long it would take you," he said.

He closed the door behind him, sealing it with his power.

She wouldn't be able to Slide beyond it, and she suspected this was a door he had actually locked.

"It was a test."

"I thought it prudent to perform a basic test."

"Why?"

"Consider it my way of testing your thinking."

"Why?" she asked again.

Ras turned to her, smiling. "Because I chose to."

"That's no answer."

He took a seat at the table, looking up at her. "It's all the answer you need, Lucy Elvraeth. You came to the C'than to learn, and yet you continue to disappear. You have been holding on to these new abilities of yours and forgetting the one piece of yourself that made you powerful."

"What piece is that?"

He tapped her on the chest. "Your heart."

Lucy shook her head. "My heart isn't what matters. All that matters is trying to better understand how to Slide, using my ability to Read, and being prepared for anything the Ai'thol might do."

Ras sighed. "If that's what you believe, then it is unfortunate."

"Why?" She felt like a fool asking the same question over and over again, but there was something about Ras that made her feel like a fool. And there was something about him that left her knowing she should be asking different questions, though she had no idea what questions those should be. He didn't intend to cause her any harm, and the longer she spent around him, the more certain she was that he wanted nothing more than to ensure her safety, but that was different from helping to train her. That was the entire reason she had come here, thinking she would learn something from him. What was she learning, other than that he would put her into rooms that were not locked, separating her from her abilities? They'd had some conversations over the last few weeks, but nothing more.

"What have you experienced when it comes to the Ai'thol?"

"I'm sure Carth has told you."

"Carth has, but I'm asking you what you experienced."

Her hand went to the back of her head, rubbing the spot where the implant had gone in. It was throbbing this morning, and she found that rubbing it seemed to help a little bit, but not entirely. Each time it throbbed, pulsing in the back of her mind, she couldn't help but feel as if she needed to do something to remove that pain, but she had no way of doing so.

Even the Healers weren't able to help her, though she didn't necessarily want the Healers to do anything for her. At this point, it was better that she continue to have her augmentation, using it to work with the women and do whatever she could to help oppose Olandar Fahr and the Ai'thol.

"Torment," she whispered.

"So you say, but was your torment at the hands of the Ai'thol?"

She frowned, meeting Ras's eyes. "The Ai'thol are responsible for what happened."

"The Ai'thol are responsible for much, but when it comes to what happened to you," Ras said, pointing to her, "I'm not convinced they are to blame. As much as you might want to give them that credit, I don't know that we can."

Lucy thought about the Ai'thol and about what she had experienced. What she had suffered at their hands had been minimal. They had attacked in Elaeavn, but some of that had been because of Lareth. How much of what the Ai'thol had done had been a reaction to someone else?

What she had experienced in Asador had been more than a reaction, hadn't it?

They had been after power. They wanted the wisdom stone.

And now?

Lucy no longer knew what the Ai'thol were after. They had gone to Nyaesh, looking for the power of the Elder Stone there, and there had been considerable attacks, but she had found the C'than far more worrisome within Nyaesh.

"I see that you aren't certain."

"That's your point? You want me to realize that the Ai'thol aren't what I believed?"

"On the contrary, Lucy Elvraeth. The Ai'thol are exactly what you believed. All I'm trying to do is get you to think through things and realize there are more aspects at play here than what you have long told yourself. Your people like to believe there is only one threat, and yet, in a world like the one we live in, there is never only one threat."

"What other threats are there?"

"That is the purpose of the C'than."

"That's all you're going to tell me?"

Ras smiled at her. "Unfortunately, that's all I can tell you."

He turned back to his desk, and he pulled some papers in front of him, flipping through them. Lucy watched him for a moment before getting annoyed and moving around so that he was forced to look at her.

"And that's the purpose of the C'than? That's the purpose of everything that happened to bring me here?"

"Not at all," Ras said, not looking up.

"Then what is it?"

"It is for you to learn to observe."

"Observe?"

Ras smiled, clasping his hands over the stack of papers. "When you were in that room, what did you experience?"

"You trapped me there."

"Did I trap you there?"

She frowned, cocking her head to the side. "No."

He shook his head. "You were not trapped. You might have believed you were based on what you saw, but when you allowed yourself to actually observe, you began to understand you were not trapped at all."

"That's your lesson?"

He smiled at her. "You've already made it clear that you don't want to learn Tsatsun, and perhaps Tsatsun isn't the right way to teach you."

"You don't think I have the talent?"

"I don't think you need to have the talent," Ras said.

He turned his attention back to the pages, going through them. Lucy looked over his shoulder but was unable to read anything on them; she wondered if that wasn't the point. Perhaps this was another test, some other way for him to determine what she might be able to observe. As she stared at them, she didn't notice any patterns or anything special about them. It was possible there was nothing there for her to even be able to determine.

"How am I supposed to observe?"

"That is something I can teach you."

"Well?"

"Well, what?"

"Are you going to begin teaching me?"

"Everything is a lesson, Lucy Elvraeth. Have you not seen that?"

"A lesson, now, and not a test?"

"There will be tests. Part of your time here demands there be tests, but there will be more than just tests. You will be challenged to observe."

"Why?"

"Because it's necessary. Because in observing, you gain an understanding. And in order for us to do what we must, understanding needs to come first."

"You want to understand the Ai'thol?"

"I think we need to understand why Olandar Fahr is taking the action he is." Ras stuffed the papers back together, and she couldn't tell if there was a hint of disappointment edging the corners of his eyes. Was she supposed to have discovered something from that stack of papers? She wasn't able to read them, and so she couldn't tell anything from them. "Before we think that we can find a way to stop them, we first must understand him. If we know what he's after, then we will be able to defeat him."

"I thought he was after power."

"If he were after power, it would have been less challenging for him to claim by now. Given how long he's been active, and the nature of power that he has already acquired, I believe there is something more to it."

"Why?"

She really needed to be asking different questions, but around Ras, she felt like a child, like when she had first gone to the library in Elaeavn. The caretakers had treated her delicately, and it had taken her time to grow into her role, to take on more and more responsibility and become useful within the library.

If there was something she could learn from Olandar Fahr, then she would need to continue to work at it, and yet how would she be able to do so?

She hadn't even seen him yet.

Only, she *had* seen someone who had seen him.

Her experience with the Architect gave her an advantage others lacked—the opportunity to better know what Olandar Fahr might be thinking.

Ras watched her, almost as if he knew what she was thinking.

"You wanted me here because of my captivity with the Architect."

"Why would you think that?"

"Because I have a perspective you needed."

"And what perspective do you think that is?"

"A perspective others have not had."

Ras smiled at her. "You are correct. Your time with the Architect gave you a unique perspective. We have not had much exposure to Olandar Fahr, certainly not enough to feel confident in being able to know what he's planning, and because of that, we have struggled to know what he might do next. Having someone who does have some experience with him, who does know what he might be thinking, is valuable."

"I don't have much insight into the Architect's thinking."

"You have more than you know."

Lucy thought back to her time in captivity. There had been no opportunity for her to really know the Architect, had there?

She had been working on trying to gain a better understanding of her abilities, and in doing so, she had been trying to shut out some of the noise of the voices, and yet, as she had done so, she had found it more difficult than she had expected. The voices had been overwhelming to her, to the point where she had heard them as a jumble.

How much of them—if any—came from the Architect?

What she had experienced with the women in the village suggested that those with augmentations like hers weren't people that she could Read, and yet, the Architect didn't haven't an augmentation like hers. His was a traditional Forger augmentation, one she'd thought she would be able to find some way beyond.

And she had, hadn't she?

He had managed to Push her, but that had been before, when she was still trying to understand her abilities, and before the implant had fully taken hold. Since then, she had succeeded in getting free.

Could the timing of her freedom matter?

Could it be tied to the fact that the implant had fully absorbed?

Lucy breathed out, looking at Ras. He was watching her, and there were some of the same questions in his eyes.

"You want me to observe myself."

"We must understand ourselves before we can know others, Lucy Elvraeth."

"And then what?"

"And then you decide, Lucy Elvraeth."

"I thought you wanted me to work with the C'than."

"What makes you think this is not working with the C'than?"

She sighed again, and once more, she couldn't help but feel as if there was something she missed, but what was it?

Perhaps that was what Ras wanted her to discover. If it was all tied to her understanding herself and trying to grasp something along these lines, then she needed to determine what it was. And if it was a matter of her observing herself, given everything that she had gone through, now was the time to do so.

"What about Olandar Fahr?"

"Eventually, we will need to turn our attention to him. There is more than what we know."

"What more?"

"I suspect he is not the only one after power."

21

LUCY

Marcy flickered throughout the village, Sliding. She did so in short bursts, and then stopped. Each time she managed to Slide, Lucy smiled to herself, pleased the other woman succeeded, wondering whether she would be able to keep it up if it came down to it. It was one thing to be able to Slide in situations like this, and quite another to do so under pressure. Then again, did she want these women to know what it was like to deal with pressure? Didn't they deserve more safety than that?

If it were up to Lucy, they wouldn't have to deal with anything else. They had been through enough already, and the more they had to be exposed to, the more dangers that existed, the more she began to wonder whether there was any way for them to remain safe.

The village was safe.

She looked around. The homes in the village were much warmer than they had been when she'd first come across it. Smoke drifted from several chimneys. The smell of baking bread and other foods mingled with the sea air, and there was a scent of happiness. Contentment. The women had made this place their own.

It hadn't even taken that long. They had been here for only a few weeks, and in that time, they had already begun to settle in, taking what had been little more than a series of homes and turning them into an organized settlement. Lucy had secured paint, Sliding it back here, and a fresh coat had been applied to many of the buildings, with others in progress.

Despite all that, she couldn't shake the sense that something more needed to be done. She'd gone with Carth, moved those strange stones out of the water, and returned here. Seeing the impact of those stones had reinforced her need to do more, but she wasn't quite sure what that was.

These women all counted on her to provide them with some protection, and the longer she was here, the more she thought she owed them. She had been working with them, trying to train them, and thinking she should be able to find some way to ensure they received the necessary knowledge to understand their abilities. The entire affair held an undercurrent of darkness, the edge of what they had gone through, that torment that they had experienced that left her not quite certain. They deserved better, and they certainly deserved more than what they had encountered so far.

For her part, Lucy wondered when she would have to reveal this place to Carth. The other woman had asked her, and Lucy had demurred so far, thinking she would keep it to herself, partly because she didn't want to reveal it to Carth yet. If she did, she worried that Carth would try to use them. She didn't need to Read Carth in order to know how the woman would want to use them, and even if she could, she suspected Carth would have some way of hiding what her plans were.

It was something that troubled Lucy quite a bit.

"You've returned," Eve said, approaching from the water's edge.

Lucy turned toward the woman. Of all of the people here, Eve had more of an edge to her. She needed to get to the bottom of that. Perhaps Ras's lesson applied even here.

"I told you I would."

"Each time you leave, we wonder if we'll see you again."

"I thought I'd come back often enough that shouldn't even be a question anymore."

"Shouldn't it?"

Lucy studied Eve and forced a smile. "Have you uncovered anything?"

"I keep trying to use this metal like you told me to, but nothing seems to work."

"It's not that I told you to use metal. I told you it's possible your ability would be tied to the metal."

"That doesn't appear to be the case."

"I'm sorry."

"Then what ability do I have?"

"Unfortunately, it's possible you won't have any ability."

Eve glared at her. "Why not?"

Lucy resisted the urge to touch the back of her head, to draw attention to her own implant. Eve's implant was in a similar location to hers, though not all of the women's were. Something about the placement of the implant seemed to matter as much as the woman who received it. There had to be some aspects to it that Lucy didn't fully understand, and the longer she was around them, the more uncertain she was that she would be able to determine the difference. If Rsiran Lareth were here, he might be able to help her better understand the nature of the metal. Even Haern might be able to help, but she had not gone to them. Going to them meant asking for help. And it meant revealing the presence of the village. What did it say about her that she wouldn't even consider returning to Elaeavn to ask someone who had a better understanding of the matter at hand?

Could she be too stubborn?

She never would have believed that about herself before, but maybe she was avoiding it. Or it could be that there was another reason, and it was less about what she was avoiding and more about what she feared might happen if she went to Elaeavn for help.

If she wanted to help these women—really help them—she needed to find answers, regardless of where she would have to go for them.

It was something she hadn't considered much, but now that she was here looking at Eve, she couldn't help but wonder if perhaps that was the right strategy. If she went to Elaeavn, asked for help from those who might understand the nature of what they were trying to do, she might be able to better understand the injury that had occurred.

There was another reason for her to go. Someone within the city was responsible for what had happened to her.

Daniel believed it might be his father, but even if it wasn't, she thought she needed to try to discover who had willingly sacrificed her to the C'than. Whoever it was obviously cared very little about the people of Elaeavn.

"What have you been able to do?"

Eve glared at her before turning away, lifting the hunk of lorcith.

"Nothing. That's the point of this, isn't it? Other people have begun to develop abilities, but me? I don't have anything."

"Why are you so angry about it?"

"Asks the woman who has all sorts of fantastic abilities."

"I'm sorry I was born with abilities," she said.

"You weren't just born with them, though. You have whatever you had before, but then more was added to it. That just doesn't seem quite right."

Lucy forced a smile. "I understand why you are upset."

Eve tossed the piece of metal away, and she turned back to Lucy. "Don't play at condescending to me."

Lucy shook her head, and as she did, she noticed something in the distance.

The lorcith moved.

It had landed near the rocky overlook that would lead down to the shoreline, and as far as Lucy knew, the rock should have remained there, but the rock was following Eve.

"You don't have to smirk at me like that," Eve said.

"I'm not smirking at you."

"Then you're making fun of me. That's worse."

Lucy shook her head. "That's not it, either."

"What is it, then?"

She pointed toward the lorcith.

Eve turned and stared at the rock, frowning. "I don't see anything."

"Move."

"You move."

"No. Move and watch what happens."

Eve shot her a look before taking a few steps.

As she did, the piece of lorcith reacted, following her as it had the last time. Lucy smiled to herself, more pleased than anything that the lorcith seemed to react. If nothing else, having some idea of what abilities Eve possessed was useful.

"How is that possible?"

"Well, we wanted to know whether or not you had any abilities."

Eve glanced over at her. "I have abilities?"

"It seems as if you have a connection to lorcith."

"That's lorcith?"

"It is. And some people of Elaeavn have a connection to it. It's considered a useful ability."

"How is controlling metal useful?"

"You'd be surprised. I've known a man who can use it with weapons."

"That could be useful," Eve conceded.

"And I suspect there are plenty of ways to use it that I don't even know about. Why don't you continue to work with it, see if you can master a level of control with it, and if you can, then we can see if there's anything more you can do."

"Why won't you teach me?"

"This isn't anything I have experience with."

There were times when she wondered if it would have been beneficial for her to have access to the metal, if only to better understand what it might be able to do. Using lorcith seemed as mysterious to her as Sliding probably did to Haern. Even though he had lived around Sliding his entire life, he had no ability to do so on his own, and even though she'd lived around people who had control over lorcith, she had no ability to do so on her own.

"How am I supposed to learn it?"

"You can work on your own, seeing if you can't figure out whether you can control it, or..."

"Or what?"

"Or we bring you someplace that you might be able to get answers."

"Where is that?"

"The only place where I know people who can control lorcith is Elaeavn."

"No," she said.

"You wanted to know—"

Eve cut her off. "No."

Lucy nodded. "Then we will work with you here. We can see what we can come up with, see if there's any way for you to gain a better understanding of how to control the metal. But you do have an ability, Eve. Regardless of anything else, that much is true." And as she said it, Lucy couldn't help but realize that everybody else around here also probably had an ability. Even if they hadn't developed it yet, they needed only the proper time and motivation in order to do so.

"Now that you have discovered what you can do, it would be helpful if you would do me a favor."

"What favor?"

"Others need to know if they have any abilities," she said.

"How am I supposed to help with that?"

"Think about what you had to do. Think about what you wanted to know. And think about the others, how much they've been through. If there's any way for them to gain access to the same sort of power you did, we should try to do it."

Eve held her gaze for a long moment, finally looking away, turning her attention back to the lump of lorcith that moved as she moved. A hint of a smile came to her lips, and though Lucy didn't fully know what the woman had been through, whatever it was had put such an edge to her that she worried she would never relax and become what and who she was meant to be.

"I will think about it."

"That's all I can ask."

Eve stormed off, and the piece of lorcith went with her. When she turned back, reaching for the lorcith, Lucy swore she saw a smile cross the woman's face.

At least there was that. Regardless of anything else that happened, having Eve find a sense of peace was important.

Others might need the same thing, and though it might not be quite as apparent as it was with Eve, some of them suffered just as much. Many of them might need a gentler touch. Lucy thought she had to find some way to help them, but how was she supposed to do that?

She Slid, making her way back to the water's edge. Standing there, she looked out over the water, wondering what it might be like beyond here. Carth would know what was out there, having sailed as often as she had, as far as she had. There was probably quite a bit beyond the sea that Carth have knowledge of, and the possibility that existed out there left Lucy filled with wonder.

She closed her eyes and Slid.

When she emerged, she did so within the tower.

Hurrying up to the library, she found Ras sitting at a table as he often did. Strangely for someone as powerful as he reportedly was, he spent much of his time in the library. Much of it seemed to be cataloging the various works that were stored here, works that Lucy had begun to suspect weren't found anywhere else.

Ras looked up when she appeared, almost as if expecting her.

"What have you uncovered?"

"Nothing. I just thought it was time for me to return."

"Did you believe I was angry with you?"

Lucy shook her head. "No."

"Good."

"You wanted me to observe myself. What do you think I can find?"

Ras sat up, clasping his hands together. When he did, he held Lucy's eyes. Something about him changed, the way that it often did, making him practically seem to glow, and he smiled at her. "What have you tried to do?"

"Honestly? I really haven't tried much. I know you want me to understand what I went through so that you can better comprehend the Architect, and in doing so, you want to better understand Olandar Fahr, but I don't know how much I will be able to help you. Some of it I don't even remember."

"Why don't you remember?"

"Because I was controlled by him."

"You think you are still controlled by him?"

"There was a time when I did. I don't anymore."

"Then you should have nothing preventing you from reaching those memories."

"I don't think it works like that," she said. She wasn't entirely sure how it worked, though she had been the one to do the Pushing and understood that it was similar in some regards to Reading. She had tried to piece together what she had done when she had Pushed. It had involved forcing her thoughts on someone else, something she didn't do very often, which made it challenging to recreate. Before, it had been done in a time of need, and now that she didn't have that same urgency, she wasn't sure she even wanted to try it.

"You know how it works?"

"I have used that technique," she said carefully.

"So I've heard," he said.

"Is this your way of challenging what I had to do?"

Ras smiled at her. "Did you have to do it?"

"How else was I supposed to ensure our safety?"

"I don't know. I wasn't there, so unfortunately, I can't

answer that for you; but as you were there, once again, if you observe yourself, you can decide if there was some other way you could have reacted."

Lucy took a seat across from him, meeting his gaze. She felt a strange stirring in the back of her mind, one that reminded her of someone Reading her, and yet she didn't think he had the ability to Read. There were times when sitting with Carth, she had the feeling the woman could Read, and still she was quite certain Carth couldn't do it. Perhaps it was little more than her ability to assess situations, one that Ras would likely share. Both of them valued Tsatsun, and both believed in playing the game, they could know their opponent.

Perhaps that was all Ras was doing. She could imagine him appraising her, trying to view her as an opponent on the game board, trying to decide how she might react, and yet the stirring at the back of her mind seemed different, not like someone playing Tsatsun.

"What would you have me do?"

"I would have you start with a memory you are certain of," Ras said. "Pull it apart. Analyze it. Decide if what you know is real or not."

"Why?"

"As I think I've told you, you must know yourself in order to know others. And once you know yourself, then you can decide if what you are observing is accurate. When it comes to Olandar Fahr, we must try to understand all various angles, as until we do so, we cannot know him."

Lucy closed her eyes, thinking through what she could try to understand. She had encountered quite a few different situations while trapped by the Architect. Many of them might or might not have been real, and as she thought about them, she couldn't help but wonder how much of what she had experienced was what she believed it to be. The more she considered it, the more she began to wonder whether she could even use that time to determine if she was in full control of her mind.

What she needed was a different memory.

What memory could she use?

It would have to be an earlier one, a memory from before she had been changed, when she was just Lucy, not Lucy the augmented Elvraeth.

As she often did, she drifted back to her sister, thinking of what had happened.

They had never been terribly close, but losing her sister had been difficult. It had been challenging for the entire family, not just for Lucy. Her parents had blamed her for what happened, and Lucy had said nothing, the same way she often said nothing.

She thought about that time, the memory of it, and…

Pushed the thoughts away.

"You were going into a dark place," Ras said.

"How do you know?"

"It's the way you winced as you were thinking of it. What was it?"

"It was nothing," Lucy said.

"Nothing? Unfortunately, I doubt it was nothing. And that nothing seems to be important to you. If it's important to you, then it's important for you to work through, if only for you to get a better understanding of yourself."

"Like I said, it's nothing," Lucy said.

Ras stared at her, and she let out a frustrated sigh before turning away from him and getting to her feet. She began to pace in the library, and yet she couldn't shake the feeling that he was right. What had happened to her with her sister was important for her to address. More than anything, it was something she could use. If she could piece together what she had experienced and borrow from those memories, she might be able to understand who she was.

Observe herself.

That seemed to be the hardest thing for her.

In some ways, she thought Carth had known about it. She might not have said what it was, but she had known that Lucy was tormented. Perhaps that was why she had not returned to Elaeavn.

No. She *had* returned to Elaeavn, though briefly. And there was no reason for her to continue to go back, no reason to risk herself like that. There was nothing for her in Elaeavn. The only thing she had there was family, but even that wasn't a reason to return. The family she had in Elaeavn wasn't the kind of family she wanted to be around. The more time she spent outside of the city, the more she began to understand there was so much more for her in the world. With her new abilities, she couldn't help but feel as if she were meant for more.

Perhaps the Great Watcher had intended all of this for her, and if so, she needed to find herself, much like Ras suggested.

It had to be something more than working as Carth's tool, her way of finding other C'than.

She thought she was starting to uncover her potential

by working with the women of the village, but it would take even more than that, wouldn't it?

And in order for Lucy to do so effectively, she would have to find a strength she had never possessed.

She wasn't a fighter. Wasn't that what she had told Carth over and over again?

And yet, if she remained passive, others like Olandar Fahr and the Ai'thol and the Architect would continue to take advantage of her, to use her. If they did so, she would find herself back where she had been.

Imprisoned.

She wanted none of that. What she wanted was to do as Ras suggested, to know herself, and to find a way to ensure not only that she was safe, but that she would never experience that sort of torment again.

What would it take?

She turned slowly. Ras continued to watch her.

She couldn't shake the feeling that he knew the thoughts racing through her head and was somehow aware of the anguish she experienced, the struggle that rolled through her. In order for her to move past this, she was going to have to face—and embrace—some of the hard parts of her past.

Was she able to do that?

She wasn't the same young woman who had left Elaeavn. She was different. Stronger. Perhaps augmented, but that didn't mean she didn't have strength within herself. All it meant was that she had a different type of strength, and she had to find some way of mastering what she possessed.

Lucy turned her attention back to the shelves, staring at them.

She would do this. She would be strong enough.

Taking a seat again, this time at her own table, she rested her head on her hands and focused, thinking back to Elaeavn.

22

HAERN

HAERN REACHED THE EDGE OF THE CITY. EVERYTHING about it left him on edge, making him feel as if he were making a mistake. He didn't like abandoning Galen. Leaving his friend—and mentor—behind left him troubled. Galen wouldn't do the same were the situations reversed, but then, Galen also was far more capable than Haern.

Did he have to leave him?

It was possible that he could go back, that he could find some other way of helping, but in order to do so, he would need to get to safety, prepare in a way that involved arming himself differently, and then he could attack.

The only problem was that he didn't have enough connection to lorcith to mount a serious attack. The Forgers had proven they were far more capable than he.

He paused at the edge of the city, checking the knives he had on him before *pushing* off with one knife, sending it streaking away then dropping the coin and *pushing* off on that. He traveled, going from lorcith to lorcith, connecting to the lorcith within each item, staying high above the ground as the wind whistled past him. He braced himself for the possibility that others might appear, but as he traveled in the darkness, there was nothing. Moving in this way was safer than traveling on foot. He continued to *push* and *pull* on coins, slipping through the darkness, the city behind him growing ever more distant.

After a while, Haern dropped back to the ground, turning his attention toward the distant city. Galen needed him. What was he doing running?

Back on solid ground, he looked around. There was a clearing here, and the sound of water rushing came from somewhere nearby. Haern headed toward it. He was thirsty, the effort of fighting his way free from the city nearly overwhelming him.

Lights in the distance caught his attention. They were too close to be the city, and not bright enough to be a village. Haern approached slowly, carefully, feeling his way across the ground. He kept his collection of lorcith coins with him, prepared for the possibility that he might have to *push* away, traveling as quickly as possible to escape from whatever this was.

As he neared, he heard the sound of voices.

Haern froze. A thicket of trees near him would provide some protection, and he *pushed* off on one of the coins, soaring high into the air and coming back down to land slowly—gently—near the tree.

"Quiet," someone snapped.

Haern froze, listening to the sounds, and heard a faint whimpering.

What had he come across?

"She's hungry, Rally."

"I don't care if she's hungry. We don't got no food, so she needs to be quiet. You know where we are."

"I know where we are. You're the one who brought us here."

"Quiet."

Haern crouched, staying near the base of the tree, trying to listen. If only he had Listening as one of his abilities, it would be easier. Even a more enhanced eyesight might be beneficial, but the fire made everything difficult for him to See through. Smoke swirled around the campfire, clouding and obscuring his ability to make out more than he had.

"At least let me go for water."

There was a moment of silence, and Rally grunted. "Be quick about it. If you're gone too long, I'm sending the hounds after you."

Haern darted behind the tree, watching. After a moment, a shadowed figure made its way from the campsite, heading toward the stream he'd come across. He stared for a moment, wondering if perhaps he should intervene but knowing that would be dangerous. Anything he might do would only end up with getting someone injured, possibly this woman.

At the least, he could figure out what was going on, couldn't he?

He crept away, and once he was clear of the trees, he *pushed* off, flying until he reached the stream, coming to land and crouching on the far side of it. He waited there until the woman approached. She appeared out of the darkness, little more than shadows, and seemed not to notice him for a long stretch. Haern cleared his throat, trying to get her attention.

With a start, she stiffened, standing frozen in place.

"I'm not going to hurt you," he said softly, standing.

"Who are you?"

"Just a traveler. Who are you?"

"You shouldn't be here. It's dangerous."

"Why? What's happening?"

"These lands have been..." She glanced over her shoulder before turning her attention back to him, shaking her head.

In the faint moonlight, Haern couldn't make out much about her features. She had an angular jaw. Dark hair and pale skin. As he stared at her intently, he thought he saw bruises on her face, though it could just be some disfigurement. He didn't take a step toward her, not wanting to threaten her.

"What have these lands been?" Haern asked.

"Nothing. You should keep moving."

"Why? Do you intend to hurt a tired traveler?"

"I'm not going to hurt anyone, but..."

She twisted her dress, tightening her fists, and was otherwise completely still.

"Is someone hurting you?" Haern asked.

"I'm fine." The woman swallowed, leaning forward just a little bit. "Are you going to stop me from filling my water jug?"

"No. Do what you need. Like I said, I'm just traveling through here. I don't intend to cause any trouble."

The woman watched him for a moment before

crouching down in front of the stream, tipping a pitcher until it was full. When it was, she stood, looking at Haern for a long moment. A question burned in her eyes. Rather than asking, she said nothing, spinning away from him, taking the pitcher of water away.

Haern watched for a long moment. Should he go after her?

Having overheard Rally, he didn't like the idea of simply abandoning her.

Haern *pushed* off on a lorcith coin, clearing the stream. On the other side of the stream, he hurried after her. When he caught up to her, he gave her space but kept close by.

The woman stiffened. "You should turn away."

"What's your name?"

"My name doesn't matter."

"It matters. What is it?"

"I told you, my name doesn't matter."

"What are you afraid of?"

"I'm afraid of you continuing to follow me."

"I have no interest in hurting you. I could help."

"Help how?" She paused, turning to him and looking him over from head to foot. Haern wondered what he would look like to her. Probably not all that intimidating. He might have his sword, but it was sheathed beneath his cloak. His knives were hidden, and they were far enough from Elaeavn that even the threat of his people wouldn't be enough to matter. "You don't look like you could be of much help."

"You might be surprised."

"Do you intend to harm me?"

"I've already said that I don't."

"Then leave me. If you don't mean any harm, turn away." She glanced over at him for a moment, and when she did, he could more easily make out what he had seen on her face. They were definitely bruises. One eye had swollen slightly, and streaks of yellow faded down into her cheek. A healing cut on her chin would have been more noticeable were it not for the injury to her eye. "You don't want to be a part of this."

Haern paused, letting her disappear. Maybe she was right and he didn't want to get involved, but as she made her way closer to the campfire, he couldn't help but feel as if he had to do something. Besides, there was someone younger there as well, and if he did nothing, whoever this man harming this woman was, he would do more to them.

Swearing to himself, Haern scurried forward, reaching the edge of the campfire. The woman had taken a seat near an older man, and two other men were there, both of them with strange deformities to their faces and powerful builds.

He stepped forward, clearing his throat.

The man looked up, and the other two jumped to their feet, reaching for swords he hadn't noticed it first. Haern flashed a wide smile, holding his hands up, his gaze drifting around the clearing before settling on the woman. She stared at him, shaking her head slightly, and hopefully imperceptibly so that the other man wouldn't notice.

"Mind if I share your fire?"

"Yes." The man glanced at the other woman, studying

her for a moment. "We've had enough trouble with strangers that we aren't interested in having someone else join us."

"I know. I've had the same difficulty. It's dangerous out there."

"You will understand, then, that we don't welcome any strangers joining us at the fire."

"It seems a shame that we couldn't travel together. Like I said, I have been—"

Two men took a step toward him. Haern stared at them for a moment. "I mean no harm."

"Then you can mean it somewhere else," the other man said.

Haern took stock of the campfire. It was larger than he had realized, and in addition to the woman and the other two men, there were wagons arranged along one side. All of them were enclosed, and the crackling of the fire did nothing to obscure the sound of scraping he heard from within those wagons.

There was a young girl here, that much he knew, but could there be more than just one young girl?

Who would do such a thing?

Haern took a step back. "Are you merchants?"

"I think we've made our intentions clear."

"I could use a little trade. As I said, I've been traveling for a while, and I'm tired. I have coin." He held out his handful of lorcith coins. In the faint firelight, the other metals gleamed, making them look almost as if they were gold coins.

The man frowned. "Leave the coins and be on your way."

"I'm not leaving the coins. I asked for trade."

"And I said to leave the coins."

"Or what?"

"Or you will find out how dangerous the road can be."

The woman sitting next to the man was shaking her head, and Haern flashed a bright smile. He might have difficulty with Forgers, but men like this shouldn't pose him too much difficulty.

"Is that right? Do you intend to set the hounds on me?" Seeing as how he hadn't seen any dogs within the camp, he wondered if these two silent men were the hounds. They certainly looked ugly enough.

"Where did you hear that?"

"What's in the wagon?" Haern said. All traces of a smile had left his face, and he readied his connection to lorcith, preparing to *push* the coins first. He could use each of the coins like a weapon, and from there, he could grab for his sword and then the knives if necessary.

Once he was done, he would have to be prepared for whatever it took. He had no idea how many people these men had abducted—and he felt increasingly certain that was what they'd done.

The man stood, shifting his hand to the side, revealing a sword. "I've given you fair warning. Leave the coins and you might walk away from here."

"And then what happens to the woman? The girl? The others I can only presume are in the wagon?"

"That is none of your concern."

"I think it will be my concern." Haern pulled his own cloak back, revealing his sword.

The other man smiled. "You really are a fool."

He tipped his hand, and the two silent men lunged forward.

They were quick, far quicker than Haern had expected, but he'd been training with Galen, and if that training had done nothing else, it had prepared him for the possibility that things wouldn't go quite as planned. In this case, he *pushed* on two of the coins, sending them streaking at each of the men. At the same time, he *pushed* one of the coins down and then *pushed* himself off, flipping up over the two men, landing behind them. He unsheathed his sword, *pulling* on a connection to the two knives that were hidden in his pockets, and *pushed* them toward the two men who had changed directions.

Both had coins implanted in their skulls, but it had done nothing to slow them.

Haern almost stumbled.

He *pushed* on a coin again, taking to the air, and then used his knives, sending them through the two men. Neither of them fell.

What sort of ability was this?

It was going to take more power than he'd realized to stop those two.

They couldn't attack if they couldn't walk, and he *pushed* on his sword, sending it twisting through the air, the blade spinning as it chopped toward one of the men's legs. It hacked through it, dropping the man to the side, and he started trying to crawl.

He made no sound.

Haern *pulled* on the sword, and then *pushed*, sending it toward the other hound, taking off one of his legs as well.

Only then did he drop.

He landed next to the first man.

"You will pay for that," the man said.

"No. You will. Release the woman."

The man held a knife to her throat, watching Haern. "Or what? You will—"

Haern didn't give him an opportunity to finish. He *pushed* on one of his coins, sending it straight toward the man's throat. He *pushed* with considerable force, and it tore through him, ripping into his throat and leaving a bloody mess behind.

Rally dropped.

Movement behind him caught his attention, and he spun around to see the two hounds trying to crawl toward him. Glancing over at the woman, he tipped his head to the side. "Is there any way to kill them?"

"Not that I've seen."

"Then this is going to be brutal," Haern said.

He *pushed* on the sword, sending it through each of the men, slicing an arm and a leg free. He carved off their heads, hacking through their bodies, trying to get them to stop moving. Even when all of that was done, there was still some movement, though it was little more than a twitching.

He turned to the woman. "How many girls?"

"How did you know?"

"I didn't until I got here. How many?"

"Seven plus myself."

"How old are they?"

"Why?"

Haern glanced over at Rally. He'd seen slavers before, but nothing like this, and certainly not with men who seemed to be almost unkillable. "I'm not here to take you from one horror to another. All I want to know is how many girls and what their ages are."

She continued to watch him, eyeing him with the same suspicion, and Haern wondered exactly what it was she had been through. Maybe she had been helped before and ended up trapped, captured by someone who was presumably offering their assistance.

"All I want to do is ensure you get to safety. Nothing more than that."

"How do we know?"

"I didn't come through here trying to find random captured girls. I was on my way home when I came across your campfire."

"Where is your home?"

"Elaeavn." He watched her, looking for any sign of recognition, but there was none. "Where is your home?"

"Not here," she said.

"Let me help."

She glanced over at the wagons before turning her attention back to Haern and finally nodding.

Haern made his way to the first wagon, jamming his knife into the lock, snapping it open. Inside were three girls, the youngest of whom couldn't have been any older than five, and they crawled away from him.

The woman appeared next to him, reaching her hand into the doorway. "It's okay. You can come out."

"Elise?" the youngest said. Her voice shook, and the woman nodded. The little girl crawled forward, jumping into Elise's arms. She carried her back, away from the wagons—and away from the remains of the two hounds along with the other man. Elise helped the other two girls out of the back of the wagon, guiding them away and toward the darkness. They were a little older, somewhere between twelve and fifteen, but still thin and frail, all bones and clearly malnourished.

Haern made his way to the next wagon, breaking open the lock much like he had with the first. Inside were four girls, all of them a little older. He backed away, letting Elise get in front to help the girls free.

The last wagon was unlocked. There were no girls within, and he searched for supplies, finding food and a stack of knives. In addition, a heavy bag of coins was tucked near the far corner.

He turned, handing the coins to Elise. "Wherever we can get you to safety, you're going to need this."

"What is it?"

"I suspect it's the money he's gained selling others."

Elise's eyes widened. "Why would you give this to me? Don't you want it?"

"I didn't help you for money."

"There's no place we can be safe," Elise said.

"That's not true."

"We've traveled through plenty of lands where he has no difficulty grabbing other girls. Most of the places were interested in buying, too. Where can we go that we won't be bought or abducted again?"

"You need to find safety."

"Safety doesn't exist in this world."

"That's not true."

She looked past him, and he turned to see the two hounds still twitching. Were their bodies in the same place he'd left them? He couldn't tell. If they were somehow able to restore themselves, he wanted to be long gone before then. And if they could do that, he had to wonder what sort of terrible magic allowed it.

It was something he wanted nothing to do with.

"I've not seen any way to get to safety," Elise said.

"Only because you haven't been given the opportunity."

"And what opportunity is that?"

There was one place he thought that he could guide them, but doing so would delay his return to Elaeavn.

Did it matter?

If he didn't help these girls, what kind of person was he?

His father would have helped, wouldn't he? He didn't know. Maybe he wouldn't, as they weren't from Elaeavn. There was one thing he did know—Galen would have helped.

The challenge would be finding a nearby city. Haern didn't know the landscape well enough to identify the easiest way to travel, and going on foot with this many people would be slow and cumbersome. At the same time, it would be worthwhile.

"We should go," he said.

"Now?"

"I'm afraid that if we don't, the hounds will pose another challenge."

Elise glanced over her shoulder before nodding. "Where do you intend to take us?"

Her voice was filled with suspicion, and he understood. Given the way she had been abused, he couldn't blame her at all. Had he not trained with Galen, and had he not wandered through Asador searching, he might not know what to look for, but as he had, he thought that he could do this.

"Not my home. I intend to help you find women who can keep you safe. They know what it's like to go through what you have suffered."

"Women? What kind of women?"

Haern glanced down at the fallen Rally. His blood poured out around him, and he was tempted to reclaim the coin. But the one that had torn his throat out would be useless to him now. And he didn't want to clean it off. Instead, he would bury it, sending it deep into the ground so that someone else couldn't find it and use it against him.

"Women who don't fear men like that."

23

HAERN

By midday the following day, they were all exhausted. Even Haern was worn out, mostly because he'd been awake for a significant duration of time, and everything in his body longed to lie down and take a rest. He didn't dare do it. Not until they were closer to safety.

Elise and the other girls surprised him. They were managing far better than he would've expected, and despite how long they had been walking, none of them had complained. All of them had kept pace, continuing the steady trek northward.

Haern wasn't entirely certain that north was the right direction, but he and Galen had traveled south, Sliding to a place where they could find the Forgers. Safety would have to be in the north, where there were cities Haern was more familiar with, though none quite like Elaeavn. Even if he wanted to bring them to Elaeavn, he didn't know that it would be safe for them the way other cities might be. His homeland wasn't welcoming to outsiders.

More than that, his homeland wouldn't have the

Binders. That was what he wanted to find for Elise and these girls.

They reached a wide river, and he motioned for them to pause. All of the girls took the opportunity to drink from the river before taking a seat and resting.

Elise turned to him. "You haven't said where you're guiding us."

There was still the same suspicion in her voice as had been there before. He would earn her trust somehow. "Partly because I'm not entirely sure. I don't know these lands that well."

"I thought you came from someplace far from here."

"I do, but I didn't travel by foot."

"By sea?"

"Not by sea. Some of my people have the ability to travel without walking." That seemed to be the easiest way for him to describe Sliding, though he wondered how she would respond to such a description. It was a strange ability, practically impossible to believe, and yet it was what it was. "I had traveled by this method and was stuck."

"Your ability failed?"

"I don't have the ability to travel in that way. Another who was with me did, but we were separated."

"And your ability to fly?"

She said it so casually that he was almost taken aback.

"I can't fly."

"I saw you when you're fighting with Rally and his hounds. You were flying."

"It's not so much an ability to fly as it is a connection to metal." Haern took one of the knives from his pocket, holding it in the palm of his hand. He *pulled* on it for a moment, letting it hover, and then he twisted it in place. "This knife is made of a type of metal that I can manipulate."

"And the sword?"

He nodded. "The sword as well. It allows me to use it in a way that grants me a certain power over it."

"And you can use that to fly?"

"I know it doesn't make a lot of sense, but…"

"It makes about as much sense as the hounds."

"What *were* those men?"

"They weren't men. At least, not any longer. Perhaps they once were, but they were used in such a way that something about them changed. They became less."

"I don't know. It seemed almost as if they became more."

"And yet they lost themselves. Rally controlled them, which meant we weren't able to go anywhere or do anything. Anytime we tried, he sent the hounds after us."

Haern's gaze drifted to her cheek. Elise nodded.

"He never struck us himself. He always let the hounds do it. He viewed it as a reward for their service."

They fell into a quiet, and Haern took a seat, staring across the river. The landscape had changed, more rolling hills than there had been before, with the occasional copse of trees. It was times like this that he wished he had spent more time outside of the city, allowing him the opportunity to know where he was and how to find the nearest village. He could use his remaining coins, travel that way, but doing so would force him to abandon Elise and the girls.

"I'd like to get across the river," Elise said.

"Why?"

"The hounds."

"What about the hounds?"

"They can't be killed."

"Anything can be killed."

"Unless they're already dead."

Haern got to his feet, looking across the river. "They won't be able to cross this?"

She shrugged. "I don't know. It's possible, but anything that makes it more difficult for them to follow us is worthwhile."

Haern looked across the river. It was wide here, wider than most rivers he'd encountered, and the only way across would involve him using his connection to lorcith. Either that or heading along the shore until they found a bridge, and that wasn't a guarantee. They could wander for quite some time before coming across anything that could be used to cross.

"When you're ready, I'll help get you and the others across."

"By flying?" Elise had a hint of a smile when she said it, and he chuckled. It was the first time she had shown any emotion other than fear or irritation.

"You're going to have to let them know I don't mean to harm them."

"Maybe take the older ones first. That way they can be there for the younger ones, and I can stay on this side with some of the younger ones until you are finished."

Haern nodded. "Whenever you're ready."

Elise took a deep breath before sweeping her gaze

around her. When she was done, she got to her feet, heading toward the other girls. She said something quietly, and one of the older girls looked at Haern before turning her attention back to Elise, shaking her head.

Approaching slowly, Haern held out his hand. "Let me show you what she's talking about." He should have known that it would be unwise to just attempt to carry them across without having a demonstration. With everything they'd been through, it wouldn't be surprising for them to be afraid—terrified, even—of him approaching like that.

Haern dropped the coin on the ground and then *pushed*.

He hovered in the air and used the connection to the coin to travel across the water. When he landed on the far side, he turned and looked over at them. Dropping another coin, he *pushed* again, coming to land on the far side.

"As I told you, he can fly."

"I can't..." Haern shook his head. "I can carry one or two at a time. If it'll make you feel better, I can take two to begin with so that you're not over there by yourself."

Two of the young women stepped forward, and Haern nodded. He slipped his arm around each woman's waist, and they grabbed on to him. He *pushed,* carrying them across the river, landing with a little bit more force than he intended. One of the women laughed as they came to land, stumbling forward. Haern *pushed* off, landing on the other side again. He made several trips, each one easier than the last. When he finally had everybody other than

Elise on the other side, he turned, ready to *push* when he saw movement in the distance.

Haern frowned, staring until he realized what it was that he saw.

The hounds.

He *pushed* quickly and landed next to Elise.

"You make it look so easy. It's almost as if you were born to do it. I could—"

"There's no time. We need to cross the river."

"Why?"

Haern pointed, motioning toward the oncoming hounds. They were moving rapidly, and he grabbed Elise before she had a chance to say anything and *pushed* off, hovering in the air just as the hounds jumped. They nearly reached him, but Haern *pushed* them across the river. When he was there, he *pulled* on the coin.

The hounds stood on the far shore, their bodies grotesque and twisted, somehow stitched back together. For a moment, he wondered if perhaps he had been mistaken and hadn't killed Rally as he had believed. There would've been no way for him to survive having his throat ripped out like that, but how was it possible these hounds still lived?

"How are they still here?" Elise asked.

"I've never seen magic like it."

"Hopefully the river…"

As they watched, both hounds took a step forward into the water.

"Run," Haern said.

"What about you?"

"I intend to stop them again."

"We don't want to go without you."

He looked at the other girls. If he failed and the hounds managed to reach them, what would happen to them? Would the hounds try to bring them back to Rally's body, or would something worse happen?

"You need to get moving. I'll slow them. I managed to stop them once."

Hopefully he could do it again, and now that he had an idea about the technique involved, he hoped that he could tear through them, ripping them apart, but a part of him worried that it wouldn't work.

Elise looked at him for a moment before turning and shepherding the girls forward. They started running, heading north, and he couldn't imagine how tired they were after everything they'd been through. They had to be exhausted, and yet despite that, they took off at a rapid pace.

Haern *pushed* off, hovering, waiting for the hounds to appear.

Neither of them emerged from the water.

Could the water have dragged them downstream?

He turned, glancing toward the girls as they disappeared, when a loud splash caught his attention.

Haern barely had a chance to *push* himself higher into the air, scarcely avoiding one of the hounds grabbing him by the foot.

He unsheathed his sword, sending it spinning at the nearest hound, trying to catch the man in the leg. As it spun, the hound lunged for the blade, and Haern adjusted the direction of the spin, managing to get the blade spiraling up and through one of the hounds. The blade carved the creature in half, but he worried even that wouldn't be enough. He adjusted, cutting it into fourths, feeling more than a hint of disgust at needing to do so.

Holding himself steady in the air like this was tiring, and he worried he wouldn't be able to manage for much longer.

The other hound jumped.

Haern didn't have a chance to react in time. The hound crashed into him, somehow reaching him where he was suspended thirty feet in the air, tearing at him, and Haern flicked the coin at the hound and *pushed*. It separated them, sending the hound tumbling, and Haern flicked another coin behind him, *pushing* off to hold himself into the air. As he twisted into position, he *pulled* on the sword, sending it at the falling hound, carving through the creature. With another *push,* the blade cut off his head, and Haern dropped to the ground.

Even headless, the hound continued to try to move toward him.

He needed to destroy these creatures, but what would it take? Fire might work, but he didn't have any way of starting a fire easily.

What if he picked up the hounds and dropped them into the river? It might be enough to wash them downstream, separate the parts and hopefully keep them from joining again.

He stood off to the side, controlling the sword, sending it slicing through the creatures. He chopped them into chunks as small as he could stomach and then started kicking the remains into the river, not wanting to pick them up. Even doing that disgusted him. With each plop into the river, it splashed, and he feared that he wasn't doing enough.

He forced himself to continue. When he was done, there was no sign of blood as there should be. Whatever had been done to the men, turning them into these creatures had drained them of all blood.

What sort of horrible magic was that?

It had to be the Ai'thol, but why?

He scanned the ground, looking for any coins he might have left, and *pulled* on lorcith, dragging it toward him.

When he was done, he watched the river for a moment, his gaze drifting across to the other side, looking for any sign of movement.

There was none.

Finally he turned, heading across land, racing toward the women.

It didn't take him long to catch up to them. Elise looked at him, a question in her eyes.

"I hope they don't follow us, but..."

"You don't know," she whispered.

Haern shook his head. "If I had some way of starting a fire, I think I would've burned the remains, but I didn't want to linger too long."

"You could have buried them."

"They went into the river. Hopefully it's fast-moving enough that it will carry the different parts away."

Elise glanced over her shoulder, her gaze going toward the distant river, before turning back to him. "If we reach the city, then we won't have to worry about it."

Hopefully that was the case. Haern had never seen

magic like the hounds and had no idea how they were able to continue to attack. How many other creatures like that existed? If the Ai'thol had developed that sort of power, they wouldn't stand a chance. Worse, if some slaver like Rally had managed to acquire two, how hard could it be for others to find?

None of them said anything as they continued across the rolling hills. Eventually, day began to fade, the sun setting, shadows rolling across the ground. They still hadn't come across even a small village, no place that they could stay, and Haern wasn't eager to spend another night on the road, but by the time the sun set fully, he realized they wouldn't have much choice.

They made their way toward a copse of trees that would provide some shelter, and the girls began to fall asleep quickly. Haern paced, looking around the camp. Other than him, Elise was the only one who didn't drop right to sleep.

He joined her at the edge of the trees, looking out into the night. "You can rest. I'll keep watch."

"You shouldn't have to do that. This isn't your fight."

"Not at first, but it is now."

They were silent for a while before Elise turned to him. "I was wrong about you. I didn't think you would help."

"I couldn't leave you like that."

"What happens if we don't make it to this city where you think we can get help?"

"We'll make it. It might take longer than we want, but we will find something."

"And if we don't?"

"I'm not going to abandon you, if that's what you're worried about."

Relief swept across her face. "We're going to need to find food."

"When was the last time any of them had anything to eat?"

"He didn't feed us often. Most of the time, he gave us water, but even that wasn't enough."

Haern marveled at the fact that they were able to keep such a steady pace regardless of their hunger and thirst. "I wish I had more to offer."

Elise reached into her pocket and pulled out the pouch full of coins. "We aren't entirely helpless."

"I don't think that you've ever been entirely helpless. Most people would have given up when faced with what you did, but you fought through it."

"I didn't fight."

Haern looked at her eye, nodding slightly. "That would say otherwise."

"That wasn't fighting. That was trying to stay alive."

"Isn't that the same thing?"

Elise fell silent, and he joined her in looking out into the night. There was a part of him that feared the hounds would somehow come after them, but if it had taken the better part of twelve hours for them to restore themselves and catch up, they hopefully had a little more time, and that was if the river hadn't swept them downstream.

"Tell me about your home," Haern said.

"What's there to know?"

"How did you end up with him?"

"He came to my village. He said he was a merchant,

and with the wagons, how were we to believe otherwise? He set up outside of the village and traded a few things, but not much."

"You didn't question him then?"

"We've had merchants like that come through my village before. We aren't on a major thoroughfare, and most who come through do so out of chance rather than intentionally. It's not often that we find someone who has much of value to trade, so when he arrived, we thought it was more of the same."

"When did you realize otherwise?"

"When he snuck into the village in the middle of the night. He grabbed three of us."

"Which of the others were from your village?" When she didn't answer, he breathed out heavily. "He already sold them, didn't he?"

"They were younger, and he said they were more valuable."

"Why?"

"Those who buy the girls like them younger. They feel they can train you."

"The people I'm going to bring you to don't look too kindly upon that sort of thing. You'll be safe."

"Safe," she said softly. She pulled her knees into her chest, wrapping her arms around them. Her eyes drifted closed, and Haern watched her for a moment. He didn't have a good sense of how old she was, but she couldn't be that much younger than him. Despite that, there was something much more world-weary about her. How long had she been a captive?

How long had any of them been captives?

He wandered through the trees, glancing at the girls. They were of all ages, some of them so small that it left his blood boiling with rage. None of them looked well fed, and most wore tattered clothing, though as he looked at them—really looked at them—he realized that much of their clothing seemed to come from various different styles. Which way would Rally have been heading?

Seeing as how Elise said she came from the south, he suspected they were moving north. If so, were there others he needed to worry about? He thought the Binders would have prevented such things from occurring in these lands, but maybe there were limitations to what the Binders could do.

Once he found them, he would ensure Elise and the others were safe.

Haern paced. He was tired—exhausted, even—but he couldn't sleep. Even if he wanted to, he doubted his mind would shut down, racing with everything they had encountered.

If Galen had survived—something that he was no longer certain had occurred—he might have already returned to Elaeavn. What would Galen think? Would he believe that something had happened to Haern? Would he send others out of the city, Sliding and trying to find him, or would he wait, knowing that Haern would be coming by foot—or by lorcith jumps?

In order to keep himself awake, Haern continued to pace, wandering around the small clump of trees. Other than the buzzing of insects, his footsteps were the only sounds in the night.

Morning came slowly, but it came. Thankfully there

had been no return of the hounds, and as the girls and Elise awoke, starting their trek north, Haern began to hope they might be able to stay ahead of them, if they were going to return at all.

He didn't push nearly as hard as he had the day before, and as they made their way, he felt his eyes drift closed with each step, and he didn't bother to keep them open. Somehow he managed to continue onward, and every so often, he would feel a hand on his arm guiding him. He would flutter open his eyes, see Elise making sure that he stayed with them, and then he would stumble onward, half awake.

By the time evening came, he dropped to the ground, barely able to go on. Elise crouched next to him. "Sleep. We'll keep watch over you."

"What if the hounds—"

"If they come, I'll wake you, but you won't be any good to us if you can't stay awake."

Haern was asleep in moments, and when he awoke, it was the middle of the night. All the girls were asleep other than Elise. He joined her where she crouched near a stream. "Thank you for letting me sleep."

"You needed it. I was afraid we are going to have to carry you half of the day."

"Has there been any sign of the hounds?"

"Nothing. I think you were successful."

"Has there been any sign of any cities?"

"Not yet."

"Eventually, we'll run into a road and we can follow that into one of the cities."

"And what if we don't?"

"We will." He glanced over at her, the question he'd been wondering about after their conversation the night before coming back to him. "How long were you captive?"

She turned away from him, staring off into the distance. "I lost track."

"How long do you think you were captive?"

"A long time," she said softly.

"I can help arrange transportation to get you back home."

"I don't know that there is a return home for me. I don't know if any of these girls can return home."

"Why not?"

"We traveled a long way."

"And I told you that my people have a way of transporting themselves. Once we get you to safety, I can return to my home and see if someone can help."

"Do you think they would?"

"I do."

She sighed. "I'm not even sure I want to return. When I was in my village, I never wanted to stay there. No one does, but at the same time, there's really no hope of escape, either. I suppose I had come to terms with the fact that I would always be there."

"You don't want to go back to your parents?"

"I'm sure my parents think I'm dead."

"Wouldn't they want to know that you're alive?"

"I don't know." She looked down at her hands, twisting them together.

"What is it?"

"It's nothing."

Haern knew better than to push. She deserved better,

and considering how she fell silent, he decided that he wouldn't cause her more distress.

"Why don't you get some rest?"

She looked over at him for a moment, studying him before getting to her feet and joining the other girls. Haern took a drink from the stream, letting the cold water wash through his mouth, and began to pace, once more making a circuit of the campsite. At least tonight he was better rested, even if it was only a few hours. Hopefully they would find a place to stop and keep the girls safe within the next day or so, but there was no one else out on the road, and the absence of people left him wondering if they were even heading toward some settlement, or if they weren't going to find anything at all.

By the time morning came, the girls awoke again, and they started off. Haern's stomach was rumbling, so he couldn't imagine how the others felt. Considering how little they had reportedly eaten during captivity, he feared they wouldn't be able to hold out for much longer.

The day passed, eventually rolling toward evening, and as it did, he was reassured by the fact that they hadn't come across the hounds again. Maybe they really *were* gone.

Every so often, he dropped a coin, *pushing* off so that he could scan the horizon, looking for a way toward civilization. Once he found a city, he could look for the Binders. Then he could ensure the girls' safety.

Near evening, he found a road.

As dusk fell, movement in the north caught his attention.

He tried to make out just what it was but struggled to

do so. There had to be something out there, though what was it?

Even if he managed to reach it, he wasn't sure he wanted to do so at this time of day. It would be better for them to be fully rested, better for them to have a chance to come at it without fearing they would be overwhelmed, and better for them to wait, but the longer he stared, the less certain he was they could wait.

Whatever was out there was making its way toward them.

"What is it?" Elise asked.

Haern shook his head. "I don't know."

"Is it… is it them?"

It shouldn't be the hounds, but he couldn't be sure it wasn't. He would've expected to have more time before the hounds managed to catch them, but he didn't know enough about the creatures to know whether or not that was true.

Haern glanced at the others with him before coming to a decision. They couldn't rest. Regardless of how tired they might be, he didn't dare take an opportunity to sleep yet. What they needed to do was stay ahead of whatever was coming in their direction.

It meant continuing on. It meant that despite the exhaustion that most of them—probably all of them—felt, they had no choice but to continue to push onward.

Haern said nothing to the others, not wanting to scare them, but continued to encourage them to hurry along. As they walked, he couldn't help but feel as if the movement in the distance was getting closer.

It was possible that it was.

As the evening drew on, he realized that he would have to make a choice. Either he could continue on their journey with the others, trying to encourage them to move as quickly as possible, or he could attempt something different.

Something different meant potentially dangerous, but it also meant the likelihood that they could reach safety.

Wasn't that what he was after?

Haern took a deep breath, glancing over before deciding.

"Keep moving. I'm going to see what is after us," he said to Elise.

"You can't leave us like this."

"I'm not leaving. I'm only taking a moment to try to ensure we are safe. I will catch up once again."

Elise watched him, and there was pain in her eyes that he couldn't stand, but he also didn't dare remain behind, not until he knew exactly what it was that they might be facing.

It left him with no choice but to head away from the others and hope this wasn't anything to fear.

24

DANIEL

Returning to Elaeavn was difficult. Daniel Slid from Nyaesh, emerging in Asador for a moment to recuperate, and then from there, he Slid onward, making his way toward Elaeavn. If he had more confidence in his strength, he would have done so in a single Slide, but traveling in this way was taxing.

Then again, it wasn't quite as taxing as he would've expected it to be.

When they emerged near the Ilphaesn Mountain, Rayen looked over at him. "Why all the stops?"

"So that we don't end up in the middle of this mountain," he said, looking up at it.

"It is impressive, though not quite as impressive as some farther to the south."

"There are larger mountains to the south?"

"Incredible mountains to the south, and even beyond that."

"Maybe I need to spend more time Sliding around the world."

"I thought that was part of what you were doing."

"I hadn't spent that much time doing it before."

He turned his attention to Elaeavn. It would've been easier had he been able to Slide with Lucy, but she had another assignment, a task that she hadn't wanted to share with him. Though it troubled him, he thought he understood. If he were captured, he wouldn't be able to betray them.

"Have you ever been to Elaeavn?"

"I've been near it," she said.

"Near?"

She pointed to the sea. "We sailed past a few times, and though your people like to think your city is concealed from the water, the angles don't quite work out as well as they believe. From a distance—and with the right spyglass—it's quite easy to make out the entirety of your city."

"When I was growing up, I couldn't imagine going anywhere else."

"Most children feel the same way."

Daniel took a deep breath. There were times when he thought it would've been easier to have stayed within Elaeavn, to have taken up the role his parents wanted for him. Had he done that, he never would have gotten involved with Carth. He never would have known about the extent of the Ai'thol. He would have feared the Forgers, the same way everyone who lived in Elaeavn feared the Forgers and the possibility of another attack, but beyond that, he would have known a relative safety.

It might be ignorance, but within ignorance was also a certain happiness.

Now that he knew the truth, and now that he had

experienced much more of the world outside the borders of Elaeavn, he would never be able to enjoy that blissful sort of ignorance again.

"I wouldn't have stayed if I hadn't believed it was worthwhile for me to do so," he said.

In the distance, waves crashed along the shore. The sound was no longer familiar to him. After having spent so much time in Nyaesh, he'd begun to forget the steady rhythms of the sea as waves crashed along the shores. As a child, he had known the distant sound of the waves along the shore. Even within the palace, it was possible to hear that sound, to listen to it as the waves struck, and to be lulled into a certain sense of comfort by it.

He reached out his hand, waiting for Rayen to take it, and stepped forward in a Slide.

It carried him to the shores of Elaeavn. From here, the steady washing of the waves along the shoreline came to him. Along with it were the occasional sounds of seagulls as they swirled overhead. As it was early evening, the sun having set, leaving the sky darkened, dozens of voices out in the streets drifted toward them. Here along the shore, there weren't nearly as many.

A darkened shape slithered out of the shadows, and Daniel froze.

It took a moment for him to See that it was nothing more than a black cat.

Rayen laughed at him. "All that for a kitty?"

"Cats are viewed differently in Elaeavn."

"And why is that?"

"Superstition, mostly."

Rayen made her way toward the cat, crouching down in front of it. It circled around in front of her before rubbing its face up against her hand. She glanced up at him. "I don't see anything dangerous about this little kitty. He's hungry. Don't your people feed them?"

Daniel shook his head. "No one feeds the stray cats."

"No one?"

"There are plenty of rodents and scraps they manage to find even without anyone feeding them." And he wasn't about to tell her that cats could be both lucky and unlucky, depending on how many there were. Thinking about it left him feeling a bit foolish about the superstition.

"That seems cruel," Rayen said. She stood, and the cat wound around her ankles, rubbing up against her. "In my homeland, we keep cats as pets. One like this would be prized."

"Why like that?"

"Because it's all black, of course."

Daniel chuckled. "Do your people think the shadows favor it somehow?"

"Is that any different than the way your people view cats?"

He frowned before shaking his head. "I suppose not."

"Some places I've traveled have even larger cats."

"We have those, too. They roam through the forest." The idea of getting too close to some of the animals in the forest made him uncomfortable. He could Slide from them and had never been attacked, but he didn't really want to see any of those creatures, either. No one did.

"I suppose you find them unlucky as well."

"No. Just dangerous."

"Cats are skilled hunters."

"Maybe we can train them to hunt the Ai'thol."

Rayen glanced down, looking at the cat for a long moment. "I think this one is too little."

"Right now it's too little, but wait until it grows up."

She looked over at him. "This kitty will get quite a bit larger?"

Daniel smiled to himself before shaking his head. "I shouldn't tease you like that. The feral cats in Elaeavn stay about the same size. Most of them are small like that one, but the larger cats are out in the forest."

"What if the kittens are in the city and the full-grown adults stay out in the forest?"

"That's unlikely."

"Does anyone keep these animals as pets?"

Daniel shook his head vigorously. "No. I couldn't even imagine anyone willing to do that."

"Then how do you know?"

"Well—"

Rayen started laughing, leaning over and petting the kitten again before standing and turning her attention to him. "I can see the little kitty makes you nervous. I won't pick on you anymore."

"I find that hard to believe."

"Fine. I won't pick on you *much* more."

Daniel resisted the urge to turn away from the cats. As Rayen suggested, it was a foolish superstition, and it was one that he shouldn't abide by anymore. He was old enough now that he should be comfortably certain there was nothing dangerous about these cats—other than the fact that they often came in large groupings.

He shivered, pushing away those thoughts.

Rayen watched, amusement curving her mouth. "Where now?"

"Rsiran Lareth is going to be within the forest."

"You didn't want to Slide us there?"

"With the protections placed around it, it wouldn't be easy for me to do." Lucy probably could Slide beyond those protections now, but he wasn't able to do so. He could reach Elaeavn, and from here, he could walk into the Aisl, but more than that was beyond his ability to Slide.

"Did you want to come to the city?" she asked.

Daniel looked up toward the palace, his gaze drawn almost unintentionally. It had been a long time since he had visited, but he doubted much had changed. There was something about the palace, looking up at it from this angle, that he always found strange. The palace had been designed to blend into the rock, much the same as everything in the city had been designed to blend in, concealing it from the outside world so that anyone sailing past wouldn't see it easily. The only problem was that within the city, the palace seemed to float from certain angles, jutting out from the rock, giving it the appearance of hovering in the sky, almost as if it were blessed with abilities of its own from the Great Watcher.

"Ah. I see."

"What do you see?"

"That's your home, isn't it?"

"It was, but it hasn't been for quite a while."

"I thought Elaeavn has been your home?"

"I have been away from the city itself for quite some time. My parents wanted me to lead, but that was never what I wanted."

"Leadership takes many forms. I never wanted to lead either, but Carth encouraged me to be more than I thought I could be."

Daniel continued to stare up at the palace. Had he remained, he would have been on track to assume his father's position on the Council. Strangely, with the training Carth had provided, he was better suited now than when he had been here.

"We can go to the forest," he said.

"Perhaps a better use of time would be for us to travel to your home."

"There's nothing for me there."

"Will they be angry if they learn that you visited but did not come to see them?" Rayen asked.

"They won't even know that I was here."

"But if they learn that you came?"

"Even if they learn that I came, it won't really matter to them."

Rayen studied him for a long moment before shaking her head. "No."

"No what?"

"I'm not going to let you leave without visiting them."

"I'm not going to go and visit with them." He crossed his arms over his chest, watching her. There was movement nearby, and he glanced to see whether another cat was making its way toward them, though he didn't see it. He must have seen something. What was it?

"Why be so stubborn about this?"

"Because it doesn't matter."

"Do you dislike them?"

Daniel pressed his mouth together, frowning. "I'm not certain how I feel about them. My father in particular. If he was involved in what happened to Lucy…"

"You won't know until you visit."

"And he'll be angry that I left. He wanted me to serve the Elvraeth."

"We can't always be what our parents want. My parents never wanted me to master the shadows."

Daniel frowned. "Why wouldn't they? I thought the ability was highly valued by your people."

"Do you know anything about my people?"

Daniel shook his head, realizing that he didn't.

"Carth came from a time when Ih-lash still was more than just a memory. Even she didn't live there for much of it. Her parents brought her away, saving her from the destruction. But the power of the shadows lived on."

"How?"

"At first, it lived on with people known as the Reshian. They were hunted, sacrificed in a way that I still don't fully understand, and because of that my family wanted to protect me, to keep me from using my magic out of fear that I might draw the wrong kind of attention."

"They were afraid of losing you?"

"More that they feared for themselves. They might have told themselves there was a different reason for it, but that was not the case. They were afraid, and because of their fear, they were willing to let others suffer."

"How would they let others suffer?"

"They let others suffer because they were unwilling to risk anything. They thought that by hiding, they could avoid losing themselves."

"The way you say it suggests that something else happened."

She nodded. Her gaze swung around her, taking in the city. Darkness clouded her features for a moment, and she looked over at Daniel, a hint of sadness still on her face. "My parents were lost because they never were willing to fight."

"How?"

"Does it matter how?"

"Was it the Ai'thol?"

"That would be easier, wouldn't it? It would explain my desire to fight them, but no. The Ai'thol weren't involved. There are other evils in the world, Daniel Elvraeth. It's not only the Ai'thol we need to fear."

"I've seen other evils in the world."

"Have you? One thing that you haven't done, as you have said, is travel extensively. Without seeing anything other than your own slice of the world, it is difficult to say that you truly understand the darkness that can exist. Unfortunately, you have begun to know that the world is a dark place, and in time, I suspect you will be exposed to much awfulness. For now, you can't claim you have seen the same evils."

She turned away from him, heading down the street, and Daniel raced after her, wanting to catch up and apologize. It seemed as if he needed to do so, that she was angered by something he'd said, but why? What would have bothered her so much?

When he reached her at the corner of the street, he grabbed for her arm, and she shook him off. "I don't need your reassurance."

"I wouldn't have said that you did."

She frowned at him and suddenly spun, streaking forward on a surge of shadows. When she stopped, a pair of men converged near her.

Daniel was frozen at first.

Could these be Ai'thol? There had been Forger attacks within the city before, but never quite like this. Always in the past they had been more coordinated, and when the attack had come, they had involved much greater danger than this. Two men didn't pose any real threat.

And then he saw their swords.

They unsheathed, moving rapidly, and Rayen practically smiled as she pulled out her own sword, twisting backward, slipping on shadows that swirled around her, though they didn't conceal her nearly as much as they once had.

Daniel grabbed for his own sword, preparing to Slide, when three men converged on him. Where had these come from?

"You've made a mistake," Daniel said.

"Have we?"

He Slid, emerging behind the nearest man, kicking outward. The man stumbled forward, and Daniel spun, swinging his sword around in a rapid arc, catching the other man on the arm. He smiled tightly, twisting and forcing Daniel to redirect. He Slid again, righting himself.

Had he not had the training he'd undergone over the last few months, working with Carth on a regular basis along with others who had significant fighting skills, he might have been outmatched. Not only were they skilled but they seemed able to anticipate where he Slid, tracking his movements.

It would be a simple matter for him to Slide to Rayen, grab her, and then Slide somewhere else, but doing so took away the opportunity for him to learn more about this attack.

He Slid, spinning around, bringing his sword in a sharp arc. He jabbed outward, hoping to catch one of the swordsmen in the chest, and just barely managed to do so.

The other men slipped backward, away from his blade, and Daniel Slid forward, swinging his sword around, spinning the blade as he prepared to attack again.

Something caught him from behind, and he staggered.

Sliding as he stumbled, he came out in a roll. When he did, he brought his blade around, pushing outward.

A sense of energy filled him, something unusual. He tried not to pay that any mind as he continued to spin with the sword, hacking at the man as he came toward him. What he needed was to stop these three.

And he didn't know how Rayen was managing.

Why stay on the ground?

He took a step, Sliding to the nearest rooftop, pausing for a moment to look down. Rayen seemed to be doing reasonably well, shadows spinning around her and wrapping around each of the other two men, but they were able to part the shadows much more efficiently than Daniel would've expected.

She didn't need his help, but she did need him to keep these three off her.

The men gathered themselves, taking the time that he gave them to adjust, and he Slid.

This time, he appeared in the midst of them. He jabbed, Sliding again, emerging once more on the rooftop, taking a moment to assess the situation before Sliding once more. Back and forth he went, pausing for the barest moment as he did, and adjusting his attack in those moments.

During one such Slide, he caught one of the men on the arm. He dropped his sword, and Daniel spun, slamming his sword into the man's chest. He Slid away, taking a moment to focus on the other two. They ignored their fallen partner, and he Slid down to them, attacking the nearest, hacking at his leg before Sliding back. He spun, Sliding to the other side, swinging toward the other man. With only two to focus on, he required less energy, and he was able to dart from place to place, using his connection to Sliding in order to do so.

One of the men came too close, and Daniel managed to jab his sword into his shoulder. The man switched arms, fighting just as well with his off hand.

What sort of fighters were these?

Daniel didn't have an opportunity to consider it for too long. He had to Slide back, getting away for a moment before darting forward once more. He caught one of the men on the leg, slicing along his thigh. It barely slowed the man.

He didn't want to have to kill them, but it appeared as if they weren't going to give up easily. If he didn't stop them altogether, they would cut him down, and it seemed as if they would move on to converging upon Rayen.

Twisting once more, he brought the blade around, catching one of the men on the shoulder. He grunted, staggering off to the side, and Daniel realized that it was the one he'd gotten in the leg.

A few more Slides, and both men had dropped their swords.

Daniel glanced at the fallen man before stepping toward them, holding his blade outward. "What is this about?"

Neither man answered.

"Why attack us?"

They weren't from Elaeavn. Even if their obvious skill with the sword didn't give that away, the lack of green to their eyes did. More than that, they wore drab-colored cloaks, and their hair was cut short, but there was no scarring as he would have expected for one of the Ai'thol.

Were they Ai'thol, he would've expected a different type of fighting.

Perhaps they represented the other sort of evil in the world that Rayen suggested existed.

A soft groan caught his attention, and he Slid to the other end of the street, watching as Rayen wrapped both of the men in shadows, dragging them down. He glanced over his shoulder, but the other two had disappeared.

"What do you think this was about?" he asked her.

She shook her head. "I don't know. Neelish sellswords shouldn't be here."

She crouched down next to one of the men, pulling away his sword and then grabbing a pair of knives from sheaths hidden beneath his cloak. She searched him, taking a coin purse off him and then continuing to look for other weapons. When she was satisfied that he had none, she moved on to the other man, removing three knives from him, along with a smaller coin purse.

"You're going to take their money?"

"They would have failed in their mission. They didn't earn it."

Daniel laughed softly. "Why are they here?"

"That's the question, isn't it?"

She got to her feet, her gaze arcing along the street toward the other fallen sellsword. "You killed him?"

"I was trying to stay alive."

"Carth will be quite disappointed."

"That I still live or that I didn't kill the other two?"

"That you killed one of the sellswords."

"Why?"

"That's a story you will have to ask Carth."

Rayen's gaze drifted toward the Floating Palace in the distance. She frowned as she stared. "I know that you don't wish to go home, but we need answers, and if there are sellswords in the city, we need to see what the ruling Council knows about them."

Daniel stared at the fallen sellswords for a moment before turning back to Rayen and finally nodding. "We can go, but I can't guarantee that they will know anything."

"Why not?"

"Because the Elvraeth who live in the palace don't generally take much of an interest in the rest of the city."

"Even though they lead?"

"Leadership takes many forms."

Rayen laughed darkly. "That it does. Come on, Daniel Elvraeth. Let's see just what your parents know about the workings of their city."

25

DANIEL

Daniel slid to the courtyard outside of the palace. There was a certain familiarity in coming here, though he had no interest in doing so. The grass that had once been here had long since died away. A few trees grew, though they were pruned so that they didn't grow too tall, and they remained hidden by the rest of the palace. If they were too large, they would disrupt the image the Elvraeth wanted to maintain, that of the palace floating. These days, the palace's appearance gave it a certain formidability in the eyes of those within the city.

"This is it?" Rayen asked, looking around.

"Were you expecting something more impressive?"

"The palace of the Elvraeth has something of a reputation," she said.

"I'm not sure how much of that reputation is earned and how much of it is manufactured."

"Indeed," she said. "There have long been rumors of powerful Elvraeth councilors, but from what I have witnessed myself, there aren't all that many, are there?"

"Not any longer." There was a time when he would have denied the accusation. "Are you ready?" he asked.

Daniel breathed out for a long moment, looking around as he prepared to Slide into the palace. As he attempted to Slide, he met with resistance and released Rayen's arm.

"What is it?" she asked.

Daniel looked up at the palace. He motioned to one of the nearest windows. Bars crisscrossed over top of it, blocking access. "Do you see the window there?"

"I do."

"These rooms were designed in a way that should protect against anyone like myself from accessing them."

"Heartstone."

"It is. It prevents me from Sliding past it."

"But it doesn't protect the castle from everybody."

Daniel shook his head. "I suspect Lucy would be able to Slide beyond it, much like Rsiran can."

"Are there others who have the same ability?"

Daniel shrugged. "Most who have any ability to Slide do so frequently and willingly, but there isn't really a way for them to Slide into the palace."

He headed toward the main doors, nodding to a pair of tchalit on either side. They were guards, the sort of guards who looked out for the safety of the Elvraeth family, and traditionally they had been the only ones who had been granted permission to carry swords within the city.

They stepped in front of him, blocking access.

"The palace is closed to visitors. You should return in the morning."

"I am Daniel Elvraeth. I am permitted entry into the palace."

He noticed a hint of hesitation in both of the men. He understood why they would hesitate. His name would be recognized, though they might not know whether he was actually allowed within the palace. For that matter, Daniel didn't know if he would be allowed entry. It had been so long since he'd been here that perhaps his parents had banished him.

"Daniel Elvraeth?"

Daniel nodded.

The two men stepped aside.

Rayen glanced over at him, a half smile on her face. He resisted the urge to say something to her, not wanting the kind of comments that he knew she would make. Instead, he strode forward, opening the door and stepping inside the palace.

It was strange being home, if that was what this was anymore. There was always a sense of pomp and formality about the palace, and it had been designed to elicit a specific response. Marble stretched from wall to wall, with massive pillars rising periodically along the hall. Portraits of the original Elvraeth founders hung along the walls, but mixed in with them were lorcith sculptures of such exquisite detail that he marveled at them, even from this distance. Many of them—probably most of them—had been made by Rsiran Lareth, surprising given his father and others' view of Lareth.

Then again, there was no denying his skill with metal. One of the sculptures represented one of the Elder Trees, and it stood on a pedestal at the far end of the hallway, catching a hint of moonlight that drifted into the window. There was something about that sculpture he could feel, almost as if it stored some residual power.

"My father sits on the Council, but he will be unlikely to share anything with me about the workings of the city." His mother might, but at this time of night, he would need to awaken her to get those answers, and he didn't really want to do that. It would be better to come back in the morning, and he considered simply doing that, but the body of the fallen Neelish sellsword suggested that he needed to do something else.

"Is there anyone else you know?"

"There is one other person who might be of use. Cael Elvraeth."

Rayen snorted. "We should have started there."

"You know her?"

"Carth regards very few people as highly as she views Galen. And because of that, his bride is known to her—and therefore to me."

"You could've told me that."

"I could have, but then we would have missed the opportunity to experience the thrill of battle."

"I'm not so sure that was much of a thrill."

"Not for the Neelish sellsword who thought to challenge us. You have to admit you enjoyed the challenge."

"I didn't really enjoy it, but…"

Rayen shrugged. "How else will you improve if you don't challenge yourself?"

"By training and sparring," he said.

"There is something to be said about a real fight. Sometimes you need to encounter something more, an opportunity to draw out the full ability. If not, then you never really understand your potential."

"You have an odd perspective on this."

"I have a realistic understanding of the need to continue to improve. There is nothing odd about it."

Their feet thudded on the marble as they made their way through the palace. When they reached the end of the hall, Daniel pointed toward the stairs, heading up. It would've been easier for him to Slide, and he thought that he might be able to do so within the palace, now that the heartstone wasn't trying to prevent him from accessing it, but there was a part of him—probably the Elvraeth part that he'd been raised to respect—which warned him off from trying to Slide through the palace itself.

When they reached the landing, he continued up. He knew where to find Cael Elvraeth, though he had never sought her out during his time in the palace.

"If Galen is here, maybe we can ask for his help," Daniel said.

"Galen had been retired for a long time."

"What was he like when he was still an assassin?"

"He was one of the most feared men in the world."

Daniel paused at the door leading into Cael Elvraeth's portion of the palace. Each of the ruling Council members had a section of the palace that was granted to them. Cael's was probably smaller than most, seeing as how she didn't have any extended family of her own. Her father was gone, and she had no relatives other than Galen. The two of them had never had children, though there had always been the murmurings that they should have.

Daniel took a deep breath before knocking. He stood for a moment before the door opened, less time than he would've expected.

Cael stood before him, wearing a lovely robe around her shoulders, her hair pulled up into a bun. A necklace hung around her throat, made of lorcith and with incredible skill. She tilted her head to the side, and Daniel felt a faint fluttering in the back of his mind.

She was Reading him.

She was a skilled Reader and rumored to be one of the most powerful. Having been around Lucy, he wondered how Cael compared. She Read him, quickly overcoming his barrier, and doing it so softly and subtly that he wouldn't have been aware of it had it not been for his experience with Lucy over the last few months.

"Daniel Elvraeth," she said, tipping her head in a nod. She turned her attention to Rayen, her mouth pressing into a tight line. "Rayen Shadow Born."

"Do I know you?" Rayen asked.

"She Read you," Daniel said softly.

"I suppose I should have prepared for that," Rayen said. She flashed a smile, opening her palms in front of her and shifting her body so that she looked at Cael. "Then you know why we're here."

"I know you've come looking for Rsiran, but unfortunately, I won't be of much help."

"Why not?"

"Because I don't know where they are holding him."

"Holding him?" Daniel and Rayen shared a look, and he turned his attention back to Cael. "Who's holding him?"

Cael frowned. "You don't know?" There came another soft fluttering in the back of his mind. It was gentle, though not so gentle as when Lucy was working within his mind. Could Lucy be even more powerful than Cael? Then again, Lucy had been augmented by the Forgers, using their knowledge over the Elder Stones to grant her increased abilities, so that shouldn't be terribly surprising. "You didn't know. You didn't come to ask where he is. You came to ask for his help. Oh, Daniel Elvraeth, I am sorry. Perhaps I shouldn't be the one to tell you that he's gone missing."

If Rsiran wasn't here, then he would need the next best person. "Where is Haern?"

"I don't know. Galen has been working with him, trying to train him, for what I presume is an opportunity to go after Rsiran if it presents itself, though he has been trying tactics outside of what most would approve of."

"Such as what?"

"Such as…" There came the same fluttering in the back of his mind once again, and Daniel braced himself, knowing there was nothing he could do to prevent her from reaching into his thoughts, grabbing anything she wanted. Cael didn't seem to have any hesitation about doing so, either. She overwhelmed any attempt he made at placing mental barriers; perhaps it was best if he didn't even try. They could communicate more effectively that way. She would know why he was here, what he needed, and then she could tell him what he needed.

"You attacked the sellswords."

"I would say we were attacked by the sellswords," Daniel said.

"That is unfortunate. They are here to guard the shores, to help ensure that the Forgers don't pose a threat."

"Do you believe the Forgers can be stopped by sellswords?" Rayen asked.

"They are the most capable swordsmen we know of." Cael turned to Rayen before glancing at Daniel. "At least, that we knew of. Perhaps we should have gone to Carth and her Binders before."

"And what do you know of the Binders?" Rayen asked.

"I have been with Galen for decades. I know what Galen knows."

Daniel wondered how Rayen might react, worried that she would be angry, but he needn't have been. Rayen surprised him by barking out a loud laugh, shaking her head. "Of course you would. And Galen is well known by the Binders. For a time, he was the only man who was granted access to them."

"For a time."

"Now we have others who have spent quite a bit of time around us, though they have a different purpose," Rayen said, glancing at Daniel before turning her attention back to Cael. "The sellswords won't be of much use when it comes to the Forgers."

"They are of more use than my citizens."

"There are plenty of your people who have abilities."

"They might have abilities, but they don't have experience using them. Not all of them have wanted to understand how to fight, Rayen Shadow Born."

"And yet, had they taken the time, most of them would have been more of a threat. The Forgers wouldn't have been nearly as terrifying if they had developed their resistance to them."

"We can debate the point of our defenses another time. For now, I think that I must escort you to the Aisl."

"Why to the Aisl?" Daniel asked.

"If you came looking for Rsiran, then I must help you find the one person who can provide some answers about what took place."

"Why can't you tell us what it was?"

"Because there is much for you to understand, and it's possible you might be able to help."

Daniel shared a glance with Rayen, before turning back to Cael. "What happened?"

"We will answer those questions and more when we reach the heart of the Aisl. I think you need to speak with Jessa."

Daniel swallowed, suddenly nervous. If Rsiran was missing, he could only imagine that he had been somehow taken by the Ai'thol, and if that were the case, and they hadn't heard about it, where would they have taken him?

They hurried from the top level of the palace, stepping outside, and once back out into the moonlight, beyond the guards, he looked around, waiting as Cael joined him. He grabbed her hand and Rayen's and Slid.

Reaching the heart of the Aisl forest was easy. As soon as he emerged, he breathed in familiar air. Something was different than the last time he'd been here. It was partly that the Forgers' poisoning had changed the energy coming off the Elder Trees, but there was something else.

It was late, but even at night there was still a vibrancy to the heart of the Aisl forest. Flames crackled along the perimeter of the clearing, blocked off so that the flames couldn't spread, and they cast their light outward into the night, smoke rising slowly and twisting up into the sky.

He looked over to see Rayen watching him, an intrigued expression upon her face.

"I don't know that Jessa will be all that excited about an interruption at this time of night," Daniel said.

Cael shook her head. "She hasn't been sleeping well the last few months."

"Months?"

How could it have been months that Rsiran had been missing? Had Carth and Lucy known? Perhaps that was what Lucy had been doing all this time—trying to find some way of helping Lareth.

They made their way across the clearing, reaching the base of one of the Elder Trees. Daniel Slid up into the tree with the others, and from there, he paused in front of Jessa's door. He'd only been here once before, but there was something about Jessa Lareth that intimidated him.

"Go ahead," Cael said.

"I..."

The door to the home opened. On this level, the home was built into the tree, onto a platform that had been fixed in place, the Elder Tree massive and allowing multiple homes to be built along its branches. Pathways were worked between the branches, the intertwining bows allowing the people to make their way from place to place, unencumbered by restrictions that would otherwise have been found within the trees.

Jessa stood before him. She looked weary, her deep green eyes heavy, her graying hair swept back into a braid. Much like Cael, she wore a long robe that hung on her shoulders, covering them, and when she saw him, she frowned. "Daniel Elvraeth." Her gaze flicked to Rayen and then Cael.

"Jessa Lareth. I—"

"Come in. We can talk once you're inside."

Daniel stepped inside, joining Rayen and followed by Cael. When she was inside, they closed the door. A hearth crackled, the strange magic of how the Elder Tree allowed fire to burn, giving a certain warmth to this place. He took a seat on a comfortable chair, perched in front of the fireplace, watching the flames.

"You came because you heard about Rsiran," Jessa said, standing near the fire, mixing a pot that smelled like spiced tea.

"Actually, we didn't," Daniel said.

"You didn't?" Jessa turned to him, watching him for a moment before glancing to Cael. "If they didn't come because they knew he was missing, then why are they here?"

"Perhaps you could ask them."

"I am asking you."

"Do not be angry that my husband has been working with your son."

"I'm not angry that your husband has been working with my son. I'm angry that it's necessary."

"And do not blame me for the necessity of it," Cael said.

"I don't, I just..." Jessa breathed out heavily, turning her attention to Daniel. "As you have learned, Rsiran is missing."

"That's what I've heard."

"I had thought..." She shook her head. "Perhaps it doesn't matter what I thought. I'm sorry, Daniel Elvraeth. Rsiran is not available, and neither is Haern."

"Where is Haern?"

Jessa glanced at Cael. "You didn't tell him?"

"I didn't need to tell him. Your son will return."

"My son has been gone for the last three days, and typically his training sessions are much briefer than that."

"He is with Galen."

"Galen can't promise he's safe."

"Galen never promised that no harm would come at all. He only vowed he would train your son. He intends to ensure he has every opportunity to survive, though your son needs to listen."

"Your husband seems to have been quite excited to have been training my son."

Cael took a deep breath. "I can't deny that something has been different for Galen. And it's not so much that Galen is excited about it. It's more about a sense of purpose. Within the city, he has been allowing me to fulfill my purpose, and in doing so, he has neglected something that would have fulfilled him. I have tried to encourage him to find other ways of reaching fulfillment, but he is a difficult man."

Rayen grunted, nodding. "I have heard that he is. The two of you argue as if you're old rivals when in fact you're allies. There is much good that has come from Galen returning to this world. Carthenne has finally found purpose again."

"Carthenne has always had purpose," Jessa said.

"She has purpose, but she has lacked a partner."

"And Galen is her partner?" Jessa asked, looking to Cael.

Cael smiled sadly. "There are aspects of his life I have learned to deal with. Unfortunately, not all of them please me, primarily the fact that he and Carthenne share a bond that he and I don't. I have come to grips with it, much like you need to come to grips with the fact that your husband has a purpose in what he does."

"I haven't come to terms with that."

Daniel stepped forward, getting between the two women once again. "Will one of you tell me what happened with Rsiran?"

Jessa took a deep breath, bracing herself and turning toward the hearth. "Have a seat, Daniel."

"I think I'll stand."

Jessa glanced over her shoulder, arching a brow at him. "Take a seat."

Daniel took a seat, and Rayen sat next to him, glancing over and grinning.

Jessa turned her attention to the fire, not looking over at him. "I understand that Haern and Rsiran found you in Nyaesh," she said.

"They did."

"And I understand that you were fighting with Carthenne."

"We were."

"After they returned here, there was an attack."

"What sort of attack?"

"The sort that they weren't prepared for." She turned back to them, taking the teapot off the coals and pouring a cup before handing it over to him. When she was done, she offered one to Rayen, who shook her head. Cael took the offered cup, inhaling deeply.

"What happened?" Daniel asked.

"We had captured one of the Forgers," Jessa said. "And by we, I suppose I mean my husband and son. They were interrogating him, looking for answers, trying to uncover anything they could that would help them learn just what the Forgers might be doing. They had been pressuring our borders, and there was some reason behind it, though we didn't know what."

"Did you figure out what it was?"

"No. They decided upon a different tactic, thinking perhaps they could use him."

"How did they intend to use him?"

"They thought to release him, wanting to see where he might go. Unfortunately, he managed to get away from them."

"How?"

"I don't really know. Galen was involved," Jessa said, glancing over at Cael. "Along with Haern and Rsiran. There was an attack, and from what Haern tells me, my husband was stabbed, and then he was taken."

"Where did they take him?"

"I can only imagine they took him to wherever the headquarters of the Forgers are."

"The Ai'thol," Rayen said. When Jessa looked at her, she shrugged. "You keep calling them Forgers, but that is a misnomer. They are the Ai'thol. The Forgers are but one arm of many. Much like the Hjan were an arm of the

Ai'thol. All of them are your enemy, and all of them are dangerous."

"Fine. The Ai'thol," Jessa said, seeming to struggle with saying the word. "Either way, Rsiran is now missing. He was taken, and we don't know where he's gone."

"And Haern has been looking?"

"Haern has been training. He's determined to uncover what happened to Rsiran, even if it means taking on the Forgers—the Ai'thol—himself."

"He won't be able to stop them," Rayen said.

"Probably not, but Galen has been working with him as well, and the two of them—"

"The two of them would still not be enough," Rayen said.

"Where is Haern now?" Daniel asked.

"He has been away for a while. I don't know when he'll return."

Daniel glanced over at Rayen. With Rsiran missing, and Haern not here, who would they go to with their questions about the metal?

26

HAERN

HAERN WASN'T NEARLY AS TIRED AS HE HAD BEEN, BUT THE effort of walking over the last day had taken something out of him. There was something to be said about traveling using his abilities rather than on foot, and as he headed away from the girls and Elise, he dropped a coin, *pushing* off on it. He sailed through the air, *pushing* on one after another, summoning the coins back to himself before moving onward. He feared leaving the coins behind, knowing that if he were to do so, he would quickly run out of them. He had only so many to use, and already he worried he would run out of them before this was all done.

He traveled overhead, making his way toward the movement he had seen. It came from the north, the direction they had been traveling, and thankfully, Elise and the others were guiding themselves somewhat to the west. It would prevent them from colliding directly with whoever these oncomers were, and it would give Haern a chance to investigate without whoever he might encounter realizing where he'd been.

Jump after jump carried him, leaving him flying as Elise had said.

There was a certain freedom in traveling like this. And it was one that he found himself relishing, to the point where he thought he enjoyed this even more than he would Sliding. His father would have known this technique, but with his other abilities, he had no reason to travel in such a way.

Night had fallen in full by the time he started to get close to the movement he had seen. He approached carefully, slowing, but staying in the air, determined to reach these oncomers as quickly as he could. As he went, he paused, taking stock of how many there were and their position.

Nearly a dozen, all of them men, and all mounted.

That meant soldiers, but soldiers from where?

He looked for any other signs of danger but didn't come across any. There didn't seem to be anything else that implied these men were like Rally, and they were moving steadily, keeping the horses going across the land in a direction that would eventually have ended with them meeting up with where Haern had been guiding the girls.

From the looks of it, it had to be coincidental. It didn't seem as if they posed any sort of danger, though it was possible that he was reading this wrong.

He continued to watch, remaining in the air, concerned that they might change directions at any moment, but even more concerned that they might identify him up in the air. They shouldn't, but all it would take would be for one of them to glance up.

He watched for a while, tracking their movements, and when it became clear that they were nothing more than common soldiers, he observed for a while longer. Holding himself in the air taxed him, but he thought it necessary in order to know if there was anything to worry about. He didn't recognize the markings on their helms, but there were enough men that he'd have to be concerned were they to head toward the women.

They veered off, turning away from where the women would have traveled. Haern followed to make sure they didn't change direction again, and when he was content that they didn't, he turned back.

Once he reached the women, they could rest for the night. He could keep watch, and they could rest without fearing that something might happen to them.

As he traveled, he saw no sign of the women.

Had he miscalculated?

He didn't think so. He was certain he knew which direction they had been traveling, and yet he wasn't able to find them.

Haern backtracked, making his way once again in the direction he had traveled. He found footsteps, but nothing else to identify where the girls had gone.

Maybe it was a mistake not to have left something of lorcith with Elise. If he had, he would've had the opportunity to track her down. There weren't many places they could conceal themselves. Out here in the night, there was nothing but the darkness, and it would be difficult for them to hide from his Sight.

He continued to search, pushing himself higher and higher into the sky, challenging himself. He'd never gone quite this high before. In the distance, he caught sight of something unexpected.

It wasn't the women he was searching for—at least not yet. Instead, the twinkling lights of a distant city caught his attention. The city was large and sprawling, easily large enough to be the kind of place where he could find help. It was probably the same place the soldiers had been heading. Now all he had to do was find the women and get them to safety.

From there, he would return to Elaeavn, likely having to answer Galen's questions—if Galen had survived.

He pushed those thoughts out of his head.

Now that he'd found the city, he didn't want to disappear in a different direction and lose sight of it. He might not be able to find it again.

When he had nearly given up hope, he finally saw them not that far from him. With his enhanced Sight, he should have Seen them before now, but somehow he had not.

As he started to make his way down, he realized they weren't alone.

Haern unsheathed his sword as he dropped to the ground, preparing to fight. He didn't want to have to, but he didn't want these girls to be attacked again. They'd already been through so much, and he had committed to keeping them safe. Had he made a mistake going after the movement he thought he'd seen?

When he landed, he gave himself a little distance before approaching. Elise stood off at the front of the line of girls, and there were three figures arranged in front of her, all of them dressed in dark robes.

This, at least, was something Haern recognized.

Forgers.

At least he understood how they could suddenly appear. They would have Slid, though why?

There was nothing around them, not even a road, so there shouldn't be any reason for the Forgers to have come—unless they had somehow followed him.

That wasn't likely. If they had followed him, there would've been signs of them before. With their ability to Slide, they would have tracked him down long before now. At least they hadn't managed to find them while he was essentially unconscious from his exhaustion, but had they waited for his absence to attack?

It could be he was giving them too much credit.

At the sight of the Forgers, every thought he had, every ounce of hatred he felt toward them, came flooding back to him.

Without knowing whether Galen lived or died, Haern resented them.

They were responsible for what had happened to someone he cared about. They were responsible for capturing his father, abducting him, and possibly killing him. And they were responsible for every bad thing that had ever happened in his homeland.

Haern suppressed those thoughts. It did no good for him to feel this way. All it served was to satisfy his sense of vengeance. It did nothing to ensure the safety of these girls he'd promised to protect. And Haern was determined to do so.

Clearing his mind, he forced himself to think in a practical sense. First off, he had to figure out why they had appeared in the middle of nowhere. If it was only about lorcith, they should have found him first. He was the only one to have it on him. There was no reason they should have discovered these girls—unless they had come after the sense of lorcith Haern had been using. That would explain the possibility of finding them, but none of the girls would've had lorcith with them.

Only… they did.

He hadn't been focusing on it, though he should have. There was a sense of lorcith nearby, and surprisingly, he hadn't noticed it before.

It wasn't Elise.

One of the younger girls, a dark-haired girl with frail features by the name of Catherine, had one of his coins. He could feel it on her.

Had he known that, he might have been able to use it to track them.

As he approached, he could overhear Elise talking.

"We're just trying to get to safety."

"You're out late. As you are probably aware, it can be dangerous on the road for young women like yourselves."

"We are aware. We are lucky to have gotten away, and were it not for help, we would have been…" She glanced over her shoulder, her gaze sweeping over the other girls before somehow making Haern out in the darkness. When she did, her eyes widened slightly.

"They don't need your escort," Haern said, stepping forward. He was outnumbered. If the Forgers had any control over lorcith, any advantage he had would be removed, which meant he needed to focus on a different way. He doubted he'd be able to talk his way free, which meant he was likely going to have to fight. These girls deserved his willingness to fight.

"You have an escort from Elaeavn?" one of the Forgers asked.

He said it with such derision that Haern tensed. He gripped his sword, holding on to it and focusing on the lorcith within it. He might not have much of an opportunity if it came down to fighting.

"I have offered them my protection. If you think to challenge that, then you may be my guest." He stepped forward, holding his sword at the ready.

The nearest Forger grinned. "One of Elaeavn who is armed. An exile."

Haern kept a straight face. Maybe they didn't know that Elaeavn no longer exiled their people, or maybe they did know and they were saying it for the girls' benefit. Either way, he wasn't about to give them the satisfaction of any sort of reaction. It was easier and better for him to ignore them.

"Armed and who knows how to use the weapon," Haern said. "If you'd like to find out, be my guest, but trust me when I tell you that you won't be pleased by what you find."

The Forger standing in the lead glanced at the others with him. "There is one of you, and yet there are three of us. There's only one man we know who would dare such foolish odds."

At least they acknowledged his father. Maybe he could convince them to reveal whether they knew anything about him, including if his father still lived. Could a chance encounter provide him with information he'd been seeking?

It seemed almost too much to hope for, and yet hope was all he had at this point.

"What if I am that man?"

"You aren't him. We have enough experience to recognize him." The Forger glanced at the girls before turning his gaze back on Haern. "Besides, this one doesn't take slaves."

"Neither do I."

"Then you've taken playthings." He glanced at the girls before leering at Elise a long moment. "I can't say that I blame you. This one at least has something appealing about her, but the rest are far too young. We will buy them from you."

Haern couldn't believe what he was hearing, and the soft murmuring behind him from the girls told him they didn't believe it either. More likely than not, they feared that he would agree to sell them. They had seen him protect them and probably knew that he had fought the hounds, but would they trust him?

After everything they had been through, trust would be difficult for them.

It was still possible he would be able to obtain information from the Forgers, and more than anything, that was what he wanted. He wanted—no, he *needed*—to know more about what the Forgers had done with his father. If he could uncover that piece of information, then he might finally be able to make the next move.

In order to find his father, he needed to find the man responsible for what had happened.

"They're not for sale."

The sigh of relief behind him told him everything he needed to know. He hated that he had even given them a moment of questioning, that they had to worry about the possibility of him offering to sell them to these Forgers. They deserved better than that.

"Everything has a price. And even if they don't, do you really think that you can withstand us?"

"It's up to you if you want to test me. You already said you fear one of my kind. Maybe I'll give you reason to fear another."

"I doubt that."

Without his Sight, Haern wasn't sure if he would have noticed what happened next.

The Forger began to shimmer and motioned to one of the other Forgers, just enough that Haern realized he was the one to fear.

He *pushed* on the knife hidden in his pocket, sending it streaking away from him, straight into the Forger before he had a chance to Slide.

It was the only surprise he would have over them. He spun, sending the sword out with a *push*. The lead Forger reacted, Sliding and disappearing for a moment.

Haern didn't give them the opportunity to react again. He *pushed*, sending the knife away from him, using that to target the remaining Forger. There were two left, and all he needed to do was remove the threat of one of them, and the odds would be more in his favor.

He *pushed* on the knife, managing to catch the other

Forger, striking him in the chest. Two Forgers were down.

That left only the lead Forger.

Where was he?

Haern spun around, *pulling* the knife back to him, readying for the next attack.

The last Forger was near Elise.

The man grinned at Haern. "Impressive. You will pay for their lives, but first, I think she will pay for their lives."

The Forger began to move his sword.

Haern *pushed* on his knife, trying to catch the Forger but not sure if he'd be fast enough. At the last moment, another thought came to him, and he *pulled* on the coin he still felt in Catherine's pocket. The knife streaked toward the Forger while the coin did the same.

The Forger avoided the knife, Sliding back a step, his sword coming up and puncturing Elise's stomach. Blood bloomed around her dress, and Haern cried out. The coin struck the Forger in the temple. He continued to *push,* sending the coin *through* the Forger with as much strength as he could manage.

The Forger dropped his sword, but the damage was done. Elise was injured, her belly punctured by his sword, and she grabbed for it, wrapping her hands around her stomach, sinking to the ground.

The Forger Slid, disappearing.

Haern raced toward Elise. She moaned as he lifted her. "I'm so sorry, Elise."

"No… you gave us a chance."

He moved her clothing to the side so that he could evaluate the injury. He had no real knowledge of healing, nothing like he needed, but he wasn't about to stand by and do nothing.

He searched for signs of the Forgers coming back, but there was no one there.

The sword had gone through her belly, piercing her back. It was deep enough that he doubted it would be survivable without Healing, and he had no way of getting her to the kind of Healer he thought might provide an opportunity for her.

Haern scooped her from the ground, looking at some of the older girls. "I need to get her to safety. There's a city not far from here. If I walk with her, there's a good chance that she won't survive."

"Leave me," Elise moaned.

Haern shook his head. "I'm not going to leave you here. You deserve more than that."

"They deserve a chance to survive. Without you…"

"Without *you*, they wouldn't have the opportunity to survive," Haern said.

"They need you. Get them to safety."

Haern wanted to scream. Instead, he turned his attention to the oldest of the girls. They couldn't be more than fourteen or fifteen, still young, but old enough that they would have to find a way to take charge. "I'm going to take her to the city and find her a healer. I'll return for all of you, but in the meantime, here." He held out the sword, along with his two knives, waiting for the girls to take them.

"I don't know how to use it," the nearest girl said.

Haern shook his head. "Most of the time, it's not about

knowing how to use it, it's about intimidating those who think to attack."

"What happens if they return?" another asked. This was Joanna, a flaxen-haired girl no older than fourteen, and yet she managed to have strength in the question and didn't ask with as much fear as he would've expected.

"You run. Move as quickly as possible. Follow the direction of the moon," he said, pointing to the sky. "It will take you toward the city. I won't be long."

"Go on," Joanna said.

Haern let out a relieved sigh. Joanna and the other girl turned to the rest, shepherding them together. He was thankful they seemed to be taking charge. After what they'd been through, it wasn't a guarantee that they would be strong enough to resist, and the fact that they showed such fortitude impressed him.

Dropping a coin, he *pushed* off.

With the urgency he felt, Haern was moving more rapidly than he ever had before, flying through the air, feeling it whip past him, unmindful of anything that might be below. Every so often, he glanced down, afraid that perhaps there might be Forgers returning, but there was no sign of them.

In the distance, the lights drew him.

As he neared, Haern began to slow. He was tempted to come flying into the city, but if he did that, it would raise the wrong sort of questions, and possibly draw attention in a way that would pose dangers to the people he was trying to protect.

Where was he going to find a healer?

Depending on the city, it might be more difficult, but

he could start at a tavern, look for evidence of a Binder, and hopefully they would have someone who could help.

Reaching the edge of the city, he decided against dropping back down to the ground. There was no point in it. He was already out of sight, and this way he could find his way toward someplace where he could get her help.

Elise had stopped moving, stopped making any sound. That was a problem. How long would it be before she was gone?

Elise deserved more.

He raced forward, continuing to *push* and *pull* on the coins. The sound of music caught his attention. Music usually indicated a tavern, and though he hadn't had all that much experience in taverns, certainly not as much as his uncle Brusus, he knew enough to recognize that would be the most likely place for him to find the help he needed.

Dropping to the ground, he raced toward the door, still holding on to Elise.

Inside the tavern, he paused. The sound of music drifted to his ears, loud and boisterous. Haern looked for signs of the Binders.

There was only a single man making his way around the tavern.

A singer at the back of the room glanced in his direction. She had dark eyes and dark hair, and her warbly voice pierced the din of the tavern, drifting to his ears.

She was singing of sorrow and sadness, and as he listened, he wondered just what she had experienced. Whatever it was sounded as if it were a torment.

As he looked around, he realized that he wasn't going

to find anyone who would be of any use to him. There was no one here who looked as if they were with the Binders.

All along, that had been his plan. Find the Binders, find help, and then use the Binders to ensure that the girls were safe. If he couldn't even do that, then he didn't know if he would be able to provide any safety for them.

Elise moaned, the most movement she'd made since he had brought her here. He carried her from the tavern, deciding that if nothing else, he would find a traditional healer.

Racing along streets, he practically collided with someone.

It took him a moment to realize that it was the singer from the tavern. A thick cloak covered her shoulders, and a dark ribbon wound through her hair, holding it back. She was shorter than he had thought when he had seen her in the tavern.

"You," he said.

"What happened to her?"

"We were attacked. I was hoping to find help back there, but..."

"Why back there?"

Haern hesitated before answering. He glanced over his shoulder toward the tavern before turning his attention back to the singer. There was no point in revealing too much to her, was there? If he did, he would only end up with more questions, and he wasn't sure they were questions he had any answers to.

"It doesn't matter," he said.

"It does matter. Why were you there?"

"Friends of mine once told me that if I needed help, I could find it in a tavern."

"What sort of friends?"

"Friends."

The woman stared at him for a long moment before starting to smile. "If you tell me what sort of friends you refer to, it's possible I might be able to help. I don't want your friend to die any more than I suppose you do."

Haern debated whether or not to say anything. It was possible she might be able to help. Maybe the singer knew where to find a healer within the city. "Can you show me where I could take her?"

"Only if you tell me what your intention is."

"My intention is to see her saved. I need to do it quickly."

"Why?"

"Because there are others who need my help, and the longer I'm away, the more likely it is that something will happen to them." He debated how much to say, but this *was* the reason he'd come. "Does the term Binders mean anything to you?"

The singer stared at him for a long moment before taking a deep breath and shaking her head. "Come with me."

"Where you going to take me?"

"You came looking for the Binders, didn't you?"

27

HAERN

The singer led Haern through the streets at a rapid pace. Haern was thankful that she was moving so quickly. Each moment they delayed seemed to be a moment that Elise didn't have.

"What happened to her?" the singer asked.

"We were attacked."

She shot him a look. "I can see that. Who attacked you?"

Should he be honest with her? He didn't know if she sided with the Forgers. There were certainly plenty of people who allied themselves with them, fearing that if they didn't, they would suffer, but at the same time, if she was with the Binders, it was unlikely she was with the Forgers. Carth certainly wasn't.

"We came across Forgers."

She stared at him for a moment before nodding. "Hurry," she said.

They reached the end of what appeared to be an alley, and the singer knocked twice on the door before it came open. Once it did, she hurried inside. There were others inside the room, five in all, and all of them women.

"Is this—"

"This is the Binders in Dreshen."

At least he had the name of the city. If only he knew enough about the geography to know where it was in relation to Elaeavn.

"Who is this, Mindy?"

Mindy—the singer—glanced over to Haern. "He came into the Spotted Cow, looking for us."

"How does he know?"

Mindy shrugged. "I don't know, but it seems as if he has some experience with the Binders farther to the north."

One of the women jumped to her feet, hurrying toward him, glancing down at Elise. "How do you know about the Binders?"

"I've spent time with Carth and Rayen."

In this case, honesty seemed to be the right strategy, and he worried that if he didn't tell them the truth, they wouldn't offer help to Elise. As it was, he feared that the longer he was here, the more the others with him would suffer.

"Carth is dead," one of the other women said.

"Quiet," the first Binder said.

"She's not dead. I saw her."

"You saw her?" She stepped forward, getting into his face. She was thin, and her nearly black eyes glared at him. "Where?"

"It was in Asador. We were trying to..."

"Trying to what?"

"Trying to save someone."

"It's possible she would be in Asador," one of the others said.

"She's dead," the dark-haired Binder said again.

"Maybe she wanted us to believe she was dead."

"I have the sense that she was trying to conceal herself," Haern said.

"Why?" Mindy asked.

"I don't know. I think she's trying to find information, but…"

They hadn't offered to help Elise yet, and that troubled him. If they were Binders, wouldn't they want to offer their help as quickly as they could? They had to know that Elise needed their aid, but they hadn't even bothered reaching for her.

Maybe this had been a mistake.

"Is there anyone here who can help, or do I need to keep looking?"

"We can help," Mindy said. She met the lead Binder's eyes and nodded. "Take her to the back room, and we will be with her shortly."

Haern glanced behind the grouping of Binders and headed through the doorway. Once there, he found a bed and set Elise down on top of it. When he was done, he stood, looking around. The room was sparsely decorated, with nothing but a washbasin and a wardrobe for decorations. A staircase at the back of the room led up, and he again began to wonder if perhaps he had made a mistake. Maybe these weren't the Binders.

He should be more careful. Anything he said or did

ran the risk of revealing Carth to those who might want to do her harm.

One of the Binders entered. She had pale skin, deep brown hair, and eyes that sparkled with a vibrant green.

His breath caught.

"You're from Elaeavn," he said.

The woman cocked her head to the side, staring at him for a moment. "And why would you say that?"

"Your eyes."

"You don't think that anyone else can have green eyes?"

"It's not that, it's just..."

The woman ignored him and came to stand next to Elise, touching her forehead. Her eyes darkened for a moment.

She might deny that she was from Elaeavn, but the nature of her power had to be similar.

Not only that, but could she be a Healer the same as Della and Darren? If she was, then he might have found someone who could be of help to Elise, and he could begin to relax.

"I imagine they asked you what happened," the woman said.

"They did. She was attacked by one of the Forgers."

"Forgers?"

"Yes."

"What's a Forger?"

Haern frowned. How was it possible that they wouldn't know what a Forger was?

"Dark robes. They use implants to augment their abilities. Seem as if they want to rule."

She nodded to herself. "We call them the Ai'thol."

"We always called them the Forgers, but I think they're the same."

"Perhaps they are, then." The woman pressed her hands on either side of Elise's belly. She closed her eyes and pressed her hands together, squeezing them, and Elise began to moan. As she worked, Haern could make out the way the skin stitched back together, reforming much the same way as it did when Darren performed a Healing.

There was no doubt in his mind that it was the same.

"How did you get your ability?"

"Why?"

"I just wondered. It's an impressive ability."

"Some of us can Heal. Others have different talents."

Haern stared at Elise for a moment. "Can she stay here?"

"Now that we've healed her, we're not forcing her to leave."

"There are others I need to help."

"What others?"

"I left them behind to save her."

"How far away?"

"Not far. Can I bring them here?"

The woman glanced to the door behind her. "You will have to ask the others. That is not my area."

Haern patted Elise's hand before heading through the doorway and standing for a moment. Three of the Binders remained, though none of them were Mindy. He wanted to thank her for bringing him here but wondered if perhaps she had to get back to whatever it was she had been doing, her Binder role.

"Can I bring the others here?" he asked.

"How many others?" one of the women asked without looking up. She was sitting at a table, writing on a sheet of parchment, a lantern glowing next to her.

"Eight or so."

"There are eight more like that one?"

"They aren't like her. They aren't near death. They're starving, but..."

"You may bring them," one of the other women said.

Haern glanced over to her, noting her dark hair that reminded him of the healer, but she didn't have green eyes or any other features that would otherwise suggest she was similar. "Thank you."

None of them answered.

He stepped out into the street. The night was cool, and the wind caught his cloak, sending it fluttering. He *pushed* on a coin, dropping it to the ground and then hovering in the air as he tried to get his bearings. He'd traveled quite a bit through the city, and now he wasn't entirely sure which direction he had come through.

Could he use lorcith?

Since reaching the city, he hadn't tried to use a connection to the metal. There hadn't been a reason, but more than that, he been so focused on helping Elise that he hadn't even thought about it.

As he strained, searching for evidence of lorcith, he felt it in a surprising quantity.

It was all around him.

How could there be so much of the metal here?

It would make it difficult for him to determine where the other girls were, and he decided to push away those thoughts, focusing instead on getting out of the city.

He traveled in the direction he thought he'd come.

Elise was alive. That was as much as he could hope for at this point, and hopefully he could keep her that way.

He traveled until he found the girls. They were moving quickly, jogging for the most part. When he landed in front of them, Joanna held her sword up before seeing that it was him. She tried to hand it to him, but he shook his head.

"Keep it."

"Won't you need it?"

"Maybe, but I have other ways that I can fight. You keep it and defend yourself."

"Did you find her help?" Catherine asked.

Haern turned to her, meeting her youthful gaze. "I think so."

"Think?" one of the other girls asked.

"You remember the women I said I was going to try to find?" Several of the girls nodded. "I think I found them. They had one with them who had the ability to Heal."

"She's going to live?"

Haern looked toward the city. "She was alive when I left."

"Why did you leave, then?"

"I didn't want to leave you out here for too long."

"How far do we have to go?" one of the younger girls asked.

"It's not far."

He stayed with them as they continued, though they didn't run as quickly as they had been now that Haern was back with them. When the city came into view, they hurried their steps. At the edge of the city, Haern motioned for them to slow.

"We have to go quite a ways in the city, but I think now that we're here, you will be safe."

"What about you?" one of the others said.

"I'll also be safe," Haern said, smiling. "I need to return to my home. My job isn't done. I'm trying to find someone important to me."

"Were they taken by these Forgers?" Catherine asked.

Haern nodded. "Unfortunately, he was. We did everything we could to try to protect him, but it wasn't enough. And the Forgers are powerful."

He guided them through the streets, weaving toward the distant location where he had left Elise. As he went, he had a sense that he was followed.

Every so often, Haern would pause, looking behind him, but he saw no evidence of anyone behind him. Maybe it was nothing more than his imagination, but he didn't think so.

Rather than heading directly toward Elise, he decided to take a different path and began to wind away from where he had been heading. Every so often, he would look behind him, searching for evidence that someone was following, but never came across anything.

"What is it?" Joanna asked as they traveled.

"Just a feeling," he said.

"Why do I get the sense that we aren't going to like that feeling?"

"We're fine," he said.

"What happened?"

"I think we're being followed."

"By who?"

"I don't know."

"Do you think it's the Forgers?"

He didn't answer, partly because he wasn't sure how to answer. It was possible the Forgers had managed to find him, but how would they have done so?

"Haern?"

"It's fine."

"What if they *are* following us?"

They paused near a series of tall buildings, and Haern looked up. He was tempted to *push* upward, to see if he could glimpse anything from overhead, but doing so would leave the girls in danger.

Instead, he continued to navigate them through the streets.

There had to be another option.

What they needed to do was find someplace they could go that would conceal them, but where would that be?

Not only conceal them, but they needed to go someplace they could get help if needed.

First, he needed to know if he was actually being followed. If it was nothing more than his imagination, then traveling away from Elise only took them farther from where they needed to be, but at least he felt as if he were proactive. He didn't want to be the reason that something happened to them.

They reached a square. Buildings framed it on all sides, and long grass grew within it. He motioned for them to follow him, and they headed to the center of the square, standing there for a moment, looking around. It gave Haern a chance to determine whether they were being followed or not. Out in the open like this, it would be hard to follow someone without being spotted.

There was nothing. No sign of anyone who might be following, no evidence of danger. So why didn't he feel any safer than they had been?

"Haern?"

He raised a finger to his lips, silencing the girls.

Dropping a coin, he *pushed* off, hovering in the air. He remained like that for long moments, looking around, and waited, afraid he would find someone watching from the shadows.

He was being paranoid, he knew it, but with so many depending upon him, he didn't know that he had any choice.

As he began to lower himself, a flicker of movement caught his attention.

Had he not been so on edge, he wasn't sure he would've even noticed, but in this case, he was tense, afraid he had overlooked something.

The sense of movement occurred again, and Haern shifted his attention, looking to see where it had come from. It was down one of the alleys, and as he stared, hoping for his enhanced eyesight to help him, he Saw another flicker of movement.

Forgers.

He was sure of it.

Did that mean that the Forgers were moving openly in the city?

When he had been here before, he hadn't seen any

evidence of it, but then again, he had been so focused on Elise that maybe he had overlooked it.

Dropping to the ground, he *pulled* his coin to him and looked at the girls. They needed him to protect them, but how was he going to do that?

Perhaps he needed to trust the Binders, use them and whatever help they could offer, but for some reason, he feared that he had made a mistake in coming here.

Without any other allies, he didn't have any choice.

He motioned for them to follow him as they headed toward the alley. He made a point of guiding them away from where he'd seen the Forger, and as he did, he watched for evidence of the flickering, the telltale sign of the Sliding the Forgers used.

There was none.

A part of him considered trying to claim his sword again, but he decided against that. Instead, he would use the coins. They would work as an adequate weapon, and he focused on them, ready to *push* upon them, but there was no sign of the Forgers as he went.

Twisting through the streets, he found his way toward the place where he'd left Elise.

"She's here?" one of the other girls asked.

"She's here," Haern said, pausing in front of the door. Something felt off.

He spun, looking for signs of the Forgers, but there were none.

It was just his imagination. He had to put away those thoughts, be ready to move on, and once he did, then he could help these girls.

He knocked, but no one answered. Haern opened the

door, looking inside, but there was no sign of the Binders. He motioned for the girls to follow, and they joined him inside the home but found it empty.

Where was Elise?

"Where is she?" Joanna asked.

"I don't know. She was here, and there were several others."

The bedding had been changed, and there was no evidence of blood, making it look as if no one had been here.

Were they trying to make it seem as if he had been imagining it?

Where had they taken Elise?

He had been gone long enough that he wondered if perhaps they had been attacked. Maybe they had felt the need to move her for their own safety and for hers, but to where?

Movement near the door caught his attention, and Haern turned to it.

Not just movement. Sliding.

"Behind me!" he shouted.

Several of the girls started whimpering, and he tried to position himself so that they would be safe. He *pushed* on coins, sending them at the suddenly appearing Forgers.

They flickered in and out of existence, more rapidly than he could follow.

He turned and realized what was happening.

They were grabbing the girls.

Haern swore under his breath. Where were they taking them?

Probably the same place they had taken the Binders—and Elise.

One of the Forgers shimmered too slowly, and Haern *pushed* on a coin, sending it slamming into the man's shoulder. The Forger spun, and Haern dove, grabbing for him, keeping him from taking one of the girls—Catherine, he realized.

Slamming the Forger to the floor, Haern punched, driving his fist into the man's face. He twitched before falling still.

Jumping to his feet, Haern spun around, readying another pair of coins, but it was too late. The room was empty other than him.

The Forgers had taken all of the girls.

He grabbed the fallen Forger, lifting him, and dragged him to the back of the room. Once there, he turned his attention to the stairs again and carried the man with him, climbing the stairs quickly before pausing. It was an unfinished space, and there was another door.

Haern took the man there, dragging him, half expecting another Forger to appear, but there were none.

Once on the rooftop, he looked around. At least here, he wouldn't be surprised, and he could use his coins to *push*, but where would he go?

He had escaped the Forgers in one city only to encounter them in another. And there were far more Forgers than he would've expected.

Worse, he feared what they intended to do with the girls.

Haern slapped the fallen Forger, striking him on either cheek. The man began to stir, and Haern held him in place, *pushing* down with one of his coins. If only he hadn't left his knives with the girls, maybe he would have a weapon.

His knives.

His sword.

There might be significant lorcith in the city, but he *knew* those weapons. He had either forged them himself or helped in the process, and because of that, he was connected to them in a way that he wasn't bonded to other lorcith.

It had to matter.

As the Forger awoke, Haern continued pressing down on the coin, practically forcing it through his skin. The man cried out, and Haern clapped her hand over his mouth.

"You're going to be quiet until you tell me where they brought them."

"You made a mistake."

"You attacked people that were under my care."

"Which was your mistake."

"Where are they?"

"You won't find them."

"And why not?"

"They will be far from here by now."

"No." That didn't fit with what he knew of the Forgers. He had a hard time believing that they would suddenly run from the city. "Where are they?"

"Probably dead."

Haern *pushed* on the coin again, forcing it down into the man's shoulder. "Careful, or you're going to be dead first."

"I welcome death."

"You might welcome it, but I think I'll draw it out."

"You don't have it in you to draw out death."

"Don't I? I trained with a man who taught me many techniques of torture. I doubt you want to know just how easily I could torment you, but I'm more than willing to share with you those techniques." He continued to *push* on the coin and grabbed for another, setting this on the Forger's forehead. He held it there, *pushing,* though without much force. The Forger's eyes widened. Haern could feel him trembling and worried that he might try to Slide away, but sitting as he was on top of the man, he thought he could keep him from Sliding away from him.

Just how long would he be able to prevent him from doing so?

Not as long as he wanted. Eventually, Haern suspected the Forger would find some way to escape him, and all he wanted to do was prevent him from doing so for as long as possible.

"Where are they?"

"You can't think to save them."

"Don't tell me what I can think to do."

"You made a mistake. You've made an enemy that you know nothing about."

"I know more about you than you realize. It's you who have made an enemy you know nothing about."

"Oh, we know plenty about those from Elaeavn. Your people fear violence."

Haern pressed the coin all the way through the man's shoulder. He cried out, and Haern kept his hand clamped over the man's mouth. "What was that? Like I said, I've trained with a man who has taught me various torture techniques. I don't think you want to know anything about them."

He continued to *push* on the other coin, squeezing it down, sending it toward the man's skull. With a little more pressure, the coin would tear through his head.

There was another sense of lorcith that came from within the man himself. He shifted his focus, *pulling* on it.

This lorcith was wrapped around his spine.

The man began to scream, and even his efforts at suppressing the noise failed. The cry was piercing and painful, a tormented sound that did nothing to diminish Haern's determination.

"I see I have found something you respond to," Haern said.

"Stop. Please."

"Where are they?"

"I don't know. If you stop, I will help you find them."

"If I stop, you will turn me in to your friends. I think it's better I continue to hold on to this." He *pulled* on the lorcith again, dragging it away from the man's spine, unmindful of the fact that he continued to scream. Haern braced himself, ignoring the cries, anger filling him that made it so that he felt no remorse. This man deserved nothing but his rage. "Tell me where they are, and I might take mercy on you."

"They will be within the temple."

"Temple?"

Haern turned, letting his gaze drift around the city. If that was where they had taken the girls, then Haern was determined to head there. In the distance, he saw a building that rose higher than the rest. The temple. That was where he had to go.

When he turned his attention back to the Forger, the man somehow Slid, leaving Haern to crash down to the rooftop.

28

HAERN

HAERN MADE HIS WAY THROUGH THE CITY, *PUSHING* OFF ON lorcith. He traveled as quickly as he could, wanting to reach the temple. Visions of what they were doing to the girls kept drifting into his mind, and he was determined to get to them, to rescue them. But even when he found them, how was he going to break into a place fortified by the Forgers?

He couldn't do it alone.

He had to believe the Binders hadn't betrayed him. If he thought otherwise, then any help that they might have would already be gone. Haern hoped they hadn't betrayed him but had been attacked and had moved, avoiding the possibility of the Forgers finding them.

Which meant he needed to find where they had gone.

He raced back toward the distant tavern he had encountered when he'd first come to the city. Once there, he landed, entered, and looked around. As before, all the tables were occupied, and a single servant meandered through, bringing drinks. There was no sign of the singer, and Haern frowned, making his way toward the servant.

"What happened to your singer?" Haern asked.

The man glanced over at him, looking him up and down. "Why?"

"She took something of mine."

"We're not responsible for any lost items."

"I'm not trying to make you responsible. I'm just trying to find her. Where did she go?"

"How should I know? We're not responsible for her, either."

Haern tensed, squeezing his hands into fists. He wanted to grab the man, slam him against one of the tables, and force him to help, but that would do nothing other than make him feel a little bit better.

Instead, he hesitated. "Do you know if she had other jobs?"

"Most of our singers have other jobs. We aren't the only tavern in town."

"Can you at least tell me her name?"

"Why?"

"So it's easier to find her."

There was a part of Haern that feared she had given him a fake name, and if so, then he would be even more inclined to believe that everything had been a scam, including the possibility that they were Binders.

Haern cocked his head, waiting for the servant to answer, and finally he shook his head and sighed. "She called herself Mindy Lee."

"Do you know if she's from here?"

"We have many people that come through Dreshen. I can't tell you if she's from here or not."

"Do you think she's from here?"

"Like I said, we have many people who come through here, and I can't tell you if she is or not."

Haern suppressed frustration that continued to surge through him. It was mixed with a nervous sort of energy that made him feel as if he needed to hurry. He needed to find the girls before something happened to them. As he had no idea what the Forgers intended with them, he didn't know how long he had.

Maybe they were no different than Rally, intending to use them, to enslave them, sell them off, but that had never been his experience with the Forgers.

The servant took a step back. "Are we done?"

"I guess we are."

The man glared at him as he spun around, disappearing.

Haern backed out of the tavern, feeling a sense of helplessness. He had come here thinking he would find the Binders, thinking that he would find help for Elise and the others, and even if he had found the Binders, he wasn't convinced he had found help.

Once out in the street, he looked for anything that might give him a clue about where Mindy had gone. He continued through the city, searching, before shifting his focus to lorcith.

There was quite a bit of lorcith all around, and despite that, he needed to ignore it, to focus on the lorcith he had made. Had Galen not helped him train to push away the sense of the metal all around him, he might not have been able to do it. Instead, he was able to push the surrounding metal to the back of his mind, leaving only the lorcith he had a hand in creating. As he held on to that sense, he focused on the various aspects of it. There was the lorcith of the knives and the sword. They seemed to be far away from him, but still together. That gave him hope that the girls either still had the weapons or they were still in the city. Then there was the sense of lorcith that came from the coins. A few had been scattered, left throughout the city. That surprised him as he had thought he had grabbed the coins as he had been traveling, but maybe he hadn't.

Then there was another coin.

That was the one that he wanted—and needed—to find.

He let the focus of that coin draw him. He didn't *pull* on it; instead, he let it *pull* him. He wandered through the streets, focusing on it, moving toward it. At one point, a building got in his way, and he had to drop a lorcith coin and jump over it. When he landed, he waited a moment before the sense of the lorcith coin returned. When it did, he continued onward.

As he went, he felt increasingly certain that he was heading in the right direction, and yet he was moving away from the temple.

Was that a good sign?

Continuing this way, he paused and felt the sense of lorcith once again. It was close enough he thought that he could get to it.

Haern closed his eyes, focusing on lorcith only, ignoring all the other metal he detected within the city around him, determined to find where they had brought Elise.

As he went, the sense of her coin was closer.

Up.

His gaze darted to the second story of a nearby building, and he saw movement shadowed in the window.

Pushing off on a coin, he reached the rooftop. Once there, he paused.

He could feel the coin in the room below him.

Haern hesitated. How was he going to get in there and get to Elise?

He had enough experience with the Binders—and with Carth—to know the Binders were talented, possibly enough that they would be able to overwhelm him. Then again, they wouldn't have the ability to *push* on lorcith.

Plus there was the woman he had encountered. He was certain that she was from Elaeavn, even if she didn't know it. Her ability to Heal, along with her green eyes, gave her away. She *had* to be from Elaeavn.

He looked for a way down. A trapdoor led into the building, and Haern tested it, not surprised that it was locked. He shoved one of the coins into the lock and twisted, using his connection to lorcith to help him. A loud snap sounded, almost too much in the night, but he ignored it and lifted the trapdoor, hurrying down the stairs. Once down, he paused, focusing on the sense of lorcith. It was near.

A door blocked him from whatever was on the other side.

Haern reached for the handle.

It would be much easier if the doors weren't locked,

but at least he had a way to get past them. Once again, he put a coin against the door and *pushed*. The leverage forced the door open, a loud crack too noticeable in the quiet around him.

Jumping into the room, holding on to his connection to the coins, he prepared for the possibility that he would need to *push* on the coins, but there was no one here other than Elise.

She lay motionless on the bed. Her hands clasped over her stomach made it seem almost as if she had died, but he could tell that her breathing was regular. It was just her eyes that were closed.

Haern let out a relieved sigh, heading over to Elise. It wouldn't be long before the women arrived, and when they did, he wanted to be prepared for the possibility that he would need to disappear quickly.

Scooping her off the bed, he turned to the door and saw one of the Binders framed there.

"How did you find us?"

"Why did you take her?"

"You led them to us."

"Led who?"

"The Ai'thol."

"I didn't lead anyone. I was trying to help others, and I thought you were going to help."

"We did."

"You saved her, but you sacrificed the others. The Forgers—or Ai'thol, whatever you want to call them—have them."

"Then they are lost."

"They're not lost. They're at the temple, and I intend to

go get them."

"As I said, they're lost."

"Aren't you willing to fight? The Binders I know were willing to resist."

"You claim to know the Binders, but you know nothing."

She took a step toward him, and Haern noticed something.

It was a shimmer. A Slide.

His gaze darted toward her eyes, but hers were a deep brown, almost a black.

He shifted his focus, realizing that there was other lorcith in the room with him.

Not just in the room with him, but within the woman.

"You've been augmented by them."

She froze, meeting his eyes. "What did you say?"

"I can feel it. They augmented you. Are you with them?"

She glared at him. "You know nothing."

"I know what I can feel. I feel the metal within you." He *pushed* on it, and she stumbled backward, a muted scream coming from her. The metal was wrapped around her shoulders, an unusual location, though he didn't really know where the Forgers preferred to place the implant. In the case of Lucy, hers had been buried in her head. He wasn't sure how many of the other Forgers had something similar, though he suspected it was more than just Lucy. And then there was the Forger he had encountered out on the roof. His implant had been along his spine.

"Do that again and you will die."

"I told you I'm trying to help. There are eight young

girls who have been taken by the Ai'thol. I intend to get them back."

"Eight?"

"I told you I was helping others."

"We didn't know you were helping eight."

"What did you think I was doing?"

"You brought her to us."

"And I told you that I was going to bring others to you if you were willing to help." He maintained his connection to the lorcith within her, ready to *push* if it came down to it. He thought he could react before she had the opportunity to Slide, though having never tested whether he could prevent someone from Sliding using their connection to lorcith, he didn't know if that was true or not.

"You don't get to make comments like that."

"And why not?"

"You accuse me of an augmentation from the Ai'thol, and you use their magic against me."

Haern laughed. "Use their magic against you? They've stolen the magic of my people, much like you've now stolen the magic of my people."

He watched her, half expecting her to attempt to Slide, but she stood motionless.

Another appeared at the doorway.

Haern glanced over, recognizing Mindy. "I imagine you weren't expecting me."

"You shouldn't have come here."

"You shouldn't have taken the person I entrusted with your care."

"We did nothing."

"You did. You abducted her. And here I thought you

wanted to help."

"You don't understand."

"Then help me understand. If I don't understand, make it so that I do."

"You can't understand."

Haern glared. "I understand that some of you have been augmented by the Forgers—the Ai'thol. I understand the girls I promised to protect have been abducted because you betrayed me. And I understand you took someone from me, hiding her here. Do I have it about right?"

"As I said, you don't understand."

Haern *pushed* on coins, sending them circling around him. He was prepared to attack if it were necessary. Would they try to stop him from carrying Elise out of here? If they did, he was ready to use the coins in whatever violent way necessary to get her to safety.

"Stop and we will help you," Mindy said.

"Now you think I should believe that you are interested in helping?"

"We helped her, didn't we?" She pointed to Elise. "You don't understand what we risked to do so."

"As far as I can tell, you risked nothing."

"We risked the safety of our people. That isn't nothing."

Haern glared at her. "Tell me what happened."

"You can sense the metal," Mindy said.

Haern nodded. "I can."

"And the Ai'thol have not given you that ability?"

"No. It's an ability some of my people have."

"None of us had any abilities," Mindy said.

"No?"

She shook her head, glancing to the other woman. Haern maintained his connection to lorcith within her, prepared for the possibility that he might need to *push* on it, if only to prevent her from Sliding away.

"They experimented on us. They bought us, turning us into slaves, and brought many of us here. They used their strange magics, their control over metal, and forced their power into us." She glanced at the other woman. "None of us wanted that power. It was imposed upon us, regardless of whether we wanted anything to do with it."

"You have a choice now."

"We don't, not the way you would believe. We do everything in our power to keep ourselves safe. That involves working together, staying together, but it usually doesn't involve helping outsiders."

"You claim that you're Binders."

"Because we've heard the name."

"So you're not Binders."

"No more than I imagine you actually know Carth."

Haern glanced down at Elise. He shook his head, studying her breathing. He needed her to wake up, but maybe she wouldn't. It was possible she was injured enough that she couldn't awaken.

"I fought at her side, and despite what you might think, she does live."

"How is that possible?"

"It's possible because it's true."

Mindy glanced at the other woman. "In all the time we've been here, we believed Carth to be nothing more than a rumor."

"I can assure you that she is not a rumor." A thought came to him. "And if you oppose the Ai'thol, I imagine that Carth would welcome you."

"Are you sure?"

"I don't claim to know her as well as some, but my mentor considers her a close friend. If we can rescue these girls, I can put you in contact."

There was a part of him that wondered whether or not that was a mistake. It was possible that doing so would only end up with him exposing Carth to danger, though as far as he knew, Carth wasn't afraid of anyone.

"First, I'm going to need your help."

Mindy took a deep breath. "We've been resisting them for a long time."

"Then continue to resist. Help me. Let me get these girls back. Don't let them be tormented by the Ai'thol."

"Rescuing them will be difficult."

"Maybe, but if what you say is true, they are at risk of the same thing happening to them as happened to you. Is that what you want?"

"We don't want to have others experience that torment," Mindy said, rubbing the back of her head.

When she did, Haern frowned to himself. "What ability were you given?"

"You wouldn't understand."

"I think I might. What ability was it?"

"I have the ability to know what another person is thinking."

"We call it Reading," he said.

"There's a name for it?"

He nodded. "There is, and there are others who have

that same ability. They come from my homeland, though I don't know why they would have given you those abilities."

"We were experimented on."

"How long ago was this?"

"A year or so."

That didn't make sense to him. Why would they need to experiment? As far as he knew, the Forgers had mastered the connection to lorcith long ago, having used it in the attack upon Elaeavn.

Something here didn't quite fit.

"Help me and I will put you in contact with someone who can help you," he said.

The two women looked at each other before nodding.

Haern set Elise back down on the bed. "How many will be willing to help?"

"I don't know," Mindy said.

"How many are you willing to ask?"

"There are a dozen of us in the city."

"Then we should ask all of them."

He glanced over to Elise, feeling like he should be doing more for her, yet if he could get help for the girls, then he was doing everything he needed to do, and then maybe—just maybe—he could figure out what exactly the Forgers were after.

Leaving the room, one of them closed the door, though now that he'd broken the lock, there was no way to seal Elise within. At least they couldn't keep her here. If it came down to it, she could escape.

At the bottom of the stairs, Mindy brought him to a large room where he found several other Binders—or whatever they were. They weren't Binders, not yet, but if they served the same ideals, then they could be.

Two of them jumped to their feet when he appeared, looking to Mindy and the other but saying nothing.

"He needs our help," Mindy said.

"Why should we help him?"

"Because his friends have been taken by them."

"If they've been taken, then there's nothing that we can do," one of them said.

"I've told him otherwise."

"You would speak on behalf of all of us?"

Mindy turned to the woman. She had long black hair, high cheekbones, and a narrow nose. "He can help us reach Carth."

The other woman frowned, her brow furrowing. "How?"

"He knows her."

"He claimed that before, but we have no reason to believe it."

"No reason other than the fact that he knows her," Mindy said again. "We need to trust."

There was something about their comments that left him uncomfortable. He couldn't tell if they were still keeping something from him or if there was something else taking place here. Regardless of the outcome, he wasn't about to reveal where Carth could be found to these women.

Mindy glanced over, and he was reminded of what she had told him about her ability. If she was a Reader, then would she know what he was thinking?

Most of the time, he was able to seal his mind off from

Readers, and he thought he could do so even now, but if she had some way of getting past those barriers, of bypassing his defenses, then maybe he wasn't nearly as safe as he thought.

He would have to be careful.

"How do you propose that we get into the temple?" one of the women asked.

"Well, I've seen that some of you have the ability to Slide," Haern said. "That's how I would start. From there, we can determine if there is anything more that we can do."

"How do you even know they're still there?"

"He controls the metal," Mindy said.

"Like they do."

"No. I do it differently," Haern said.

There was something unsettling here, but he needed their help. The longer they offered to help, the less certain he was that they had pure intentions.

What would happen if they tried to use him?

There might not be anything he could do.

Worse, he didn't know how—or why—they would try to use him, but if nothing else, he would be ready.

"And once we're there?" one of the Binders asked.

"Once we're there, I will find those I promised my protection to, and if anything or anyone gets in my way, I will destroy them."

He swept his gaze around the room, fully intending all of them to take the brunt of it, and when he was done, he looked lastly to Mindy. For some reason, he had a feeling she was the one he needed to worry about the most.

"When will we start?" he asked.

29

HAERN

THE SLIDE CARRIED HAERN TO THE STREET OUTSIDE THE temple. Darkness swirled around him, almost as if the shadows were alive, but that didn't seem quite right to him. He remained motionless, looking over at the Binder who had carried him here, half expecting her to disappear, but she didn't.

The effect of the Slide was no different than when he'd traveled with those from Elaeavn. There was a stirring sense of movement, and when they emerged, standing outside the temple, the air had a strange stench to it.

"What now?" he asked.

"This was your plan."

"The plan was for me to get here, and then to go from there to find the others."

"Then find them."

"Do you intend to abandon me here?"

"We promised our help, didn't we?"

"You did, but I have a sense you aren't thrilled about it."

"And why should we be? We sacrifice much doing this, and we draw attention to ourselves."

"It seems to me that you already have attention drawn to you."

"Not like this."

"I promise I will act quickly," Haern said. He pushed away the sense of lorcith he felt all around him, including what he felt from this Binder, and focused on the sense of the coin he'd forged. Not only the coin, but he honed in on the sense of the knives and the sword. All of that connection filled him, drawing to him, and he fixed the location in his mind.

He stared at the temple. Up close, there was an energy to it, though even from a distance, Haern had felt as if there were a bit of an energy radiating from the temple. Whatever energy there was seemed dangerous to him, and he worried he would end up trapped inside, or possibly worse, experimented on by the Forgers within. If that happened, he didn't think he'd have any way of getting free.

And it was possible these Binders would end up trapped as well. He'd seen the way Forger magic worked and wondered if perhaps they had some way of holding them, confining them. If they did, he ran the risk of entrapping others while trying to save these girls. Was that a trade he was willing to make?

He could be upset that they had taken Elise, but in doing so, they had moved her away from the Forgers, protecting her from the possibility of an attack. He should be thankful, not angry.

And he *was* thankful. Now, all he wanted was to find a way to get beyond here.

Holding the lorcith coins in his hand, he prepared for the possibility he would need to *push* them. Though with Forgers involved, and in a place that they controlled, it was possible he wouldn't be able to use the coins in the way he was accustomed.

Pushing off on one of his coins, he hovered in front of the temple. He didn't want to go in through the front door, and as he floated, he realized the rooftop might provide the best entrance. Shooting higher into the air, he dropped down on the roof, searching for signs of any other movement around him.

A door led inside, and Haern tested it, surprised to find it was unlocked.

The moment he went into the temple, a strange power seemed to envelop him, leaving him with a sense of emptiness.

He strained to ignore it, and on a whim, he used the same technique his father had taught him about sealing off his mind using lorcith, trying to protect himself from the emptiness he detected.

The sense began to fade. He could ignore the hollowness he felt.

Stone steps greeted him, and darkness threatened to swallow him, but thankfully with his Sight, he was able to make his way down. He watched for evidence of any of the Forgers but saw none.

Continuing down the stairs, he paused every so often, focusing on the sense of lorcith, but it didn't seem to be moving. It was still there, and the longer he focused on it, the further into the temple he realized it was located.

Descending rapidly, Haern took the stairs two at a time. He tried to go as softly as he could, trying to keep his footsteps from thundering along the stairs, wanting to reach the girls before anything else happened to them.

At one point, he heard movement and paused.

Where were the other Binders?

They were supposed to have come, but they hadn't followed him, or if they had, he saw no sign of it.

Another few steps, and he noticed movement.

He stopped, looking around him, realizing he wasn't alone anymore.

Wrapping himself with his connection to lorcith, he took a few more careful steps down. He circled around and around, and then came face-to-face with a dark-robed Forger.

Without giving the man a chance to react, he *pushed* on one of the coins, slamming into the man's forehead and all the way through.

It was brutal and bloody, and he'd had little choice. Haern regretted having to be so brutal. It didn't feel right attacking like that, and yet, if he hadn't, he would have been the one injured.

Continuing down the stairs, he could still feel the sense of the lorcith below him. He wasn't sure how far he would go, or even how far this temple extended, but the stairs seem to be leading him forever downward.

Something was wrong.

The Binders should have joined him by now.

If they abandoned him, he didn't like the chances of making it out of here successfully—or alive.

Another few stairs, and someone suddenly appeared in front of him.

He hesitated, frowning as he realized that it was a woman.

In all the time he had faced the Forgers, he'd never encountered any women among them.

"What are you doing here?" she asked.

"Where are they?" he asked.

"Where are who?"

"Where are my friends? I know they're here."

The Forger continued to look at him, and then she began to shimmer.

Haern *pushed* forward, the coin starting to rip toward her, but she managed to avoid it. She Slid away from him, forcing him to chase.

Only how was he going to chase her? She had Slid away from him, and now they knew he was here.

Haern raced down the stairs, still holding on to the connection to lorcith. It was there, faint and vague, but he knew he was getting close. He had to be.

Only… first he had to get to it.

Another few steps, and voices nearby caught his attention.

They came from above, one of them female, and likely from the Forger he had just encountered. Haern ran down the stairs, no longer trying to be silent.

At the base of the stairs, he froze. There was the sense of lorcith, but it was no longer near him.

Had he gone too far?

He should have been able to detect lorcith he had a hand in creating, but the further he descended the stairs, the harder it was for him to detect where it was.

And, strangely, there was no other way out other than through the base.

Which meant he would need to either go back up the stairs, or he would figure out another escape route.

Haern hurried forward. Doing so brought him into the heart of the temple, which made him uncomfortable, but what choice did he have?

A door blocked his way out, and Haern tested it, finding it locked. He shoved a coin into it, as he had when reaching the Binders, and forced the door open. It came open with a loud crack, which now would give away his location more than anything else. Haern hurried down the stairs, and at the base of them, he looked around for anyone else but didn't find them.

It was just him.

Taking a deep breath, he thought through how he was going to find the girls. They had to be here, but where would he come across them?

Nothing but walls of stone surrounded him.

A shimmering came from one side of him, and then from another.

He looked around, trying to find a way out, holding on to his connection to the lorcith coins, but each time the shimmering appeared, another Forger emerged from their Slide.

He was trapped.

One of them was the woman he had seen. He tried to

send the coin, but she held out her hand, and the coin stopped in midair.

More and more Forgers began to surround him, the majority of them women.

What was going on here?

The woman waved her hand, motioning to the others, and they Slid toward him, surrounding him on all sides, holding him in some sort of confinement, and he couldn't move.

A part of him was tempted to continue to fight, to attack, but if he did that, he would end up dead. At least this way, there was the possibility that he would find out something, though what could he learn here?

One of the Forgers grabbed him, and they Slid.

Haern braced himself, and they emerged inside a brightly lit room. Walls of shelves surrounded him, all of them with stuffed with books. A brightly glowing hearth occupied one end of the room, comfortable-looking chairs beside it.

This didn't strike him as some sort of torture room, but he wasn't entirely sure what it was. The Forger said nothing, though at this point, considering what he had done, he supposed there was nothing for the Forgers to say. He had already shown what he was willing to do, cutting them down, showing no mercy. Other Forgers appeared, all of them emerging in this room. His time was short.

One of them was the woman. When she arrived, she looked at him, making a steady circle before taking a seat at the far end of the room. "Why have you come here?"

"I came for the people you abducted."

"That *we* abducted? You have it wrong."

"I don't have it wrong. I know they're here."

"I'm not denying the fact that they are here. What I deny is that we abducted them."

"What do you mean?"

"Who are you?" the woman asked.

"It doesn't matter."

"Oh, but it does. It matters a great deal. Who are you?"

Haern looked over at her, shaking his head. "I said it doesn't matter."

"The less inclined you are to answer, the more inclined I am to force an answer. Is that what you want?"

"How do you intend to force an answer?"

"The same way you intended to force your way into our temple."

"I'm not alone."

"No? What help do you have?"

At this point, seeing as how the Binders had abandoned him, he felt no remorse about sharing anything about them. Would it make a difference? Probably not to this woman. He had a sense that she didn't care. Still, he said nothing.

"I would like to know where your help is."

"Why? So that you can attack them and abduct them, too?"

"Again, we have not abducted anyone."

"There are several young women trapped within your temple that would say otherwise."

"Do you believe we are responsible for trapping them?"

"I know you are."

"You know nothing other than violence. I've seen it in other men, and I recognize it in you."

"I've seen the violence from your kind, too."

"My kind? And what is my kind?"

"Forgers. Ai'thol."

Haern looked around him, knowing he had to get out of here as quickly as possible. The longer he was here, the more likely it was that something would happen to the other women.

At the same time, he couldn't shake the thought that the Binders had somehow betrayed him. He focused on the sense of lorcith. There was some nearby, though not nearly enough for him to reach it and use it. Without access to lorcith, how was he going to get out of here?

The woman watched him. "What is it you intend to do?"

"I already told you that I'm going to free my friends."

Haern surveyed the inside of the room. It was plain, nothing but stone, and he couldn't determine whether there was an easy way out. What he wouldn't give for his father's ability to Slide now.

He really had to stop comparing himself to his father. Rsiran had ended up captured no differently than Haern, and in Rsiran's case, he *should* have been able to escape. Haern was accustomed to his weakness.

Turning his attention back to the woman, he met her gaze with a glare. "You were experimenting on those girls."

"You have been woefully misinformed."

"I don't think so. I know what the Ai'thol do."

"And what do you think that the Ai'thol do?" She leaned toward him.

There was a certain intensity in her gaze, and Haern was forced back a step, unable to meet her eyes. He couldn't help but feel as if there was something he had missed.

"You have come to our place, our temple, and you have attacked. You are lucky I allow you to live."

Haern searched for how many other people were in the room with him. What sort of effort would he have to exert to free himself from this?

Possibly more than what he could manage. He noticed two others, but they were by the door, and unfortunately for him there was no lorcith around them.

"Are you going to attack me? Are you going to do to me the same as you did to those women?"

She watched him, a hint of a smile on her face. "You would challenge me. Interesting. Not many come here and are strong enough to challenge, but then, not many are so foolish, either."

"I'm not afraid of what you might do," he said.

"Not yet, but you will be. Tell me where they are and we can make this quick."

"Where who are?"

"The others who accompanied you. When you share with us their location, we can ensure your suffering is short-lived."

"I don't know what you're getting at."

"Perhaps you understand better than you know. I will give you a little time to reconsider."

She disappeared in a flash, Sliding away in a shimmering of color. Movement near the door caught his attention.

The two people he had thought were guards approached, and each of them grabbed one of his arms, forcing it down onto the armrest of the chair. Haern tried to fight, but there wasn't anything he could do. He was bound to the chair, ties wrapped around his chest, holding him in place. As he thrashed, struggling to move and get away, his captors jammed something through his hand and into the wood of the chair.

Haern screamed.

Pain raced up his arm, hot and throbbing, the kind of pain he could barely withstand.

He couldn't even fight. Tears streamed down his face, and he tried to blink them away, to ignore them, but there was no ignoring the pain rolling through him.

"Why?"

The word came out as a choked sound, painful, and as it did, he began to feel something else.

Not just pain, but a strange tugging sensation.

It reminded him of what it felt like when he was *pulling* on lorcith, only in this case, it felt as if whatever they had jammed into him was *pulling* some part of him away.

Were they *pulling* off his powers? Could they be using his magic against him?

The two men held his arm down, preventing him from jerking his hand free.

Someone else appeared in a flash. There was something almost familiar about this person, though why should that be? A shrouded hood covered their face. A strange odor radiated from them, something of heat and fire.

He waited, and the newcomer grabbed the two rods slammed through his hands and bent them over, wrapping them around the armrests.

The ends of the metal touched.

It was almost as if an electrical current shot through him.

Haern screamed again.

He tried to bite it back, tried to hide the pain he felt, but he couldn't. There was nothing in him but pain.

"Do you recognize it?"

"What?" he cried out, trying to suppress the pain and the tears within him.

"Do you recognize the agony?"

Haern blinked, managing to clear his eyesight, and looked up, trying to See through the darkness, but he couldn't. There was something about that voice that sounded familiar.

"Does it hurt?"

The newcomer tapped the metal bars wrapped around his hands, and with each tap, another surge of pain raced through him, an electrical current that left him in renewed agony.

"I will teach you the nature of pain. You will come to embrace it."

The man disappeared, suddenly flickering out of existence, and Haern was left with the other two men standing near him. He waited for them to say something, but they didn't. They walked away from him, leaving him tied to the chair, the strange metal rods wrapped around his hands forcing him to remain there.

He looked around. He was alone here.

He tried to move, but every time he did, pain shot through him once again.

Trapped. That was what he was. He might not be in a cell, but he could no more move now than were he in the same kind of cell his father had placed the Forger in.

Haern looked up.

The Forger.

That had to be who he had seen. But how?

Somehow—some way—he was going to have to find his way free, but he wasn't sure what it would take.

If he couldn't move his hands, what could he do?

He kicked at the chair.

With each kick, pain throbbed through him, and he realized that he was trapped, wholly and completely. He had to find a way to fight through the pain.

Either that, or he had to embrace it.

He was reminded of something Galen had taught him, a warning that he would need to understand the agony he doled out. But could he?

He had experienced the poisons Galen taught, coming back from them each time. In this case, what he needed to withstand was something else. He needed to withstand torture.

Not only would it be torture, but it would be self-inflicted.

Freedom. That was what would be promised to him if he succeeded.

He would not remain trapped.

He focused on the pain in his hands. The metal sent a strange shock through him every time he moved his hands, almost as if it were trying to prevent him from using them, but his legs were free. He tried to stand and found that he could lift the chair, though barely. Doing so caused the pain in his hands to surge again.

He sat back down, breathing heavily. Tears continued to stream down his face.

Haern didn't know how long he sat there. Moments stretched onward, minutes passing into hours.

He tried again. This time when he got up, he managed to stand for a few moments, long enough that he could feel the weight of the chair as it clung to him, enough of a presence that he thought he could deal with the pain, but then the shocks began to roll through him again. His whole body spasmed, and he sank back down, collapsing into the chair.

Panting, not yet defeated, Haern continued to hold on.

Every so often, he could swear there was movement near him, but he wasn't sure. How much of this did the Forgers know about?

They were probably watching, prepared for the moment that he made his escape. And when he did, he didn't doubt that they would react, converging upon him, maybe piercing his feet or his legs with another metal rod to complete the torment.

If they would come, let them.

Haern stood again, screaming. He held on to the chair, pain surging through his hands, and when the shocks began to convulse him, he collapsed, dropping down on the chair.

It creaked, but only a little bit.

The pain abated after what seemed like hours.

Coughing, spitting out a trickle of blood, he stood again, and again he dropped onto the chair.

This time, the pain didn't hit him until his hands jerked forward when he crashed into the chair. It was different than the electrical pain, a tearing sensation, almost as if it were ripping through his bones. He screamed.

Once again he stood. When he dropped onto the chair, it shattered.

He lay there for a long moment. The only thing that got him moving was the thought that the Forgers might come into the room.

Haern crawled forward. Sections of the chair hung from the metal bars wrapped through his hands. He didn't have the stomach to try to break them free, and instead let them dangle, something that could be useful as a weapon if it were necessary. He made his way toward the door, reaching for the doorknob, wondering if perhaps he might find some way to get free.

Every time his hand hit the door, another jolt of pain shot through him.

He had to fight through this. He had to survive. If he couldn't, he would let down the girls.

That as much as anything motivated him.

He was responsible for them. He had freed them from their captivity, and then he had been the reason they had gone to the Binders, and he would be the reason that they were saved.

Haern found the door handle, and he wiggled it until it popped open.

The man on the other side of the door turned toward him, and Haern screamed, smacking him with the board attached to his hand. He collapsed on top of the man, ignoring the electrical shocks that raced through him, slamming the board into the man's face over and over again until it was a bloodied ruin.

Even then, he didn't stop. How could he? If this man—this Forger—got up, they would drag him back, and Haern didn't know if he had the strength to withstand whatever they might do to him.

When he was certain the man wasn't going to move again, he dragged himself off the floor, continuing forward. It was a tile floor, and stone walls lined either side of him. Pain and weakness coursing through him made him stumble along the hallway, staggering forward until he reached a branch point.

Haern closed his eyes, focusing. Lorcith. That was what he needed, wasn't it?

He looked down at his hands. Blood had clotted around the metal, staining the bars that slipped through them. They had pierced the wood, and if he could find someone who could pry the metal free, he could remove this from his hands, and then…

The sudden sense of lorcith called to him.

It was nearby, and up.

Haern staggered along the hallway. When he reached the stairs, he started up them. He dragged one hand along the wall, pain shooting through him, but that same pain kept him awake. It kept his mind alert. A trail of blood worked along the wall as he went, and too late, he realized that he shouldn't have been touching the wall.

When he reached the landing, he came across two men.

Haern launched himself. He kicked one man in the head, spinning the board attached to his hand at the other, fighting through the agony. He crashed into the man he'd struck with the board, falling on top of him, and he swung the board over and again, blood spraying from him the same way it had the man below.

When he was convinced they weren't going to get up, he paused and looked around. This was too noisy. Not only would there be the sound of his screams, but there would be the sound of the attacks, the steady thump and kick each time he knocked down one of the attackers.

Reaching the stairs, he staggered up them, stumbling onto the next landing.

Lorcith was near.

He could feel it. Not only could he feel it, but he could almost call it.

What lorcith was this?

He *pulled* on it.

As he did, the pain in his hands intensified, the electrical shock racing through him, as if he somehow were using the metal piercing him to add to what he was doing.

He released the attempt to *pull* on the lorcith. Instead, he let it draw him toward it, following the sense of it rather than trying to *pull* it to him. It might not be possible for him to *pull* it anyway if it were something large.

When he reached the end of the hall, he found the

staircase that led up and down. Up was the sense of lorcith, but as he stood there, there was another sense, and he frowned, hesitating.

Down also had lorcith.

Should he go there?

He couldn't tell, and with as much as his hands hurt, he no longer knew what to think. He tried to focus, but he couldn't. All he could think of were the sense of lorcith piercing his hands and the sense of lorcith in the distance.

What he needed to find was whether any of the lorcith felt more significant. Not only more significant, but did any of it feel familiar?

As he stood there, swaying in place, he couldn't help but think that up was where he needed to go.

Was that safe? Up meant higher into the tower. Up meant closer to the Forgers. Up meant that he might end up trapped.

Down might be safer.

The longer he stood there, the more uncertain he felt.

Finally he headed toward the stairs. Lorcith pulled him, and he answered, some distant part of him reverberating with the sense of lorcith, and he feared ignoring it, feared that if he chose not to answer, he would end up in even more pain.

All he knew was pain.

If he could end that, if he could find some way of removing the pain, he wanted to do it.

Pausing at the top of the stairs, he feared that he would come across more of the Forgers, but there was no one. Haern staggered down the hall, stumbling as he went, and he reached the door.

It was a simple door. On the other side of it, the sense of lorcith called to him.

A familiar sense of lorcith.

He *pulled* on it gently.

Coins.

That was the only thought that rolled through his mind.

Coins.

They were *his* coins. If they were here, it meant the girls were here.

It meant he was close.

Trying the door, he found it locked.

Haern slammed his shoulder into it. Again. And again.

The door popped open.

He stumbled forward and skidded to a stop.

The Forger, the same man he and his father had tormented, stood waiting. A dark smile crossed his face.

30

LUCY

Lucy had spent considerable time in Elaeavn, both in the city and in the forest, and yet, going back, even within her mind, was difficult. With everything that had happened to her in the time since she'd left, she was no longer sure if she could return as easily as she'd thought.

Somehow, she had to find the answers within her mind. The more she thought about it, the more uncertain she was she could get to the bottom of what she knew to be trapped within her mind. It was almost as if she were blocking it out, trying to force herself to think of anything else. She had to find a way past the block to uncover more about herself.

The answers were there.

They were visions, and more than that, they were a part of her, part of who she was.

She thought about her sister.

That was the one thing she dreaded—and had avoided for a long time.

She focused on her, thinking about Cara and times

they had spent together. She hadn't spent much time thinking about her over the last few years, trying to block those memories from her mind. There was a mystery to what happened to Cara, and yet Lucy had never considered it.

Perhaps that was why Ras wanted her to know herself.

If she couldn't know herself, she couldn't know anything else.

"Why are you hiding from me?"

Her sister had been under the bed, and Lucy had noticed her sneaking around, hiding, and yet Cara hadn't wanted to come out.

"You're going to laugh at me," she said.

Lucy let out an exasperated sigh. "What makes you think I'm going to laugh at you?"

"Because you always laugh at me."

"I don't always laugh."

"Often enough," she said.

"Then stop doing such foolish things."

Her sister shook her head. "They're not foolish."

"Are you going to tell me why you're here?" Lucy looked around her room, and it was as she remembered, but then, as this was nothing more than a vision, her recollection, it *should* be as she remembered.

"Father has visitors."

"He often does," Lucy said.

"These visitors are talking about something."

Lucy sighed. "If that's all you're going to say, then—"

"That's not all I'm going to say. Why won't you even give me a chance to talk with you?"

Lucy dropped down on the bed. She remembered

being tempted to Slide away, and even in the memory, she couldn't help but feel as if she were far more exasperated with her sister than the young woman deserved. At this point, Cara was barely ten, and Lucy had been fourteen, feeling as if she were not only the big sister, but as she was coming-of-age, she was the more mature one.

Perhaps it had been misplaced. Now that she understood what she'd gone through, she no longer knew whether the confidence she'd allowed herself to feel was true confidence or misplaced arrogance.

"What you want to tell me, Cara?"

"I just thought you'd want to know what they were talking about."

"Why would I care what Father is talking about?"

"Because it has to do with the Council."

Lucy glanced toward the door and could make out the faint murmuring of voices from the other side, but as she wasn't much of a Listener, she wasn't able to determine much beyond that. It was considered rude to spy on her father, but she didn't even want to do so. She had no interest in the Council business, and yet there were times when she appreciated the fact that her father had some influence over the Council. It allowed them to live the way they did, in rooms that were far larger than so many within the palace were allowed to have. Most who were within the palace had small quarters, staying in them because they didn't want to lose their access to the palace and to the Council. It would've been better for many of them to have taken up residence in some of the homes surrounding the palace, as the people who lived in those homes often lived in far more luxury than those within the palace itself.

"I'm not sure I care what the Council is doing."

"They're talking about *him* again."

Lucy tensed. *Him* always meant Rsiran Lareth. It was one topic of conversation that managed to get her father worked up every time, and yet she had never really understood why. Lareth was harmless, at least when it came to the Council itself. He had helped Elaeavn. Everyone knew that.

Even at this time, Lucy remembered thinking how foolish it was for her father to be so caught up in the things Lareth had done, and yet some of that was because of her interest in Rsiran, wanting to better understand how to Slide, and knowing that without him, the city would have been claimed by the Forgers long ago.

"I think we have to ignore that conversation," Lucy had said.

She found herself pausing the memory, trying to understand what she had been thinking of, and why this was the memory she'd chosen to work with anyway. This memory was strange for her to come back to, though it did tie into what had happened.

Had she paid more attention at the time, she might have better understood the way her father had been a part of some greater scheme against Rsiran, and perhaps they might've been able to prevent what had happened to him —and because of that, to her.

Then again, Rsiran was never really in any danger from her father. Her father didn't have enough influence or authority to cause him any trouble, though he might feel like he did.

She pulled herself back into the memory, thinking through it.

It was a strange thing to approach this way. It was a matter of trying to piece through what she had observed when she was younger, working through her own memories.

With her ability to Read, there was no reason she shouldn't be able to turn her power of observation internally like this.

"You ignore it. Then again, you ignore everything. I've been telling you what I've seen."

"And what have you seen?" Lucy snapped at her.

She cringed at that memory. Why had she been so hard on her sister? Cara had good instincts, and even now, Lucy realized she should have paid more attention to what her sister had observed.

Not only did it have something to do with Lareth, but it had something to do with her father and whatever role he might've had with it.

"That's what I came to tell you," Cara said, crawling out from underneath the bed and crossing her arms over her chest. Cara was weakly gifted. She had medium-green eyes, and the braid in her brown hair hung over one shoulder. The set to her sister's jaw suggested her irritation, an emotion Lucy remembered all too well.

She had wanted Lucy to pay attention to her.

It was more than that. She had wanted Lucy to *listen* to her.

And she had not.

She should have listened, should have paid attention, and should have known her sister wouldn't have fabricated a reason to come to her. Still, she had ignored Cara.

Her sister stood across from her, stomping her feet and cocking her head to the side. The one ability she did have was Listening, and though it was rare, it was not always all that useful. The palace was constructed in such a way as to mitigate Listeners, and most people had known how to pitch their voices low enough to prevent anyone from Listening where they shouldn't.

When the door to the room opened, her father glared at them. "The two of you need to be quiet," he had said.

Lucy remembered nodding and turning away from her sister, shutting her out the moment her father had closed the door.

It was a mistake. And it had been the last time her sister had spoken to her.

She rested her head on her hands. It embarrassed her that she had spoken to her sister like that, that she hadn't given her the opportunity to tell her what she had seen and heard. She couldn't help but wonder if perhaps there was something more to it that she had failed to fully grasp.

She had looked back, thinking about her sister, but was there something more she might be able to uncover? Her fall had been a mystery, and yet, thinking about what she remembered, she couldn't help but wonder if perhaps there was an answer to that mystery.

Lucy remembered the way her father had been angry at her, and his strange reaction after her sister's death.

Why would that have been the case?

Thinking back, Lucy couldn't help but feel as if it wasn't a typical mourning response, but then, how would she know what typical was? When it came to her parents, it was difficult for her to tell. Her father was always a reserved, almost cold, man. With what had happened to her sister, it wasn't surprising that he had struggled.

Her sister had come for her help.

That was the part of all of this that left Lucy troubled. She had ignored her sister, had betrayed her. Something about what she had overheard was important enough for her to risk Lucy's irritation.

Lareth. It had something to do with him, and it had something to do with her father and the Council, which meant that Daniel Elvraeth's father would likely be involved in whatever it was.

She didn't force herself back to think about the way she had reacted when her sister had been found. It was strange for her to have been so far outside of the city. Cara wasn't one to spend all that much time outside of the palace itself. For whatever reason, she had been found near the shores of Elaeavn, at the base of a pile of rocks.

Lucy breathed out. She hadn't been permitted to see her sister. Considering that she had fallen, and what Lucy had experienced in the time since her sister's death, she imagined there was good reason to keep that from her. Why show someone as young as Lucy such pain? Strangely, she couldn't help but wonder if perhaps her sister had been hidden from her for another purpose.

She never would have believed that before. The more she thought about it, the more certain she was that there was more to what had happened with her sister.

Had Ras known?

She opened her eyes, looking around the library. The lanterns glowed softly, and yet now she was the only one here. At some point while she had been focusing on her memories, he had departed, leaving her alone.

She worked through those memories, trying to come up with an understanding, and yet she wasn't sure whether there was anything that she could uncover.

It was another reason for her to return to Elaeavn.

The women needed her to return, if only to find more of a way to help them. Until she better understood how to help them reach their abilities, she wasn't sure whether there was anything she would be able to do.

As she thought about it, Lucy wondered if she would need to confront her father to learn if there was more to Cara's death than what Lucy remembered.

Sitting there for a moment, Lucy wondered if perhaps this was what Ras had wanted. He had told her that she needed to observe herself, and in order to do so, she had found that she had to think almost as if she were trying to Read herself, something that felt strange. The technique might be odd, but she couldn't deny that it had been effective. She'd never had a recollection of her memories quite like that one.

Could she find other memories the same way?

Other than her sister, there had been no memories of her childhood that she thought would be quite as useful to find. There were memories she needed to uncover, though. She thought the time of her captivity, the time after the Architect had claimed her, was important for her to understand, but how was she supposed to do so?

Her memory of that was so hazy, and she wasn't even sure where to start.

Observe herself.

Ras's directive drifted back into her mind, but how was she supposed to do so?

Those answers were buried, and the more she dug, the more she wasn't sure whether there was any way for her to uncover what she had hidden deep within her mind.

She could start with something she knew. There were plenty of experiences with the Architect she was certain were accurate, but where to begin?

Why not start with the first time he had Pushed her?

That time had been painful, an awareness that her mind was beginning to be pulled away from her, that she was no longer in control. If she could parse that, maybe she could remember what had happened to her and figure out just how much he had used her.

She had blocked those memories from her mind and hadn't given them much thought, not wanting to remember what it was like when she had been forced to do what the Architect had wanted.

The first time she had experienced it was outside of a small village that had been destroyed, making it seem as if Lareth had been responsible.

That was significant, wasn't it?

She tried to remember what he had said to her, but that conversation came back to her faintly, a vague impression rather than anything real.

It was almost as if the Architect had somehow sealed off those memories from her.

Knowing the man as she did and knowing the kinds of

things he might have done to her, it was possible he had somehow found a way of preventing her from remembering what happened.

And yet, as she focused on the past, she could feel the way she had been Pushed.

It was there, a faint sensation. The more she focused on it, the more certain she was that she had been used even earlier than she had believed.

Even in that village, a place where the Architect had moved lorcith around as if it were nothing, she remembered the influence within her mind.

Could she trace that influence?

If she could, maybe she could find something there—buried perhaps, but even buried would be useful to her. If she could find the Architect's influence within her mind, she might be able to uncover what he had done to her.

It was there, a vague sensation. The more she thought about it, the more certain she was that she could figure out just what he had done to her.

He had used her, but then, Lucy had known that.

Had the visit to the village been real?

She had never considered that he might have falsified that.

Lucy traced those memories, Reading herself, forcing herself to think about what she had experienced, flashing back to that time, trying to find out if there was anything there that she might be able to use.

And as she did, she found… nothing.

Either he hadn't influenced her at that point, or his touch was so subtle that she wasn't even aware of what he had done.

She focused again, thinking back to what she had experienced, and what she had seen, and when she did, she could feel no influence within her mind.

That surprised her.

Lucy dug deeper. She remembered the way the lorcith had been strewn around the village, the way it had been used to destroy everything.

Why use lorcith?

She had believed that the Ai'thol had done so in order to blame Rsiran, but what if the Architect had told her the truth, and he really hadn't had anything to do with what had happened?

And if not him, then she needed to figure out who else might be responsible. Could the answer to who was responsible be buried within her memories?

The Architect might have shared that with her, and if he had, then she needed to dig deep enough to know.

Picking through her thoughts, she worked through them to discern whether there was anything she might be able to uncover about what the Architect had done. The more she thought about it, the less certain she was that she could come up with anything. He had been there, digging through her mind, and yet as she worked, she wasn't able to figure out what exactly he'd done or how she had been influenced.

Observe herself.

Ras's suggestion drifted back into her mind, and she focused.

She had to be able to Read something.

For some reason, this place and time was important to the Architect. He had shown it to her with a purpose, and whether that purpose had to do with his fear of Lareth or whether it was all part of some plan to convince her that Rsiran was responsible, she wasn't sure.

The more she focused on this memory, the more certain she was of one fact: the Architect had believed Rsiran was responsible.

Could Olandar Fahr have planted that memory for the Architect?

There was another possibility, but it made no more sense to Lucy than anything else.

What if it wasn't Olandar Fahr who had done this? What if there was someone else who was responsible?

It certainly wasn't Rsiran, but who else would gain from it?

Someone who tried to pit Rsiran against the Ai'thol.

Could the C'than have been active for that long?

Ras suspected that there was another person of power active, but it seemed almost too much for her to believe that one person had been active long enough to have impacted the Architect's life. And she knew from the Architect that he had suffered and blamed Rsiran for his suffering.

What if the faction of the C'than *had* been active long enough to be responsible for what happened to the Architect? If they had, why wouldn't Olandar Fahr have discovered that before now?

It was possible that he had known something, though he had been so focused on what had happened with Rsiran that perhaps he had overlooked some other faction working against him.

Ras wanted her to find out anything she could uncover about the Architect, and maybe this was the key.

As she focused on the image of what happened, she looked around at the destruction here. There was something about it that troubled her.

More than anything else, it was different than what she had witnessed with the Ai'thol. Her experience with the Ai'thol hadn't been of the destruction of villages. They were destructive, and they were deadly, but had she ever seen them use their power like this, in a way that completely destroyed villages and left nothing behind?

That troubled her.

Before, she had believed the Ai'thol responsible for this, thinking that the Ai'thol had used this as a way of trying to make it seem as if Rsiran were to blame, trying to build hatred for him.

Lucy focused on what she had seen. Enormous control over lorcith would've been required, a use of power unlike anything she had experienced before.

Not only was this not Rsiran—there was no doubt in her mind he wasn't responsible for anything like this, even if it had been a village of the Ai'thol—but it wasn't the Ai'thol as she had once believed, either.

This was what the Architect had feared.

He had feared Rsiran, but he feared Rsiran because he believed him responsible for what had happened to his people and those he cared about. It was understandable given everything he had gone through, and now she realized that he blamed Rsiran without knowing that his blame was misplaced.

Could the Architect know there was some other

power and believe Rsiran worked with this other power? More than that, could Rsiran actually be working with another power?

The only person Lucy knew of whom Lareth had spent any time working with was Carth, and other than that, she knew very little about what he had been doing. He spent so much of his time outside the city that Lucy had no idea what he was up to.

Still, what she knew of Rsiran and what she knew of Haern and his family suggested this wasn't anything Rsiran would do.

This was something else.

In order to understand, she had to dig deeper. She tracked through her memories, looking for when the Architect might have begun using her, and she found it.

It was a trace of a touch, barely enough for her to be aware of, and as she paid attention to it, she realized she could Read past it.

It was difficult, but the more she focused, the more certain she was that she could find her way beyond what had been done to her. As she Read beyond that, she saw what had been done.

It happened in a flash.

Memories tumbled through her mind, everything she had experienced in the time that she had been Pushed pouring back into her. She would have to work through them, trying to understand what had happened to her, to figure out just what it meant, but the more she thought about it, the more certain she was that she was right and that she had removed the influence of the Push.

What had the Architect had her do?

As she worked through those memories, she had visions of others that flashed through her mind.

She had thought the Architect had used her to make it seem as if she were responsible for attacking other villages, to make it seem as if people of Elaeavn had been the ones to have attacked, but that wasn't the case.

He had used her to hunt down Rsiran.

Hadn't there been memories of violence?

They were gone now.

Those memories had been placed there by the Architect.

Why?

The more she focused, the more she realized that wasn't even the case.

The touch was subtle, and yet it was definitely there. What had happened to her was a Push, someone placing a memory, forcing her to believe that she had been responsible for something she hadn't done at all.

Lucy's breath caught.

Everything she had thought had happened because of the Architect and the Ai'thol was wrong.

That didn't mean the Ai'thol were blameless. Far from it. It only meant that someone else was out there, someone who was trying to make it seem as if she were working on their behalf, someone who wanted her to believe that the Ai'thol were terrible. Who would do so, and why?

She searched through her memories, trying to Read them, but wasn't able to determine who was responsible for it and how it had been done.

She would need to work through her thoughts more,

would need to try to Read her thoughts in order to better understand what had happened and how, but for now, all that mattered was that she had them back.

Her memories were once again her own.

There had been an element of torment, and the Architect had used her, Pushing on her, forcing her to serve, but he had also tried to teach her.

That was the part of all of this that surprised her the most. She wasn't expecting to have learned from him, and yet he had wanted her to better understand her abilities.

There was one particular memory that came drifting to the surface.

"Why are you doing this to me?" she had asked.

"Because you need to have control." He paced in front of her, and she recognized the cell where she'd been held. She thought she had been there in between attacks, but that hadn't been the case at all. She hadn't gone anywhere.

Whoever had placed those memories within her mind had come from the Ai'thol.

"Why do you care if I have control?"

"Because I need to know if it's possible," he said.

"Whether what is possible?"

"Whether control is even possible."

Lucy turned away from him. Now that she remembered it, she remembered how strong she had thought herself, how hard it had been for her to turn away from the Architect. Even then she had begun to Read him, and it was possible she knew more about the Architect than she was aware of. He didn't have the same type of augmentation as she did and wasn't able to protect his mind from her.

Rather than knowing all of his thoughts, she was only aware of his amusement. It surprised her that he would be so amused with her, and yet, his mirth seemed to stem from her stubbornness more than anything else.

All this time she had believed that he had been responsible for hurting her, and yet now that she had her memories back, she had no sense of that from him.

Perhaps he hadn't done anything to harm her. If so, then she needed to better understand why he had been working with her, and what he'd wanted from her.

Control.

"Why would you fear it's not?"

"Because this is different than the blessings we place."

"Blessings?" She spun to face him, crossing her arms over her chest. It was a moment of defiance she wasn't sure she was strong enough to maintain, and yet she had done it. Even now, Lucy felt proud of herself.

"You may not view it the same way." He ran his hand below his chin, tracing the scar that was there. "But trust me when I tell you we do. We understand the value of the blessing, and just how much it means that we have been granted the opportunity to take it on."

"Then why do you care if I have any sense of control?"

"Because what was done to you is different. I would like to know if it's so different that it's not useful to us."

"Why would you think it wouldn't be useful?"

"Because if you can't gain the control that you need, then you are of no value to the Great One."

"He's not so great."

"He's much greater than you can ever imagine," he said.

"What makes him so great?"

"If you want, I could bring you before him. I'm sure he would be interested in knowing how you have been used. I'm certain he would be interested in helping you understand your blessing."

Lucy had touched the back of her head, something she still did. "It's not a blessing."

"Only because you don't understand it. In time, I'm sure you can begin to, and when you do…"

Lucy had turned away again, and this time, she made a point of ignoring him. She suspected it angered him, but she didn't care. All that mattered was that she ignored him, ignoring what he was trying to do to her and the way he was trying to use her.

The only problem was, she wasn't sure how she could fully disregard him.

When he left her, she found herself staring at the wall. He had wanted her to have control, and part of that was allowing her to master her ability to Read, and to do more than just that. He wanted her to be able to Push.

That surprised her, but she could feel it even now, even in the memory, aware of how he had wanted her to have that ability.

What surprised her even more was the fact that he wasn't worried about her having the ability to Read or to Push. Not only had he wanted her to have it, but he'd wanted her to have enough control to be of use. The Architect believed that when she did, she would be useful to Olandar Fahr.

There were so many memories for her to sort through. She had been captured by the Architect for a long time, and in all that time, it was possible she had gained knowledge from him. That knowledge would be useful to her even now, a way for her to not only know what the Ai'thol and Olandar Fahr were planning, but also to better comprehend how they had wanted to use her.

More than that, it would help her better understand what else might be responsible for what had happened.

Here she had thought they only had to worry about Olandar Fahr, but what if there were two factions that were equally dangerous—and they were caught in the middle? It meant people she cared about could be squeezed by both sides. And it meant many people in the world might suffer because of this pursuit of power.

Lucy looked around the inside of the library, and for the first time since coming here, she thought she really understood what Ras had wanted of her. He wanted her to observe herself, but what he really wanted was for her to reach into those memories, to learn whether there was anything stored there that might be useful for them, a way for them to uncover the real truths.

And if she could, the C'than might be able to continue to act in the way that they had for centuries. Ras had said the C'than maintained balance, yet she had never really understood it before. If there really was another opponent at play, finding this balance was of critical importance.

Lucy breathed out. In order for her to do all of that, she would have to know herself.

She might have freed the memories she had lost when trapped by the Ai'thol, and she might now have that part of her back, but that didn't mean she knew what she needed to do.

The more she thought about it, the more certain she was there was something buried she needed to find. It involved her knowing herself as Ras had said.

There was only one way for her to know herself.

Lucy shifted in her seat, looking around the library. The lanterns glowed with a soft light, no longer as bright as they had been. It was as if Ras had turned the light down enough to give her the opportunity to dig within herself.

What did he want her to learn?

That was the question that plagued her, and the more she thought about it, the more certain she was that she needed to answer that first; only then would she be of use to the C'than—if that was what she wanted to do.

To find herself, she was going to have to go back to Elaeavn.

Perhaps she might finally have answers as to what had happened to her sister, why her sister had been lost. Even if she didn't, would it matter? Did that mean that Lucy couldn't find herself?

She didn't think so. More likely, going back to Elaeavn would only open more questions.

There was another reason for her to go, and if she did it, it would not only be for herself, but for the women in the village.

Lucy took a deep breath, focused, and Slid.

31

LUCY

Lucy emerged at the edge of Elaeavn, standing in a small courtyard. She had chosen this place for the same reason she had often been drawn to it when she was in the city, as it was a place where she and her sister had spent time, a way of being out of the palace, away from the watchful eyes of her mother, and away from her father and his temper.

It was something he had tried to hide, but he was never all that skilled at hiding his anger. In the time since she'd left the city, Lucy had forgotten about it—until Ras had forced her to think inward.

The city felt no different than the last time she had been here.

For some reason, Lucy had expected things to be changed, but then, perhaps that was only because she had changed so much that she expected everything to change along with her. She no longer was tied to the city, though she had never truly been attached to it. With her ability to Slide, she had been able to leave at any point, but it had taken an accident and the attack for her to muster the strength. Even that hadn't been *her* strength. It had been the strength of others on her behalf.

The courtyard had a few statues within it, though most of them were cracked and crumbling. Parts of the city had changed over time, rebuilt and modified, bringing back the splendor that had once been here. The city was old, and in time, stone changed, fading, cracking, and new sculptures appeared, an attempt to revitalize things.

But not in all parts of the city. Some parts were left to squalor, and strangely, she found that many of those places were some of the more important parts of the city.

This square was one of them.

Parts of the square had been rebuilt, as if those who had once spent time here had known it would be important to have this place, but others were not, and she had always found it interesting how there were new sculptures mixed with the old. It was the old ones that always drew her eye.

Lucy took a deep breath, letting it out, and wandered out of the square onto the street. Elaeavn surrounded her.

The city itself was unique, set along a seaside that stretched up to a peak. There was Lower Town, a part of the city that once had been more run-down and decrepit, but over the last few years it had become revitalized, with people choosing to move there. Shop owners had begun to migrate from the Upper Town down to Lower Town. It was one of many changes that Lucy had observed herself over the last two decades, watching as shops she had once visited with her parents when she was young had left the

Upper Town, moving away from the palace—and the Elvraeth.

As with any change, that had angered her father.

Lucy had never fully understood it, though she suspected it had something to do with diminishing the authority of the Elvraeth. As he sat near the Council, and he had hoped he would one day sit upon the Council, he didn't want any change that would diminish the authority of the Elvraeth Council as they ruled over Elaeavn.

Unfortunately for her father, the people of the forest had changed the dynamics. Many within the city looked to Rsiran and Jessa now, viewing them as de facto rulers, and because of that, the Council was viewed by many as merely a way of trying to mitigate Rsiran and Jessa's authority.

She glanced up toward the palace. From where she stood, the illusion of it floating was diminished, but it still jutted out from the rock, and from certain angles it would seem as if it floated completely.

Even though she didn't want to go to the palace, that was where she needed to visit.

Eventually, she would need to question her parents. In order to know herself and to verify what she had observed, to find those answers, to uncover what Ras wanted her to uncover, she thought she needed to do so, but there was another way to get the answers she needed.

It didn't involve going to them or others of the Council. Not yet, at least.

Eventually it would. The longer she thought of it, the more certain she was that she would have to challenge the Council. Given what had happened to her, and the likelihood that some of the Council had been involved in the attack on Rsiran, there would have to be an intervention. She wasn't sure whether it would be from her or from Daniel, or perhaps it would even involve Cael Elvraeth.

One thing she could do was go to the library.

She focused, Sliding into the palace.

There was a time when thinking about Sliding in the palace was beyond her. The heartstone should have limited her, but the stronger she grew with Sliding, the more she began to realize there weren't that many things that would prevent her from using her ability. Ras managed to do so, though he was tied to the power of an Elder Stone in a way that she didn't fully understand. It was possible Ras was unique.

She didn't even need an anchor in order to Slide beyond the protections built around the palace. She emerged outside the library and hesitated. She could have Slid all the way into the library, but doing so might have brought her face-to-face with one of the caretakers before she was ready. She didn't fear the caretakers, but she did know they weren't thrilled when she Slid into the library, partly because they were suspicious of the ability the same way that people of long ago had been.

Pushing open the door, she stepped inside.

The scent of the library was distinct. It was that of the mustiness of books hundreds upon hundreds of years old. There were centuries of records, most of them depicting the time of Elaeavn, describing the Elvraeth out of a need to determine who had the right to rule. There was a whole section of the library depicting who was related to who, and in many of those works, there was a debate about which of the families were most senior. All claimed they were Elvraeth in order to rule.

When she had been here before, she had viewed the library as impressive and enormous. She'd believed that very few places would ever be able to rival the library, thinking that serving as a caretaker in Elaeavn would have been a noble profession. Having been to the library in the tower of the C'than stronghold, and having heard of the library in Asador, she no longer believed it was quite as impressive. More than that, the works collected here were all tied to the Elvraeth and to Elaeavn, whereas the works in other places related to the rest of the outside world, connecting things in a way that Elaeavn never had.

It was a shame, really. Elaeavn had remained isolated for so long that they had never really understood how they could—and should—be a part of the outside world.

Perhaps there were answers as to why that had been the case.

If there were, they were probably buried in some of the oldest sections of the library.

"Can I help… Lucy Elvraeth!"

She turned to Jamis. He was a thin caretaker, impossibly old, and had been pleasant. Of all the people who had been here, he was one who had always offered her a certain level of help. It was because of him that she'd had a future as a caretaker at all. If not for him, she might never have been granted a position, and though she no longer wanted that, she still had a fondness for him.

"You've been missing."

"I was never missing," she said.

"No? You aren't one of the lost?"

Lucy frowned. "The what?"

Jamis waved his hand. "It doesn't really matter."

"It does. What were you getting at?"

He got up from his table and tottered over toward her, maneuvering between the tables. "Nothing other than the fact that there have been reports of missing throughout Elaeavn."

Lucy's heart began to flutter a little faster. Could it be as easy as that? She had come here, wanting to find out what she might be able to uncover about the women who had been abducted by the C'than, and the first thing she did when coming to the library would reveal what she needed? It seemed almost impossible to believe that it would be so easy, and yet here Jamis was, telling her about others who had been lost.

"And you call them the lost?"

"Perhaps there needs to be a better title, and perhaps if you have returned, then they will as well. Many believe that they weren't really lost."

"How many are missing?" What if there were more than those she knew about? What if she hadn't found everyone she needed? That would mean she wasn't finished with finding the remnants of the C'than.

"We aren't sure of the extent of the missing, but the likelihood is that there are dozens," he said.

Lucy stood fixed in place. Dozens. That fit with what she had experienced, and it fit with the numbers she had found outside the city, women who had been trapped by the C'than.

"Are they all women?"

Jamis pressed his lips together in a tight frown. "No. That would be odd, wouldn't it?"

Lucy sighed. If they weren't all women, then what had happened to the men?

It was more that she had to uncover. With everything she had gone through, everything she had experienced, she thought there had to be some way for her to find the key to what had happened to these lost, but she wasn't sure where even to start.

"When did they start going missing?"

"The lost have been gone for months."

Months. That fit with her experience.

"I wish there was something we could do for them. Many of the parents suffer, and if it weren't for having each other, they might be even worse off."

"What do you mean that they have each other?"

"The mothers gather."

"Where?"

"Why, at the Garden of the Servants."

Servants of the Great Watcher were the closest thing Elaeavn had to religion. She knew exactly where that would be.

She thought about the women she knew who had been captured, and if the family members missed them as much as how Jamis made it sound, it seemed to Lucy they should return to Elaeavn. But none of them had wanted to do so.

It was difficult to understand the reason why, but she suspected many of the women had been altered so much they didn't feel as if they belonged in Elaeavn any longer. Lucy understood that.

"They believe the servants can ask the Great Watcher for assistance."

Lucy looked around the inside of the library, and once again, she couldn't help but feel how small everything was. It was so different than when she had worked here, so different than when she had believed it to be a place of enormous power. The longer she was here, the more she felt aware of just how she had changed. It wasn't that this place had altered, but she had been through so much.

"Thank you, Jamis." He smiled at her, and Lucy stepped out of the library, leaving him. She debated Sliding off to the Garden of the Servants but decided otherwise. From here, she had to find out whether or not what she had observed of herself, the way she had looked inside, was real.

Lucy Slid, emerging within her childhood room.

The room was little different than what she remembered. There was a bed and a wardrobe. Within the wardrobe, she suspected she'd find her clothing. The bed had stacks of boxes upon it. More boxes were along one wall. The table Lucy had used to study was taken up as well.

Her parents had moved on.

Then again, they must have thought that she was lost, and if so, they likely doubted she would ever find her way back.

She stepped over to the door, pulling it open. As she did, she half expected to find her parents, but they weren't here.

Perhaps it was better that they weren't.

The main room of their quarters was relatively large

compared to some within the palace. Her father was a fairly senior man within the branch of the Elvraeth, and because of that, they were given rooms that were nicer and larger than many others. The hearth was dark, and she approached it slowly, hands raised, feeling for any hint of warmth that might suggest they had been here recently, but there was nothing.

She turned her attention to the shelves. Like many of the Elvraeth, her father had bookshelves stuffed full of various books on different topics. For the most part, she suspected her father did so as a way of looking more cultured than he was. It was all about perception. With her father's position within the Elvraeth, he was often the one to host certain meetings, and because of that, there would be others within this room who her father would want to impress.

Lucy skimmed the shelves, looking for any sort of information that might help her, but came up with nothing.

Then again, that wasn't the reason she had come here.

If only there was some way to know more about what her parents might have done. The longer she thought about it, the more she realized something. She'd come here wanting to know whether she could trust her own observations, thinking that she should question her parents about what she had remembered of her sister, but why would she even need to do that? Was there anything in what her parents might tell her that would convince her that she was right?

More than anything, she remembered how they had treated her, the way they had belittled what had happened, to the point where she was the one who had felt the most guilt at losing her sister.

It wasn't to say they didn't mourn her loss. They did, but they also blamed Lucy to a certain extent. Perhaps the key for Lucy was not in asking others to help her determine whether what she observed was accurate, but in trusting herself.

How would Ras feel about that?

Lucy looked around the room again. It had been so long since she'd spent any time here, and even longer since this place had been home—really home.

It was no longer home to her, and she wasn't sure if it ever could be again. The longer she was here, the more certain she was that this place was not for her anymore.

Taking a deep breath, she focused on the distant sense of the tower. And then she Slid.

32

DANIEL

THE CENTER OF THE CLEARING CONTAINED THE FORGE, taking up a large portion in the center of the Elder Trees. It was quiet at this time of day, the forge not yet up and running, and no smoke emerged from the chimney as it had the last time he'd been here. He stood before the door, feeling uncertain.

"Are you going to go in?" Rayen asked.

Daniel stared at the door. It was solid oak, weathered from its time out in the open within the clearing, and stained almost black. If they were able to convince Neran to come with them, Daniel wasn't sure whether he'd be able to offer as much insight as they needed. "I worry we'll disappoint Carth."

Rayen laughed softly. "Carth won't be disappointed. I doubt you could ever disappoint her."

Daniel cocked a brow. "What do you mean by that?"

"What I mean is that she holds you in esteem, Daniel Elvraeth."

He held her gaze for a moment before turning back to the door, knocking, and waiting. After a moment, the door opened slowly and Neran stood on the other side. He was dressed in a weathered shirt and pants. His hair was balding, and moderate green eyes looked out at Daniel, wrinkles deepening along the corners.

"Can I help you?" He glanced from Daniel to Rayen.

"I'm Daniel Elvraeth, Master Neran. We came with a request. We have need of someone who has a knowledge of metals."

"I take it you need this because of her." He nodded to Rayen. "Were you the one who left with Lucy Elvraeth?"

"I did."

"Where is she?"

"Off working on something important."

"More important than trying to uncover how to remove the implant the Forgers placed?"

"She's come to terms with the fact that that will be unlikely. Now she has moved on to acceptance."

Neran frowned and scrubbed a hand across his face. "What is the request?"

"There is a strange metal alloy the Forgers are using."

Neran's gaze drifted toward the Elder Trees. The metal embedded within the bark gave the trees something of a shimmery appearance. That was the source of the strange energy Daniel had detected, though as far as he knew, even Rsiran hadn't known the purpose of the metal.

"They have always used a strange metal," Neran said.

"They have, but they have begun to vary their

approach. There's one they have recently begun to use that prevents Sliding." It was a gamble sharing that with Neran. The other man might feel much the way that many of the older people from Elaeavn felt about Sliding—the same way his father felt about it.

"That ability is all that keeps us safe."

He breathed out a relieved sigh. "Without it, the Forgers have an easier time of trapping those of us who oppose them."

Neran scanned the inside of the trees. "There is nothing I've been able to do with these trees. I thought Rsiran would have come up answers, but unfortunately, it's beyond even him. With his absence, I've been the one responsible for ensuring the safety of the forest, but I no longer know whether I'm doing an adequate job at that."

"I'm sure you're doing as well as you can, Master Neran." This wasn't going at all how he needed it to go. They needed Neran to come with them, to study the stone, and to figure out what the Ai'thol were after.

"I do as well as I can, but it's not the same as what Rsiran would do. He recognized something about lorcith I haven't. While I can hear the metal and can use it, I don't have the same connection to it as him." Neran took a deep breath, letting it out in a heavy sigh.

"Will you help us?"

"I'm an old man, Daniel Elvraeth. I'm not fit to fight anymore."

"We're not asking you to fight. I don't know that it's even necessary. What we need is someone who can help us understand what it is the Forgers"—he glanced over to

Rayen—"intend to use these metals for. What we really need is to know if there's some way of us overpowering it."

"How long will you need me to be gone?"

"I don't know. Returning is nothing more than a Slide away."

Neran glanced over his shoulder, looking at the cold forge. "This has been a Lareth forge for the last twenty years. It's a strange thing to leave it empty."

"I'm sure one of the Lareth will return to work at the forge again," Daniel said.

Neran smiled sadly, and there was something in the expression that told Daniel he wasn't entirely certain whether that was true. With Rsiran's absence, the one who had built this forge was gone.

"I should take some time to prepare," Neran said.

Daniel shared a look with Rayen before nodding. They needed to be getting back. There was no telling what the Ai'thol were after or when they might attack again. The sooner he could get Neran to Nyaesh to study the stone, the better.

When he and Rayen left Neran, he turned to her. "Before we leave, I'm going to try to visit the palace."

"Do you need my company with this, or can I stay here?"

"I think I should do this myself. What will you do?"

"I haven't spent any time within this forest. I have something of a curiosity about aspects of it."

"Maybe you can figure out what's going on with the Elder Trees."

"Seeing as how Rsiran Lareth has examined the trees already, I have a hard time believing I will uncover something of use."

"Just because Rsiran studied them doesn't mean you might not have something to offer. You've traveled extensively, and it's possible you'll know something he might've missed."

Rayen arched a brow at him, and he shrugged.

Daniel took a step, Sliding back to the palace.

In the daylight, the palace caught the rising sun, giving it a majestic appearance. The pressure from the heartstone bars over the windows pushed upon him, a reminder that he wouldn't be able to Slide all the way into the palace, though as he usually did when arriving here, he had no interest or need to Slide all of that way. He nodded to the guards, both of them different than the ones the night before, mentioning his name briefly before they stepped aside.

At least his name still granted him access to the palace. Making his way from one section of the palace to another, he entered the wing his side of the family occupied. All families within the palace were descended from common Elvraeth ancestry, but his particular branch liked to claim they were among the oldest and still purest of the Elvraeth. His connection to his abilities was really no different than any others', though. In some ways, Daniel was weaker than many of the other Elvraeth.

Voices at the end of the hallway caught his attention, and Daniel approached slowly, almost cautiously, reaching the Great Hall and looking inside.

Servants carried food from the kitchens, setting it on long tables with members of his family all arranged around them, many of them sitting quietly, introspective, but others murmuring softly to each other.

An elevated platform at the far end of the room was reserved for the heads of the family. Boris Elvraeth—his father—sat alone on the elevated platform. A pair of servants dressed in the forest green of the Elvraeth household continued to ensure that his father had everything he needed.

Where was his mother?

Daniel approached carefully. Occasionally, people would glance over at him before returning to their food, but as he made his way through the tables, conversation began to die down. Daniel no longer fit in, and it was more than just his dress that set him apart. When he'd been in the palace, he'd been forced to come to these meals regularly. They served as a time where the head of the family would demonstrate their position, serving as a reminder. He understood the gamesmanship, even if he didn't agree with it.

He approached the elevated platform, watching his father eat. One of the servants set a tray of meat and cheese down in front of his father, and Boris waved his hand, sending the servant away.

"What do you want?"

Daniel smiled to himself. His father would have known that he was coming. Not only was he a skilled Reader, but he was a Seer. His ability there was considered unrivaled. It made him dangerous to his enemies.

"I haven't seen you in over a year and that's how you greet me?"

His father looked up then. He had deep green eyes, the depths of color within them so typical for the Elvraeth, and he paused, setting the biscuit he slathered with jam down on his plate. "Am I supposed to rejoice in your sudden appearance, Daniel? You abandoned your family."

"I did so to help Lucy Elvraeth." Seeing as how his father and hers were friends, that should carry some weight. "And I would have thought you would be pleased to see your son."

"I would be pleased if you thought to assume your responsibility." His father turned his attention back to the biscuit, chewing it with his gaze lowered to the table. "Why have you been gone so long?"

Daniel was tempted to question his father about his role in what the C'than had done, but this wasn't the place. "The Forgers—"

His father slammed his fist into the table softly. It was enough to disrupt the conversation that had returned to the room, but only for a moment. "Do not speak of the Forgers. They have posed no threat."

Daniel kept his face neutral. There were many among the Elvraeth Council like his father who believed that the Forgers had truly posed no threat in the twenty years since their last attack. How did Cael manage to navigate the personalities? All they had to do was look out and see how those within the Aisl had prepared, to wander beyond the city itself and into the forest, and they could see the evidence of the attack. But too many of the Elvraeth had no interest in doing so. As long as the main part of the city, the traditional part, remained intact, there was no interest in trying to explore anything different. And why should there be? All they cared about was keeping things as they were.

"Fine. I will speak of the Ai'thol."

"Am I supposed to recognize this term?"

"If you were paying attention, perhaps you would."

His father looked up slowly. "Did you come here only to insult me, or was there some other purpose for your visit?"

"I had hoped to have a conversation with you."

He finished his biscuit, licking his fingers clean before waving to one of the servants, who brought in a pitcher of freshly squeezed juice. The servant poured a glass of amber juice, and the sweet smell drifted to Daniel's nose.

"Why did you really come?"

"Because I needed help."

"What sort of help?"

He almost told his father that he hadn't come to him for help but that he'd come to Cael Elvraeth, but he decided against it. There was already enough antagonism between his part of the family and Cael's.

"I needed help from one of the guild members."

"The guild?" His father looked up at him, meeting his eyes for a moment. In that brief moment, Daniel had the sense of a fluttering within his mind that passed as he placed a barrier in front of his thoughts, preventing someone from Reading them. His father was a skilled Reader, but Daniel knew he could prevent his father from getting into his mind, although there was always the possibility that he would slip past—or that he had somehow managed to increase his knowledge over the last year.

The real challenge would be preventing him from Seeing something about him.

"Why would you want one of the guild to help?"

"Attacks outside the city have begun to use various metals."

His father's mouth twisted up in a look of disgust. "I suppose that is to be expected. After the guilds decided lorcith should flow openly, others would find reason to use other metals. Did they think that was the only one with any power to it? The Great Watcher granted us lorcith, but word has come to us over the years of other metals of power."

That surprised Daniel. The one thing he never would have accused the Elvraeth of being was worldly. "What other metals of power are you aware of?"

His father turned his attention back to his food, continuing to pile it into his mouth. "Many over the years have thought to send us examples of their work. None of it has really mattered," his father said while chewing.

Was he referring to the C'than? "What examples have been sent?"

"As I said, doesn't matter."

Daniel decided not to push. All he would do would force his father into a defensive position, and that wasn't what he wanted. It was time to try a different approach. "Where's Mother?"

His father set his hands down on either side of his plate, looking up at Daniel. "This is breakfast."

"I realize it's breakfast. Where is she?"

"Your mother has decided she would prefer not to enjoy breakfast with the rest of the family."

"Just today, or is this an ongoing thing?"

"As you have been away for a while, I will not take it as an insult that you question me in such a way, but do not patronize me."

"I'm not trying to patronize you, Father. All I'm trying to do is—"

"I know what you're trying to do."

Daniel took a deep breath. "And I know what you tried to do." He straightened, meeting his father's eyes. "I know of the C'than. You're the reason Lucy was—"

His father stood up, the chair he'd been sitting on flipping to the floor with a loud crash. The conversation within the hall went silent again. His father leaned forward, meeting Daniel's eyes for a moment. "If you weren't my son, I would have you exiled for leaving."

"That punishment has been forbidden," Daniel said.

"And a mistake at that. As you are my son, I will tolerate your questions, but only because I hold out a sliver of hope that you will one day recognize you are needed to sit at these tables."

"I think we both know that day has passed. Soon yours will as well."

"Is that a threat?"

"It's a statement of fact. You remember those, don't you?" He was pushing too hard, but anger boiled up in him. If his father *was* partly responsible for what had happened to Lucy, he needed to be called out on it. "There's a war out there, Father. The Council may wish to ignore it, but it's real. Eventually, the Elvraeth will have to come to grips with their place in the war. The Forgers may have left this portion of the city alone, but it's only through the efforts of those who live in the Aisl that the city has been safe." Daniel's voice was rising. "I've traveled much outside of Elaeavn. I've seen places where the Forgers have continued their attacks. I've seen places where the Ai'thol who lead them have overpowered other cities. All in the name of gaining additional power. Eventually, they will turn their attention back to Elaeavn. Our sacred crystals are far too much of a prize for them to abandon."

"I see no evidence that they have continued their attacks. Perhaps they've already gotten what they need."

All eyes were on him now. This wasn't the time or place for this discussion.

Daniel started turning away before hesitating. "What was that?"

His father shrugged. "What was what?"

"What did you say?"

"I said that I see no evidence that they have continued their attacks. Do you think that we are so ignorant as to the happenings within the forest?" His father marched around the table, standing at the edge of the elevated platform, keeping himself looking down at Daniel. "We aren't nearly as isolated as you would believe us to be, Daniel. We have heard the stories. There have been no attacks on the Aisl. None since—"

"Since Rsiran was taken."

"Yes."

"You don't have to be so excited about that."

"Who said anything about being excited? He's a

disruptor. It's because of him that we have maintained whatever battles with the Forgers we have over the years."

"Another possibility would be that it is because of him that the city has been safe from the Forgers over the years."

"We'll never know, will we? What if he only encouraged them to continue paying attention to our people? What if we would have been left alone had Lareth not pressed the attack?"

After what he'd seen, Daniel had a hard time believing that the Ai'thol would leave anyone and anything alone if attacking them served the purpose of power they sought. Rsiran might be many things, but he was serving Elaeavn, regardless of what the Elvraeth Council believed. Without him, without the pressure of his attack, they wouldn't be safe.

And it was something his father might not ever really understand—or appreciate.

Regardless of whatever news they might hear out of the Aisl forest, it was different traveling there himself, speaking to the people who were impacted, walking the perimeter where Rsiran had placed the lorcith bars that created a barrier. Without doing that, how could anyone understand the extent of the danger posed by the Forgers?

Something that his father had said triggered an idea, though he wasn't sure what to make of it.

What if the Ai'thol already had what they wanted from here?

The same had happened in Nyaesh. The Ai'thol had come, destroyed the wall around the palace, taking the stone that had already been infused by the Elder Stone.

Could they have done something similar here?

"Tell Mother that I visited," Daniel said as he turned away.

He hurried from the room, ignoring his father as he attempted to Read him, pushing his barrier into place to ensure that there was no pressure in the back of his mind. He raced through the halls, back out to the courtyard, where he emerged into bright sunlight. With a step, he Slid, emerging in the heart of the Aisl forest.

He paused, looking around. The Elder Trees growing all around him, rising high into the sky, glittered with the metal that had been implanted in their trunks. He stared at them, feeling the strange pressure, the energy he'd been aware of the moment he had come here.

"Rsiran wasn't able to come up with any way of undoing the damage that has been done," Jessa said, coming up from behind him.

Daniel turned to her, seeing the sadness still burning within her eyes. This was a woman who had lost much over the years, and now she suffered with the possibility that her husband was tormented by the Ai'thol—or worse, dead. "I know he focused on removing it, but did he ever try to figure out what it was?"

"When it comes to the Forgers, we often don't know what they intend."

"This wasn't the Forgers."

"What do you mean?"

"The attack wasn't the Forgers. At least not at first." He frowned, looking at the trees. The Ai'thol had come and attacked. Their presence here had been for a purpose, but what was it? "This was the C'than. Or part of them."

Daniel's gaze drifted from the base of the massive tree all the way to the branches hanging high overhead. Despite the metal embedded within the trunks of the trees themselves, there was nothing about the tree that looked at as if it were dying. Leaves remained bright and vibrant.

"What if destruction was never their intention?" he whispered.

"You don't think they would destroy?"

He tore his gaze away. "I don't know that destruction has ever been their purpose."

"Daniel, you weren't alive during the last attack, but I can tell you that they want nothing more than to destroy. When they came to the city before, their attacks destroyed much of it, all as a diversion for coming here, intending to tear down the Elder Trees."

He had heard that often enough as a child that he believed it to be true, but there was something off about that belief. And with what he saw now, there was something about the possibility that they wanted nothing more than to destroy that didn't feel quite right.

"What if they aren't trying to destroy the trees at all, Jessa?"

"What do you think they're trying to do, then? Look at this. Look at what they've done to our trees. They want to change them, much the same way they attacked others, trying to change that. They will destroy them."

"Maybe it's not about destroying at all. Maybe it's about using them." Why hadn't anyone seen that before? Daniel hadn't returned after the attack, so he hadn't considered it before, and even if he had come back, it was possible that he wouldn't have noticed it. It might have taken him having seen other things in the world, having seen the way that the Ai'thol destroyed in Nyaesh, to recognize that there was something more taking place. He didn't even know if he was right, but if he was, and if this was about more than simply destroying the Elder Trees, then the longer they left them alone, the more likely it was that the Ai'thol were gaining access to power they should not.

"Using it?"

Daniel looked all around. "When I returned to the city, I felt the energy here. It was different than anything I had felt before."

"What sort of energy?"

"I'm not even sure how to describe it. All I know is that when I came, it felt different. It wasn't that there was a loss of something, though perhaps that was a part of it. Instead, this was a sense that something had changed. I wonder if you might recognize it if you were to leave the city for a while and return."

"Even if we recognize that the power is different," Jessa said carefully, "what does that matter? The attack was meant to weaken us."

"That's just my point. What if the point wasn't only to weaken Elaeavn, but to strengthen the C'than, and the Ai'thol discovered it and turned it to their advantage?"

He started toward one of the nearest trees, making his way slowly and carefully. He didn't recognize the metal that had been embedded into the bark, but if Rsiran had been here analyzing it, then the person most likely to succeed had already done everything possible to uncover the secret of that metal. If Rsiran hadn't been able to decipher it, no one would be able to do so.

He ran his hand along the surface of the tree, not touching it—he didn't want to get his hand too close to the surface—but just above it. As he did, there was a sense of energy that crackled along his palm.

"It's a siphon," he whispered. Jessa stood behind him, eyeing the tree, but almost as if she were hesitant to get too close. He turned to her. "I think it's pulling power from the trees."

"Like I said, destroying them."

"And what if it was never designed to destroy?" Daniel looked from tree to tree, his gaze drifting around the clearing. If all of them were like this, emanating the same sort of energy, he could easily believe that this was a sort of siphon, drawing power from the Elder Trees, stealing it and funneling it somewhere. But where?

"If it wasn't meant to destroy, why would they have gone through such effort here?"

"It's about power. Everything they've done has been about collecting power." He nodded to the trees. "Our Elder Trees and our sacred crystals are but one type of power. There are others throughout the world. Things that are referred to as Elder Stones. They have collected power from them as well."

And a siphon made a whole lot more sense than simply trying to destroy. The Ai'thol wanted power, but they didn't want limitations to their power. If they were able to use the power within the trees without destroying them, that would be far more valuable to them than merely killing the trees.

"If it's meant to siphon power off, then where would they be collecting it?"

Daniel frowned. That was the real question, wasn't it? They wouldn't be satisfied just taking power. It had to be about sending it somewhere.

But where?

33

DANIEL

"I UNDERSTAND YOU AREN'T INTERESTED IN DEPARTING quite yet."

Daniel looked over to Rayen, shaking his head. "I don't know that I can." They stood in the middle of the clearing, and his gaze went from tree to tree, searching for something that would explain where the power went. The longer he stood here, the more certain he was that was the key. And the longer they were here, the more sure he was that he needed to get those answers. They needed to uncover just what it was the Ai'thol were after here.

"It fits," Rayen said.

"What?"

"This attack." She turned to him, forcing him to meet her gaze. Darkness swirled around her eyes, the shadows drifting around her, making it up into her face and giving her something of a haunted—and quite lovely—appearance. Standing here beneath the trees, the shadows swirling everywhere, he imagined that she would be quite powerful with the shadows, though Rayen made it sound as if she didn't need any shadows for her to have power. "The Ai'thol take what they can, but not all situations allow them to claim power from the Elder Stones. At least, not easily."

"Because taking would involve destroying."

"Because taking sometimes isn't possible. There is a place to the south that Carth discovered early on, a place where the Ai'thol first made their presence known to her, and in that land, acquiring and controlling one of the Elder Stones would be nearly impossible."

"Why?"

"Because it is a part of the water. There is something about the land itself that imbues the water with the power. It grants a certain imperviousness to the shadow blessing."

Daniel smiled. "So if I go to this place, I wouldn't have to fear you attacking me with your shadows?"

"Do you think I have no other tactic than the shadows?"

Daniel smiled to himself. "I don't, but I do find it amusing."

"And you will find it amusing when you're lying on your back, my sword to your throat."

"You won't do that."

Rayen drifted toward him, shadows swirling around her. "I won't?"

Daniel shrugged. "You don't want to hurt me. You like me too much."

She glared at him for a moment. "I think you get ahead of yourself."

Daniel smiled. The longer he spent around Rayen, the

more he enjoyed that time. There was something easy about being around her, simpler than being around Lucy, especially in the time since her augmentation. Not that he blamed Lucy. She was trying to understand what she had become, and she was to understand her connection to power. She had told Daniel there could be nothing between them, and he respected that.

At the same time, he hadn't stayed because of Lucy. He had stayed because he had wanted to better understand the Ai'thol and his role in stopping them.

"How did they acquire the Elder Stone there, then?"

"I'm not entirely certain. Carth believes they managed to claim a supply of the water. It would provide them with access to that Elder Stone magic, but it would be limited. It's easier for them to acquire an Elder Stone altogether, sort of like taking the Elder Stone from Nyaesh."

"But they didn't take the Elder Stone from Nyaesh."

"No. They were constricted, but even that limitation has granted them access to power they didn't have before. Now they have the stones infused with power from the Elder Stone, they have the next best thing. It's possible that power will last them long enough to be dangerous, and it's even more possible the longer they have access to that sort of magic that they will be able to acquire additional resources, enough that eventually they will take the Elder Stone itself."

It was like the sacred crystals. They could be claimed, and the power that was within them might be granted to whoever stole them. The Elder Trees were different. You couldn't uproot a tree and remove it without destroying it. It was similar to the shadows he'd experienced in the temple.

"What if they managed to find some way of trapping the shadows?"

Rayen shook her head. "As far as we know, they haven't managed to do so yet."

"And if they do manage?"

"They will be far more formidable than they already are." Rayen made her way toward one of the trees, tracing her fingers along the surface of it. "There is power here, as you said."

"You couldn't feel it the moment we came here?"

"No." She turned to him. "I find it interesting that you could."

"Maybe it's because I'm from here."

"Perhaps. What else do you detect?"

"Not as much as I would like. If they're siphoning this power off, we need to figure out where it's going and if there's any way we can redirect it."

"There's another alternative," Rayen said.

"I don't think we can destroy the trees," Daniel said. "That is what you mean, isn't it?"

Rayen shrugged. "When it comes to stopping the Ai'thol, we need to dig them out at the roots. If that involves sacrificing a hint of power, then so be it."

"Doing so would weaken us. We don't want to weaken those who might resist the Ai'thol."

"If we can't figure out where this power is draining, it might not matter."

He frowned to himself. "There has to be a purpose to

siphoning this power off. Perhaps if we can figure out where it's going, we can find where they trapped Lareth."

"We have never been able to uncover the Ai'thol headquarters. Carth has searched but failed. Now she focuses her energies on trying to locate as many of the Elder Stones as possible. That will be the key to defeating the Ai'thol. They come after that power, and if they manage to acquire it, they become that much more difficult to stop."

What would happen if they had access to the power of the Elder Trees?

Daniel didn't even know what that power did?

The Elder Trees represented some of the most ancient abilities of the people of Elaeavn. Because of the power of the Elder Trees, his people could Slide, had a connection to lorcith, and abilities similar to that. The Ai'thol had already proven they had a way of gaining those abilities. For the most part, they did so using lorcith or other metals, but what if they had another way of reaching them?

Daniel Slid to the center of the clearing, reaching the forge, knocking briefly until the door opened and Neran looked at him.

"I'm about ready to go, Daniel Elvraeth."

"I don't think we can go quite yet," Daniel said.

"Why not?"

Daniel nodded to the trees. "We need to understand something here."

"We cannot remove what they've done."

"What if it's not about removing it but redirecting it?"

"What do you mean?"

"What I mean is that I think that there's a possibility the Forgers placed whatever they did here along the trees order to steal the power from them. What we need to do is figure out where they took that power and what they intend to do with it."

Neran followed him to the nearest Elder Trees. "This is the smith guild tree."

"This one connects to lorcith?"

Neran nodded. "Only those who are members of the guild will know their own tree."

"But if they see you by it…"

"Most who are members of the guild make a point of visiting each of the trees. Doing so gives you the opportunity to bask in the power from each one, though we haven't been able to do that much over the last few months."

"Which one is tied to Sliding?"

"You would have to be a member of the guild to know that."

Daniel looked around the clearing. He had never attempted to join any of the guilds, though he did have the ability to Slide. There had been no point in it for him, other than the fact that he was Elvraeth and had wanted to understand the connection he had to that ancient ability.

"Why are you telling me this?"

"If you're right, then the Forgers have gained far more than we ever would have imagined."

"They didn't need the Elder Trees to have that ability," Daniel said. He looked over to Rayen. She stood off to the side, shadows swirling around her, drifting from her feet all the way around the tree itself. As they did, they wound up the base of the tree before drifting back down. It was subtle, but for some reason, Daniel was aware of it. "Why would they need the Elder Trees? That's what I'm struggling to understand. The Ai'thol have had the ability to use that before."

"By tapping into lorcith."

"Yes."

"What if they seek another way?"

"What do you mean?"

"You have mines filled with this metal nearby?"

Daniel nodded. "We stopped near Ilphaesn on our way. You saw the mountain and the mines that wind deep within it."

"The proximity is interesting."

"Why is that?" Neran asked.

"You have these trees tied to ancient traits. It's no different than the powers we had in Ih or Nyaesh. They're connected to the land themselves."

"You think the trees are somehow infused with lorcith?"

"I'm not entirely certain, but it would make a certain sort of sense. There would logically be some sort of connection between these trees and the metal, especially if the metal itself is what allowed the Ai'thol to have such power."

Daniel wasn't completely convinced, but it was worth investigating. "Can you feel the energy here?" he asked Neran.

Neran continued to hold his hand above the surface of the tree. His fingers were thick and strong, though the knuckles were now bent and twisted. Somehow he still managed to hold a hammer, to work at the forge, and to possess considerable power. Daniel marveled at that.

"There is something here, though I don't know that I can fully explain what I detect."

"If I'm right, then what you're sensing is the Forgers attempting to siphon off the power of the trees. If we can find where they focus that energy, maybe we can redirect it."

"And then what?" Neran asked. "The moment that we redirect it, the Forgers will realize it, won't they?"

"Probably."

"And then they will attack."

"We can't fear them attacking."

"You don't have to fear them because you can Slide. You have powerful friends. The rest of us would be stuck here. The fortifications Rsiran placed are no longer as stout as they once were, and we would fear the next attack. And then the next. Eventually, we would fall. The Forgers would take this power, and—"

"We can't allow them to steal from us, Neran."

The old blacksmith clenched his jaw, breathing in noisily. "I can feel it."

Daniel grabbed Neran, taking Rayen with his other arm, and he Slid, emerging at the base of the Ilphaesn Mountain. From here, the sound of waves crashing far below drifted up to his ears. The cliff was violent here, the water below a dangerous froth, but there was something about coming here, standing along the rocks, and allowing himself to feel the energy as it swirled deep below.

"I don't know that I will ever adjust to that sensation," Neran said as they emerged from the Slide.

"Hasn't Rsiran Slid you many times?"

"Not many times. I made the mistake when he was young of making him feel as if it were something he should be ashamed of rather than something he should take pride in. I made many mistakes when he was young."

Neran turned away, looking out over the violent water as it crashed along the rocks below. Daniel looked to Rayen, and they shared a glance for a moment. He let it pass. That wasn't why they were here. Instead, he focused on the energy he had felt within the Aisl. Could he feel it here?

If he could, perhaps the Ai'thol had redirected power to the mountain, trying to infuse the lorcith with even more strength. A part of him didn't really expect that to be the case, but it was worth investigating. Then again, the longer they were here, the more the time he spent away from Nyaesh and trying to understand what Carth wanted him to discover, the less likely they would be to prevent another Ai'thol attack.

"Can you detect anything?" Daniel asked Rayen softly.

Shadows drifted away from her, stretching back toward the Aisl forest. They were thin and wispy and stretched faster and farther than he could follow.

"You've taken us beyond the range of what I can pick up on."

Daniel closed his eyes. The energy wasn't there any longer.

"Neran?"

"I detect nothing."

Daniel grabbed Neran, taking Rayen, and Slid. He emerged at the edge of the forest. They were closer than they had been before, but still not so close as to step across the barrier. As he stood there, the trees growing thicker the further into the forest they went, he focused on the sense of power, looking to see if there was anything here that he could detect.

"How were you able to Slide?" Neran asked.

"What?"

Neran nodded toward the ground, and Daniel noticed one of Rsiran's lorcith bars embedded deep into it.

"He placed those barriers before he was captured. I've been adding to them, but I take more time than Rsiran to prepare such protections. The lorcith is a barrier that should prevent anyone from Sliding across it, but you traveled from the Aisl to Ilphaesn."

Daniel frowned. He hadn't really thought about it, but he hadn't struggled to Slide from the Aisl to Ilphaesn. He had Slid to the city, but then would that have been protected in the same way?

He thought that it might be. Why wouldn't Rsiran have placed his protections around the entirety of the city?

"I don't know. Maybe something about the protections has changed."

"Not so much that it would allow those of the Sliding guild to bypass them." Neran studied him for a moment. "Perhaps something about you has changed. You have been outside of the city for quite some time. Did the Forgers augment you as well?"

Daniel shook his head. "I would've known."

Rayen was watching him, and there was something to

her look that left him uncomfortable. Daniel turned away from it, focusing instead on the energy within the Aisl forest. That was the reason they were here, and if he could figure out what he was picking up on, maybe he would understand where they were siphoning that power.

"Do you detect anything here?"

Neran stepped toward the border of the forest, his hands pressed out in front of him, and shook his head. "I don't. Whatever is here would be too subtle. It might not be possible for me to make out anything. With the protections Rsiran placed here, it's possible I won't detect anything at all."

The protections were meant to keep people from easily Sliding into the forest and to serve as a warning to those within the forest of someone trying to penetrate the barrier, but could they have another purpose?

He could easily see how Rsiran would have used them to hold the power within, but that involved Rsiran knowing there was something to trap here.

Daniel took a step forward, crossing through the barrier. As he did, there was a gentle tingling across his skin. On the other side of the barrier, he paused, focusing on the heart of the forest. There was still no sense of it.

Could he be too far away?

Daniel motioned for Neran and Rayen to join him, and they tried, but a barrier prevented them.

Daniel stepped back across the barrier, grabbing them, and Sliding them back across. "Was Rsiran trying to keep everybody inside?"

"No, but it seems as if he has prevented most from crossing," Neran said.

"How did Haern leave the city?"

"I wasn't involved in Haern and his planning."

"You wish he would have involved you?"

"Haern needed to do this on his own. It's a sign of his growth that he wanted to do it at all."

Taking the others, he Slid deeper into the forest again, emerging back at the heart. Once here, the sense of energy struck him once more.

Daniel began to make his way from the heart of the forest, walking back slowly, focusing on the energy as he did. At the edge of the trees, the energy began to ease, the power that he'd felt flowing starting to abate.

Why would it change there?

He started forward again, back into the trees, and once he reached the boundary, he felt the same energy once again.

The boundary of energy seemed to be at the ring of trees, though why should that be?

Rayen was watching him, and she joined him. Power swirled around and away from her, questing toward the Elder Trees and then away from them. The frown on her face began to deepen. The shadows shifted, disappearing into the ground for a moment before she gasped.

"What is it?" Daniel asked.

"I feel it."

"Where?"

"Beneath us."

"How is it beneath us?"

"I'm not entirely certain." Shadows swirled around Rayen, once again drifting toward the ground before returning to her. "All I can tell is that the power is there. I don't understand where it could be concentrated beneath us."

"There is a cavern deep beneath the ground," Neran said, approaching them. He was frowning, and his mouth pressed into a tight line, as it seemed as if he were trying to try to understand what he was detecting. "The Forgers should not have been able to reach it."

"What do you mean?"

"It's someplace that Rsiran knew about and he entrusted me with a key to finding it."

"What sort of key?"

Neran studied them for a moment before turning away. As he headed back into the heart of the Aisl, Daniel paused for a moment before following. Rayen grabbed for his arm. "Are you certain this is the person you want to trust?"

"There's no reason that Neran would have to betray us."

"You'd be surprised at reasons people might have for betrayal, Daniel Elvraeth."

He watched her for a moment before shaking his head. Neran wouldn't do that. But he didn't really understand what Neran was after or why he would hide something from others within the forest.

When he caught up to Neran, the other man was standing in front of the forge, pausing with his hand in front of the door. "Were it not for great need, I probably would not have revealed this to you."

"You haven't revealed anything," Daniel said.

"I wasn't prepared to show this to you. Rsiran did not want this known by anyone other than himself."

"And what is it?"

"You will see."

Neran stepped inside, waited for Daniel and Rayen to follow, and motioned for them to close the door. Once they were inside, he headed toward the anvil, standing in front of it. "Can the two of you help me move this?"

"Move the anvil?" Daniel asked.

Neran nodded.

Daniel glanced over at Rayen, who shrugged. Shadows stretched from her, and he grabbed on to one while Neran grabbed the other, with Rayen standing off to one side, shadows swirling from her and stretching into the anvil. As they worked, they managed to move the anvil, but only a little bit. It moved slowly, almost painfully slowly. When they pulled it away, a section of the ground looked different. There was a large plate of metal set into the ground. It wasn't lorcith, though Daniel didn't recognize what kind of metal it was.

Neran grabbed a prybar from his supplies and began to lever it beneath the piece of metal. When he was done, he nodded again to Daniel and Rayen, and the two of them helped him pull the plate off the ground.

When they lifted it away, a narrow stairway led deep into the earth.

"This has been here?" Daniel asked.

"Rsiran didn't want to be the only one who had access to this place, but at the same time, he didn't want it to be easy for others to reach."

"Where does this go?"

"Down."

"I see that, but where?"

"I've never been in it, so I can't really answer that for you. All I know is that it leads down into the earth."

And beneath the heart of the forest. This forge sat at the center of the forest, and Daniel suspected the anvil was at the center of that.

He glanced at Rayen, taking a deep breath, and then started down.

34

DANIEL

THE SMELL OF EARTH SURROUNDED HIM, FILLING HIS nostrils, almost an unpleasant odor. He barely had enough room to navigate down the rungs along the ladder built into the wall. The other side of the narrow tunnel pressed against his back, hard-packed earth lined with some metal that carried a strange aroma. Not lorcith, no more than the plate that Rsiran had used aboveground had been lorcith. With Rsiran's connection to lorcith, it surprised Daniel that he would've chosen something else.

Then again, perhaps using something else made it less likely that anyone would detect what he had here.

The stairs continued to go deeper and deeper. Darkness surrounded him, but he had no fear of the overwhelming darkness. There was no point in fearing it as, though he couldn't see anything, he didn't feel as if he were in any danger of falling. The opening was far too narrow for him to lose control.

For a while, he tried to count the steps, but he lost

track. There was a sense of movement above him, a vague and distant sense that came from Rayen over him, and he hurried down the stairs, trying not to get kicked in the head as she followed him.

And then the pressure on his back eased. Daniel squeezed the ladder, trying to hold on to it so that he didn't lose track of where it was in the darkness. Maybe he had been unprepared. He should have grabbed a lantern or something before descending down here, but he'd been so focused on what he intended that he hadn't really thought it through.

Reaching the last rung of the ladder, he hung suspended for a moment.

"Daniel?"

"Just a minute."

"What is it?"

"Everything sort of ends here."

"How does it end?"

"There's no more of this ladder, and from here there is nothing but a drop of some sort."

He didn't know how far he'd have to fall. If Rsiran was responsible for this, it wouldn't be so far as to be dangerous, but where was he going to end up?

There was nothing to do but let go and trust that he wouldn't fall too far.

Daniel released his grip.

In the darkness, there was a moment of terror as he continued to fall, dropping farther and farther until his feet connected with hard-packed ground. There was no cushion, and he tried to absorb the blow, managing to catch himself and rolling forward so that he didn't end up injured.

Getting to his feet, he turned as Rayen dropped, the sound of her much more coordinated fall coming to his ears.

"That was interesting," she said.

"I'm not so sure interesting is how I would describe it."

Daniel waited for Neran to drop down, and it took a moment for him to reach them. He appeared as little more than a shadow in the distance, difficult for them to make out, and when he landed, Rayen was there, helping him to his feet.

"Now what?" Daniel asked.

"Do you detect anything?" Rayen asked him.

Did he pick up on anything? He didn't think so, but he'd been so focused on getting down here safely that he hadn't turned his attention to anything else around them. He turned away from the presence of Rayen and the others, trying to envision the energy he'd felt before, and the sense of it came to him slowly. It was there, faint, but definitely present.

As he picked up on it, he realized that it was focused downward much as Rayen had suggested. Daniel continued to hone in on that sense of energy, trying to get a sense of whether it went anywhere else or was merely directed this way.

He couldn't come up with anything.

Rayen approached. He felt her almost as much as he could See her, though the fact that he could See anything in this darkness surprised him. Normally in darkness this profound, all he would make out would be gradations of shadows. While he did have some awareness of those shadows, he could make her out much more easily than he would've expected.

"Can you detect anything?" he asked.

"It's here, but I don't know where the power is focused."

"Why would Rsiran have this here?" he asked Neran.

The other man was there, just off to the side, near enough that he thought he could reach him if needed. Could he Slide out of here if it were necessary? Now that he'd been here, Daniel couldn't see why he wouldn't be able to, unless the metal used to line the tunnel made it too difficult.

He took a step, Sliding, emerging nearer to Neran. That answered the question of whether or not he'd be able to Slide.

"Rsiran had a reason for this place," Neran said.

"I'm sure he did. What did he intend for it?"

"There is—"

"Daniel," Rayen said, cutting off Neran before he could answer.

He turned and realized that Rayen was standing at the far end of the cavern. He could barely make her out, noticing little more than shadows, and Slid over to her. When he emerged, she touched him on the arm.

"Can you feel it?"

"What do you want me to feel."

"A presence here."

"As in someone else is here?"

"No, this is different. This is a different sense of power. I'm not entirely certain what it is."

"I don't see anything."

"I suspect it's on the other side of this wall."

Daniel studied it. There wasn't anything obvious here, and if she detected something, perhaps it was a doorway of sorts.

Daniel ran his hands along it, feeling for something that might trigger an opening. If this was someplace Rsiran had put here, it was possible there wasn't even a doorway. With his ability to Slide, he wouldn't need a door.

But then, hadn't Neran said that Rsiran had wanted to ensure this wasn't lost to their people? That didn't sound like the sort of thing that suggested Rsiran wanted to hide whatever was here. If that was the case, then there would have to be some way of reaching the other side.

"Did he tell you whether there was some way to open this?" he asked Neran.

The other man approached. "I do not know how to access anything else. This is where he brought the sacred crystals."

"He did *what*?" Daniel asked.

"That's what I was trying to tell you. After the attack on the trees, Rsiran decided to move the sacred crystals. For a long time, the crystals had been within the trees, but after the attack on the city, he eventually moved them back to where they had always been."

"Perhaps that's all I detect," Rayen said.

How could he have done that? What if no one had learned what happened to the crystals? "Wait here."

Daniel Slid, emerging in the clearing above. The sudden change—the flash of brightness all around him—was almost too much. He shielded his eyes, looking around as he searched for Jessa. He Slid up to her home and emerged on the branch outside of the door, knocking quickly and waiting only a moment before it opened. When she stepped out, Daniel grabbed her, Slid, and emerged once again inside the darkened chamber.

Jessa gasped. "How did you know this was here?"

"Why did Rsiran hide this?" Daniel asked.

"Did you tell them?" she asked Neran.

"They have a right to know."

"They don't have a right to anything," she said. "Rsiran brought the crystals here to protect them, not to risk exposing them again."

"But by bringing them here, he prevents others from having the opportunity to reach them."

"It was a temporary plan, just until he knew what the Forgers intended."

"But he's gone. What would have happened had we not come looking?"

"There are others who know of this," Jessa said.

"How many others?"

"Enough that we don't have to fear the crystals disappearing altogether."

Daniel glanced over to Rayen. His eyesight had adjusted once more, but he still wondered why Rsiran would have done this. "What's the key to getting to the crystal chamber?"

"There is no key," Jessa said.

"There has to be something. Otherwise, how would we be able to reach it?"

"Rsiran ensured that the crystals would be safe. He didn't want anyone else being able to reach them before he managed to do so."

"Why?"

"He didn't know who to trust."

The words hung in the air for a moment. "That's not quite true. If he trusted you, then he knew someone he could trust. And I imagine he told others who had the ability to Slide here. Even if he didn't tell others who could Slide, he would have had to have alerted someone who could reach here."

"Sliding isn't the key to finding the crystals."

"Then what is?"

Jessa studied him for a moment. As she did, Daniel wondered again how it was that he was able to see her quite so clearly. He shouldn't be able to See her that well with the dim light, but she was more than just gradations of gray as he would have expected.

"Why are you doing this?"

"Because I'm convinced that the Forgers"—it was difficult for him to refer to them as Forgers anymore, having come to believe that the better term was Ai'thol, but those of Elaeavn still didn't understand it quite as well—"are using the power of the Elder Trees. That energy is funneled downward. We followed it. And there has to be some way that we could intervene."

Jessa watched him for a long moment before pushing past him, and when she reached the wall, she pressed her hands on either side of it. At first, Daniel wasn't aware of anything, but the longer she held her hands upon the surface of the door, the more he felt a strange surging. It wasn't anything he would've expected.

The wall clicked and began to slide open.

"Rsiran did this?"

"It's keyed to something I possess. Others have something similar."

"What is it?"

Jessa shook her head. "I'm not going to share that with you. I've shared more than I intended to begin with, so be thankful that I did, but I am not going to tell you all of the secrets."

"Why does there need to be so many secrets?" Daniel asked.

"You travel with one of the Binders, and you question why there needs to be secrets?"

"What's a Binder?" Neran asked.

"She is a Binder," Jessa said, nodding to Rayen. "They accumulate information, acting as a spy."

"Some of our Binders are spies, but the rest merely consolidate information. At first we did it to combat the Hjan, something that I think you should be thankful for. Over time, that purpose has evolved, much like Carth has evolved."

"You have evolved to become even more spies," Jessa said.

"As I said, we aren't—"

"Is this necessary?" Daniel said.

He touched Rayen on the arm and took a step forward, into the opening in the wall that Jessa had created. Once through, everything began to change. The energy he'd been feeling swirled around him, far more potent than it had been before. That surprised him, but not nearly as much as the energy concentrated here. A haze obscured his Sight, making it so that he couldn't See anything easily.

Underneath the haze, there was something more, and it took a moment for his eyesight to clear for him to be able to make out a faint glow.

He'd been around that glowing light before.

The sacred crystals.

If they were here, then what was the haze that surrounded everything?

That haze seemed to be the key to all of it, but why? What exactly was it?

"Jessa?"

"I can't see anything very well," she said.

"Neither can I."

"This is troubling," Jessa said.

"When was the last time you were here?"

"I came with Rsiran when he moved the crystals. I haven't been here since."

How long had it been? Months since the attack, long enough that whatever the Forgers had been after had had an opportunity to take hold.

He stepped forward into the haze, feeling the power as it swirled around him. It was a sizzling energy along his skin, an electrical sense that left everything tingling. Daniel pressed forward, determined to power through it, and once he did, he stepped out into a bright, glowing blue clearing.

The five sacred crystals were arranged on pedestals,

and the circle of crystals seemed to push back the energy that swirled around them. He didn't know if that was intentional or whether there was something else he needed to be concerned by, but standing here, he didn't feel the same sense of energy as he did on the other side.

There was still some connection, though it was different.

Rayen followed him, shadows swirling around her, protecting her, isolating her from the energy. Maybe he should've waited for her to have gone with him, and he could have used those shadows to defend against that energy, but at the same time, there shouldn't be any reason for him to need to protect himself against it. The energy wasn't harmful to him—at least, it shouldn't be harmful to him. It was a part of him and his people. It might have been channeled in an unusual direction, but it didn't change the fact that this was still their energy.

"These are the crystals?"

Daniel nodded. "These are the sacred crystals of Elaeavn. They are our Elder Stones."

"You have more than one Elder Stone," she said.

"I suppose we do. Why do you think that is?"

Rayen shook her head. "I don't know. I'm not sure that Carth knows. It's unusual for one land to have more than one Elder Stone, and in your case, the Elder Stones are different. They grant a variety of abilities, not just a single one."

"And yet they are all similar," Daniel said.

"Are they?"

"Most of the abilities from the crystals are tied to our senses. Sight. Mind. Listening. When augmented, those abilities allow for different aspects of them." He'd seen it with Lucy in the way that she was able to Push, a variation on Reading. He wasn't sure what variation there would be with Sight, but there was likely some augmentation to it. More than that, the sacred crystals and the Elder Trees were tied together.

"It is unique. But then, the Great Watcher is unique among the elders," Rayen said.

"What do you mean?"

"Nothing more than rumor. The elders are felt to be powerful beings. Each of them was responsible for one aspect of the world, granting their favor over it. In the case of Lashasn, it was that of fire. It came from the volcanoes deep within the land, and the people there were touched by fire, given the ability to use it and manipulate it. The people of my land were gifted by the darkness in the shadows. We have been blessed, and some of us even more so, able to use the shadows in a way that allows us to protect ourselves and our people. Other lands are different. I mentioned one where the power was in the water, granting a certain strength and immunity to shadows."

"Why would there need to be an immunity to shadows?"

"We don't know, but Carth suspects it's tied to the elders who touched the land. Not all of them got along. There is a balance. A counter."

"And what's the counter to the Lashasn Elder Stone?"

"We aren't entirely certain. We continue to look, and it's possible that the Ai'thol have already uncovered that, but we don't know," Rayen said.

If the elders had a way of balancing each other out, then a single one wouldn't grow more powerful than the others.

"Other than the Elder Stones, there is no evidence for the elders' existence," Daniel said.

"Isn't there? Our peoples are all different, and most believe that difference is tied to the elders who helped settle that land. In the case of your people, you were given the blessings of the Great Watcher, a being viewed as one who sits above the world, looking down upon it."

"He does sit above the world looking down upon it," Jessa said, joining them within the circle of crystals. "When you have an opportunity to hold one of the sacred crystals, you understand the role of the Great Watcher. Some of us more than others."

"And you?" Daniel asked.

Jessa shook her head. "My experience was mundane compared to some. But Rsiran, on the other hand, had a significant experience. In his, he was sitting above the world, given the opportunity to look down, and from there he was able to See many things, not the least of which was the connections to metal all throughout the world."

"All metal or only lorcith?" Daniel asked.

"You'll have to ask Rsiran, but it was more than just lorcith."

"Was that what it was like for you?" Rayen asked.

Daniel shook his head. "When I was given the opportunity to hold one of the crystals, none of them glowed for me."

"What do you mean?"

"There's something to the sacred crystals that alerts you that you have been granted permission to handle one. The crystal would pulsate softly to indicate that power was accessible. Some never have the opportunity to know the strength of their people."

Rayen stepped away from him, making a slow circuit of the inside of the ring of crystals. Daniel watched, curious, as she stopped at one and the other and then another. Each time she stopped, Rayen looked down at the crystals, studying them, before turning on and moving to the next.

"Do you remember which crystal pulsated for you?" Daniel asked.

"When you're given the opportunity, it's disorienting," Jessa said.

"What would happen if we let her draw power from one of the crystals that didn't want anyone to have it?" Daniel asked.

"Rsiran isn't sure that's even possible," Jessa said.

Neran joined them, but he stayed just inside the ring of crystals, his gaze darting from one to the other. He looked at them almost suspiciously and seemed far more uncomfortable than the rest, as if he didn't want to be here.

"The Ai'thol must believe it possible."

"Whether or not they believe it possible doesn't matter. The crystals decide who is granted that opportunity."

"What if they have some way of forcing it?"

"His grandfather thought the same thing," Jessa said. "And Rsiran remained unconvinced."

Daniel began to turn, and he froze as he watched Rayen reaching for one of the crystals.

"What are you doing?"

"Look at it. It's so beautiful. The way it's pulsing, it's almost as if it…"

She grabbed the crystal.

There was a flash of blue light that faded. When it was done, Rayen stood in the middle of the circle, the crystal back on its pedestal. It had been nothing more than a heartbeat, and yet Daniel knew what had taken place.

One of the crystals had allowed Rayen to handle it.

"What happened?" She looked around, seeming dazed as she spun in place, looking at each of the crystals before pausing and turning her attention back to Daniel.

"It seems as if you were granted permission to handle one of the crystals," Daniel said.

Jessa's mouth set in a tight line, and she glared at Rayen. "You should not have done that."

"I didn't do anything."

"You held one of the sacred crystals."

"She was granted permission, the same as you," Daniel said.

"You don't know that."

He turned away. *He* hadn't even been able to hold one of the crystals, and now Rayen had? "What did you see?"

"I was making the circuit of the crystals and that one"—she began to spin around, pointing at one crystal before turning her attention to another and finally frowning—"or whichever one it was began to pulse. It became brighter and brighter, practically demanding that I handle it."

Daniel might not have had one of the crystals call to him, but he'd heard stories about them often enough that he understood what Rayen was describing. It was the same as others who had been granted the opportunity to hold the crystals had experienced. And if she had been given permission by the crystal, then there was no reason she shouldn't have been able to handle it.

"The crystal granted her permission," Daniel said.

"The crystal didn't do that," Jessa said. "She forced herself on it."

"I'm not sure that she would have been able to force herself upon a crystal. All I'm saying is that—"

"All you are saying is that you think this woman should have been given the opportunity to hold one of the sacred crystals, something that few within Elaeavn have been able to do despite the fact that Rsiran has offered it to as many as want to."

"How many are called to them?" Rayen asked.

"It's less than one in every twenty who are drawn to a crystal."

Daniel was surprised by the numbers. He knew it wasn't common to be able to hold one of the crystals, but he had thought the likelihood would have been higher than that. If it really was only one in every twenty or fewer, he shouldn't feel quite so bad that he had failed when it had been his opportunity.

"Do you feel any different?"

Rayen looked around for a moment before shaking her head.

"It can take some time. When I was given the opportunity to hold one of the sacred crystals, it took months for me to understand the full depths of my abilities," Jessa said.

"And what happened? How are you changed?"

"My gift was one of Sight. When I was able to hold one of the crystals, it began to augment my ability, and with that, I have since had an even greater ability with Sight."

"None of that was dark back there?"

"Not for me," Jessa said. She turned to Rayen. "As you aren't of Elaeavn, it's possible that any ability that you develop will be different."

"How so?"

"I don't really know. There is one among us who might be able to answer, but even she might not be able to provide the information that you want. You will have to wait and see what changes for you."

"Now that we have the crystals taken care of, how about we figure out what that energy is?" Daniel said.

"That's just it. It wasn't here when I came with Rsiran before. Whatever is out there, whatever that energy is, it's not supposed to be here."

"Do you see this?" Neran was crouched near one of the pedestals, facing outward, his gaze staring away from the glowing blue of the crystals almost as if he were trying to see beyond them and toward the energy.

Daniel joined him, crouching next to him. "What do you see?"

"I'm not entirely certain. The energy seems to focus here." He glanced to the next pedestal. "And there. And all around us."

"How so?"

"It's swirling around us, and as I look at it, I can't help but feel as if the energy is focused here on the pedestals."

Daniel crept forward and positioned himself right in front of one of the pedestals. He ran his hands along the outside of it, feeling for the energy the same way he had felt for the energy up above.

Neran was right. The energy did seem to concentrate in the pedestal, and not only that, but it traveled through it, and downward.

"What did Rsiran make these pedestals out of?" Daniel asked.

"Rsiran didn't make them. These were the original pedestals that were here."

"That were here?"

She nodded. "You don't realize that?"

"Realize what?"

"We are in the original crystal chamber."

"But that was within the palace."

"The one the Elvraeth used was connected to the palace, but it wasn't the original chamber. This is."

Daniel stared, unable to take his eyes off the circle of pedestals and the power around them. He marveled at them, trying to figure out what he was seeing. And if they were once more in the original crystal room, how was it that Rsiran had connected it to the heart of the forest?

More than that, if they were joined, then it was possible that the crystals and the Elder Trees weren't separate Elder Stones but were somehow interconnected in a way he didn't fully understand.

More than ever, he wished Rsiran were here.

Maybe he needed to offer to help Haern find his

father. If nothing else, Rsiran would help provide answers.

He glanced over to Rayen and then to Neran, coming to a decision. He would bring Neran back to Nyaesh, allow the other man to investigate the stones, but then Daniel would return, determined to find Haern—and Rsiran. Then they could understand what it was the Ai'thol intended by siphoning off the power here.

35

HAERN

STAGGERING FORWARD, HAERN COULDN'T TAKE HIS EYES off the Forgers. His mind didn't work quite right. Pain continued to roll through him, but it was more than just the pain. It was the idea that this man was responsible for not just his suffering, but that of the girls that he had come here to save.

As he approached, the Forger smiled widely. A scar working through his dark hair seemed new. Another augmentation? The flatness to his eyes made them look empty and hollow.

He reached for the man, straining, and held out the boards with the metal bars through them. The man ignored them.

"Why?" It was the only thing Haern could get out, and it was the one question he thought he needed the answer to the most. If he could understand why this Forger had used the young women, he…

What?

What could he do? He was defeated. He might have

found the Forger, but what did he think he could do now that he had? With the boards attached to his hands, the metal bars through his palms, there wasn't anything for him to do. It was a miracle he was still able to stand.

More than anything, he wanted to collapse.

"I didn't think that you would make it here."

"I'm sorry to disappoint you."

"Disappoint? Oh, on the contrary, this is exactly what I wanted."

He staggered toward the man, holding his hands out. The Forger continued to grin, and Haern spun toward him, trying to bring one of the pieces of wood toward the man's face, but he Slid, moving off to the side and emerging from his Slide before Haern was able to reach him. Haern stumbled, staggering, the sudden change in direction causing pain to shoot through his hands. He didn't know how long he'd be able to withstand this attack, but he would continue to fight.

"Why did you attack the girls?"

The Forger Slid again, appearing behind Haern. He reached the door, kicking it closed.

Some distant part of Haern's mind knew that the Forger was locking him in, trapping him here with him, which meant he would need to grab on to the Forger in order to escape.

"You have come to my temple, and you have violated the safety I have offered and provided those who come here."

Haern staggered again, sweeping toward the man. This time, as he started to Slide, Haern swung the board, watching as the faint light that started to shimmer around the Forger coalesced, telling Haern that he was going to Slide, but also where he was going to emerge from the Slide.

He connected.

Pain shot through him, but the cracking sound of the board over the Forger's head was satisfying, and he continued forward, trying to slam his entire body into the man, but the other Slid away.

Haern got to his feet. His gaze darted around the room. There were chairs all around the walls, and banners hanging from overhead. The air smelled of flowers and spice, nothing horrible about it.

Where had the Forger brought him? No. That wasn't quite what happened, was it?

Haern's mind wasn't working the way he knew it should, but he realized that no one had brought him here. He had come of his own accord, following the sense of lorcith.

And if there was lorcith here, he could use it.

He focused on the Forger, and when he emerged from his next Slide, Haern was there, ready, and he brought the board around, slicing with it as if it were a sword. He caught the Forger under his arm, with enough force that the other man grunted as Haern did, spinning off to the side.

Stumbling again, he intended to crash into him, but the other man managed to stagger back before Sliding.

Where was he going? Haern followed the sense of the Slide, tracking the way the strange shimmering appeared. If he could follow that, he might be able to figure out where the Forger might come out next.

Turning slowly in a circle, he came across him.

It was little more than a slight thickening of the air. He wasn't sure why he was even aware of it, and for a moment, he wondered if it were nothing more than his imagination. It was possible that with as much as he hurt, with as much pain as now filled his body, he was imagining things.

If so, he would attack the hallucinations.

Another spin, and this time he could swear the Forger was coming out of a Slide nearby. Haern spun again, bringing the board around. As he did, he connected.

There came a crack as he caught the Forger underneath his chin.

The man staggered back.

If he could Slide, why would he remain in this place?

"Where is my father?" Haern asked when the man emerged from another Slide. He didn't attack this time, holding his hands out, his arms off to either side. The electrical shocks surging through him continued, but he had begun to ignore them. He wasn't sure how long he would be able to do so, but with each shock, he found he was able to push it out of his mind and ignore the sensation.

"Your father is lost."

"He's not lost. I'm going to find him."

"You won't be able to find him."

"Don't say that!"

Haern staggered forward again, swinging his boards.

The Forger smiled at him. "Unfortunately for you, it is the truth. Your father is lost."

"No!"

The Forger grinned.

Distantly, Haern knew the man was playing him, that he was tormenting him so he could get the reaction he wanted, and it was working. Haern had to react. It was his father, after all, and he had lived for too long without Rsiran in his life.

When the Forger started to shimmer, the translucent air seeming to fold, Haern launched himself.

Pain coursed through him, and he could barely stand it, but he threw himself at the Forger, crashing into him just as he Slid.

The Forger tried to Slide, but Haern was there, holding on to him, his arms wrapped around the man's neck. The Forger grabbed on to the metal rings through his hands, pulling on them. Pain rolled through him unlike anything he had ever experienced. His whole body threatened to convulse, to rebel against what the Forger was doing, but Haern ignored it. He had learned how he could ignore it, having forced himself to do so when escaping from the chair.

He squeezed, holding on to the Forger, arms wrapped around the man's neck, legs brought up around his waist, and the Forger collapsed to the ground. Haern rode him down to the ground, staying on top of him. The Forger gasped for air, but Haern squeezed again. Rage filled him. Hatred for this man nearly overwhelmed him.

He would destroy him.

"Haern?"

The voice came from somewhere near him, and he had no idea why one of these Forgers would know him, and he rolled the Forger over, keeping himself on the man. He squeezed, hands wrapped around the man's neck, wanting nothing more than to tear away his last breath. He didn't deserve to live.

And yet, he refrained. If he killed the man, he would no longer be able to find out what happened to his father, and any chance of recovering Rsiran would be gone.

That as much as anything made him hesitate. He eased back but continued to squeeze, digging his fingers into the sides of the man's throat. This was someone who had tried to kill him. This was someone who had attacked his people. And he had done so more than once.

"Haern?"

There it came again.

The first time he'd heard his name, he could almost believe it was imagined, but this time, the soft and gentle way his name was said suggested perhaps it wasn't an illusion. Maybe this *was* real.

Haern looked around. He tried to blink away the pain, the tears, but there was nothing he could see. The room was empty, wasn't it? Chairs lined the walls. Banners hung from overhead. Otherwise there was nothing but blurriness around him. There wasn't any light, nothing that he could see through, and as he lay there, looking around, trying to make out what it was that was calling to him, Haern shivered.

The voice had sounded so familiar.

He looked at the Forger. His breathing came out slowly, raggedly, and he was wheezing. All Haern could think of was that this man had been responsible for what had happened to his father.

More than that, this man had been responsible for

Haern leaving Elaeavn, and because of him, Haern had come after the girls, finding them, rescuing them.

Something Galen had said worked its way into his mind, drifting to the forefront, overriding anything else he could think of. It was surprising coming from Galen, a moment of hearing the other man talk about believing in something of a higher power, but in this case, that was what Galen had said.

"Haern?"

This time there was no denying it.

He released his grip on the Forger, getting to his knees. It was painful. Staying where he had, holding on to the Forger, his hands wrapped around the man's neck, there had been less pain than there was now. Moving sent renewed pain rolling through him. Nausea filled him along with it, and with each movement, every time that he tried to do something—anything—he found he could not. He stayed on his knees for long moments. The pain continued to work through him, and he shook, jerking each time the old sense of electricity rolled through him. When it finally passed, Haern took a few breaths before opening his eyes.

He remained on his knees. The Forger was near him, and he didn't know if he had killed him.

The sense of others nearby drew his attention, looming close to him.

It was more than just the sense of others nearby.

Lorcith.

He *pulled* on that sense, focusing on it, and felt for the sense of his coin. He had forged these coins, they were his, and he had given them to Elise and the others to hold while he went looking for them.

Elise.

That was why he was here. If he could find her and the others, he could rescue them from this.

"Elise?"

Why was she here?

How was she here?

His voice came out hoarse, but he managed to get it out. Staggering to his feet, he looked around. There would have to be more than just this Forger here, wouldn't there? He couldn't have been the only one in the room, but then, Haern had the sense that the Forger had drawn him here, wanting him to be present for whatever dark reason he had in mind.

The coin was close. He turned, looking for it, and saw nothing more than a glowing brightness in front of him.

"Haern. I'm here. What… what happened?"

"Elise? You need to get moving. The Forgers—"

"We're safe."

"How?"

"They didn't want to hurt us. The others—"

Something else moved, drawing his attention. There came a different sense, a powerful explosion, and as he focused on it, he realized it came from deep beneath him. Somewhere deep within the tower, the temple rumbled.

"What happened with the others?"

"The others were going to hurt us."

Would the Binders have done that?

A hoarse cough caught his attention. Haern turned, barely gritting through the pain rolling through his hand,

and the Forger lying on the ground started to laugh, a dark and horrid sound.

"The Binders? Is that what you believed, Lareth? There are no Binders here."

No Binders? But *weren't* they the Binders?

Then again, who had suggested that? Had it been them, or had it been Haern?

The more that he thought about it, the more his mind managed to clear, the more certain he was it had been his fault. Was he the one who had suggested that they were Binders?

"They were protecting us, Haern," Elise said, her voice distant, weak.

No. He couldn't believe that. He didn't want to believe that. Even if the Binders were not what they had made themselves out to be, he couldn't believe the Forgers had any interest in helping these women. He had known the Forgers too well, had faced them too often, to believe that they would have any motivation to help someone else.

It meant that they were somehow coercing Elise and the others.

He had seen how the Forgers had the ability to do that but hadn't expected them to be able to use it on someone so quickly—or perhaps not on so many at one time.

If it wasn't this Forger, then it had to be another.

He reached for the man, finding him lying on the ground.

"You lost, Lareth," the man said.

Haern grabbed his head, and he slammed onto the ground.

He got back to his feet. Why couldn't he see anything?

There had been chairs. Banners. There was the Forger. But now there was nothing. All around him was darkness. He couldn't see a thing, and the more he tried, the more he strained to see into the darkness, the worse off he was.

They were poisoning him.

That was the only thought that rolled through his head, and it was one that made sense. Galen had taught him to recognize poisons, and in this case, the poison they were using had to be something attached to him. His hands.

Whatever metal they had used was reaching into his bloodstream. The longer it was there, the more likely it was he wouldn't be able to recover from it.

Somehow, he had to get these bars off.

He should have forced the Forger to take them off before he did anything.

"Elise?"

She was here, but where?

Then again, she'd seen his brutality. She'd seen the way that he had slammed the Forger into the ground, and why would she want to be around him any longer?

"Please, Elise. Help me."

Someone was there, arms wrapping around him. Haern tensed, every part of his being wanting to rebel, to resist, fearing that touch, mostly because he had been exposed to such dangers ever since coming to the temple.

"I'm here," she whispered.

"How?"

"They… they brought me."

The Forgers had done this to her. Anger surged within him. "What about the others?"

"The others are unharmed. They protected us. They brought us here."

"Not protected. Not yet."

"Haern?"

"They did this to me."

"Because you attacked. They told us—"

Haern tried to look toward her, but he couldn't find her. All he could feel was the sense of lorcith flowing from her, and he was thankful that he hadn't lost that.

Surprisingly, there were shades of light that swirled around him, and as he tried to see through it, he found that areas of lorcith seemed to glow a little brighter.

"I need you to bend these bars. I need them out of my hands."

"I don't know if I can."

"Please."

Elise moved her arms, and he wanted nothing more than to have her slip her arms back around him, to comfort him, to feel the welcome touch of someone. After feeling pain for so long, he wanted that relaxation.

It was not to be.

Pain jolted his left hand.

He started to jerk away before his mind overrode instinct, realizing Elise was trying to pull off the metal bars as he had asked.

He didn't know if he screamed or not, only knowing pain continued, an unrelenting sense of torment, almost as if Elise knew exactly what she was doing to him but continued to do it.

And it was gone.

Long moments passed while he panted, each breath a

struggle, straining to try to gather himself to control his response, and finally, the pain began to abate.

"Is it done?"

"As much as I can, Haern."

"It's a bar of metal. All you need to do is pull it out."

"I don't know what they used on you, but I wasn't able to pull a bar of metal out. Something remained in there."

He swallowed, thinking about what had happened to Lucy. She had been changed, augmented, however intentional or not by something similar.

"Do the other."

He braced himself, and this time he didn't think he jerked away. When she grabbed for his hand, pulling on the metal bar, he tried not to resist and thought he managed. When the pain flooded into him, he bit back a scream, though perhaps not as well as he believed. His throat felt ragged, some part of him exhausted from shouting, and he tried to silence himself, not wanting to draw any more attention to them than he already had. He didn't want to be the reason the Forgers came after them, but he also didn't think he would be able to withstand the pain he was feeling for very much longer. He might have asked Elise to do this, but the longer she worked, the further she pulled out the metal in his hand, working it out, the more he…

The pain began to ease.

He breathed out. Could it be over?

He didn't know. Hopefully, but even if it wasn't, he was thankful that she tried.

"I got as much as I could on the side, too," Elise said.

"I'm sure you did well." His voice was hoarse, ragged,

and he lifted his arms, wondering if he would even be able to move his hands. Would the pain be too much for him?

He was able to move more freely than he had before, and he waved his hands around, thankful that he no longer had the board attached to them.

Then again, those had served as weapons, and he had been able to use them to protect himself. He looked around, but still saw nothing more than the bright light all around him.

Whatever they had done to him had changed him. He was certain of it and knew it had poisoned him in some way. His only hope now was that it hadn't been anything permanent.

He touched the left hand where the bar had gone through. The skin felt strange where the metal had pierced him, but it was more than just that. It was almost as if where the metal had been had somehow changed.

Pain throbbed in his hands, but it was different now.

If this had poisoned him, then he needed time to see what effect the poison would have, and hopefully, it wouldn't be anything too significant so he would have time for recovery, though it was possible the Forgers had created some way of poisoning that had no recovery. They knew he was working with Galen; he couldn't help but think that they would use that as an opportunity to get back at Galen for everything he had done to their people.

"I'm sorry. I did as much as I could, but I couldn't get everything out, Haern."

He looked toward Elise, though he couldn't see her

easily. "You did well. I don't think you could even do anything more."

Now that he could move without pain, he looked around. It might be only his imagination, but it seemed as if his vision were starting to clear a little bit, and now he no longer saw only brightness. He was able to make out faint outlines, and he reached toward the nearest, realizing it was Elise.

His hand brushed her cheek and her breath caught. "I'm sorry, I wasn't trying to—"

Elise took his hand, pressing it up against her cheeks, holding it there. "You startled me, that's all."

"We need to get moving. I don't know what's going to happen when he comes around or when more of the Forgers appear, but I don't want to be here."

"They didn't want to hurt us," she said.

"Maybe not, but they wanted to use you the same as the Binders—or whoever they were—intended to use you."

How would they find a way of getting to safety?

They needed to get moving, get out of here, and then where?

Rumbling echoed again, and he felt the sense of it filling him.

"The Binders are attacking the temple," Haern said.

Haern took a few shallow breaths. With each breath, everything started to clear even more. Eventually, he felt as if he might finally be able to see again. The effect of the poisoning would clear, and from there he should be able to make out where he was and figure out some way of escaping.

"Where are the others?"

"They're back here."

Elise took his hand, guiding him, and he didn't resist. He could see the shadows, the faint outline of everything around him, but nothing more. As she guided him to the back of the room, he heard the soft whispers of others around him.

"It's okay," Elise said.

"We saw what he did," one of the girls said. Haern didn't recognize the voice, and he couldn't see well enough to make out who might have spoken, but some part of him withered as she said it.

"That man is the one who abducted my father," Haern said. "He's holding him captive somewhere, and he's the reason I left my city. I came looking for my father, and now…"

Now he didn't know if he ever would find his father. The Forger wasn't going to tell him, and some part of Haern knew that even if he did, it probably didn't matter. He wasn't going to be able to find Rsiran like that. If the Forgers had him, what hope did he have of ever getting into their fortress?

Even with Galen, they wouldn't have been enough.

An idea came to him.

"Are any of you harmed?" he said.

There came another soft whisper, and it was Elise who answered. "Everyone is fine, Haern. They didn't want to hurt us."

"They were going to use you. You're bait."

"Bait?"

"They wanted to draw out the Binders. And it worked."

Haern turned away, the faint outline that he was able to see enough for him to make his way. "I'll be back."

"Haern?"

"Keep them safe," he told Elise.

Stumbling forward, he reached the place where the Forger lay. He still hadn't moved, but then again, Haern had slammed his head onto the ground with enough force to crush his skull, so it was possible he wouldn't be able to get up. He crouched near the man's feet, grabbing on to his ankle, and simply held it.

He waited for long moments, watching the Forger as he breathed. Every so often, there came a faint rumbling from deep within the temple, but that passed. How long would it be before the attack reached them here? They might be powerful, but so far, the Binders hadn't managed to penetrate that deeply into the temple. It might take them a few hours to reach into it. The sense of lorcith he detected was far below him, and he paused only a moment to wonder why he felt that sense so acutely now. As he focused on it, he could feel the lorcith coins Elise and the other girls carried on them, and if he wanted to, he could *pull* on that sense, draw it to him—or him to it.

The Forger continued to breathe slowly, but gradually, his breaths became increasingly rapid, until he was coming around. That was what Haern needed. He continued to hold on to the man's ankle and wait.

It didn't take long before he awoke. When he did, he immediately started to move.

Haern kept himself low, gripping as tightly as he could

onto the Forger's ankle. If his own experience meant anything, the Forger wouldn't be able to focus on anything other than the pain throbbing in his head. That was a distraction Haern counted on, believing the Forger wouldn't know there was someone else there, someone clinging to his leg, someone who would be holding on while the Forger Slid.

The Slide started, beginning with a folding of the air, turning it more translucent, and then it began to shimmer. He waited. Though he knew that he wasn't thinking quite as clearly as he should, all he wanted was to follow the Forger, hopefully to wherever his father was trapped.

The Slide dragged him, tearing him from this place to another.

When they emerged, Haern continued to hold on to the Forger. He looked around, searching for any way to recognize where they were, but he saw nothing.

The air stank. It smelled of fire and ash, but there was another odor mixed with it, equally unpleasant. It was pungent, a sour, sulfuric sort of smell, and his nose wrinkled.

Maybe it was nothing more than the abrupt change from the floral and incense aroma of the temple, but he could scarcely stand it.

"You," the Forger said.

Haern turned his gaze to the Forger, who had his neck bent, looking at Haern.

"You have made your last mistake, Lareth."

"This is where my father is, isn't it?"

"Your father is gone, Lareth."

"I don't believe that."

"Don't you? You also didn't want to believe he could be captured, but I have proven he can. And now his son will share his fate. I suppose there is some cruel irony to that, but given everything your family has done to mine, I find it difficult to care."

"My family has done nothing to yours."

"Oh, Lareth, how naïve you are."

The Forger got to his feet, moving far more easily than Haern would've expected. And here he'd thought that the other man had been too injured to do anything, but maybe that had been partly an act.

He needed to use this Forger to get back to the temple. The longer he was away, the more likely the Binders—or false Binders—were to reach the others.

What had he been thinking?

He hadn't. He had wanted to figure out where they were keeping his father, but maybe he hadn't needed to Slide with the Forger in order to come up with that.

It might've been better—safer—for him to have held the Forger, forced him to reveal his secret, but then, it was equally possible that the Forger would not reveal anything.

"Where is this?"

"This is a place you will never escape."

Haern held on to the Forger, keeping him from Sliding, and yet the Forger did nothing to try to move, not attempting to kick Haern off, and simply allowed him to hold on to him.

"This is your hideout."

"Hideout? You make it sound as if we were little more than criminals, Lareth. The Ai'thol serve a noble purpose."

"There's nothing noble about the way you hurt others."

"We don't hurt. We provide order. Stability. How many places have you visited where lawlessness is the rule? The Ai'thol aim to provide order."

"The Ai'thol only want to serve as the law."

"How else could we provide order if we didn't?"

The Forger stared at Haern for a moment, and then he jerked his foot free, standing back, watching Haern, a dark gleam in his eye. "And here I thought I would have to work harder to bring you here. Now that you're here, you will find, much like your father, that there is no escaping from this place."

"I'm not going to escape."

"Oh?"

"I'm not going to need to escape," Haern said, getting to his feet and looking around him. There was nothing but stone, and it reminded him somewhat of Ilphaesn. The air stank, which was another clue. He needed to piece together everything he could, so that if the Forger didn't tell him where he was, he could come up with it on his own when—and if—he managed to get out of here. "I'm not going to need to escape because you are going to take me back."

The Forger laughed darkly. "Lareth, you have not yet begun to understand. But you will. You will."

36

HAERN

THERE WAS LITTLE WARNING OF AN ATTACK.

Haern felt a sense of movement behind him and realized a moment too late that it came from the sense of lorcith.

Why should there be lorcith surging near him?

He spun around, his gaze sweeping around him, and as he did, he realized that there were several others near him. Many of them had lorcith on them.

As he turned, trying to understand what was taking place, he realized that the sense of lorcith wasn't *on* them. Whatever lorcith he detected was *in* them.

All were armed, and the weapons they carried weren't lorcith blades. If they had been, he might have an advantage. There was nothing here that he thought he could use. He hesitated a moment, straining to reach lorcith, hoping that if nothing else, he could find perhaps a coin, a knife, a sword, but why would the Forgers make that mistake?

He knew they wouldn't.

One of the Forgers Slid toward him, and Haern pushed out his hands, bracing himself, and the Forger went flying away when he emerged from the Slide.

Strange.

Maybe there was someone else here.

How could someone else be here? How could someone else fight alongside him?

They couldn't.

Which meant that it had been him.

He looked over at his hands. Now that his vision had cleared, the changes to his palms were clear. The metal went through, but there was no more blood, and it seemed almost as if the metal had smoothed over his palm. It hurt when he clenched his hands into fists, but not like he would have expected. Every so often, the electrical jolt still came through him, but now he was able to ignore it.

When another of the Forgers Slid toward him, Haern *pushed* again.

This time he did it intentionally.

He focused on the lorcith he detected within the Forger, and with it, he sent a surge of his connection to the metal outward, and the Forger went tumbling head over feet, rolling across the room.

The connection to lorcith was far greater than he had ever had before. Could the metal they had used on him have changed him?

That was the only explanation. It was the same way Lucy had been changed, her own natural abilities augmented and perhaps even added to. Though he didn't want to gain abilities in such a way, he couldn't deny the usefulness.

If he could continue to employ this, he might be able to—

Something struck him from behind, and Haern went staggering. Catching himself, he turned around, swinging his arm, but he swung into nothingness.

He was struck from the other side, and again he went staggering.

They were Sliding into him from all sides.

How many Forgers were here?

Haern focused on what he could detect of them, and faintly, the awareness of several Forgers drifted to him. There were five—no, *six*—and they surrounded him. The longer he waited, the more Forgers appeared.

A troubling idea came to him.

What would happen if the main Forger appeared?

Olandar Fahr.

He'd heard the name but didn't know anything about him other than that he was powerful. Then again, if he found him, he might be able to find his father.

He needed to do something quickly. The only thing he thought he might be able to do would be to grab the Forger who had brought him here and force him to bring him back to the temple.

Could he figure out which of the Forgers that was?

He turned slowly, and as he did, he detected the lorcith within that Forger.

It was faint, a trace amount, but as he detected it, he *pulled* on it.

A muted cry was his reward.

The Forger slammed into him, and Haern was ready, having braced for it, and he wrapped his arms around the Forger, grabbing the man.

When the next attack struck him, a surge of lorcith that suddenly appeared, Haern spun around, letting the Forger take the brunt of it.

"Call them off."

The Forger laughed again. "You don't understand."

"Call them off," he said.

"And why would I do that? There is no way you will make it out of here. There are too many of us, and while you may have gained an understanding of lorcith in the time since you and I met, you aren't strong enough. Rsiran Lareth isn't strong enough."

At the mention of his father's name, Haern squeezed, choking the Forger, silencing him. Rage and anger filled him, and he turned, spinning around at each of the Forgers as they tried to Slide toward him. He *pushed*, sending them away, and found it was simply easier to create a shielding around him, a bubble that he continually *pushed* against; the Forgers couldn't Slide past it.

That would be useful, but only if he managed to survive.

He dragged the Forger with him, *pulling* him across the ground as he made his way through the chamber. Again and again Forgers tried to reach him, but he was still able to hold out against them. Eventually, Haern suspected he would fade. The moment he did, he would suffer an attack he might not be able to resist, but for now he would get through here.

More than ever, he was certain his father was here. If

he could reach Rsiran, rescue him, then he wouldn't need this Forger to bring him out. He could have his father bring him.

Haern almost let go of the Forger but realized his father wouldn't know how to find the temple.

He *was* going to save those women.

He reached the doorway. It was ornate, carvings and symbols along it incredibly decorative, and he paused, staring at it for a moment before hurrying through. If he could get through this, there might be time to look and understand those symbols later. For now, all he needed to do was get out of here. Once through the doorway, an orange light glowed in the distance. The tunnel continued forward, sweeping high overhead, much higher than was necessary. Was this only for decoration, or could there be another reason that they had carved it in such a way?

The Forger started to moan, and Haern wrapped his arms around the man again, squeezing once more. There remained the temptation to do more than just choke him out, but he resisted. He needed this Forger, and until he got back to the temple, until he was able to help those he had promised to help, he wasn't going to be the reason that they suffered. Not again.

At the end of the wall, he paused. There was another doorway, this one arching quite a bit higher over his head, enough so that he had to crane his neck to see the peak. Once through, heat slammed into him.

Lava.

That was what he had seen from a distance, and that was the cause of the soft glowing, but how was it he hadn't felt anything before now?

He backed up through the doorway, and as he did, the air temperature dropped considerably.

They must have used something to prevent heat from escaping. Impressive.

Sound from behind him caught his attention, and Haern continued to push outward with his lorcith barrier, marveling briefly at the fact he was able to do something like that at all. He went back to the doorway. He had no idea if he was heading in the right direction or if there were other places within the Ai'thol hideout that he would find his father, but there hadn't seemed to be anything else when he had been in that first chamber. This had been the only way.

Unless there was another way by Sliding.

Most of the Forgers had the ability to Slide, and they wouldn't need halls or stairs or anything. If they could Slide through here, then they wouldn't be limited in any way.

Yet, he had a hard time believing all of the Forgers could Slide. What would they do if they were injured? He and his father had injured the Forgers often enough that there would have to be some other way for them to navigate their hideout.

The walkway along the lava was probably twenty or thirty paces wide, wide enough that he could stay away from the edge of it, but curiosity called him forward. Why would the Ai'thol choose this place?

It was a strange location, and even if he managed to escape, he wasn't sure he would be able to figure out why they had made this their hideout. How many volcanoes existed? And this might not even be an open and active volcano. It was possible they used a place that was inactive. If this was deep beneath the earth, buried, he might never have found it on his own.

The Forger moaned again, and Haern resisted the urge to choke him out. Let him come back around. With his newfound control over lorcith, he wondered if he could prevent the Forger from getting away from him. Maybe there was no way he could.

He followed the path, winding along the lava, staying away from the edge. He wanted nothing to do with it. Heat continued to build, pushing on him, and after going for a while, he began to wonder if he would be able to withstand this. Or would the chamber be too much for him? Would the heat overwhelm him?

Another opening loomed in front of him, as tall as the last. Haern paused at it, focusing on a sense of lorcith, but detected nothing.

He continued onward, passing several other massive doorways much like the last, and at each of them he paused, focusing on the sense of lorcith, but he found nothing.

Finally, he came to a smaller doorway.

There was no sense of lorcith, but he was drawn along, hurrying forward, expecting he could find something here. There had to be something, didn't there?

Doors along the hall caught his attention. At the first one, he paused, leaning up against it. He tested the handle and found it locked. Haern considered forcing his way in but continued on. There were other doors much like it, all of them locked.

When he had made his way halfway down the hall, he understood what it was.

Cells.

His heart hammered. Could *this* be where his father was?

If so, could he rescue him?

He didn't know how much time he had left, and the longer he lingered, the more likely it was someone would reach him. If more and more of the Forgers appeared, he wasn't sure how well his new control over lorcith would protect him. It was possible he would be forced away.

There was nothing to do but start.

Racing forward, he reached the first door, slamming himself against it. He hammered at it with his shoulder, ignoring pain that surged through him with each crash into the wood. When it finally splintered and popped open, he looked inside and saw an old man sitting in the center of the room. The man had a long beard, wrinkled skin, and hollowed eyes. He looked up at Haern before turning his attention back to the ground.

Not his father.

Haern made his way down the hall, reaching the next door, and when he did, he slammed into it much like he had the first. It took fewer blows this time before he managed to get it open, and when he did, he froze. An older woman sat in the middle of the room, much like the man in the other room had. She looked up, greasy hair falling in front of her face, obscuring her eyes.

A part of him wanted to go to her and help, but that wasn't why he was here.

Dragging the Forger with him, he continued onward,

reaching the next door. He knew how much force was required to slam into it and threw himself against it, again and again. The door crashed open.

There was another man in this room, his dark skin making age difficult to determine, and his head shorn. Wounds were healing on his face, and yellow bruises ran along both arms.

Haern turned away. Door after door was the same. Each time he kicked one open, looking inside, he expected to come across his father, but each time he was disappointed. There was no sign of Rsiran, and each room had someone inside, making him wonder why the Forgers held so many people here. In several of the cells, people lay unmoving. Their bodies were wasted, and the stench within the rooms left him thinking that they were dead.

Haern started to count how many people had already died by the time he opened the cell and gave up when he got to double digits. Nearly half of the cells.

How could the Forgers leave them like this?

The man he was dragging began to come around.

Haern dropped him on the ground, propping him near one of the walls. He held on to the strange connection he now had to lorcith, *pushing* so he wouldn't be able to Slide, and waited for the man to come around. When he did, Haern nudged him with a toe.

"Still fighting, Lareth?" the man asked, his gaze lingering down the hallway before turning back to Haern. "You see you can't succeed. You will join the rest."

"Where's my father?"

The Forger attempted to Slide, and when he did, he slammed into the barrier Haern now held.

The Forger turned to him. He tried to Slide again, the translucent shimmering that came with each attempt drawing Haern's attention. He *pushed* the Forger back, throwing him against the wall before *pulling* him once more toward him.

"Did you intend to give me a gift?"

"Ah, Lareth. If only you understood everything taking place, but all of this is so far beyond you."

"Where is my father?" The Forger attempted to Slide again, but once again, Haern held on to him, *pushing* him back. "You gave me this ability. I'm not going to let you succeed."

"How do you intend to escape?"

"Where is he?"

The Forger stood, far more casually than Haern would've expected, and he let his gaze drift along the hallway. "How many doors have you opened? How many more do you think you can open before others get here? How long do you think you can withstand our attack?"

"As long as I need to."

He noticed Sliding coming from down the hall; there wouldn't be much time remaining. The moment someone else Slid to him, the others would follow. Already it was likely they had discovered where he had gone.

It was time for him to finish this, but he was not about to leave without his father.

Haern *pulled* the Forger to him, and he shifted the focus of how he used his connection, continuing to *push* outward, holding him in place. The longer he worked with lorcith in this way, the easier it was.

"You're going to help," Haern said.

"Help? I don't—"

Haern *pushed* him, sending him into one of the nearest doors.

It crashed open, and Haern *pulled* on the Forger, preventing him from falling on whoever was inside. He glanced past the Forger, realize that it wasn't his father before moving on to another. It was easier to *push* on the Forger, to use his body weight to crash into the doors, and as he did, he managed to open one after another. All of the cells were occupied, something that didn't surprise him at all. What surprised him was just how many cells were here.

So far, none of them held his father.

When he reached the end of the hall, he realized there were no more.

Had he come all this way to fail?

The Forger looked at him, a sneer still twisting his mouth, and Haern had a sinking feeling he might not succeed. Where else could he go? He dragged the Forger with him as he made his way along the hallway, staggering forward.

"You see how you will fail, Lareth. You see that your fate will be much like your father's."

"He's here. Tell me where he is."

"I've already told you where he is. He's gone."

"He's not gone. My father is too strong to be defeated by you."

"And who says he was defeated by me? I am not the one you need to fear. And I am not the one who destroyed your father."

Haern stopped in the middle of the row of cells,

holding on to his connection to lorcith, and looked around him. Could his father be gone?

He had planned on finding his father, thinking that all he needed to do was find the Forgers, to figure out where they would bring Rsiran, and then he could rescue his father, bring him back to Elaeavn and his mother. More than that, he needed his father to help get him out of here.

Instead, he failed.

The Forger laughed, the sound ripping at some part of Haern.

He had been a fool. He should have known better, should have known that his father could not survive captivity that long. The Forgers wanted to destroy him. How could they not? His father had hunted them for years, tracking them, tormenting them, removing them as a threat.

When they had an opportunity to return the favor, it was not at all surprising that they would do so.

It had been a long time. Long enough no one could have survived in captivity.

And he had seen what happened to others in these cells, the way the Forgers had been willing to leave them, to torment them until they died. So why should he think his father would be any different?

It came from believing his father was incredibly powerful, but he was still only a man. There was no way anyone could survive captivity like this, not even his father.

Perhaps that had been his mistake.

Haern dragged the Forger with him. When he reached the end of the row of cells, he turned to the Forger. The faint shimmering of movement started to draw his attention, enough that there would be other Forgers appearing.

He waited.

When they appeared, he *pushed*.

Haern was relentless, sending them tumbling into the lava, ignoring their screams as they fell, knowing they deserved a fate far worse than that.

One after another they appeared, and each time, he used his connection to lorcith, *pushing* the Forgers away from him, letting them fall into the lava. He stopped listening to their screams, hardening himself.

His father had been right. The Forgers deserved everything he could do to them.

He turned to the Forger he held. "You will return me to the temple."

"I will not—"

Haern *pushed,* sending the Forger toward the lava, before drawing him back. "Bring me back to the temple, and I will release you. You can come slinking back here and do whatever it is you need to, but know that if you don't, this will be your fate." As if to punctuate it, one of the Forgers suddenly Slid, and Haern *pushed* on him, sending him stumbling into the lava. "Do you understand me?"

"Do you think I fear death?"

"I think you intend something, and whatever it is you intend can't be accomplished by dying. So yes. I do think you fear death."

The Forger started to laugh, and Haern *pushed* on him again. He let him linger at the edge of the walkway overlooking the lava. He held him in place. How long would he be able to hold on? He wouldn't be surprised if he suddenly failed. This new connection might be significant, but he had no idea whether it would be indefinite.

"I don't want to tear down everything within your hideout."

"This is not a hideout. This is—"

Haern *pulled* the Forger to him. "I don't care what this is. All I care about is getting back to the temple."

He had been gone a long time now. If he wasn't going to be able to save his father, then at least he could fulfill his promise, save the young women as he had told them he would, and return to Elaeavn.

He dreaded telling his mother what he had found. But she deserved to know. She was a strong woman, and she had faced so much, dealt with his father disappearing often over the years, and managed to hold everything together in the Aisl in his father's absence. Haern had the sense she had never wanted that life for herself, that she would have preferred to have settled down, to have his father with her, and not have to wonder every time he left whether he would return. If nothing else, now she would no longer have to worry.

Eventually, Haern would come back here. His father deserved that. With enough people who could oppose the Forgers, Haern would return with strength, and he would destroy everything they stood for.

He would take up that mantle for his father.

For the first time in his life, Haern thought he had the strength needed to do so. Now that he had this connection to lorcith, maybe he *could* pose a real threat to the

Forgers. With Galen training him—if he survived—he could learn what was needed to defeat them.

Another couple of Forgers appeared, and they tried to circle him, but with his connection to lorcith, he dragged them into the lava. He felt no remorse.

"This is your last chance." He *pushed* on the Forger, sending him to the edge once again. He let him lean forward, holding him in place.

"I will return you to the temple," the Forger said.

Haern *pulled* him back and waited. "If you take me to the wrong place, I will end you, and then I will find anyone you care about and end them."

"Your father already has." The Forger started to Slide, and Haern released the connection to lorcith, allowing him to Slide him. When he emerged, he looked around, half expecting that the Forger would bring him someplace deeper into the mountain, or possibly even drop them into the lava, but he did as he'd promised, and they appeared within the temple, back where he had left the others.

Haern stepped back. "Go."

"You won't hold me here?"

"I told you I would release you."

The Forger attempted to Slide, and he hesitated before turning back to Haern.

Haern *pushed* on him. "Don't make me regret allowing you to leave."

With that, the Forger Slid away.

37

HAERN

THE INSIDE OF THE TEMPLE LOOKED AS HAERN remembered.

Chairs lined the walls, and banners hung overhead, symbols upon them that he didn't recognize. A set of chairs near one end of the room sat upon an elevated dais, and the women were all gathered around, watching him with suspicion when he arrived.

Elise stepped forward, regarding him with a strange look, and Haern took a deep breath, trying to hold on to the sense of lorcith, sealing it all around him. Several of these women had coins that he'd forged, and now that he was back, he felt the sense of that lorcith far more acutely than he had before.

"What happened?" she asked.

"I went looking for my father," he said.

"Where is he?"

"It's possible he no longer lives." The ground rumbled, and he turned his attention to the door behind him. The false Binders were still out there. Facing the Binders was very different than facing off against the Forgers and the augmentations they used to change themselves.

"We need to get moving," he said.

"How? You said it's not safe."

"I don't know that it is safe, but we don't have much of a choice."

"Where would you have us go?"

Where could he bring them? He had thought that he was getting them to safety by coming here, believing the Binders would provide that safety, but unfortunately, that did not seem to be the case.

And if the Binders weren't able to protect them, he would have to do it, wouldn't he?

That meant Elaeavn, but the people of Elaeavn did not tolerate outsiders very well.

Where else could he go?

There were other cities that he knew were trustworthy. Places where the Binders *would* help these women.

That meant delaying his return home. When he had wanted nothing more than to find his father, to save him, that would have mattered. Now, with the likelihood that his father had already passed from this world, the only thing he would be delaying was telling his mother what had happened.

"There is a place we can go," he said.

"You said we could come here."

"And I thought we could. We're going north, to a place called Asador. From there, those of you who want to return home will be able to do so." Haern didn't know if the Binders in Asador would actually allow that or not, but he believed they would. Carth would ensure they had some way of getting back to their homes, and those who didn't want to would be able to work with the Binders. "I can help. I want to help."

Elise looked at the others with her. The steady rumbling from below continued, and there came with it the sense of lorcith. The Binders were carrying something, though he didn't know if it would be something he could use against them.

When another explosion rocked the tower, he made his way toward the door, standing there for a moment, listening outward.

The sense of darkness loomed down the stairs, and he realized he couldn't remember coming up these stairs in the first place. He must have, but that time was nothing more than a blur. He'd not been able to see anything, his vision blinded, only the sense of lorcith drawing him.

As he peered out into the darkness, he realized something about his Sight had changed. There were lines across his vision, and through them came a sense of pulsing power.

It was lorcith, but it was something else too.

Could the temple hold lorcith within the walls?

If this was a temple of the Forgers, then he thought it could, but how had he not noticed that before?

Maybe that was why his vision had been a blur.

Haern *pushed* on that sense.

It was faint, but he was able to use it. He didn't know if he would be able to do the same without his new connection to lorcith, but the longer he stood there, the more certain he was there was lorcith here. Not just here, but everywhere. The sense of it flowed throughout these walls, through floors, through everything.

Strangely, the sense of lorcith wasn't profound. It was faint, a trace amount, barely enough for him to do anything more than recognize it was present.

Considering what he knew of the Forgers, they had to be aware that there was lorcith within the walls, but if it was intentional, why wouldn't they have used a greater concentration?

Why so little?

He breathed out heavily, glancing behind him. Elise and the others stayed where they were, not approaching, and he realized they might not come.

Footsteps sounded on the landing below him.

If only he had a coin, a knife, something with lorcith he could use to help carry him down, he could reach the landing, figure out what the Binders were doing, and then return.

But did he need that?

With the lorcith in the walls, he could use that.

He *pushed* and dropped down the flight of stairs, cushioning his landing with a *push* off the lorcith within the ground. There was movement below, and with that movement came the sense of lorcith.

Haern erected a bubble around him, using the same technique he had when he had faced the Forgers. It might not work against the Binders, but then he felt the connection to lorcith and wondered if maybe their experiments had been similar to what the Forgers did.

He glanced up the stairs, checking for movement

before turning his attention back below. The attack was still further down the stairs.

Blood on the walls caught his attention, and he realized that it had to be his blood. A trail from where his hand ran along the length of the wall weaved up and down the stairs.

It was a wonder he was still on his feet, but even more impressive was that he didn't feel bad. After everything he had experienced, and the fact that he had been fighting for as long as he now had, he was tired, and his hands throbbed, but nothing more than that.

Hesitating for a moment, Haern couldn't help but feel as if that were a problem.

He shouldn't feel better with Forger metal implanted in his hand.

What if they had *wanted* him to have the metal implanted in his hand?

It was something he would have to consider later.

Haern *pushed*, jumping off and letting himself drop so that he descended to the landing below.

Three women approached.

He recognized one of them, having seen her at the house, but the other two he didn't know.

"You," Julianne said. "You left us."

"You abandoned me," he said.

"We did what we were asked to do."

"You abandoned me. And you were responsible for what happened to those women."

"Careful," she said.

Haern focused on the sense of lorcith and could feel it

from somewhere within her. It was faint, twisted, but it was there.

Maybe it wasn't lorcith at all but one of the alloys.

As he stood there, he realized that the other two women also had lorcith within them.

They had been experimenting.

He was careful and pushed gently around him, creating a little bit of a bubble, enough that if they attempted to get too close, he could hold them at bay.

More than anything, he wanted answers. If they were trying to mimic the Binders, he wanted to know why.

The other two women he didn't recognize shifted their stances, trying to slip off to either side of him.

Haern *pushed*, blocking them from taking another step, and they surged forward, trying to reach him, but he held firm, keeping them from going anywhere.

"You're not even Binders, are you?"

"You're one of them."

"No." He looked from one woman to the next and shook his head in anger. "They made me. I wasn't anything but Sighted from Elaeavn. And now…"

Now he didn't know what he was. Something else, though what was that?

"You couldn't understand," Julianne said.

"Why couldn't I understand?" When one of the others tried to surge forward, he waved his hand, *pushing* her forward against the wall and holding her there. "Try it again and see what happens."

"They came to our lands, enslaved our people, and we went for help. We thought we found others like her, others who wanted to attack, but they didn't. They retreated, the same way that everyone retreats from the Ai'thol."

"Who did you find?"

"The people you seem to revere so much."

"The Binders?"

"Binders. What did they bind anyway? They bind themselves to fear, and they hide, avoiding those they could help, even though they have the ability to do so."

"What happened?"

"What happened is that we were willing to fight. We were willing to do what was necessary. We were willing to sacrifice ourselves if it came down to it to free our people."

He didn't know what to say. How could he argue with that? If they felt as if the Binders had abandoned them, how could he argue otherwise? It was possible that in their minds, the Binders had abandoned them.

"But now you want to force others into your fight."

"We don't force, we offer an opportunity."

"An opportunity to be changed. The same opportunity I was offered." He held his hands up and *pushed*. All of the women went sliding back. "I can't deny there is power in the augmentations, but those who receive them should agree to do so."

"You aren't going to convince us," Julianne said.

"I don't need to convince you. I intend to stop you."

"You've already made your first mistake."

He realized that she was delaying him.

There was the sense of lorcith, but now it came from above him, and far more potently than he had noticed it before.

Great Watcher!

Haern *pushed*, using his connection to lorcith to travel up the stairs. At the top of the stairs, he *pushed* again and darted into the room. He skidded to a stop, realizing there were more than he had expected.

There had to be a dozen of the false Binders, enough that he didn't know if he would be able to overpower them.

He started to *push* on the sense of lorcith but realized he couldn't do that. The lorcith he'd gifted to the girls now became a deterrent. He couldn't *push* away lorcith without impacting them.

Could he do so selectively?

Maybe he could hold on to his connection to the coins he'd made, *pull* on them, while *pushing* on the sense of lorcith he had not made.

Doing so would be far more complicated than anything he had done so far since gaining an increased connection to lorcith, but he had to try.

Haern *pushed* off the lorcith in the floor, reaching the center of the room. Once he was there, he *pulled* on the lorcith he had forged, drawing it to him, and then he *pushed*.

There was resistance, and it took him a moment to realize that resistance came from lorcith within the floors and walls and ceiling. He was trying to *push* on too much. Could he filter his connection? Could he reduce it in such a way that he didn't *push* on it quite so much?

Haern changed the focus, drawing a little less lorcith, and he *pushed* outward.

"You need to get them closer to me," he called out to Elise.

She looked over. Her eyes were wide, and he could see the fear fluttering within them.

"Bring them to me, and I can push them away."

"How?"

"I can't explain it. Bring them closer."

He continued to hold out, creating a barrier. Those with the lorcith coins he'd forged were drawn toward him, and they stumbled into the center of the temple, coming closer to him.

Elise gathered the others, attempting to bring them to her, but the false Binders were getting in the way, delaying her.

Haern jumped forward, crouching in front of one of the young girls who held one of his coins. "I need the coin back," he said as gently as he could.

She nodded quickly, reaching into her pocket.

He took it and *pushed*.

With that, he sent it streaking into the nearest of the false Binders, freeing Elise.

He *pulled* on the coin, holding on to the other connection to lorcith he had, and used the coin as he attacked, driving it around him, hitting one false Binder after another. He found he wasn't trying to kill, only injure. As he attacked, *pushing* on the coin, he wondered if perhaps that were a mistake.

If it were Forgers, he would have no qualms about killing, but for some reason the Binders made him sympathetic.

Elise continued to gather the women with her and

motioned for them to get near the center of the temple. Haern used the coin, *pushing* it around them, sending it streaking one after another, hitting one Binder after another, giving Elise a chance to get them together.

When she had the last of them, Haern backed toward the center of the temple.

There were nearly a dozen Binders, enough that he still didn't know if he would be able to stop them, but for now, in this moment, he was able to *push* against them, holding them at bay.

Faiza approached, her face bloodied, a small gash along one cheek, a sword in hand. She looked at him, coming as close as she could to the barrier that he erected. "How long do you think you can hold this?"

"I'll hold it as long as I need to get them to safety."

"Do you think this is all we will do?"

With the comment, he realized she was right.

He had attempted to find compassion, but what good would compassion do?

Others would be captured, forced to undergo the experiments the Binders attempted upon them and suffer the same way these women had almost suffered. Was that what he wanted?

There was something he could do, but it would require he be as cruel to them as he had been to the Forgers. Haern wasn't sure he had it in him. He didn't want to be that person, but what choice did he have?

"You think the Binders don't oppose them, but they do. I've been with them when they do."

"They have run. They left us exposed, and it forced us to make our own preparations."

"This isn't what Carth wants."

"Carth is dead."

"Carth lives. And I tell you this isn't what Carth would want."

It was his last attempt at trying to convince her to do something other than attack. He didn't want to destroy them, but he didn't know that he had much of a choice.

"Carth doesn't live."

"She does. I fought alongside her, facing the Forgers—the Ai'thol. She doesn't run, but she also wouldn't attack and sacrifice her people. More than that, the Carth I know wouldn't force people to do something like this. She works with those who come to her."

"You don't know Carth."

Haern realized she was trying to delay him much like Julianne had done on the landing. He turned and saw more of the false Binders coming up the stair.

"Don't make me do this."

"Make you do what?"

"You're doing to me what you would do to them. You're going to force me to do something I very much don't want to do."

"Anything that you do will be your choice, Haern of Elaeavn."

"Haern?" Elise said.

He looked over to her. Her eyes were wide as she looked around her, focusing on the girls cowering at the center of the temple before turning her attention back to the false Binders.

"Don't let them take us."

The comment pained him, filling him with agony.

One way or the other, he was going to fail in what he wanted to do.

He breathed out. The sense of lorcith was all around him, filling the walls, the floor, the entire temple, and he focused on what he could detect, letting that sense roll through him, granting him strength.

He needed to use that strength. He needed to draw upon it.

Haern let it fill him.

He pushed outward, funneling the sense of lorcith he detected from the temple all around him out through himself, through his hands and the strange metal that now penetrated them, and *pushed.*

The others went staggering back. All of them save Faiza.

She stood resisting him, and Haern met her eyes, defiance burning within them.

Pushing on the coin, he sent it toward her, connecting with her shoulder, spinning her around. He *pulled* on the coin, drawing it back, and then *pushed* outward again.

Once again, all of the false Binders slammed into the walls around. Chairs shattered. Screams echoed, and he ignored it all. He continued to *push,* forcing outward, pain throbbing through him, the same kind of pain as the electrical sensation, that jolting feeling he had known when they had first placed the rods through his hands. The air sizzled with that energy. He held on to it and continued to *push.*

At one point, Haern had started to scream.

Something dripped down his face, and he reached up to realize that it was blood coming out of his nose.

Someone touched him, and Haern jerked around, ready to attack, preparing to *push* on the coin, but realized that it was only Elise.

"Come on, Haern. They're down."

He looked around. The chairs that had lined the inside of the temple were destroyed. The false Binders lay atop them. Somehow, he had managed to rip down one of the banners hanging overhead as well. Haern swallowed, looking at the destruction, wondering how many of the women had died because of his attack.

Elise took his hand, guiding him. The others went with her, and Haern held on to his sense of lorcith, keeping it wrapped around them, prepared for the possibility he might have to *push* and attack. If it came down to it, he hoped that he had enough strength. He had drawn strength from the temple itself and wondered if he could do it again.

He lost track of how many stairs they took. After a while, they left the stairs, heading down the hallway. He passed fallen bodies and realized that they were Forgers who had died. He found himself surprised there weren't many more of the false Binders.

Those within the temple weren't fighters.

That was why so many of the Forgers had died.

What was this place?

It didn't matter. All that mattered was that he was going to get out of here, and he was going to take these women to safety.

At the bottom of the stairs, they headed out, and from there they reached the street. Faint light streaked in the distance. It was gentle sweeps of orange and red mixed with hints of blue as dawn was beginning to break. A warm breeze gusted, and Haern breathed it in.

The sudden realization of how tired he was struck him.

Maybe that came from leaving the temple. As he turned to stare at it, the sense of lorcith drifted to him, and he wondered if perhaps it had been strengthening him during the battle.

The pain in his hands started to throb, or maybe he was only more aware of it now that they were leaving the temple. Either way, it ached, a sense that he had been ignoring, and he looked down at his hands, running his fingers over the strange pieces of metal that had burrowed into his skin.

This might have been exactly what the Forgers had wanted.

They had altered Lucy, and now they had done the same to him.

Had they done that to his father?

Unless none of it was intentional.

He looked at the women and girls. Some of them were crying, but for the most part, they were quiet. Elise guided them, marching them through the street, keeping her hand on his as she did. After a while, she looked over at him.

"Asador?" she asked.

Haern looked around the city. All of this had been for his father. He had left Elaeavn, traveling with Galen, searching for information, and instead he had found something else.

His father was gone. Lost.

Which meant that he would have to fight. He would have to work with the people of Elaeavn, but also people like the real Binders, along with these women, and any others who would join with him to oppose the Forgers. The Ai'thol.

With these augmentations, he might have the strength to resist.

"Asador for now."

"And then?"

"From there I don't know. You get to decide."

"I'm going to stay with you, Haern."

He looked over at her. "Elise, you don't need to do that. You're strong enough to stay on your own."

"I might be, but I think you need someone with you."

They continued to make their way through the city. At this time of day, there were very few people out. The smells of the city struck him, a mixture of food and smoke and a strange pungent aroma that hung over everything, reminding him of the Forger hideout. When they reached the edge of the city, he looked back, noting the temple at the heart of it and feeling the pressure from the lorcith within it.

"Are you sure this is what you want to do?" Elise asked.

"I'm sure. I told you that I was going to get you to safety." He might not have been able to save his father, but this was something that he thought he could do. It might be a small step, but it would be the first of many small steps, and he would continue to take those steps, doing what was necessary. Eventually, they would defeat the Ai'thol.

38

LUCY

Once again, Lucy paced around the outside of the tower. There was something peaceful about walking along the rocks, and though she had a harder time than others, particularly Ras, she still found it soothing to pick her way along the rocks, looking for answers as she stared out into the distance, trying to gain an understanding of this place and what it meant for her.

Waves crashed along the shores, and she wanted to stand in the water the same way she once had stood within the sand, letting the water swirl around her ankles, trying to see if there was anything she might uncover that would help her find understanding, and yet, the water was much colder here.

Why should that stop her?

Lucy pulled off her boots and her stockings and waded into the water. Her breath caught, taking away most thoughts, and all she could think about was the icy cold of the water as it slammed against her.

She breathed, steadying herself, trying to gain control over herself and her emotions. She stood there, letting the saltwater flow over her ankles, and with each wave, it crested higher, slamming into her knees. Each jarring wave took her breath away.

Despite that, she didn't want to move.

Even here, with the icy cold water all around her, she found it peaceful.

When she finally adjusted to it, she stared out over the water into the distance. In all the time she'd been here, there had been no ships moving. As far as she knew, it was difficult to find this place, and were it not for Carth showing her how to reach it, Lucy doubted she would have been able to do so.

There was value in remaining concealed, but it made finding other places like it just as difficult. She needed to know if there were other places so she could see whether there was an answer as to what happened to the others, so she could know whether there was more to the lost.

She lost track of how long she stood there. All she knew was that the water was unpleasant at first, but the longer she stood, the more she began to appreciate the cold. Cold could be painful, but it could also be cleansing.

In her case, she had a need for the cleansing aspect of the water. She had spent so much time trying to figure out whether or not she could be trusted, whether what she remembered was accurate, and though she still wasn't sure, the longer she spent here, the surer she was there was something for her to uncover.

It was just a matter of her finding those answers.

She had to dig deep within her mind. Lucy needed to trust herself.

Somehow, that seemed to her to be the most difficult thing that she could do.

Why should she have a hard time trusting herself? It was more than just the fact that the Architect had forced her to serve. The Architect had wanted her to be anxious, wanted her to be unsettled, and because of that, he had wanted to leave her confused. If she weren't, then he would not have been able to control her quite as well as he was.

"You seem at peace."

Lucy turned slowly, nodding to Ras. "You told me to find a way of observing myself."

"And have you?"

"I think so. The only problem is that when I did, I'm not sure about what I uncovered."

"Why not?"

"I don't know whether I can trust what I observed."

"Why is that?"

"Part of it comes from the influence of the Architect."

"And?"

"And I was concerned he somehow managed to make it so I would not be able to trust what I remembered."

"I see how that would be difficult."

"It would be, except I am not sure if he would even have the ability to influence me."

"Why is that?"

Ras had a hint of a smile on his face, almost as if he knew the answer, and as Lucy watched him, she supposed that was true. More likely than not, Ras *did* know the answer and had been waiting for her to come up with it on her own.

"The nature of the implant. Somehow, with the implant I now have, he wouldn't be able to Push me, would he?"

"I'm not at all familiar with the nature of the implant, Lucy Elvraeth."

"I suspect you're more familiar than you're letting on."

"Perhaps," he said.

"Do these C'than know how to place this implant?"

"Unfortunately, Lucy Elvraeth, there are other types of C'than, as you have seen."

"Would you say you know how to place an implant like this?"

"No."

"Which is what I thought. And it's why the Architect was so amazed when he discovered this."

"I suspect he was quite thrilled with it."

The memories Lucy was able to reach told her that he had been. It wasn't surprising. The Architect had been excited with the possibility that he would have some way of using power he couldn't reach otherwise, and more than that, there was something about perfecting what Olandar Fahr had started, a desire to continue his work, to get the point where they would be able to use even more of that power.

"You knew I was trustworthy."

Ras joined her in the water, and she realized he was barefoot, and suspected he had planned on joining her all along. "I knew the nature of what had been done to you allowed you to protect yourself. Would it not, the others who used such an augmentation would be placed into the same sort of danger."

"Then everything I remember is accurate."

"If you say so."

"I do."

Ras tipped his head. "And what is it that you remember?"

"More than I had expected to remember."

"And with what you remember, are you able to offer any insight about Olandar Fahr?"

"He's after power," she said.

"He is."

"But as you've said, he's not the only one." The more she thought about it, the more she realized that was key to what Olandar Fahr was up to. It wasn't just that he was acquiring power—he was acquiring power with a purpose.

"What does that tell you, Lucy Elvraeth?"

She closed her eyes, and as she did, she thought back to the various images she was able to recall. There was more trapped within her, and the more she thought about it, the more certain she was she needed to understand what it was that she uncovered. The longer she spent, the more certain she was those answers would be there.

For now, she had to work through them, which meant that rather than focusing on trying to do anything too complicated, it was a matter of trying to master herself.

That was the lesson she needed. It was not just a lesson *she* needed, but a lesson that the women she had been trying to teach needed.

Here she thought finding those answers would involve

going to Elaeavn, and when she had been there, there had been a discovery, but there had also been a realization she wasn't sure she could remain. It was the same realization the others had already made. Perhaps they were farther along in their own self-discovery than she had been.

She didn't want to force these women into serving in a way they didn't want to do. Not that she could. And she had already started to help them, allowing them to find themselves, and in the case of someone like Eve, she had helped her uncover her ability, which was valuable. The more she was able to uncover, the more she was able to do, the more likely it was she would be able to help.

And that, as much as she hated to admit it, was the key.

Olandar Fahr was after power. And so too was someone else.

Whether it was tied to the faction of these C'than that had splintered off, or whether it was connected to something else, she had to come up with the answer as to what it was and whether there was anything she could do about it.

And she had to keep looking.

She had to find the rest of the lost.

They were gone, taken from Elaeavn, used by the C'than, and perhaps by whoever the C'than served.

Strangely, as much as she had struggled, trying to figure out how she could serve both the C'than and these women, the answer had come to her, giving her the solution that she needed.

She had to do both. She needed to root out the rest of the C'than infiltration, but in doing so, she was going to be able to help these other women, women who needed her support.

As much as anything, that was important to Lucy.

"It tells me that I need to keep looking. I need to understand."

"Do you think you do not?"

"I don't yet, but I think I can."

Ras nodded. "That is good."

"It doesn't matter to you that I don't want to learn Tsatsun?"

"Why should it matter?"

"Because of what Carth told me. You wanted to train her so that she could be—"

"I wanted to train Carth so that she could be Carth. I need to train Lucy Elvraeth so that she can be Lucy Elvraeth. You are different, but that doesn't mean you are less valuable. In your case, Lucy Elvraeth, you have a very distinct value to the C'than."

"It's not just the C'than."

"It is not."

She breathed out a long sigh and turned her attention back to the water. She would stay here, try to see if there was more she could find from what the Architect had shown her, however unintentionally, and then she would return to the village, to continue to work with the women there to find their own way, to understand who and what they were.

Somehow, in between all of that, she would need to keep looking into the C'than. That was the answer she needed, and the more she thought about it, the more certain she was she needed to uncover why the C'than had splintered off.

Ras continued to watch her, and she couldn't tell if he was Reading her. The way he regarded her left her feeling uncertain. She decided it didn't matter. There was nothing that she would hide from him. She had hidden enough from herself, and now it was time for her to find those answers.

39

DANIEL

THE SENSE OF POWER COMING FROM THE CENTER OF THE forest nearly overwhelmed him. Daniel couldn't shake the uneasy intuition that he had. The Ai'thol were busy with some plan he didn't yet understand. Would the people of Elaeavn lose their Elder Stone?

"Is there anything that you can do about it?" Daniel asked Neran. The old blacksmith stared at the pedestals supporting the crystals, and as he did, there came a sense of pressure that pushed on Daniel.

"Rsiran tried, but he wasn't able to do anything more with it."

"Did he know it was acting as a siphon?" Daniel asked.

"Rsiran is quite capable."

Daniel glanced to Rayen, but she had been somewhat silent ever since holding on to one of the crystals. Curiosity filled him about what sort of experience she might've had. He'd heard some of the tales, but most people who had an experience holding on to one of the crystals weren't able to easily explain what happened to them.

Power.

That, as much as anything, seemed to be the key to it.

Unfortunately for him, he had never been able to utilize the crystals. Even now, with the soft glowing light of the crystals, there was nothing about them he could use. Even if he went to one of them, there would be no power given to him the same way others were able to obtain power from the crystals. It was almost as if the crystals had some plan, but what sort of plan would there be?

He shook away those thoughts. "Rsiran is capable, but what if he overlooked it?"

"I don't think that he overlooked anything," Jessa said, glancing from Neran to the crystals before finally looking over at him. "And since the Forgers have him, I guess we won't ever know, will we?"

"Haern will find him," Neran said.

Jessa glared at him and he looked away.

Daniel didn't want to say it, but the Ai'thol were far too capable. If they had captured Rsiran, it would be nearly impossible for anyone to go after him. Even if they tried, the likelihood of succeeding and finding him alive—and still in some way surviving—was quite low.

"There is something here," Neran said as he continued to make a circuit. He had been walking around the base of the crystals, watching, and doing something Daniel couldn't quite make out. He could feel it, somewhat, though what was it that he detected?

Most likely it was nothing more than Neran using his

connection to one of his Great Watcher-given abilities, but if that were the case, why was it that Daniel would be able to detect what he was doing?

Joining him, he followed as Neran trailed around the crystals. There was nothing here that he could see, but maybe it wasn't something that he needed to see with his eyes. Maybe it was something that he needed to feel.

"What do you see?" Daniel asked.

Neran looked up, his back stooped as he leaned forward. "It's not so much what I see as what I can feel."

"Lorcith?" Jessa asked.

"There is some, but it's less than I would've expected." Neran straightened, looking around the room, and he swept his hand in a wide circle. "This close to Elaeavn, there's lorcith everywhere, which makes it difficult to know whether there's anything active, but in this place and in this case, I feel as if there is something here."

Daniel leaned toward the ground, wondering if his Sight would enable him to See something that Neran might miss.

The ground was smooth, almost polished, and there were no seams. It was all of a dark stone or tile, as if carved out of the ground itself. He couldn't tell if there was lorcith, but if Neran believed that there was, that was the reason they had come for the old blacksmith in the first place. If anyone would be able to detect the presence of lorcith, it would be a member of the smith guild.

"Rayen." When she didn't look his way, he headed over to her, touching her lightly on the arm. She startled, jerking back and lashing out with shadows that slammed into him before fading. Thankfully, the shadows didn't harm him, though that was probably more luck than anything else. "Are you all right?"

"I think so."

"What happened?"

"I'm not sure how to put words to it yet, Daniel. You are from Elaeavn, so you must understand."

"I've never held one of the sacred crystals."

"Never?"

"Has everybody from Ih been in contact with the Elder Stone there?"

"It is different. We are born with the ability or we are not."

"There are people from my home who are born with abilities, but the crystals decide who else gets to handle one of them. Those who do are often granted enhanced abilities."

"I'm not from Elaeavn, so what sort of change should I expect?"

"I have no idea. Right now, I need your ability with the shadows."

She took a deep breath, drawing herself up. "What is it that you need?"

"Neran says he detected something here. I need to know if you can detect something as well. We're looking for some way that the Ai'thol may be routing power from here."

She frowned for a long moment before nodding and turning her attention to the crystals. Her gaze lingered on them long enough that he wondered if perhaps another one might be glowing for her. If it did, would she be given even more power?

Shadows flowed out from Rayen, rolling across the ground.

"There is pressure here," she said. Jessa looked up from where she was talking to Neran and turned her attention to Rayen. "I'm not entirely sure if there's something more, but..."

Rayen continued to make her way toward the crystals.

Jessa started toward her, but Daniel moved to block her. Jessa might believe the crystals were meant for the people of Elaeavn and no one else, but if the crystals decided Rayen was worthy of holding one, who was he to say otherwise?

Rayen stopped outside of the ring of crystals. Power washed over the base of the pedestals, swirling in a steady pattern until it completed a circle. Rayen stood fixed in place, her eyes closed, and her breathing slow but steady.

"Daniel, I'm not sure that she should—"

He raised his hand, silencing Jessa. A pang of guilt rolled through him as he did, but he needed to see if Rayen could come up with any answers.

The shadows began to thin, flowing downward, almost as if going through the ground. Rayen still kept her eyes shut, so he watched the shadows, looking to see if there might be something—anything—that would explain what she detected.

When she finally opened her eyes, she looked over at him. "There's something more here."

"More?"

She nodded. "It's deep, but I can detect it."

Jessa made her way around the ring of crystals, every so often glancing over at them, her gaze lingering as longingly as Daniel suspected his did. Hadn't she had the opportunity to hold one of the sacred crystals? As far as he knew, they had given her increased eyesight, but maybe she wanted more. His father was the same way. He wanted more power, longing to hold each of the crystals —the same way Lareth had held them.

"Rsiran said there wasn't anything else here."

"Maybe he's not aware of it," Rayen said.

"He would have explored everything around here. This is the crystal chamber, after all."

"I can't tell you one way or another what your husband might or might not have uncovered. All I can tell you is that there is something more. It is deep below us, and it's something like this chamber."

Could the Ai'thol have discovered that?

"Do you think we can reach it?"

"I don't know how. I can detect something down there, but nothing more than that."

If *he* could detect it, he might be able to Slide down to it, but what exactly would that take? He wasn't sure he'd have any way of following what she discovered with the shadows, so whatever she did would have to somehow guide him.

"There might be another way," Neran said.

"What way is that?"

"Ilphaesn."

Jessa glanced at him. "Rsiran has explored Ilphaesn. There were no tunnels that led here."

"The mines lead all throughout these lands. Some of those mines are incredibly old, far older than the miners' guild knows. Rsiran knows that as well."

Daniel looked over to Rayen. With her connection to shadows, they could use that and probe through Ilphaesn, and maybe she could find her way.

"Neran, will you help us?"

"I fail to see what this will accomplish."

"If we can find where the Forgers are diverting our power, we might be able to do something to stop them."

Neran seemed to consider for a moment before nodding. "I will go with you. I can't say that we will be successful, but it is worth looking."

"You might need my Sight," Jessa said.

If he were to have his choice, there were others that he would rather bring with him than Jessa, but she probably did have better eyesight than him as she'd held one of the crystals. If they were going to go deep within the mines, then he liked the idea of someone able to See better than he might be able to do.

He grabbed Rayen, reached for Neran, and then nodded to Jessa. She grabbed ahold of his jacket, and with that, Daniel Slid.

Only after did the realization that he had never Slid so many people at one time come to him. He should have been more careful. Bringing two people was difficult enough, but bringing three was almost beyond his typical ability.

Surprisingly, he managed to Slide them to Ilphaesn without too much struggle. They emerged outside the mountain, and he looked up at the massive mountain as it rose high overhead, ending in a snow-covered peak. There were plenty of people from Elaeavn who still held Ilphaesn in almost mystical regard, but Daniel was not one of them. The fact that Ilphaesn was the source of lorcith made it valuable, and his experiences over the last year had done nothing but reinforce how important lorcith was to not only his people, but others.

"Where do we go from here?" Daniel asked.

"You've never been here?" Neran asked him.

"I don't have any connection to lorcith, so what reason would I have for ever having come here?"

Neran looked up, where a massive gate somewhere along the face of the mountain glimmered in the fading sunlight. A road wound along the side leading up to that gate, and up further from there.

"Will you able to Slide us throughout the mountain?" Jessa turned to him, studying him. "I ask because the mountain is extensive, and even when Rsiran was here, he struggled with navigating the entirety of it. If you don't think that you will be able to do it, then perhaps you shouldn't bring us with you."

"I can bring the three of you with me, and as long as we're focused, I can get us to where we need to go."

Jessa grunted. "I'm not so concerned about you getting us where we need to go. I'm a little bit more concerned about getting out."

"I know my limits."

He grabbed the three of them and Slid up to the gate. He paused only a moment before Sliding them through.

On the other side of the gate, he couldn't help but realize that despite how many times he had Slid over the last few hours, there had been no real change in how much strength he was able to draw.

Why would that be?

He had more practice Sliding these days. With everything he'd been through, he had exerted himself quite a bit more than he ever had before. If there was one thing he knew about his abilities, it was that the more they were used, the stronger they became.

"Where do we go from here?" he asked.

"Rsiran and I have spent quite a bit of time here over the years. We go down."

"What about you?" Daniel asked Neran.

"I have been here a few times, but only a few times. I was never sentenced to serve in the mines."

"That was the only way you would come here?"

"I may be able to hear the song of lorcith now, but when I was growing up, I feared it."

"Most did at the time, Neran," Jessa said gently.

"Perhaps, but even now I still have a part of me that reacts every time I first hear the song."

"What sort of song is this?" Rayen asked.

"It fills me," Neran started. He closed his eyes, tipping his head toward the ceiling of the mine. A little bit of sunlight streamed through the gate, but shadows began to fall only a dozen or so paces into the mine. "If I let it, it will overwhelm me. I can hear it even now. Some parts of lorcith sing more loudly than others, and the longer I stand here listening, the easier it is for me to distinguish distinct tones. In a place like this, it's almost like a chorus, a choir of voices, but in my blacksmith shop, the voices are different, more urgent, and they demand my attention."

"That sounds beautiful," Rayen said.

Daniel glanced over, half expecting to be met with a

sense of sarcasm, but there was none from her. She meant it.

Strangely, that reminded him of what Beatrice said of Sliding. Were they connected in ways he didn't understand?

"There are times when the song is beautiful, but there are other times when the song is frightening. The longer I listen, the harder it is for me to ignore it. There are times when I hear the song that I feel almost as if I will be pulled into it, joining the choir." He opened his eyes, looking at them, age and weariness making the wrinkles along the corners of his eyes deepen even more. "It is foolish, I realize that. It's the reason that I pause every time I go into my shop."

Daniel glanced over to Jessa. "Is it the same for Rsiran?"

Jessa had been watching Neran, her lips pressed together as she regarded him. "He never describes it quite like that. He calls it a song and tells me he can pick out individual pieces based on what they ask of him, but he never speaks of being pulled into the chorus." She took Neran's hand. "Are you sure that it's safe for you to be here?"

"I can resist it, if that's what you're afraid of."

"I'm not afraid of you losing yourself, I just wanted to make sure that this won't be too unpleasant for you. I'm sure that we can find our way through here without your getting tormented."

"If we find something, my presence might be necessary," Neran said.

He was right, and Daniel didn't like the idea of letting Neran return, or worse for him, remain here.

"Seeing as how I have not been here before, it might be easiest for me to Slide a few places on my own and then return. Once I've been somewhere, I can Slide back."

"Are you sure that you want to wander through the mines by yourself?" Jessa watched him, her gaze flickering around her. He realized that she twisted a bracelet on her wrist, almost as if it irritated.

Rayen turned to him, shadows swirling around her. One hand remained on her sword and she smiled to himself. There was no way she would need her sword in here, but he wasn't about to tell her that. "You can bring me with you."

"I think I can manage. I can travel much faster if I Slide on my own, and I will only be gone a short while before returning."

Before either of them started to argue again, he Slid, reaching the main part of the tunnel. He paused, looking into the darkness. He tried to tamp down the way that his heart raced. Even though he had Sight, it did little more than make gradations of shadows. If only he could part the shadows, then he might be able to See more easily into the tunnel, but without a lantern, there would be no way for him to do that.

Even if he had brought the others with him, he still was dependent upon what he could See. It required him to explore, and though it might take a little while, he thought he could travel quickly.

And he didn't even need to Slide very far. He could Slide a few steps each time, pausing to let his eyes adjust, noticing where the tunnels branched off. He moved through the tunnels that way, and as he did, his eyesight seemed to grow more and more accustomed to the darkness so he didn't struggle nearly as much as when he first had started. When he descended down a series of stairs, the tunnel opened up into several different branch points. From there, he paused a moment before Sliding back and grabbing the other three and returning.

"You know where we are?" Daniel asked Jessa.

"This is the start of the mine."

"This is the *start*?"

"Everything before here was always considered picked over, though Rsiran told me that wasn't the case."

"There's lorcith all around us," Neran said.

"I move relatively quickly, but I still need to know where I'm going, so if you're comfortable waiting here…"

"Are you sure your strength is holding?" Jessa asked. "I've been around men who can Slide often enough to know that the edge of your ability can creep up on you. If you overdo it, you might not know it until it's too late."

"I'm actually feeling fine."

Much better than he thought that he should, and despite the fact that he continued to Slide, there was no ongoing sense of weakness filling him.

"Which way?" he asked Rayen.

Shadows stretched away from her, and in the darkness, Daniel noted them as a darker density, a part of the cavern that was even more difficult for his Sight to peer through. It was hazier than what she had used around the sacred crystals, and she sent them off through each of the tunnels. After a while, she opened her eyes and pointed, but not in the direction he would've expected.

"That one leads generally back toward the forest."

Daniel looked over to Jessa and she nodded. "She's right. The others lead in different directions, though this one," she said, pausing and pointing to one behind him, "runs somewhat toward the city itself. Rsiran seems to think it could lead into the city, though he never managed to find a connection."

He could imagine what it would be like to follow these tunnels all the way to the city. It would be an incredible journey, far longer than he would want to spend underground, to wander through the mines, braving the darkness, weaving through the tunnels as they led toward the city.

Then again, he didn't want to do it heading toward the forest either. The forest might be closer, but only a little bit. Daniel didn't fear the dark the way some people did—those born with Sight rarely feared it—but he didn't like the idea of being surrounded by the entirety of the mountain. What would happen if he came upon a collection of heartstone? He wasn't able to Slide beyond that.

He wouldn't be able to Slide *into* it, either.

He needed to keep his mind rational, focusing on what he could See. If they could find the cavern beneath the heart of the Aisl and whatever stretched beneath it, he believed they would have a chance to understand what the Ai'thol were after.

He took a deep breath and plunged forward.

The darkness began to shift, growing increasingly dense, and despite his eyesight, each step took him deeper and deeper into it. The longer that he went, the longer he had to pause in order for his eyes to adjust. After a while, everything became a haze of gray mixed with only a hint of darkness.

There was a sense of the shadows, and it was a sense that reminded him of Rayen, enough so that he wondered if perhaps she had pushed her shadows after him, chasing him in order to ensure that he was safe. He wouldn't be surprised she would do something like that.

Smiling to himself, he continued onward. When he reached a clearing, another few branch points of tunnel in front of him, he paused a moment to fix the location in his mind before Sliding back to the others. Before his eyes had a chance to adjust to the slight change in light, he had a moment where he feared they weren't there, but then he found them.

Grabbing on to all three of them, he Slid them deeper beneath the ground, and when they emerged, he took a step back.

"Can you See anything?" he asked Jessa.

"Give me a minute."

The darkness seemed to shift, and as it did, Daniel could more easily make out Rayen, but also Jessa and Neran.

"This was you?"

"What was me?"

"Moving the shadows."

"I did, but you should not be able to see it."

"We've been underground so long, I think that's all I can See." He stared at one of the darkened tunnels. "Can you tell which direction we need to go?"

She watched him for a long moment, and then closed her eyes, sending shadows rolling away from her. There was no change in the way the shadows had shifted before, and he could more easily make them out. They rolled off, heading down each tunnel, before she snapped her eyes open. "Interesting."

"What is?"

"These two would seem to be heading in that direction, but this one," she said, pointing to the middle tunnel, "ends in a difficult to reach section. The other dead-ends, and there's no other way to go. This last one seems to head in the wrong direction, but it works its way around before making its way once more toward the forest."

"Give me a moment."

Daniel Slid, heading down the tunnel, now taking smaller Slides, afraid to go more than a few steps at a time. It was almost as if he were running, and he grew tired the same as he would if he had been. The tunnel narrowed, becoming far more difficult for him to navigate, and he slowed, squeezing through, forced to walk, and then to drag his way through. If he got stuck, there would be no way for him to Slide free, so he needed to be careful. He didn't have others' ability to Slide without moving. For him, the step took him into the Slide.

He reached his hand out, probing into the darkness, and as he did, he found a wider opening. All he had to do was get through here.

Taking a deep breath, drawing in everything around him, he forced himself forward.

For a moment, he was trapped. In that second, his heart raced, sweat poured off him, though that was just as much from the effort of Sliding through the tunnel as it was from fear. Wind whispered across his face, a strange breeze he didn't think should be within a tunnel like this.

And then he was free.

He staggered forward, stumbling into a small clearing. It was wide enough for only a few people to stand easily, and from here, he expected to find more branch points, each of them leading off into the darkness, but there was a single tunnel heading away.

Sliding back to the others, he grabbed Jessa first, Sliding her. "Stay against the wall," he said as he emerged from the Slide. He returned for Rayen and Neran, Sliding them into the small chamber. Once there, he waited.

"We're almost there," Rayen said.

"How much further do you think we have to go?"

"Not much."

"Then maybe we stay together."

Jessa turned to him. "If you're too tired to keep going, we should rest."

"It's not that I'm too tired, it's—"

She tapped him on the chest, forcing him to take a step back. "Daniel Elvraeth. So help me, if you have trapped us here—"

"I haven't trapped us here. I just didn't like the way I almost got stuck."

"What do you mean?"

He guided her to the section of wall that he had forced himself through. "I don't have Rsiran's ability to Slide without moving. When I got stuck, I was a little scared."

He turned away from her, looking down the rest of the tunnel. From what he could tell, it appeared large enough for all of them to move, but how long would it stay that way? Would it narrow like the other had?

"I'm sorry, Daniel," Jessa said, touching him gently on the back. "You've done well."

"Let's just keep moving. I want to find this place."

He started into the tunnel, with Rayen behind him, Neran behind her, and Jessa bringing up the rear. They stayed close together, and with Rayen pressing so close to him, he could feel her breath on his neck, and every so often, he would pause abruptly to startle her until she finally pushed him out of annoyance.

He started to laugh, when he realized that something had changed.

He should have noticed it before, but he hadn't. The change had been gradual, subtle, and now that he was here, now that he saw it, there was no way to regard it as anything else.

It was lighter.

"Do you see that?" he whispered.

Rayen nodded, leaning over his shoulder. "We're close."

As they continued forward, their feet scraping along the stone, another sound came to him.

He stopped, startled, and frowned.

Voices.

40

DANIEL

THE SOUND OF VOICES ECHOED THROUGH THE QUIET IN THE cave, and Daniel made a point of raising his hand, keeping the others from moving too quickly or too loudly. He needn't have worried. Almost as soon as the voices revealed themselves, Rayen had wrapped shadows around in a way that created something of a barrier, though it was one Daniel could see through.

He would have to try and understand what it was she did with the shadows later. For now, all he needed to know was who was here.

None of the guild would come this far.

"We are near enough the space beneath the crystals that this could be it," Rayen whispered.

Daniel tried to look through the darkness. He was hesitant to move too far forward, and the tunnel was narrow enough that he couldn't allow anyone else past. "I can't make anything out."

"I can't either," Rayen said.

If neither of them could, he would have to continue forward—which meant risking exposure.

This was why they had come. They had wanted to reach the space beneath the crystal chamber, but none of them anticipated coming across anyone here.

"I'm going to head out there."

"Let me do it," Rayen said.

He shook his head. "I don't think that you can move past me, and even if you could, I'm going to have the easiest time Sliding away if it comes down to it."

She reached for her sword.

"There's no need for the two of us to argue about it," Daniel said.

"I'm not arguing. I am merely preparing."

He smiled. "Watch over me."

"And why would I do that?"

"I don't know, I think you want to make sure nothing happens to me."

"You had better be careful, or I might end up letting whoever's on the other side have their way with you."

"And what if they're nothing more than members of the guild?"

"You wouldn't hesitate as much if that were the case."

"Unfortunately, I don't think they're members of the guild." His gaze darted behind Rayen, looking to Neran, who had remained silent. Jessa tried to push forward, looking over his shoulder, but he was too large for her to see anything. "Keep me covered by the shadows."

Rayen didn't have to answer, and the shadows began to swirl around him, a steady sense he was fully aware of. He could feel them and wondered why that should be. He slipped forward, careful with each step. His foot dragged along the stone, louder than he intended, and he froze.

Rayen tapped him on the shoulder, motioning him to silence, and he glared at her.

She would be far better equipped at moving in silence than he was, though he was better able to escape if it were necessary. It had to be him.

As he continued forward, he realized that he wasn't moving alone.

Rayen stayed with him.

"I need you to watch over the other two."

"Watch over them while they do what? There's nothing else in the tunnels with us. They're safe as they can be."

He didn't think that was quite true. There remained the possibility that whoever was down here would come through the tunnels, and if Rayen wasn't there, it required Jessa and Neran to protect themselves. He suspected she had enough skill that she would be able to if it came down to it, but Neran had said that he was not a fighter.

In the tight confines, would Jessa even be able to do anything? She might have a knife, but the sword had a much better reach, and squeezed in as they were, it might be easier—and better—for her to have something with a little more reach.

He unsheathed his sword, reaching past Rayen.

"What are you doing?" she asked.

"If they're caught here, I don't want her to have to fight with a knife."

"What about you?"

"Well, I don't want to have to fight at all."

"Do you intend to go in there empty-handed?"

"I do know how to Slide, so there is that."

"I'm not sure that you and your ability to Slide can counter the Ai'thol if it comes down to it."

"Now you're trying to convince me this is the Ai'thol?"

"Who do you think it is?"

Daniel sighed. He didn't want to believe that was what was down here, but it made a certain sort of logical sense. If it were the Ai'thol, they would need to be able to move quickly.

"If this is the Ai'thol, we'll need fighters. You might not be much of a fighter normally"—Daniel arched a brow and she ignored him—"but you're certainly better than these two."

"Jessa," he whispered, ignoring Rayen and her sensible comment.

She squeezed forward and leaned underneath Neran's arm. "What is it?"

"Take this. I don't know what we're going to find on the other side, but if anyone comes behind you, I want you to jab them."

"Daniel, I don't intend to—"

He pressed the sword forward, not giving her a chance to continue to argue. She took it, though she seemed to do so reluctantly, and looked at him with annoyance on her face.

Daniel turned away and started out of the tunnel, heading back along the length of it. Rather than walking, he Slid with each movement, and found that he could do that far more quietly than even trying to walk. Each time he emerged, Rayen was there, almost as if she slid forward on the shadows themselves.

"You don't have to do that," he whispered.

"Until we know what's out there..."

The tunnel ended. It was a little lighter as he had been suspecting, and when it stopped, it did so almost suddenly, and the faint light that he had been following came from everywhere.

It seemed to emanate from the walls and from the floor. He didn't see anything that gave him any sense of where the voices had been coming from.

Daniel stepped forward, and as soon as he did, he realized his mistake.

The shadows that swirled around him created a sharp demarcation. He turned, trying to warn Rayen off, but it was too late. She was already there.

Something flickered. Daniel spun, looking to see what it was that had caught his attention, but he couldn't tell.

He didn't think he was imagining it. Whatever had flickered had been real.

Rayen joined him, stepping forward, and she held her sword unsheathed, turning slowly in place.

"There's no one here," she whispered.

"I Saw something."

"What?"

He opened his mouth to answer when there came another flickering.

This time as he tracked it, he realized it came from further down the chamber. He Slid, not waiting, and when he emerged, there was another flickering.

It was behind him.

He spun, turning back toward the sense of the flickering. Rayen was swinging her sword. Her shadows swept out from her, and each time they did, they seemed to catch something, and she tossed it off before the invisible attack struck again. It came relentlessly, striking again and again, and were it not for Daniel's ability to see the shadows swirling around Rayen, he wasn't sure he would be able to make out what was happening to her. As it was, he wasn't entirely sure what he was seeing.

Movement at the other side of the cavern caught his attention, and he realized that Jessa and Neran had come from the end of the tunnel.

Sliding over to them, he turned, trying to push them back into the tunnel. "No. This isn't—"

Something tried to push out from the tunnel, a shape he couldn't quite see.

Had the Ai'thol managed to figure out how to make themselves invisible?

Every time he had faced the Ai'thol, there had been no attack that had been anything like this. Somehow, Rayen managed to hold off the attack, but for how long? At what point would she be overwhelmed by whatever it was she was dealing with?

"I need my sword back," he said to Jessa.

"You never should have given it to me."

He grabbed it and Slid, joining Rayen, slashing at whatever it was that swirled around her. He carved, Sliding, emerging from the Slide to cut again. With each attack, he was met with nothing more than air. Rayen continued to swirl the shadows around her, using them in an ongoing attack, and he tried to help, swinging the sword, finding empty air as he did.

"What is this?" he grunted in between attacks.

"I don't know. I can detect some of their power, but…"

She didn't have a chance to finish. She was forced to swing her shadows.

Then the shadows caught something.

He spun, sweeping the sword, and brought it up at the last moment.

It connected.

It was the first time that he had been successful against whatever this strange attack was, and blood dripped, but nothing else was visible.

"Can you wrap your shadows around it?" he asked.

"What do you think I'm trying to do?"

"Is there anything more that you can do?"

"I am trying, but—"

She was cut off, silenced with a sudden attack, and her eyes went wide.

Daniel tried to figure out how he could help, but without knowing what attacked her, he wasn't sure he could—or what there was for him to do.

Rayen didn't say anything. She continued to thrash, the shadows swirling around her, and they became more erratic.

Daniel grabbed her, Sliding, and slowed.

He wasn't exactly sure how to describe what he did, only that he managed to pause in mid Slide. He caught a faint shimmering and realized there was a man holding on to Rayen, hands wrapped around her neck, and he swung his sword around, carving at the man as he emerged from the Slide.

The sword cut deeply, and when it did, Rayen gasped, stepping forward, but more than that, the man attacking her suddenly became visible.

Taking his sword, he jammed it into the man's chest.

"How were they able to disappear like that?"

"I don't know." Her voice was ragged and painful sounding.

"There is another here," he said.

"Are you sure?"

"I saw them."

"How were you able to see them?"

"Not easily, but I could—"

He realized that Neran and Jessa had been silent.

Sliding, he found Jessa, but she wasn't breathing, at least not easily. He grabbed her arm and clutched Neran to make sure he wasn't overlooking anything, then Slid.

The Slide went slowly, almost painfully, and once again he paused. It was the same thing he had done before, and he found another person with him. When he emerged, he swept the sword around, but the Ai'thol attacker had somehow known what he was doing—and blocked.

"Rayen—I need you to use your shadows and try to hold them around the attacker."

"I've tried that already, but it wasn't effective."

"Try holding them in a way that seals them inside. Don't fight when they move. Let them bring you with them."

"It would be easier for me to do if I were able to see where they were."

"It makes it awfully difficult to fight when you can't see what you're fighting, but I have faith that you can manage it. Besides, I'm going to give you a target."

"Should I be thankful?"

"It depends on what it looks like when we bring this target out."

"Be careful."

Daniel Slid to the middle of the corridor. He waited. He would be the bait, trying to draw out whatever it was that was attacking them, but there was a real risk they would go after one of the others.

He made his way in a small circle, trying to bring out the Ai'thol attacker, and nothing happened. Rayen remained where she had been, standing in place, but near Neran and Jessa, sword at the ready, with Daniel watching.

It gave him a chance to look around this small chamber, try to understand what it was and, better yet, where it was, so that he could comprehend what he was facing. The Ai'thol had figured out some way of making themselves invisible, a move he had not anticipated. It was the kind of gamesmanship he shouldn't be impressed by but couldn't help it.

Could he do something similar?

The person had been visible during a Slide.

Even if he couldn't replicate it, he at least had the ability to See it. One thing he had picked up on over the years was a way of detecting when someone was Sliding, mostly so that he could be better equipped to know what they were doing. It was how he had learned to control his Slide. Within the palace, teaching someone to Slide was not nearly as welcomed as it was out in the Aisl.

"Watch for Sliding," he said.

"You?" Jessa asked.

He glanced over at her. Of them all, she might be the most able to See what was taking place.

"Not me."

Shimmering came from behind Jessa.

That was what he'd been looking for. That same shimmering he saw when someone was Sliding. That had to be it.

He turned his attention off to the side, not wanting to reveal that he might have detected what was taking place, and watched the shimmering as it moved around the inside of the chamber. In the faint light, it was easier to track, and he was thankful they were here rather than out in the tunnel. In the darkness of the tunnel, Daniel wasn't sure he would have picked up on anything.

As it was, if he turned his head the wrong way, the shimmering would disappear. He was cautious, hating that were he to look the wrong way, he would lose the attacker.

Shifting his sword, he prepared to Slide, and as he did, he realized his mistake.

There was another in the room.

Which one should he go after first?

The other one was on the far side of the room and didn't seem to be moving, just flickering, shimmering in and out. Daniel suspected that the person was simply Sliding and then emerging in the same place over and over again. The level of control—and the strength—involved in doing that was incredible.

That was the kind of fighting he needed to learn. It was a kind of fighting the people of Elaeavn should have mastered before now. Any more attackers would be more than he could track. As it was, following the two of them was almost too much.

He had to do something quickly.

He thought about it in terms of a game, trying to imagine this as some sort of Tsatsun board. It was a little cruel doing that, viewing these people and their lives as nothing more than a game, but that was the way Carth had been instructing him, training him, preparing him from moments just like this.

What did he know?

One Ai'thol was down, a sacrificial piece. Two more remained, but could that be the only move?

He thought about the way the game would play out, silently chiding himself for referring to it as a game in his mind. The first move involved attacking one of the Ai'thol, but if he attacked the one nearest the others, the other would Slide, reaching them and possibly intervening before he had a chance to do anything.

He thought about what he would do if he went after that one. The other would be able to attack, already close enough to those he'd come with.

Either move ended up with something happening that he wanted to avoid, and so he had to figure out an alternative.

First, he had come up with which piece represented the Stone—what was the objective?

The objective was to stop them and figure out what they were doing down here.

One of the things Carth had always remarked upon was that there were often many ways to win. Sometimes the way you won wasn't the most obvious.

In this case, winning might not be destroying the enemy.

There was an alternative for him. He could Slide away, taking his friends with him, and return, but if they did, so could the Ai'thol, and they would bring reinforcements.

If they were somehow siphoning power off the Elder Trees, he didn't want to abandon this place now that he'd found it. Doing so would be allowing the Ai'thol to realize what he knew.

One of Carth's lessons filtered into the back of his mind.

"What do you think you can do?" she had asked him.

The game board set between them, and he had managed to remove a considerable number of her pieces, enough that he had allowed himself to believe he might finally win.

Still, there was a moment of doubt in the back of his mind, a reminder that he was playing Carth, and no one had beaten her.

"I have you outnumbered. Outmatched."

She had smiled at him. "There is a big difference between outnumbered and outmatched."

All it had taken was a series of moves, and in that short series of plays, few enough that he could scarcely believe how easy it had been for her, she had reversed the game.

"How do you turn it?"

"You have to find a way to turn their strength into a weakness," she said.

"But you didn't turn my strength into weakness."

"Didn't I? You believed you had the numbers, and you moved accordingly, rather than playing the same game you had been."

It was then he realized how thoroughly she had gamed him. She had known all along what he was doing, and she had allowed him to take the position that he had, making him think he would be successful.

All along, there had been no chance at success.

"How do you find it?"

"You have to find it for yourself. Every game is a little bit different, much like every player is a little bit different. Prepare, but focus on the game that you're playing, and always remember the move you're making will likely be anticipated by your opponent. Find the move they don't think you'll make."

What could he do that would counter the type of moves the Ai'thol were making?

There was one tactic he could try. It was similar to what he had done when he had managed to cut down the first of the Ai'thol. If he could somehow pause in the middle of his Slide, then maybe…

Daniel Slid.

He paused in the middle of it.

It was a strange sensation, and nothing like any sort of Slide he had ever attempted before, but as he did, he found that he was able to hesitate. He saw the first of the Ai'thol, flickering in and out.

When the man flickered into existence, Daniel brought his sword around.

The sword connected, the man not expecting it, and he carved through him.

Staying in this place, that space between the Slides, he headed toward the next and stabbed his sword through him in the middle of his flickering movement.

Daniel emerged. Everything was dark.

He focused on the sounds around him. Darkness began to clear, and he saw Rayen and realized she had been using her shadows to wrap around the others, concealing them.

"What happened?" she asked.

"I got to them," he said.

"How?"

The man nearest them had fallen, two swords in hand, and he was near Jessa. Then there was the other, lying off along one wall, blood pooling around him. Neither man moved. "I paused in the middle of the Slide."

Rayen frowned at him. "You paused? Is that possible?"

"Well I just did it, so it must be."

"Rsiran could do that. He said it takes incredible control, strength."

Daniel frowned. He had never felt that he was particularly strong, but there was no denying what he had managed to do. He had cut through the Ai'thol in the middle of the Slide—and he still didn't feel tired.

Something had changed for him. There was no use denying it anymore.

The only thing that he could think of was visiting Ih. Maybe he had been touched by another Elder Stone.

Strange, considering he hadn't even been able to handle one of the Elder Stones from his homeland.

"We need to figure out what they were doing," he said.

"They were guards," Rayen said.

"Only three of them?"

"Only three that we know of, but what happens if the rest went away? Besides, three would be enough if they were invisible."

Daniel made his way deeper into the cavern. The faint light had returned, having faded when Rayen had wrapped her shadows, but now that she had released them, that light came back, swirling around them with a certain hint of power.

"It doesn't look as if they were guarding anything," Neran said, making his way around the inside of the cavern. It was a confined space, and though the walls might have a faint glow to them, there was nothing else to it that seemed all that impressive.

Daniel couldn't help but feel as if Neran were right. They couldn't have been guarding anything.

"Is this what you had detected?" Daniel asked.

Rayen stood in the middle of it, and shadows flowed outward from her, going up toward the ceiling, sweeping high overhead and then beyond. They froze there for a moment before descending once again. She turned to him and nodded. "This is the place, but I would have expected something to be here as well."

"Like you said, they might have already escaped with it," Jessa said, looking around her.

"That doesn't make sense," Daniel said.

"A distraction?" Jessa said.

That didn't fit with what he knew of the Ai'thol. Everything they did had a purpose, each action setting up another action, each move triggering another move. He couldn't help but think there was something that he didn't quite grasp.

And he needed to.

Daniel Slid and then emerged, doing it over and again, replicating what the Ai'thol had done. As he did, he flickered, moving in and out of place, in and out of place, so quickly he could barely track it.

He paused. "Was it the same?"

"It was similar," Rayen said. "You disappeared, but they were faster."

"Let me try again."

He started flickering again, phasing in and out, trying to figure out if there was any way for him to replicate what the Ai'thol had done, and as he did, he started to feel the shimmering around him coalesce, flowing toward him. He realized that not only was this similar to what the Ai'thol did, but they were forcing themselves in between the spaces of the Slide.

He paused in the middle of the Slide.

It was a strange sensation, the same strangeness he had detected when he had managed to do it before, and holding on to the pause in between Slides, he hesitated as he looked around, searching for signs of anything that might help him understand.

In his mind, he focused on what the Ai'thol had done. They had created a siphon, drawing power from the Elder Trees.

It had to be here.

What better place to hide it than in a space only a very few would be able to find?

But then, Rsiran would have been able to find it.

Only if he would have known where to look. The strange thing about Sliding was that when he paused in the middle of it, there was nothing else around, as if he were in some other world.

He moved around, spiraling out from the center of the room, before deciding that didn't seem like it was going to work. Emerging briefly, he grabbed Rayen and paused. In the middle of the Slide, she gasped.

"What is this place?"

"It's the place between. I can't See anything, but maybe with your shadows you can discover what they were hiding."

She pushed out with the shadows, and they swirled away from her, though not with nearly as much force as she normally managed. Rayen clenched her jaw, continuing to force them outward, and they slowly streamed. At one point they folded, slipping over something.

"That's it," he whispered and reached for what appeared to be emptiness, but his hand slammed into something hard and cold. He wrapped his arms around it, grabbing for Rayen, and Slid.

The sense was the same as when he had attempted to Slide with the strange metal they had used on the island. It felt as if he were trying to Slide a mountain, something impossible, and he continued to pull on it, tearing every bit of energy that he could muster, forcing it to comply, and brought himself—and whatever he held—out.

Staggering forward, the Slide fading, he looked at what he had brought.

It was metal. Slick and cold, the surface of it irregular, and it swirled with dozens of different colors.

Neran gasped. "What is that?"

"That, I think, is what they were using against us."

"Where was it?"

"It was between," Daniel said. For the first time after all of the Sliding that he'd been doing, fatigue washed over him. He sank down, looking at the ground, and stared at the strange item. It appeared to be a massive chalice, and he could imagine it filled with some powerful wine, but instead of wine, it seemed to contain power from the Elder Trees.

"We have to replace it," Daniel said.

"Replace it?" Jessa asked. "If they were using it to take our abilities—"

Daniel got to his feet, shaking his head. "What we need to do until we figure out another way is put something that can send power back, hopefully returning it to the surface." He turned to Neran. "Do you think you can make something like that?"

Neran circled the chalice, and it came up to a little higher than his waist, large enough that while he could wrap his arms around the mouth of it, it would require him stretching. He held his hand just above the surface as he circled it. "It's possible. I think that if Rsiran were here, he might be better equipped to do it, but…" He glanced over to Jessa. "I will have others within the guild work with me. It might take a few days, but we should be able to come up with something."

Daniel breathed out. They would have to deal with it for a few days, which meant they would have to defend this space for that time, though perhaps that wasn't so much of an issue. If the Ai'thol didn't know they had been here and what they had done, it was possible they would be able to get away with leaving the other chalice out.

"We can bring this one to the surface for now," Daniel said. "You can study it, see if there's anything you can use from it."

"We will need you to help us replace it," Neran said.

Which meant that he would be staying. He had intended to come to Elaeavn for a little while, long enough to find help with metals, and instead he had been the one who had helped.

He glanced at Rayen. "Will you stay with me?"

"I haven't spent time in Elaeavn. I suspect there are quite a few taverns I could visit here."

"I don't know how exciting our taverns will be."

"You might be surprised."

Daniel turned to Jessa. He realized the sadness on her face, and he thought that he recognized it. It was sadness that came from a sense of loss. He hated that they still had no idea what happened to Rsiran, but more than that, Haern still had not returned.

"Jessa?"

"He should have discovered this," she whispered.

"Who?"

She tore her gaze away from the chalice, looking at Daniel. "Rsiran. He's faced them enough that he should have been able to find this. If he would've found it, he never would have ended up—"

Daniel grabbed her hands, forcing her gaze up to his, and shook his head. "We can't think like that. We don't know what would've happened. He did what he thought was necessary."

"And what if it wasn't?" She turned to the chalice again, holding her hand over the surface of it. "All these years we have been dealing with the Forgers, and all these years he tells me that he's been learning how they fight and how he can counter them, and all these years he's not managed to stop them. He's missed out on so much. *We've* missed out on so much."

Neran stepped up to him, glancing over at Daniel. "Let me have a few words with her. I have a little experience with this."

Daniel gave them some space, joining Rayen. "It is impressive, isn't it?"

"No one has ever claimed the Ai'thol weren't clever."

"I don't know if I would've been able to stop them were it not for Carth."

"Carth?"

"Tsatsun. I thought about how she played Tsatsun, and the lessons she taught me. Had I not, I don't know that I would have figured out a different way."

"I'm sure you would have come up with something."

Daniel glanced at the fallen bodies, and a troubling idea came to mind. What if this was all part of the game?

He turned his attention to the chalice. They would have to be careful. If this was one more move, an expected one at that, then he would have to be prepared for the next move, and then the next.

"I think your Elder Stone changed me," he said.

"It took you long enough to come to that conclusion."

"What?"

"You've been different ever since we were there. You shouldn't be able to see the shadows. If nothing else, it is helpful. I don't know what else it will do to you, but your ability to glimpse the shadows seems to have connected you to greater power."

"You're saying I'm augmented?"

"If you need to consider it the same."

"And I'm going to gain powers like yours?"

"Don't get ahead of yourself, Daniel Elvraeth."

"I just figured there would be some lessons you could teach me."

Rayen started to grin. "Oh, Daniel Elvraeth, there are lessons I could teach you. A great many lessons. I wonder if you now have the stamina necessary to learn?"

He met her gaze and chuckled. "I would like to get out of here."

"Are you ready for your first lesson?"

"Soon, but first I want to get out of these caves."

"I don't know. I kind of like the dark. And I think you will find you do as well."

41

RYN

RYN WAS TIRED. THE DAYS SPENT TRAVELING, VISITING ALL of these strange locations, had grown wearisome. Olandar Fahr had continued to explore, taking her from place to place, and with the rapidity of their travels, she had a hard time remaining focused on everything she had encountered and no longer thought that it mattered. He had wanted her to know that they were visiting the same sort of place each time.

In each place, she noticed a strange odor in the air. At first, she believed it was that of an old fire, but the longer she had been around it, the less certain she was that was the case. Now she began to wonder if perhaps it wasn't fire at all but something else.

In every place that they had visited, there was destruction. Olandar Fahr had made a point of showing it to her, and yet, he had never said anything, to the point where when they stopped in these places there was nothing for him to say.

It was enough for her to know these places existed.

The longer they went, the more she began to wonder who was responsible for what had happened. At first, she thought he had been showing her because he believed Lareth was to blame for this, but that didn't seem to be the case as far as she could tell.

The longer she was here, the more she began to question whether there was some other power at play.

That was the message that Olandar Fahr was trying to show her. If there was some other power at work, why bring her here? What did he think she would be able to offer by showing her these things?

Each time they stopped, she focused on everything she could see around them, thinking there had to be something more she was supposed to find. If it was all about understanding the moves, trying to grasp the next, she would look for it.

"Another?" They stood along the shore once again with the waves washing along her feet. She had taken to standing in the water, enjoying that aspect of the waves. There was something soothing about it, and she felt that she needed the cleansing of the water after each place they visited, almost as if it would help remove what she had seen and experienced.

"I think we have to."

"Why? What haven't I seen?"

He glanced over at her, locking eyes with her. Ever since she had committed to traveling with him, she had been with him exclusively. It was strange to her that he would remain with her for so long.

"It's not what you haven't seen, but it's more about what I haven't seen." He turned his attention onto the water. "There have been terrifying reports."

"What sort of reports?"

"Of creatures that can't be killed."

Her breath caught. "How is that possible?"

"It's something my ability to see has not revealed to me. Of the possibilities, there is none that matches what is happening now."

"Why is that important? I thought your ability to see possibilities was tied to the nature of the games you've been playing."

"It is tied to that, and yet, the possibilities I can see are different. This is the first time I have ever encountered something happening that I haven't been able to anticipate. It's almost as if I am unable to observe this."

"Why haven't we looked into that rather than what you've been showing me?"

"What I've been showing you I have known about for years."

"Years?"

Olandar Fahr nodded. "Years. In all that time, I've tried to find answers, and have continued to look, searching for the cause of the destruction, and each time I think I'm getting close, I find nothing."

Now she was certain she heard the exasperation in his voice. "And that's why you're bringing me?"

"I was hoping maybe you would find something I've missed. This is all part of the game. If we can better understand the moves around us, we can better be prepared for what else needs to be done."

"What if there is no understanding?"

"Then I will be beaten."

She knew how much that troubled him. The game was important to him.

Still, it was nothing more than a game.

"How is Lareth involved in this?"

"I'm not quite sure. Yet."

She gaped at him, but Olandar Fahr ignored her. All of this and he didn't even know?

How was it possible that he didn't know?

Given everything she'd gone through, she wanted to ensure that Lareth received the punishment he deserved, and more than that, she wanted to ensure she was able to be a part of it. That was the whole point of her participating, and yet, now that she had gotten this far, she was no longer sure Olandar Fahr was going to allow her the vengeance she wanted. If he thought Lareth was going to be important for his game, then he might not allow her what she wanted.

"Where now?"

"Now it's time for us to return."

"Return where?"

"I've shown you everything I can in the outer lands."

"Outer lands?"

He nodded. "The lands that you are familiar with, the lands where I found you, are only a part of this world. There are others, and when I was still sailing, it took weeks and months to reach some of these places. Some of them took even longer—years—for me to find. I spent time searching maps, trying to gain as much knowledge and understanding of the various lands as I could. In all that time, I continued searching for answers. When I finally found them, they were like you have seen."

"Destroyed," she said.

"Destroyed," he agreed. "I don't fully understand what happened, and because of that, I need to continue to look for answers."

"I thought you said the answers weren't there."

"They aren't where I've been looking, which means the answers are where I've not been looking."

"I don't really understand that, either."

"Come," he said.

He took her arm, and they traveled.

When they stepped free, they were once more in the small room within the temple.

After the beach and the brightness of the sun, and after the waves washing over her feet giving her a feeling of relaxation, the return to the temple was jarring. It was almost disappointing to be back here, and yet, Olandar Fahr took a seat at the table, rearranging the pieces on the board. He waited for her to take another seat, and as he did, he looked up at her.

"Sometimes a move is not the move you think it is."

"How so?"

"Watch as I play this piece," he said. He slid one of the pieces along the side of the board. "Do you see what that did?"

"I'm not as skilled a player of this game as you are."

"It's not about how skilled you are but what you observe."

"You moved the piece along the outside."

"Did you see what else I did?"

She frowned, staring at the board. He had both hands resting on either side of the table, and one of them was near the piece he had moved. There was another piece that had shifted, but she hadn't even seen him do it.

"I do now," she said.

"Good. You don't have to know the rules of the game to recognize when something is done that shouldn't be. When you were with me before, what happened?"

"You were taking more turns at one time."

"And how did that make you feel?"

Ryn shrugged. "I didn't really care."

He offered a hint of a smile. "Perhaps you didn't. But then, I suspect that comes from the fact that you have no interest in playing the game."

"I don't," she said.

"But if you did care—if you worried about fairness—how do you think that would make you feel?"

"Upset that I wouldn't have an opportunity to make a move."

"Exactly. One of the earliest lessons I learned while playing Tsatsun is that sometimes the rules aren't quite what we believe."

"You mean that it's okay for you to make more than one move at a time?"

"Sometimes the key is making more than one move at a time. Sometimes the key is using one move to distract from another. I begin to wonder if that's what's happening even now."

"How so?"

Olandar Fahr shook his head. "That is what I can't see. I was hoping that perhaps you would be able to observe something."

It occurred to Ryn that there was something more to what he was telling her. "I'm not the first person you have brought to those places, am I?"

He looked up from the board. "Very good."

"How many others?"

"Many."

"Why so many?"

"Because I need to be able to find the answers, and if it's something I'm unable to observe, another might be able to do so."

Ryn held his gaze. "But you have such powerful abilities."

"I do, but that isn't the point."

"I have no abilities."

"Perhaps not."

"Who are these others that you brought there?"

"I take only those I trust the most."

Ryn had met some of the people he was closest to. There was one, a man he referred to as the Architect, who had visited with Olandar Fahr many times. He was a stern man, and yet he was also kind to her.

"The Architect?"

"Of course," he said.

"The disciples?" She knew the disciples held a special place within the hierarchy of the Ai'thol. They were men of power and able to serve Olandar Fahr in a way that many others were not.

"The disciples have many uses, but not all of them are helpful in this manner."

Ryn frowned. "You haven't brought the disciples to these places?"

"Not all of them," he said.

"Why me?"

"Because I trust what you observed, Ryn Valeron."

She stared at the game board, not able to fully grasp what he was telling her. Why would he trust her? Why would he believe what she was able to see?

Ryn still wasn't sure that what she was able to see mattered, and she didn't know whether she was observing the right things, but at the same time, she couldn't shake the feeling that she wanted to help him.

"Why would you trust that?"

"You've given me no reason not to. I think that in time, your ability to see will be even more potent."

"Is this some possibility you've discovered?"

He gave her a mysterious smile. "Maybe something like that."

Olandar Fahr continued to move the pieces around the board, and Ryn watched. He moved all of them, using both sides, and it seemed as if he were playing against himself.

Ryn sat back, watching. She didn't know the rules of the game, and the longer she watched, the more she couldn't help but feel as if she had no interest in learning the rules. It was far too complicated. When he was done, he set the pieces back, leaning against his chair, and crossed his arms over his chest.

"Perhaps it's time for me to help you see better."

"How?"

"Do you fear taking a blessing?"

She looked up from the board, worry leaving her trembling. "I don't know what a blessing is."

"Come," he said.

He stood and held his arm out, and Ryn took it.

Ryn expected to appear in some mysterious land, or perhaps in some greater part of the temple, but when they stepped free, they were in a darkened room. The air stank of a strange odor that reminded her of what she had encountered in each of the places that Olandar Fahr had brought her. She looked around, searching for any answers, but there was none. A hearth at one end of the room drew her attention. Coals glowed with a bright orange heat, radiating that heat out into the room. A metal stand rested in front of the fire, and a hammer lay against that stand.

"What is this place?"

"This is a smith's forge."

"As in a blacksmith?"

"Very good."

"Lareth is a blacksmith."

"So I've heard." There was amusement in his voice, and Ryn needed to be more careful when she'd talked about Lareth. He had tolerated it so far, but there might come a time when he grew weary of her comments about Lareth.

"Why have you brought me here?"

"Many of my followers have taken a blessing."

"The scar," she said.

She had enough experience with the Ai'thol to know that many of them had scars, and yet she hadn't been able to determine the purpose behind them. Partly that was because she had feared asking, not wanting to upset Olandar Fahr.

"The scar. The blessing we've placed has been a traditional practice, and it's one that we borrowed from others of this land."

"What others?"

"They called themselves the Hjan, but they are gone. We have borrowed much from them, including our very own Forgers. The Hjan had their uses, though. They understood the metal in ways others do not, and because of that, they allowed us an opportunity to study ways metal can grant abilities."

"How does it do that?"

"It is something we don't fully know." He smiled. "Even the Hjan and their Forgers didn't completely understand, but we continue to study."

"That's why some of them have different scars?"

"Some do. Some want different abilities than others."

"How do you determine which ability they take on?"

"There's something to the way the Forgers choose the metal, and the way the people are chosen. Not all can accept a blessing, Ryn Valeron. It can be dangerous, and until we attempt to do so, we don't know if someone would even survive it."

She shivered. "Why are you telling me this?"

"Because it's time that you decide if you would be willing to take a blessing."

She turned to face him, tearing her gaze away from the forge. "I…"

His face was hard, his eyes intense. "I can't promise what would change for you, but given your heritage, I anticipate you will be made whole." Now he did smile. "Your parents left your homeland before you had the opportunity to know it. You missed out on power that was there, and because of that, you are less than what you would have been had you stayed there."

Ryn remembered her mother talking about what it had been like, and what her family might have known, and the fact that her abilities were different than what even her mother had possessed.

"The blessing will augment what you already possess," Olandar Fahr said.

Ryn ran her hand along her face. "I don't know that I'm ready."

"The nature of the blessing has changed. We have begun to master parts of it that we weren't able to before." He took a step toward her, and she resisted the urge to flinch. "You think of the scars that you've seen before, and you fear. If that were the only blessing I had to offer, I would wait. You are too important to me."

Ryn watched him, and in the darkened room, she wasn't sure if she could read his emotions all that well. "Why?"

Rather than answering, Olandar Fahr took a step toward the darkened forge. "Recently, we have better understood the nature of the blessing, and now I can offer one to you that would change things for you. It would open up possibilities."

Her mind was spinning, and Ryn wasn't even sure whether she wanted to take a blessing. Before doing so, she thought she needed to better understand what it was and what it would do to her, and what obligation she would have once she did.

"The how doesn't matter, but as you've seen, there is danger in this world. I search for it. I don't do so alone, and I ask much of those who work with me. In your case, I would ask that you continue to observe and report back to me, knowing that perhaps you might find the answer I've been missing. If you accept this blessing, you can become my emissary, my voice. You can truly serve the Ai'thol."

The words hung in the air, and she wasn't sure what to say or do. She didn't even know if she wanted what he was offering, but she thought of what she had seen. If the blessing would give her strength she didn't currently possess, how could she choose otherwise?

It would be her way of being ready for the opportunity to confront Lareth.

Turning to Olandar Fahr, she saw a mixture of emotions on his face. There was the typical intensity, the strength she attributed to the man. But there was something else, almost hesitation. Could he be worried about her?

More than anything, that answered it for her. He wasn't trying to force her into anything. He wanted to protect her.

And he needed her help.

With everything that she had been through, everything

that she had seen, and all that he had done for her, how could she not help?

Even if it meant pain. Even if it meant danger. She would do this.

For him.

"I will."

"I knew you would."

42

DANIEL

Daniel looked around the clearing, feeling the weight of the inside of the Aisl forest, recognizing how powerful this place had been. Perhaps if they were successful at returning that strength, if Neran managed to do what he planned, they would restore the power of the forest. They would need to work quickly, but he wasn't even sure it mattered. They knew what the Ai'thol intended. That was the first step in stopping them.

He glanced over to Rayen. "How do you feel?"

"I'm fine, Daniel Elvraeth."

"Even after handling one of the—"

Rayen raised a hand, silencing him. "I'm fine. Nothing changed for me, regardless of what I may or may not have handled."

Daniel turned his gaze up to the trees. The strange metal that worked along the trunks seemed a taunt, even more so now that he understood that power was pouring away from the trees, heading through the crystals, through the pedestals, and somewhere else. The problem was that he didn't know where that somewhere else happened to be. He wasn't sure that he could know.

Now that he had been in the crystal room, he could feel the pulling so much more acutely.

"Do you still feel it?" Rayen asked.

"I feel the sense of power—and loss. Now that we have stopped them—"

"We can't stop them."

Daniel turned to the sound of the voice. An old, frail woman hobbled toward him. Her hair was nearly completely silver, and she was dressed in a flowing robe, stripes of color around it. A shawl over her shoulders matched the robe. He had never seen her before but thought he knew immediately who she was. Everyone—even in the palace—knew who she was.

"You're Della."

"I am."

Daniel looked around and saw Jessa standing on the other side of the clearing. She must have known. As far as he knew, Della was dead. Then again, there was value in misdirection, value in allowing others to believe that you were gone.

"I can see that you are working through what to make of me."

"Sorry."

"Don't be sorry. Understand that were it not essential, I would not remain here."

"Why did you come?"

"Because Rsiran needed me."

"He may still need you."

"Perhaps. And Haern has decided to follow after his

father's footsteps, though he does not yet know it. I cannot See whether that will be fortuitous or not. It is possible that we will suffer because of it." Della turned her attention to look up at the trees. She took a deep breath, closing her eyes for a moment. "They call to me. I suppose that they call to you in a similar way."

"They did. Now I'm not sure what else we need to do."

"Ah, Daniel Elvraeth, you should follow your heart."

He laughed softly, glancing to Rayen. She had stepped aside when Della had appeared, and watched from a distance. Shadows swirled around her but never came close to Della. Was that because of something Della did, or was it because Rayen refused to use her shadows against the old woman?

"I followed my heart. That's what got me into trouble."

"You followed where you thought your heart would lead you. Most young men do the same. The difference for you is that you recognize it was not meant to be." Della smiled at him. "Too many men believe they have all the answers, and they act far more confidently than they should." She took another deep breath, her gaze focused high overhead, staring at the upper branches of the trees. "They thought that they could confine our power, but they cannot."

"You know what they did?" Daniel asked.

"I can feel what they did. That is enough."

"What exactly is it?"

"You felt it yourself, Daniel Elvraeth. I can see it in you."

"You can see it or you can *See* it?"

"They are similar enough as to no longer matter. Much like I can See that you were meant to come here."

Daniel regarded Della for a long moment. She was known as eccentric, but she was also Elvraeth, the same as him, and because of that, gifted with incredible powers. As far as he knew, she might be one of the most powerful of the Elvraeth. Her opportunity to hold one of the sacred crystals had ended with her receiving a Healing ability, and it was one that had never been seen before. With the way she stared at him, her dark green eyes practically seeing through him, he wondered if perhaps she had another gift that he didn't fully understand.

"We came here to understand metal."

"You came here hoping to find word of Rsiran, and failing that, you came for Haern, and instead you have decided that Neran will be satisfactory for what you need. And now you have done something more." She looked behind her, meeting Neran's gaze for a moment, holding it for several heartbeats before turning back to Daniel. "And I can See that you needed to come here."

"Did you know I'd discover what the Ai'thol have done?"

Della spread her hands off to either side of her. "Unfortunately, that gift does not work quite like that. I can See things, possibilities, glimpses of what could happen, but I often don't know the reason behind those. Even if I did, I'm not sure that it would matter. I can't force you to make the next choice that you will make, any more than you can force me to make the next choice that I will make."

"Some people can."

Della smiled slightly. "Ah. You have experienced someone who can Push. A difficult ability, and there are some who managed to master it, but it remains tricky and unreliable."

He thought of what he had seen from Lucy when she had used the same ability, controlling the Ai'thol. Had it been unpredictable? It didn't seem that way at the time, but none of them had planned on depending upon her ability to maintain that control. They knew that would be dangerous and that were they to try to hold on to that connection, there was the risk the Ai'thol would overpower whatever hold she had over them.

"Can you tell where the power was directed?"

"That is the real question, isn't it? You and the child of Ih found answers even Rsiran, for all his gifts, could not." Della took a step back, frowning as she studied him. "I see their touch upon you. Perhaps more than a touch. Interesting. There was a time when the powers of the elders did not mingle, when the Council was intact, but perhaps that time is no longer."

"Della?"

Could she have grown senile?

"What do you know of the Council?" Rayen asked, breaking her silence. She approached Della almost reverentially. It was the most reserved he had seen her, regarding Della carefully. The shadows no longer swirled around Rayen. They were balled up within her.

"I know much, child of Ih."

"What is this Council?" Daniel asked.

Rayen didn't look over at him, but he could feel how she shifted her focus toward him. "The Council of

Elders. Carth has spoken of it, though even she won't elaborate."

"Carthenne is wise. When I first met her, I must admit I did not recognize her wisdom, but the longer she's active, the more certain I am that she knows exactly what she's doing."

"How well do you know Carth?" Daniel asked.

"There aren't many who have held the Elder Stones."

"Della?"

Her mind had to be slipping. Even in Elaeavn, there were hundreds of people who had held one of the sacred crystals. He didn't know what it was like in other places, or with other Elder Stones, but he suspected that it was similar. How could it not be?

"He seeks to rebuild the Council," Della said.

"He?"

Della turned to look at him. The clarity within her deep green eyes startled him. No. Her mind could not be slipping, not with the way that she looked at him. "The Council of Elders."

"What exactly is the Council of Elders?"

Della glanced up at the trees once more, breathing deeply, before turning and motioning for Daniel to follow. He did so, letting her guide him out of the heart of the Aisl forest, away from the pressure that he felt upon him, pressure that came from the trees and the power that the Ai'thol siphoned off, sucking the strength away.

As they walked, Della looked around her. "Few know what Rsiran saw when he held one of the sacred crystals. He spoke to Jessa and Brusus, though I don't know whether they shared that with Haern. One could not fault them if they did not, especially as there is good reason not to share."

She spoke to Daniel as if he should know what she was talking about. "What did Rsiran see?"

"Everything."

"Everything?"

"Rsiran had a unique experience, but then, Rsiran has always been somewhat unique. He was motivated not by a quest for power for himself, but for those he cares about. His people. I wonder if perhaps that was why the Great Watcher favored him."

She continued onward, and Daniel realized that they were making a winding path, sweeping outward and away from the trees. They spiraled in a circle that grew ever wider as they went, and for a moment, he wondered if there was a purpose behind it before realizing that Della was doing something as they walked.

Maybe it was just his imagination, but it seemed almost as if the forest brightened as they passed, growing ever greener with each step. Could she be Healing the forest as they walked?

That seemed strange, but then, so did everything about Della.

"How did Rsiran see everything?" he asked.

"He sat alongside the Great Watcher."

"I saw something similar," Rayen whispered.

Della turned to her. "Did you? What exactly did you see?"

"I wasn't sure. When I felt the crystal calling to me"—she flushed but held Della's gaze—"it seemed to carry me into the darkness. From there, I had a sense of knowledge, of everything, and connection."

"Did you?" Della asked, stepping toward her.

Rayen nodded slowly. "What does it mean?"

"Only time will tell what it means. The visions we experience when holding one of the crystals are difficult to fully understand." She looked toward Daniel, watching him for a moment. "Many feel as if they are somehow lessened if they aren't given the opportunity to hold one of the crystals, and yet that was never the intention, at least from what I can determine of the crystals."

"The crystals don't want me," he said.

"You have been blessed by birth, Daniel Elvraeth. Do you need one of the crystals to prove that to you? They cannot unlock something within you that already lives there."

He held her gaze for a moment before looking away.

"You have asked about the Council of Elders, and considering what you face, I think it's time that we share what we know. Isn't it, Carthenne?"

Della turned, and Daniel watched a strange shimmering and felt a surge of power. It was nothing like he'd ever experienced before, and the moment it happened, Lucy and Carth suddenly appeared before them.

Carth took stock of the situation quickly, no sign of uncertainty to her, but Lucy had a harder time. For as powerful as she had become, the augmentations changing her into something else, a part of her still remained the same girl that Daniel had followed from Elaeavn.

"Healer. What is this?"

"I thought it best to bring us together once again."

"How?" Lucy whispered.

Della smiled. "You are lucky to live in a time where you don't get to feel the pull of someone influencing your Slide."

"You did this?" Carth asked.

"I did. I thought it time for us to speak about the Council of Elders."

"They don't need to know about the Council."

"That is where you're wrong. With everything taking place, they almost have everything they need."

"They won't have everything," Carth said.

"They have already unlocked nearly enough. They now have the Great Watcher drawn into it."

"How?" Carth turned so that she could turn her attention to the trees, back toward the heart of the forest, Daniel realized.

What did Carth know?

For that matter, what did Della know?

"We have thought that not speaking of it protects us, but I fear that it does not. We need the help of others, the help of those who might be able to add to what protections we can place."

"Carthenne?" Rayen asked.

Carth took a deep breath. "Must we do this here?"

"Where else would you have us do it?"

"I would have us do it where we can sit and converse, where we can explain just what is at stake. Seeing as how you brought me here, I think it's only fitting we find the others who have some involvement."

"I would agree."

Della turned toward Daniel and Rayen, and he was suddenly forced into a Slide.

He'd never felt anything like that before. Not only had he been forced into a Slide, but he had no control over it, nothing that allowed him to determine where he went or where he would emerge. When he emerged, he was prepared for the possibility that he might need to Slide again, ready for the chance that he might need to fight, already reaching for his sword.

It was unnecessary.

It was a tavern. Music drifted from the corner, a lutist playing a bouncy song, a singer joining in. Smells assaulted him, mostly savory meats and breads, but there was the mix of ale over top of it.

A man appeared, staring at him and glancing at Rayen. The fluttering in the back of Daniel's mind suggested he was a powerful Reader, though his pale green eyes hinted at something else.

Daniel glanced at Rayen. There had to be a reason they were here. "Della sent us."

"She sent you here?"

"She forced me to Slide."

The man frowned for only a moment. The green within his eyes flared brighter, and the faint sense of someone attempting to Read him tickled the back of Daniel's mind. He fortified his barriers, but he no longer knew if the barriers he could hold were enough against those who could Read strongly.

"Give me a minute."

The man hurried away, and Daniel glanced to Rayen in time to see Carth and Lucy emerge from a Slide. Color flushed Lucy's cheeks, and she sucked in a quick breath. "I tried to resist her, Carth, but she is—"

"Powerful," Carth said with a smile. "I have always known she is more than she appears."

"What is this?" Rayen asked.

"It appears to be a tavern, Rayen. Considering our history together, I would have expected you to have more than a passing familiarity with it."

Rayen grinned. "I recognize that it is a tavern, Carthenne, but perhaps you can share with me why this old woman thought to send us here?"

"I think we're going to have to wait for her to arrive."

"Della—"

There came a drawing sensation from him. It was almost as if he were Sliding, and yet he wasn't sure that he even moved. When it passed, Della had appeared within the tavern.

"I am sorry that I had to use you once again, Daniel Elvraeth, but the need was great."

"You used my ability to Slide to bring you here?"

"Yes."

"How? I mean… how?"

"I would have borrowed from Lucy, and yet the connection between us is different. I suspect that's because of her augmentation, though perhaps our Elvraeth connection binds us more closely." Della took a seat on one of the stools, and when the man appeared again, he carried several mugs of ale, followed by another woman who set a tray of food down the table. She cast her gaze around the table before tapping the man on the shoulder for a moment.

"I don't know that you should be here," she whispered to him.

"I think they're here because I am," he said.

"We are here for Brusus," Della said. "And there is another that I'm waiting for."

"Who?"

"When I can find him, I will bring him here as well, but so far he is out of reach to me."

Daniel glanced over at Rayen. "Haern?"

"One of the unfortunate traits of Haern and his father is their inability for me to find them as easily as others. Their connection to lorcith masks them. It wasn't always that way with Haern, but he has grown far stronger over the last few months, and it has allowed him to hide from me."

"Who, then?"

Della smiled tightly, and once again there came the fluttering of power from within Daniel, almost as if he were going to Slide, but it didn't feel as if he moved anywhere. He looked over to Della, and her gaze was locked on him, her eyes so deep a green that they might as well be black, and colors began to shimmer. Wind started to whistle, whipping around him, and there came something else. A drawing sensation.

It passed quickly, though not nearly as quickly as he would have liked. When it was gone, another person had joined them.

"Galen?"

Galen had about as much reaction as Carth had when she had suddenly been drawn. "I suppose that's one way to return me to Elaeavn."

"Where is Haern?" Brusus asked.

"We were separated. The Forgers thought to attack."

"How many?"

"A dozen. Perhaps more."

He said it so casually that Daniel blinked. "You took on a dozen Forgers by yourself?"

Galen looked over at him before his gaze surveyed the rest of the people at the table. One hand remained at his side, and it seemed as if he were rolling a dart between his fingers. Several bruises on his face were only beginning to bloom with color, and sections of his cloak had torn.

Whatever he had faced had not been easy.

As far as Daniel knew, Galen didn't have significant abilities. He was Sighted, but it took more than that to deal with the Ai'thol.

Then again, Galen had been an assassin. He had faced people of power for much of his life, and he had survived with just his enhanced eyesight. Maybe it didn't take anything more.

"Had I not been training with Haern, I might not have shaken off the rust, but thankfully, I managed to escape."

"Where's Haern?" Brusus asked again.

"Your nephew should have been here before me. He was to leave, heading out on his own, and I would've expected him before now." Galen looked at the others before turning back to Brusus. "I take it from your reaction he has not returned."

"He has not."

He turned to Della. "Can you—"

"I cannot reach him the way that I reached you."

"Is this a rescue mission, then?"

"No." Della leaned forward. "This is to help you understand what's at stake."

"We understand what's at stake."

"Unfortunately, I don't think that you fully understand it. Perhaps Carth has begun to grasp it, but I wonder if even she knows. I have been trying to understand, searching through the visions that I have, and piecing them together."

"What have you uncovered?"

"Something that frightens me very much," Della said. "We have been worried about the Forgers—or Ai'thol, however you may call them—chasing Elder Stones."

"That's what they've been doing for the last twenty-some years," Carth said.

"I suspect the pursuit has been longer than that. How many stones do we know of?" She leveled her gaze on Carth. "There is that of fire. That of night. That of knowledge. And that of healing." She held her hand out and ticked off her fingers for each one of the Elder Stones that she mentioned.

"And there are the crystals."

"The crystals are not an Elder Stone."

"They're not?" Daniel asked.

Della glanced in his direction. "We have believed that they were, much like we have believed that the Elder Trees serve as a stone, as our people have been granted abilities over the years because of those powers. And yet, our people have long believed we were touched by the Great Watcher."

"What is the Great Watcher but an elder?"

"I'm not so certain the Great Watcher sat upon the Council of Elders," Della said.

"There's that term again. What is this Council of Elders?" Daniel asked.

It was Carth who answered. "In all my years of searching, I have come across that term a few times. Most of the time it happens in cases where there are relics found, collections of artifacts that date back centuries, sometimes thousands of years. I've never understood it, other than to believe our people once had our gods watching us."

"Not our gods," Della said. "We know of the Elder Stones—fire, night, wisdom, healing, and the fifth."

"What's the fifth stone?" Daniel glanced from Carth to Della. "If it's not here, what is it?" When neither answered, realization dawned on him. "You don't know."

Carth shook her head slowly. "I don't know. And it's possible that the Healer doesn't know, either."

Della settled her hands on the table. "None of my visions have revealed that to me. I have searched, knowing that will be the key for us understanding exactly what it is that they intend, but unfortunately there is no clear answer."

"Does Rsiran know?"

"It's possible he saw something when he held the crystals. Rsiran was given the gift of the Great Watcher, the ability to sit above the world, to know the world, to know the way that power lives within it. If any were able to understand what the fifth stone would be, it would be Rsiran."

"Why are you convinced that there are only five stones?" Brusus asked.

"There are five trees. There are five crystals."

"There aren't any more than that?"

"Five," she said again.

"Then what's the purpose of the crystals and the trees?"

"They hold the power of the elders. That is the purpose of the Great Watcher. Oversight."

"Then why would they want to attack the trees?" Daniel couldn't quite understand what the connections were, only that he seemed caught up in something that was beyond him. They were talking about gods!

"What has your experience been with the crystals?" Della asked him.

Daniel shrugged. "I wasn't able to hold one, so I don't really have an experience."

"Exactly."

He frowned. His mind churned, thinking about the various possibilities and moves, already beginning to put it into terms of a Tsatsun game. He wasn't sure if that was the best way of organizing his thoughts, but after training with Carth for as long as he had, it was the way his mind had begun to work.

He had not been able to hold one of the crystals, and it seemed as if the crystals themselves had always made a choice. Rayen had been able to hold one. And then there was the sense he'd had when visiting Ih. The shadows had engulfed him, claiming him, surrounding him with power.

His breath caught.

He glanced at Della and then to Carth. He could see the same look of understanding on Carth's face as had to be on his.

"What is it?" Brusus asked.

"Are they using the trees to remove the restrictions on who can handle the stones?" Daniel watched Della for confirmation. "The attack on the trees was never meant to destroy them, was it?"

"I have wondered if the man who leads the Ai'thol—"

"Olandar Fahr," Carth said. When Della frowned, Carth leaned forward. "His name is Olandar Fahr."

"I have wondered if Olandar Fahr does not yet know if destroying the trees will destroy his intention. So he found another way for him and his people to reach for the stones. They can take the power from the stones, and they can use it, no longer dependent upon the restrictions that the Great Watcher has long placed."

Daniel tried to understand, but this was far more than what he thought he could make sense of.

"We must find the fifth stone," Della said.

"I've been looking," Carth said. "There are no rumors of a fifth stone. In all of my travels, there has been nothing."

"You knew that there were five stones?"

"Not quite the way that the Healer is saying, but I recognized there was a finite amount. Her argument does make sense."

"And you think Rsiran knows where the fifth stone is?" Brusus asked.

"Think of what Rsiran told us after his experience holding the crystals. He sat at the hand of the Great

Watcher. He may not recall everything that he saw and everything that he knew, but it's in him."

"And if there is anyone who can draw it out, it would be Olandar Fahr," Carth said. "I've met him. I have seen how brutal he can be. And I know that regardless of what we might plan, he will already have a counter for it. He is nothing if not prepared."

"Then we need to find something unexpected," Rayen said.

"While it may be unexpected to us, it's unlikely to be unexpected to him," Carth continued. "As I said, he is nothing if not prepared."

Somehow they had to find a way to overwhelm this man, but what would it be? How would they ever figure out some way of doing so?

If they didn't, what would happen if this Olandar Fahr managed to acquire the power of the Elder Stones?

"What of this Council of Elders?" Daniel asked.

"The Council is comprised of those the Great Watcher has deemed worthy," Della said.

"Worthy?"

"Ages ago, there were those who held each of the Elder Stones. They were given the ability to use that power, but only at the approval of the Great Watcher."

"Let me guess, there were five of them," Daniel said.

Della smiled. "There were five. One for each Elder Stone."

"What was the purpose of the Council of Elders?" Brusus asked.

"Guidance."

"Not guidance," Carth said. "With power like that,

there would be more than guidance. There would be ruling."

"Perhaps," Della said. "And yet, if the right person was selected, they would prove to be a wise ruler. It was a time of peace, at least from what I can See from my visions. It was a time when those with power understood that they needed to use it judiciously. It was a time when those with power understood that though they may have it, they should not necessarily wield it."

"But if Olandar Fahr is trying to rebuild the Council of Elders, there will be others with the same power as him."

"He doesn't want to sit on the Council of Elders," Carth said.

"I thought you said he wanted power." Brusus frowned as he glanced from Carth to Della.

The various moves played out within Daniel's mind. He thought about Tsatsun, the way the game was played, the way that it was won. How would Olandar Fahr intend to move the Stone?

There would be only one way.

"He doesn't want to be on the Council of Elders. He wants to lead it. He wants to rule over it."

"You said there were five members on this Council," Brusus said.

"Five members on the Council," Daniel said. "But it's the Great Watcher who decides who is granted that power." He turned to Della, fixing her with a stare. "That's what this is about, isn't it?"

"I suspect that it is."

When Brusus shook his head, Daniel met his eyes. "Don't you see? He doesn't want to sit upon the Council of Elders because that's not where the power is. The power is in deciding who has it. He wants to be the Great Watcher."

Lucy shifted slightly, looking uncomfortable. Not for the first time, he wished he had the ability to Read her as well as she Read him. "What is it?"

The others turned toward her and she shook her head. "It's about Olandar Fahr."

Carth frowned at her.

"He's after power, but I think there's a reason he's after power," Lucy said.

"What reason is that?" Della asked.

"He's not the only one chasing power. I think there's another."

Carth paled, and Daniel realized Lucy hadn't shared that with her. What was going on between the two women? "If there's another, then he's playing a different game than we knew." Carth got to her feet and started pacing.

"What do you fear?" Rayen asked.

"I worry that those we've thought are a different kind of Ai'thol aren't that at all. What if they're all tied to this other Olandar Fahr is facing?"

Daniel's breath caught. "Does that mean we're the Stone?"

Carth met his eyes but said nothing. She didn't need to. The worry on her face was clear.

EPILOGUE

RSIRAN COULD BARELY MOVE. HIS ENTIRE BODY HURT, PAIN that he had come to know far better than he ever wanted. It was the kind of pain that filled him, staying with him, and it was the kind of pain that carried with it a promise of more.

Every so often, he managed to roll over, but when he did, everything hurt anew.

He lost track of how long he'd been here. Each day was the same. Occasionally, someone would come, abuse him the same way as Olandar Fahr had, demanding information about the sacred crystals, the Elder Trees, and various other items that they thought he might be able to provide.

He refused to answer.

The longer he'd been here, the more he had come to understand the reasoning.

There was something Olandar Fahr needed from him, but so far, he hadn't managed to get it. Rsiran wasn't going to be the reason he acquired knowledge that had been forbidden to him, and he wasn't going to be the reason the Elder Stones fell into his control.

When the door opened, Rsiran barely looked up. He sat in the middle of the floor, staring at it. He had taken to making marks on the floor, using his body to conceal them, trying to keep track of how long he'd been captive here, but he had lost track.

"Do you still believe that you will one day escape?" The deep bass notes of Olandar Fahr's voice shook him.

Every time he had come to visit, there had been new pain, new wounds inflicted upon him, and yet, Rsiran welcomed them. Either the man would eventually choose to destroy him, or he would not. As far as Rsiran could tell, Olandar Fahr needed him for something.

If he could keep him from getting what he needed, he would consider that a victory.

"It doesn't matter," Rsiran said.

"Your people believe that you will return and lead them."

Rsiran looked up at Olandar Fahr. The pain made it difficult for him to focus, but he'd grown accustomed to pain. There were times when he felt as if he had known pain his entire life, and there were times when he wondered if perhaps it wouldn't be better for him just to lie back, relax, and let the pain overwhelm him. Maybe he could finally rest and be at peace.

Yet, if he did that, what would happen to Jessa?

She was the reason he kept going. She was the reason he had always kept going, wanting to be there for her, to protect her, and to protect those they cared about. As much as he had fought, he thought that he had managed to succeed. Because of his fighting, he had delayed the Forger attack. He had prevented them from gaining a foothold, and it was because of him that they had managed to keep the Ai'thol from becoming even more powerful.

"My people are more than just me."

"If your people were more than just you, they would have attacked. You see, one thing we have come to understand is the role you play. You have always thought you served as a layer of protection to your people, but you have diminished them. If only you would have allowed them to learn, to fight, to prove themselves, perhaps they would have been strong enough."

The words sat within him, and he let them fill his mind. There was nothing untrue about that. "Did you come to torment me with that?"

"I came to offer you an opportunity."

"What opportunity is that?"

"An opportunity to make a choice."

Rsiran looked back down to the ground. His gaze skimmed along the tile that he had scratched, digging his nail into it over and over again with each passing day. He had come to learn that there was one direction that allowed him to scratch most easily, to make his mark upon the tile, so that he could keep a tally of his days. Dozens upon dozens of days had been spent in captivity. All of them had been passed in torment, waiting for the moment his captors would choose to end it.

He worried that his people would decide to trade for him. If they did, they might give up something that they could and should not. He wasn't that valuable.

"What choice would you have me make?"

"I think that I would rather show you."

Olandar Fahr grabbed him, lifting him easily. Rsiran tried to fight, but there wasn't any strength left within him. When he was dragged out of the room, he attempted to Slide but found that he still could not.

Either Olandar Fahr had some way of preventing him from Sliding, or they had been dosing him with slithca—or something like it. In all the time that he'd been captive, he had never detected what they did to prevent him from reaching his abilities, but there was no questioning that he had been separated from them. Every time he thought they were close to returning, they would fade once more, the torture renewed.

He focused on lorcith, on any metal, and while he had a sense of it, he wasn't able to do anything with it. Every time he tried to *push* or *pull* on the metal, he failed. Maybe that was the effect of whatever they had been administering to him too.

Worse, what choice had he but to take the offered food and water? The alternative was death, and while there were times he wanted nothing more than to die, he also wasn't willing to actively participate in his own death.

Perhaps that was a mistake.

They headed down a long hallway. The walls were smooth, made of a dark stone, and there was a sense of lorcith within them. It was everywhere here, though it was not plain lorcith. There was something else with it, as if they had added something, an alloy most likely, but it was one that he wasn't able to identify.

At the end of the hall, heat pressed upon him.

"Where are you bringing me?"

Olandar Fahr chuckled. "I told you. A choice."

"Why do I get the sense that this isn't a choice at all?"

"Ah, Lareth, have you no faith?"

"I didn't take you for someone who had faith."

"Then you haven't been paying attention."

Rsiran tried to think of his previous conversations with Olandar Fahr, of which there had been many, but they all blended together. Most of them dealt with his interest in the crystals. He spoke of the Great Watcher often, but there seemed to Rsiran a distinct lack of understanding about what the Great Watcher meant to Rsiran and his people.

That was to his benefit. If Olandar Fahr knew more about the Great Watcher, if he knew that Rsiran himself had stood alongside him, the knowledge of all creation flowing through him, he would want that for himself. This was a man who chased power, but worse, he was a man who knew how to use—and abuse—the power that he acquired.

In the distance, a reddish glow caught his attention. Rsiran found himself staring off into the distance, trying to make out what he saw but failing.

It probably didn't matter anyway. When this was done, whenever Olandar Fahr had shown him what he intended to show him, he would most likely return him to the cell. More days would pass. At least he was seeing something other than the same familiar walls. It bothered him that should be excitement for him, but even more than that, it bothered him that he feared losing the record he'd kept of the number of days he'd been here.

They Slid.

It was a strange sensation, Sliding again. It had been months since he had, and even longer since he was the one in control of the Slide, and he felt the familiar sense of movement, the shimmering of colors, and the sense that he could step off the Slide, away from it, and remain in between. Very few people understood that there was someplace in between, but as they emerged from the Slide, Rsiran couldn't help but think that Olandar Fahr knew there was.

Heat pushed on his back. There was movement all around him, and the sense of flickering, that of dozens of people Sliding, all of them flickering in and out, and he realized that Olandar Fahr had paused in the middle of the Slide.

"This is what you wanted to show me?"

"Ah, but Lareth, you failed to understand what you're seeing."

"I see just fine. You think to impress me with your control over Sliding."

"I prefer the older term for it."

"If you prefer to call it Traveling, then go ahead. I will call it what I know."

"And I will ask you to watch."

There were more and more people flickering around him. Dozens of them. They all appeared, concentrated in this space.

"What is it that you want to show me?"

"Just a moment, Lareth."

They Slid again, completing the rest of the Slide, and emerged with a bright red glowing behind him. It was the source of the heat, and with it, he suddenly knew where they were. All this time, and he hadn't discovered that?

"Look," Olandar Fahr said.

Rsiran stared in the direction the man pointed, and as he did, his breath caught, his heart hammering.

"Haern?"

Olandar Fahr chuckled. "Yes. Your son has tried to come for you on his own. And now this is your choice."

"What choice?"

"Provide the information that I seek, or watch me cut down your son."

"No."

"You would prefer to see him die? I assure you that I would have no qualms in doing so."

Rsiran continued to stare, watching, and as he did, he tried to call out, to reach for Haern, but Olandar Fahr pulled him into a Slide, stepping off the Slide and into the place in between.

"That is your choice, Lareth. Choose, but I will only give you a few more moments to do so."

"You will call your people off?"

Olandar Fahr stared at him. "I promise only that I won't attack him."

"That's not enough."

Haern wasn't strong enough of a fighter to hold off the Ai'thol like that. He might have gained some skill, and if he had continued his training with Galen, then it was possible he would be able to fight, to hold off some of the Ai'thol, but with the dozens Rsiran had seen, there would be no way for Haern to survive.

"That is all I can offer."

The choice was easy—disturbingly so. He wanted nothing to happen to Haern, and everything he'd done over the years had been to protect his son from the possibility of this.

"What do you want to know?"

"You know what I want."

"The crystals?"

Olandar Fahr tipped his head in a nod.

"Even if you claim them, there's no way that I can make them work for you."

"I'm not asking you to make them work for me. But you will help me acquire them. You, the only man who has held each of the crystals of the Great Watcher, will do this. If you don't, then your son…"

The threat lingered, and there was nothing Rsiran could do but agree.

"I'll do it."

"Of course you will, Lareth. I knew you would make no other choice."

With that, they stepped forward, continuing the Slide.

Grab the next book in The Elder Stones Saga: The Coming Chaos.

The leader of the Ai'thol has worked for centuries on his plan to control the power of the stones. The final steps in that plan come into focus.

Altered and augmented by his new connection to the metal lorcith, Haern must use this ability to protect the women he's brought with him from the dangerous city of Dresden. A series of attacks suggests a control over metal that even Haern might not be able to withstand. Worse, the source of the attacks might be closer than he knows.

Daniel's search for the remaining stone brings him to a surprising place. Once there, it becomes increasingly clear how little they know about the stones—or how to protect them. Answers require he learn how to master aspects of his powers that have been beyond him, but are essential for what is to come.

Lucy begins to suspect another threat that rivals even Olander Fahr. Learning more about this threat requires that she chase the one person she fears most. If she can't find—and face—the Architect, they won't know what Olander Fahr intends in time to stop his plan.

Separated from the Great One, Ryn wants to understand her blessing, but she's tasked with much more. Searching for answers reveals a deeper divide within the Ai'thol. As emissary, she shouldn't be the one to fix it, but in the Great One's absence, she might be the only one who can.

Power begins to gather to stop a great danger for more than the power of the Elder Stones is at stake.

ALSO BY D.K. HOLMBERG

The Elder Stones Saga

The Darkest Revenge

Shadows Within the Flame

Remnants of the Lost

The Coming Chaos

The Shadow Accords

Shadow Blessed

Shadow Cursed

Shadow Born

Shadow Lost

Shadow Cross

Shadow Found

The Collector Chronicles

Shadow Hunted

Shadow Games

Shadow Trapped

The Dark Ability

The Dark Ability

The Heartstone Blade

The Tower of Venass

Blood of the Watcher

The Shadowsteel Forge

The Guild Secret

Rise of the Elder

The Sighted Assassin

The Binders Game

The Forgotten

Assassin's End

The Dragonwalker

Dragon Bones

Dragon Blessed

Dragon Rise

Dragon Bond

Dragon Storm

Dragon Rider

Dragon Sight

The Teralin Sword

Soldier Son

Soldier Sword

Soldier Sworn

Soldier Saved

Soldier Scarred

The Lost Prophecy

The Threat of Madness

The Warrior Mage

Tower of the Gods

Twist of the Fibers

The Lost City

The Last Conclave

The Gift of Madness

The Great Betrayal

The Cloud Warrior Saga

Chased by Fire

Bound by Fire

Changed by Fire

Fortress of Fire

Forged in Fire

Serpent of Fire

Servant of Fire

Born of Fire

Broken of Fire

Light of Fire

Cycle of Fire

The Endless War

Journey of Fire and Night

Darkness Rising

Endless Night

Summoner's Bond

Seal of Light

The Book of Maladies

Wasting

Broken

Poisoned

Tormina

Comatose

Amnesia

Exsanguinated